EARLY'S IDAHO

A FIVE-GENERATION DIARY, 1775–1905,
WITH AN EPILOGUE WRITTEN IN 1954

DOUG FISKE

THE MINIDOKA PRESS
ENCINITAS, CALIFORNIA

THE MINIDOKA PRESS

Early's Idaho is an historical novel. The principal characters and story are fictional. Any resemblance to actual persons, living or dead, is entirely coincidental.

theminidokapress@gmail.com

Cover illustration by Michael Custode

Published in the United States of America by The Minidoka Press
ISBN-10: 0996784705
ISBN-13: 978-0-9967847-0-2

For families everywhere

1

When I was a boy in Smithland, Kentucky, the quickest way to get from one place to another was to ride a swift horse. Then, by the time I became an old man in Hawkins, Idaho, a pilot named Yeager had flown a rocket plane faster than the speed of sound. Things change—sometimes for the better. Before I pass on, I figure it's worthwhile to leave a record of my family's time.

I'm Early Hawkins, from the third generation of the Hawkins line born in Kentucky. In 1775, my great-great grandfather, George Hawkins, was among the men who passed through the Cumberland Gap with Daniel Boone into the country west of the Appalachians. They cut a trace through the wilderness and founded Boonesborough on the south bank of the Kentucky River. Later, when George thought it safe, he returned to Virginia and brought his wife, Meredith, and son, James, to Boonesborough.

In 1792, James Hawkins and Jay Craig, another young man from Boonesborough, built a broadhorn and floated down the Kentucky to its mouth at the Ohio River. There they founded the town of Port William. James married Catherine, a settler's daughter, and was later joined in Port William by his younger brother, Nathan, and Nathan's new bride, Claire. In Port William, Catherine gave birth to Craig and Jenny, and Claire gave birth to John.

In 1805, the two young families built a large, sturdy broadhorn, sold their land and interests in Port William, and floated nearly 400 miles down the Ohio to Smithland, a new settlement at the mouth of the Cumberland River. They bought 300 acres of bottomland that stretched south from the Smithland plat. They cleared the land, built cabins and a barn on a rise above the flood plain, and started to farm.

Keelboat and flatboat traffic on the rivers prompted James and Nathan to build a riverside warehouse just below Smithland. Goods going up or down the Ohio and Cumberland often needed temporary storage where the rivers met. The warehouse quickly became as busy as the rivers. Nathan returned to Boonesborough and brought George and Meredith back to Smithland. By then 55, George welcomed giving up farming in favor of operating the warehouse. Meredith loved being with her children and grandchildren.

Some 30 years earlier, when George left his Virginia farm for the frontier, his sense of history and family got him started keeping a record. He noted events, often placing them against the backdrop of the times, or he wrote about the times themselves. Each generation since George's has had its recorder. The responsibility to keep the record, and the leather-bound books themselves, passed from father to firstborn son down through the generations.

Besides the record, George read and collected books. To the great surprise of Boone's other trailblazers, George toted a satchel of books through the wilderness to Boonesborough. By the time he reached Smithland years later, George had gathered what Meredith called his "heavy library." One of the things George liked about living in Smithland was that the rivers brought new people, goods and news to him nearly every day. On some days, books were among the goods.

As George's firstborn son, James was his generation's recorder. He made many journal entries during the early years in Smithland. I have included some of his entries here, along with others from later generations.

The year 1811 was so overwhelmed with extraordinary events that James waited until early 1812 to record them.

James Hawkins, February 1812. The year past was like no other I have seen in my 38 years on this Earth. Early spring brought a flood that covered our bottomlands and left our warehouse deep in mud. Planting was delayed on everything but our high ground.

In April, a comet appeared in the northern sky and remained visible every cloudless night as it moved south, reaching its greatest brightness in October. Many people looked upon the comet as a bad omen. It was even enough to unsettle our animals. Whether it affected wild animals, I cannot say. Perhaps it was just a coincidence that immense flocks of passenger pigeons darkened the sky and stripped whole forests bare. And no one could explain why great numbers of drowned squirrels floated down the Ohio.

Summer brought intense heat, drought and parched crops. August saw Tecumseh and his Indian warriors heading downriver, passing Smithland in their canoes. They were angry with the still-growing encroachment of white settlers and sought to confederate with southern tribes to fight the whites.

In middle September, there was a near-total solar eclipse. It fueled the fears of those who prophesied doom when the comet appeared in April. As if to manifest the doomsday predictions, in the dark of night on December 16th, a great quake split the Earth not 75 miles from Smithland. The trembling collapsed the chimneys of our cabins and sent us scrambling for safety out into the cold. Great destruction and fear prevailed throughout the county. Milder shocks followed the first large shock, and the trembling continued nearly daily.

We continue to be deeply affected by the embargo. River traffic is down by half. There are only domestic markets for any produce and goods. Many feel war with Britain is coming. Here in the West, the British continue to arm Indians and incite them to attack white settlers. Our county militia rides patrols daily to allay Indian attacks.

Of the events of 1811, I see only one that might portend well. A day or two following the first earthquake shock in December, a most unusual vessel paid a call at Smithland. Although in the aftermath of the quake townspeople were busy with repairs, the visitor caused every cabin, warehouse, tavern and inn still standing to empty its people into the streets. Most ran to the riverbank to gape in wonder at the boat, but some ran away in fear.

The boat lay at anchor in the Cumberland just off the foot of Court Street, with her engine emitting a regular, bass-toned throb. Her deep draft prevented her from tying to the bank as flatboats do. She was a steam vessel, fueled by wood or coal burning in her furnace. She was perhaps 150 feet bow to stern, with a beam of about 30 feet. She had paddlewheels at her sides and a tall chimney that belched thick black smoke. Escaping steam hissed as valves released it. If all that was not enough to provoke wonder, she was painted a bright sky blue.

People on board hailed those of us on the bank. Some Smithland boatmen launched skiffs and, with a few oar strokes, pulled alongside. Aboard was the captain, Nicholas Roosevelt, his wife, Lydia, their young daughter, Rosetta, their infant son, Henry, their huge Newfoundland dog, Tiger, a few servants, and a small crew.

Mr. Roosevelt told us the boat was named *New Orleans* for its destination city. John Daniel, a Smithland ferryman, scoffed and said that any flatboat or keelboat could float to New Orleans. Others doubted the *New Orleans'* usefulness. Mr. Roosevelt smiled and directed the crew to weigh anchor. With steam hissing, the engine throbbing and black smoke billowing from the chimney, the pilot, Andrew Jack, turned the bow downstream and steamed to the foot of Cumberland Island. He rounded the point, turning west into the Ohio. With no evident effort, he proceeded—upstream! Mr. Roosevelt's guests buzzed with excitement. The *New Orleans* moved smoothly against the current, rounded the head of the island and returned to its starting point. Cheers rose from the riverbank. The *New Orleans* had turned the minds of even the deepest skeptics.

Some townspeople invited the Roosevelts ashore. They expressed gratitude but allowed they had to continue downstream. Mr. Roosevelt added it was not by chance that he had stopped briefly at Smithland. He had two partners in the business venture represented by the *New Orleans*—Robert Fulton and Robert Livingston. Mr. Livingston asked Mr. Roosevelt to stop at Smithland in Livingston County, Kentucky, because it was probably the closest he would ever come to setting foot in the county named in his honor. For those townspeople who might not have known Robert Livingston's accomplishments, Mr. Roosevelt regaled us with some of them, which I repeat here: delegate to the Continental Congress; one of five on a committee to draft a declaration of independence from England; Chancellor of New York, and as such administered the oath of office to George Washington in 1789; and President Jefferson's Minister to France, and as such negotiated the Louisiana Purchase with Napoleon in 1803.

2

If the events of 1811 were not enough to stir a dull observer, February 1812 brought a discovery sufficient to sicken him. Lilburne and Isham Lewis, who are neighbors in Smithland and nephews of Thomas Jefferson, brutally murdered a slave boy. Previously a respectable Livingston County citizen, Lilburne

Lewis then dismembered, or forced another to dismember, the slave boy with an axe. The murder occurred in December on the night of the first earthquake. The body parts were burned and hidden in the masonry of a rebuilt chimney. A fortnight ago another great quake collapsed the chimney anew and revealed the body parts to a passing dog. The dog began to feast on the head. The discovery of the dog eating the slave boy's head led to Lilburne and Isham Lewis' indictment.

May 1815. River traffic has risen substantially since the end of the war. Among the flatboats and keelboats are an increasing number of steamboats.

Captain Henry Shreve touched the bank in the *Enterprise*, bound from New Orleans for Louisville, and then on to Pittsburg and Brownsville. Captain Shreve is of the opinion that the Fulton-Livingston monopoly of steamboat commerce on the lower Mississippi will fall. The way will be open for the free rise of steamboat freight and passenger service on the Mississippi and every other navigable river. In light of that event, he admired our position where the Ohio and Cumberland meet.

November 1815. John Bell has built a fine inn on Riverfront Street in town between Mill and Walnut, a clear sight across the Cumberland from Salt Point. The principal structure is built of red brick in the Georgian style. It is two stories high and has at its rear two milled-lumber structures with an interior courtyard that give Bell Tavern a U shape.

There is a fireplace to warm nearly every one of the 40 rooms. The Bell family members are resident innkeepers. The tavern is the finest building in Smithland and is certain to become a place of rest for many travelers on the rivers.

April 12, 1817. The steamboat *Washington* wooded up at Smithland today. She is Captain Shreve's boat. He expects to complete a Louisville-to-New Orleans round trip in about 40 days. The *Washington* is an unusually large boat, having two decks and displacing 403 tons. Its boilers are up out of the hold on the first deck.

May 1819. A steam-breathing dragon has descended upon Smithland. The *Western Engineer*, a government expedition steamboat, is a 75-foot sternwheeler with a serpent's head at the bow. Her destination is the junction of the Yellowstone and

Missouri rivers. The serpent's head, with its steam passage, is intended to impress the Indians of the Far West.

Craig Hawkins, March 1822. It is a proud and exciting time for us. We commissioned a steamboat to be built at New Albany, Indiana. Although at 160 tons our boat is smaller, we modeled it after Captain Shreve's *Post Boy*, a 230-ton side-wheeler. We named our steamer *George Hawkins*, in honor of our recently deceased grandfather. As odd as it might seem to call a boat "she" when it is named for a man, that is what we do. She measures 114 feet long, 22 feet wide and draws 3-1/2 feet when light. The draft is shallow enough to nose her into the bank so we can load freight and board passengers on a ramp that passes from the main deck to dry land. The main deck holds the boilers, freight and deck passengers. The second deck accommodates cabin passengers. The pilothouse sits atop the cabins just aft of the chimneys.

Cousin John and I spent a fortnight on the rivers with Captain Shreve learning to pilot and maintain a steamboat before taking delivery on the *George Hawkins*. All of Smithland, alas, nearly all of Livingston County turned out for our arrival at the mouth of the Cumberland.

We plan to ply the rivers between Cairo and Nashville, and perhaps as far as Louisville up the Ohio, dependent on the opportunity to carry passengers and freight.

May 1825. Captain Hall and his steamer *Mechanic* make frequent stops at Smithland. About midnight on April 29th, Captain Hall was surprised to be aroused from his sleep by the arrival of the Mississippi River steamer *Natchez*. To Captain Hall's utter astonishment, from aboard the *Natchez* to board the *Mechanic* came the Marquis de Lafayette, the French general who fought alongside George Washington in the Revolution. Although the war was 50 years ago, it is not forgotten, especially by an educated man like Captain Hall.

General Lafayette, his hosts and party sought passage up the Cumberland to Nashville, where they expected to visit General Andrew Jackson and others. The *Natchez* at 206 tons could not pass Harpeth Shoals at this stage of water. At 116 tons, the *Mechanic* can pass the shoals in a drought year.

A week later, after a pleasant visit to Nashville, General Lafayette returned to Smithland aboard the *Mechanic*. Word of the General's earlier transfer had spread through town, and we anticipated his return. The trustees formed a welcoming committee, and the whole town turned out to greet and honor the General. He had a carriage tour of Smithland, was the guest of honor at a fine dinner and spent a restful night at Bell Tavern.

Word came down the Ohio that at about midnight on Sunday, May 8, while carrying General Lafayette to Louisville, the *Mechanic* was snagged and rapidly sank at Deer Creek on the Kentucky side, about 125 miles below Louisville. The General was roused from his sleep and quickly taken ashore but not before he tumbled into the river and nearly drowned. He subsequently and correctly absolved Captain Hall of any fault, a relief even to an honorable man who lost a fine steamboat.

July 1826. Sad news reached Smithland that the nation has lost two great patriots to whom it owes a deep debt. John Adams and Thomas Jefferson died within a few hours of each other on July 4th, 50 years to the day after the signing of the Declaration of Independence.

April 1832. Having fathered three daughters, I was beginning to think my immediate family was destined to consist of only the gentler sex. Anne has changed all that by giving birth to a boy. He was kicking and screaming before the midwife could smack his bottom. We named him Will, and he seems to have strength enough to live up to it.

October 1836. Stanley Gower has bought Bell Tavern and renamed it for himself. Gower House is still the finest inn in Smithland and a favorite stop for many travelers on the Cumberland and Ohio rivers.

April 1837. We have taken the *George Hawkins No. 4* on her first run up the Cumberland. The Smithland shipyard has built a fine boat. The engines came down the Ohio by steamer from Pittsburg. Also from that place came the new bell. It is big, an alloy of tin and brass and looks the color of pewter. It likely weighs 250 pounds. It is about three feet in diameter and height. It is not tolled. It hangs stationary, mounted in a cast iron frame and bolted to the roof. The clapper is pulled against the bell's side. The bell has a deep, rich, resonant tone. It is not as immediate and alarming as a firehouse bell. Not that it cannot be heard from a distance when it signals an imminent departure, it just is not shrill.

May 1838. Inspection revealed flaws in the *George Hawkins No. 4*'s machinery that if left untended could cause a complete breakdown. But rather than build a new boat, we decided to keep the *Hawkins* running. She is such a fine steamer that it seemed a shame to scrap or sell her before her time had come. She needed major work that could not be effected at the Smithland shipyard. Inquiring about costs for the work, we found the best offer came from Cincinnati. Although that place is a full 500 miles up the Ohio, to effect the repairs there was still to our advantage.

John and I and as small a crew as could manage the boat made the journey expecting to return to Smithland in two to three weeks. I thought young Will would enjoy and learn from a steamboat trip to a big city like Cincinnati. He had no reluctance about leaving his lessons behind, but parting with his mama and playmates caused some sorrow.

With the repairs admirably done, and having performed a test run with the renewed *George Hawkins*, we prepared to leave the Cincinnati landing late in the afternoon of Wednesday, April 25th. Departing the landing immediately following the *Hawkins* was the *Moselle*, a fine new boat that, under the command of Captain Perrin, had just completed a trip from Saint Louis to Cincinnati in the record time of two days and 16 hours, beating the previous record by several hours. Captain Perrin went to extraordinary lengths to maintain the public's thoughts of the *Moselle* as the fastest steamboat on the river.

As we proceeded down, the *Moselle*, already heavily loaded with excited passengers, proceeded up to board more passengers before rounding and making haste for Saint Louis, her scheduled destination. We had not been under way more than 15 minutes when we heard the most horrifying explosion from upriver. We reversed our course and sped against the current to investigate the origin of the explosion and to see if we could render aid. We had been running at top speed for perhaps another 15 minutes when we began to see debris floating down. We slowed so we could maneuver and avoid a collision. To starboard we saw what appeared to be a large section of decking. A man's corpse, bloody and headless, lay across it. That sight left no doubt as to what had happened. Before the wreck came into view, we knew the *Moselle* had exploded. And we knew we were about to see much suffering. Exposing young Will to such horrors gave me pause, but people needed aid.

On our larboard side, we saw a floating barrel that had been cleaved in half on the long dimension and finished to keep its shape regular. It floated with the open side up and appeared to be stuffed with bedding. John eased the *Hawkins* to larboard, and I reached for the barrel with a pole hook. As I drew it to the hull, I was astonished to see an infant tucked in the bedding. My first thought was that it was dead, but as I lifted the barrel aboard, the baby turned its head, squirmed and began a long yawn. I had awakened a peacefully sleeping infant.

We kept upstream and continued to scan the river, but the center of attention on board the *Hawkins* became the infant in the barrel cradle. Will was particularly taken with the baby. It was dry and unhurt, and if that was not astonishing enough, the infant was completely content. We determined the baby was a girl and as long as she made no demands, we could turn our attention to aiding the *Moselle*.

The wreckage floated half-sinking just ahead. Only the section behind the paddlewheels was still partially intact. The entire forward half was completely torn away. There were corpses and body parts strewn on the Ohio bank, blown there by the explosion. We launched our yawl and began to pull survivors aboard it and the *Hawkins*. There were screams and wails and moans of agony all around us. We gathered perhaps 20 or 25 survivors, some injured and some not. There were no boats on either the Ohio or Kentucky shore, and the few people who were there had launched log floats to render aid.

The *Moselle* had proceeded about a mile above the Cincinnati landing to Fulton to bring more passengers aboard. Here, outside Cincinnati proper, the light population was quickly overwhelmed in its ability to help the dazed and wounded. Others from the surrounding area reached the site and helped. We did the best we could on the river and, satisfied there were no more survivors afloat there, we ferried our passengers to the near Ohio shore.

The scene on the Fulton landing was chaotic. There was copious blood and great suffering. Husbands searched for wives and children, mothers for babies, children for parents. Some of the voices were colored with an Irish brogue. Others frantically spoke what I soon learned was German. Will and I walked among the people searching in vain for anyone who knew the infant girl I tenderly carried. She now persistently announced her hunger and discomfort. In this scene of deep grief, pain, loss and anguish, my immediate task was to satisfy the fundamental needs of an evidently orphaned baby girl. Having fathered three daughters and a son, I had some acquaintance with infant care, but in the present circumstance I was not properly equipped to answer an infant's hunger. Among the homes along the river, I managed to find a woman with an infant of her own. Under the circumstances, the young mother required no persuasion. She volunteered to temporarily serve.

We stayed for two days, helping wherever we could and trying to find the baby's parents. Mr. Broadwell, the *Moselle*'s agent, said that most of the deck passengers were Irish and German emigrants on their way to Saint Louis and then farther west. He speculated that as many as 250 people perished in the tragedy and that the baby girl's parents most probably were among them. No one came forward to accept the child, so it became a choice between leaving the infant to become a ward of the city or taking her home to Smithland.

The people of Cincinnati were aggrieved and preparing for a public funeral for victims of the disaster. With the mayor's blessing, we left Cincinnati with the infant and a hired wet nurse. As we steamed down the Ohio, Will and I wondered how his mama and sisters would react to a new family member. Of course, they accepted the infant girl instantly. We named her Beth.

3

December 1838. Hundreds of Cherokees are encamped at Mantle Rock in our county. Ice on the Ohio prevents their crossing. Many have died, and the suffering is awful. Their forced removal from the remnants of their ancestral lands seems to be President Jackson's personal vendetta.

June 1840. Following a design I observed in Cairo, we have floated a wharfboat at our landing just below Smithland. We built a warehouse and an area fairly resembling a passenger terminal on the decks of barges that measure 25 by 100 feet. We boldly labeled the walls Hawkins Wharfboat—Smithland, Kentucky, on both the shore and river sides. Rather than nosing into the river-bank, steamboats tie to the wharfboat, which rises and falls with the river. Transfer for passengers and freight is easily effected.

April 1842. The *Fulton*, Captain Bill Forsythe's Pittsburg sidewheeler bound for Saint Louis from Louisville, tied to our wharfboat today. Among the passengers was a man who, judging by his speech, was British. That was surprising because the velvet waistcoat and gold chains and pins he wore beneath his frock coat made him look more like an American riverboat gambler than an English gentleman.

I first heard a crew member who was tending to the gentleman's baggage address him as "Mr. Dickens." I then heard the woman who accompanied the gentleman address him as "Charles." Something akin to a bolt of lightning struck me square in the forehead. Mr. and Mrs. Charles Dickens were standing amid the hogsheads and crates on the Hawkins Wharfboat in Smithland, Kentucky!

I took the opportunity to introduce myself as the proprietor and asked whether I could be of service. Mr. Dickens said he understood there was comfortable lodging and excellent food nearby. He mentioned that their party had been plagued by bedbugs in previous hotels and found the fare aboard the *Fulton* lacking. I said I was sorry for their unfortunate experience and recommended the Gower House, which I was certain he, his personal secretary, Mrs. Dickens and her maid would find altogether comfortable. I asked if they wanted a carriage. They consulted and Mrs. Dickens said that on such a beautiful spring afternoon they would walk. She asked if I could arrange for their baggage to be sent. I responded that certainly I could. Mr. Dickens tipped his hat and graciously thanked me. He then asked if I would perhaps like to join him for a stroll after they had taken their evening meal. I responded I would and asked if meeting him at the Gower House at 7 p.m. might be suitable. He replied it would. Mrs. Dickens smiled and nodded, delicately took Mr. Dickens' arm, and they turned and walked toward town and the Gower House.

I arrived at 7 to find Mr. Dickens standing out front gazing at the river and waiting for me. I had brought along my copy of *Oliver Twist*, which I had bought and read a year or two earlier. I asked Mr. Dickens if he would be so kind as to inscribe it. He replied he would but only if it was the copyrighted edition published in London rather than a pirated American edition. I handed it to him to have a look. He turned to the title page and discovered it was a British first edition. He explained there is no international copyright law between Britain and America, so authors are pirated on both sides of the Atlantic. He said he earns nothing from stolen work published in the United States and has no recourse. I said I had bought my copy from a bookseller in Nashville. Mr. Dickens judged him an honest, legitimate bookseller and said he would be happy to inscribe my edition.

With that, we stepped inside the Gower House's lobby, Mr. Dickens removed the pen at the registration desk from its inkwell and opened the cover of *Oliver Twist* to its first page. He turned to me and asked whether I was married and, if so, were we blessed with children? I replied that my wife, Anne, and I were the proud parents of four daughters and a son. He said he and Mrs. Dickens had two girls and a boy, but, sadly, had to leave them behind for this trip to America and now missed them so.

He began to write and dipped the pen back into the inkwell twice before finishing. He rolled a half-moon blotter over the fresh ink, closed the book and handed it to me. I thought it impolite to open the cover and read the inscription, so I waited until after our stroll.

We walked first by lamplight along the riverfront, then wove our way through the streets and lanes of town to the base of the hills and back. Our conversation flowed smoothly from one topic to another. At the outset, I said I hoped he did not mind my saying so, but I was surprised he was such a young man. He said, oh, not *that* young. He and his wife had just celebrated his 30th birthday in February, so he had three full decades behind him.

I countered I had four and then some, and he asked whether they were all in Smithland. I replied, yes, that my folks had settled here in 1805. I continued to say that my brother and I had built our first steamer in '22, the wharfboat just two years back and also that we farmed the bottoms. He said with some surprise that we must be very busy and asked if we had help. Oh, yes, I replied, on the steamer and wharfboat, and the farm. He turned and raised an eyebrow. "Slaves?" he asked. I replied that no Hawkins family had ever owned slaves, here or elsewhere. I added with emphasis that slavery is not something we abide. He said he was pleased to hear it, that he regards slavery as an intolerable evil and is surprised to no end that it survives in America, of all places. The moral and economic arguments are specious, he said. Beneath them lies the true reason: racialism, pure and simple. I said I agreed, but that it is not a belief I can shout from the rooftops in Kentucky without endangering myself, my family and my livelihood. I added I was sure the day would come when the issue would tear America apart. He replied he was afraid I was correct.

Mr. Dickens spoke of some of his experiences since arriving in Boston in January. He had special affection for Cincinnati and spoke highly of a Choctaw Indian chief he had met aboard one of the steamers. He also said he had met and become friendly with Washington Irving. He asked if I had read that author's work. I replied I had read *A Tour of the Prairies* and that our children never tired of Anne's or my reading aloud from "Rip Van Winkle" and "The Legend of Sleepy Hollow." With that, we had completed our circuit of Smithland and returned to the Gower House. Mr. Dickens thanked me, and I assured him the pleasure was mine. We bade each other good night and parted.

In the morning, the Dickens party was among the first to board the *Fulton*. They looked pleased and well rested. Mr. Dickens thanked me again for the lodging recommendation and our evening stroll. They were at the rail of the *Fulton's* boiler deck after the boat had rounded and headed downstream. I waved goodbye, Mr. Dickens tipped his hat, and Mrs. Dickens waved in reply.

When I had returned home the previous evening, I opened *Oliver Twist* and read the inscription by candlelight:

> *For Mr. Craig Hawkins of Smithland, Kentucky.*
> *May you and yours enjoy long and happy lives.*
>
> > *In friendship,*
> > *Charles Dickens*

March 1849. It seems that half the men east of the Mississippi have gone to California to search for gold.

May 1849. Saint Louis newspapers report fire at that place has taken several squares near the river and 23 steamboats lying at the levee. Four people died, and the loss is said to be $5 million.

July 1854. The city of Paducah, 12 miles below Smithland at the mouth of the Tennessee River, has initiated service with the New Orleans and Ohio Railroad. The leaders of Smithland decided that steamboats serve passenger and freight transportation more than adequately, and discouraged the railroad from establishing a line to our town. It subsequently went to Paducah. With permission from the state legislature, city leaders there invested $200,000 of public money in the railroad.

January 1856. As has been our custom for many years now, we gathered at the Smithland homeplace on New Year's Day. We had Hawkins kin from Livingston and nearby Kentucky counties, from across the Tennessee River in the Purchase and across the Ohio River in Illinois. Some came by horseback, some by wagon or buggy, and some by steamer. With three generations of grampas and grammas, aunts, uncles, cousins, and brothers and sisters, we had more than 50 people. We did manage, however, with our buildings and boats, to sleep everyone without having to send one soul to an inn in town.

With that many people, we had a flood of news, stories and announcements to catch up on. Even in consideration of all that competition for attention, Will's news was the most surprising. We had gathered in the warehouse for the midday meal. After the last slice of pie was eaten by the smallest child, I called for the group's attention. I mentioned what a happy occasion it was this day as it is every New Year's Day to see the success that has grown from George and Meredith Hawkins' pioneering into Kentucky. Then I opened the floor to news and announcements.

Will came about sixth or seventh. He stood on a riser in front of the room and asked Beth to come up and stand beside him. As is his way, with no hesitation, in a firm and straightforward manner, with great confidence, Will announced that he and Beth were to be married. A curious mix of gasps and cheers rolled through the room. My own reaction mirrored that of the families. It was at once shock and joy. There had always been a bond between Will and Beth. It was there from the moment we pulled her from the Ohio River as a sleeping infant in a barrel cradle.

In a way most unusual for a young boy, Will doted on Beth. He was proud and protective and encouraging. As they grew older, Will never shunned Beth as most boys do with kid sisters. He included her in everything. Anything the boys did, Beth did. She had spunk and grit, and if her size ever held her back, Will was there to help.

Although strong and having a firmness of purpose, Beth is a wisp of a girl. I doubt she weighs more than a sack of grain. She looks like a willow sapling—straight up and down, with a still thinner branch here and there. Her walk is like a heron's, stepping lightly on graceful stilts in the shallows near the river's edge. Beth is no longer a child. She is a delicate, yet strong young woman. Her red curls, green eyes and freckles give her Irish heritage away better than any courthouse birth record ever could.

And here she stood nearly 18 beside my son, Will, a young man I for the life of me cannot figure how I was good enough to produce. He must have gotten most of himself from his mama. Now near 24 and the best pilot on three rivers, he had rivermen of long experience deferring to him when he was 16 and not yet old enough to hold a pilot's license. Will is a courageous young man. The air about him is not bravado. It is not brash and impulsive. It is knowledge, confidence and certainty beyond his years.

My handsome son is to marry my lovely daughter. The gasps told the thoughts that a brother was to wed his sister. The cheers were the recognition that they were not kin and that a more perfect union could not be imagined.

July 1857. Beth has lost a child from her womb before it achieved even two months in age. Doc Sanders attributes the loss to the delicacy of Beth's form.

June 1858. Our bottomlands are underwater. We come and go from our high land in river skiffs. Tragically, Beth has lost another child. We brought Doc Sanders by skiff. He told Beth that she will be fine, but if she wants to be a mother, next time she is with child, she will have to stay in bed from the moment she is aware of the child until the day of its birth. I wonder if a woman of Beth's spirit can endure the inactivity. But a woman of Beth's determination, I know she will.

Will Hawkins, April 1860. Heeding Doc Sanders, as soon as Beth knew she was with child, she stayed to bed. We determined that if she and the child were to survive nine months this way, we would have to make it an active and joyous time, rather than treating her condition as an illness. Beth took up handcrafts. She knitted and sewed and made fine lace. She read books from our collection and newspapers that came by steamer from near and distant points. I was not surprised to see Beth carve and whittle dolls, but others were. She kept up with autumn tasks like coring and pitting fruit to be put by. We played card games and reminisced about things we did as children. Our sisters and brothers-in-law and their children visited often. All of us kept Beth's spirits up.

The baby came in April. He was an extremely small boy. Doc Sanders said the infant came at least a month too soon. Beth was exhausted from the birth. Through sheer determination, on her third attempt, she had become a mother. My admiration, love and respect for her, which I hardly thought could grow deeper, did deepen.

In a moment of hesitation and giddiness fueled by exhaustion just after Doc Sanders cut and tied the cord, Beth allowed that she was almost afraid to hold our son because he was so tiny and delicate. With a girlish giggle, Beth said it was like handling a plucked chicken. That brought relief and laughter to the birth room. In the spirit of the moment, we named our son Earl Lee. It was a short step to Early. He would struggle to survive, and he would succeed.

4

November 1860. The tension has been rising like yeast bread since long before I was born. The economic needs of a relative few Southern planters were held by most to justify enslaving African people. Europeans find slavery abhorrent, especially in a country whose Constitution has among its purposes securing the blessings of liberty. Dickens came to America in part because slavery existing here strained his belief, and he had to see for himself.

The compromises mandated by Congress bought time. They postponed the inevitable. People like John Brown, Frederick

Douglass and Dred Scott made certain that the basic evil of slavery would not fade from public conversation.

Abraham Lincoln of Illinois has been elected President. Our kin there say he is a good man. He must be—he was born in Kentucky! Now he bears an awesome responsibility. The sovereign state of South Carolina threatened to secede from the Union if Mr. Lincoln was elected. Because the Democrats split their vote, Mr. Lincoln has been elected, and most people think that South Carolina will make good on her threat. We are headed for civil war.

December 1860. Claiming denial of its states' rights, South Carolina has seceded. Other cotton states are sure to follow. There is much talk in town and on the rivers. Which states will declare which way? What will become of our country? What will happen in our lives?

Feelings in Smithland fall on all sides. Some declare for the Union, some against it, and some want neutrality. Our families are in this last group. Most in Paducah and the Purchase side with the South. Elsewhere generally in Kentucky, the feeling is strongly Union.

Every night for as long as I can remember, we have left oars and a river skiff lying among the willows on the bank below the wharfboat. On the mornings the skiff is gone, we know to take another to the Illinois shore and bring it back. They row to freedom by first crossing to Cumberland Island, then dragging the skiff on greased skids over to the Ohio, then rowing to a rest on Hamletsburg Bar and then finally to the Illinois shore.

April 1861. With a telegraph key at the Smithland *Times*, news reaches us soon after any distant event. On the 15th, word came across the wire that Fort Sumter in Charleston harbor had fallen to the Southern forces after more than two days' bombardment. Seven states have formed the Confederate States of America.

Like most in Kentucky, Beth wants neutrality. She signed the women's petition against civil war. I enlisted in the Home Guard. I will not fire on my neighbor without provocation, but should my neighbor trespass against me, I will defend myself and mine to the fullest of my ability.

I know of families split brother opposite brother, father against son. No such instance exists in any Hawkins family. Most stand steadfast by the Union. Others declare neutrality but lean Union. Our nephew, Josh, came home from school with these facts from his lessons: In 1850, the Kentucky State Legislature voted to send sections of Kentucky marble as the State's contribution to the General Washington monument being built in Washington City. The inscription read, "Under the auspices of heaven and the precepts of Washington, Kentucky will be the last to give up the Union."

June 1861. Our immediate neighbor, Tennessee, has left the Union to become the 11th state in the Confederacy. Many see the Southern cause as hopeless. The Union has every advantage—population, wealth, industry. For the South to contend it will prevail is foolish. Jeff Davis predicts a war "the like of which men have not seen." Sensible men see that Mr. Davis will lose that war, but only after a terrible price has been paid on both sides. Why cannot people resolve their differences without taking up arms?

We will see further economic effects immediately. Through traffic on the rivers is already down. Now there will be no boats to or from Nashville, and no boats above the Tennessee state line on either the Cumberland or Tennessee.

September 1861. The *Charley Bowen* leaves Evansville Tuesdays at noon on her twice-weekly run to Cairo. Depending on the stage of water, the number of hails she answers coming down, and the time she spends at each landing, the *Bowen* ordinarily reaches our wharfboat early Wednesday morning. She connects with Cumberland and Tennessee river packets for mail, freight and passengers, and continues down to Paducah and Cairo.

By late Wednesday morning September 4th, the *Bowen* was long overdue. There was no telegraphic news from above that she was delayed. She finally came into sight just before noon. By then, even the most patient passengers on the wharfboat had lost their tempers. Many had wandered off, saying they would return at the sound of the *Bowen*'s whistle. With no ice, perishable freight on the wharf was nearly ready to feed to the hogs.

It was immediately evident even from a distance that something was amiss on the *Bowen*. She was proceeding slowly and with great caution, but at the same time blowing her whistle and clanging her bell in alarm. One action, or lack of it, was at odds with the other. She passed the head of Cumberland Island and rounded in a clumsy manner opposite the wharfboat to put her bow properly upstream. As the *Bowen*'s deck hands tossed her lines to our men, I saw that Captain Dexter rather than a pilot stood at the wheel in the pilothouse. William Bently, the clerk, shouted from the boiler deck, "Blinn has collapsed. He needs a doctor." I recognized the name. I know Enos Blinn. He is my friend and a fine pilot.

I sent a rouster scurrying to tell Doc Sanders that we would be by shortly with an emergency patient. The *Bowen* had barely dropped her stage when John Dexter and another clerk fairly ran down the ramp carrying Enos unconscious, face-up in a litter. He looked whiter than the canvas. They loaded the litter on Tom McCandles' dray, and Tom cracked the whip over his mule team to run helter-skelter up to Doc Sanders.

Word soon came back that Enos was gone. The rivers had lost a good man. Captain Dexter had come down from Evansville with only one pilot and, for the present, the *Charley Bowen* was without a pilot for her run to Paducah and on to Cairo. That state of affairs was something of a predicament in Smithland these days. Henry Dexter is a Union man, and the *Bowen* is a Union boat flying the Union flag. If any man challenges that flag, Captain Dexter carries a four-pounder aboard to protect it. Although there were no hostilities in Smithland, there was considerable Southern sentiment. Finding a licensed pilot in Smithland to stand at the wheel of a Union boat was not an easy task.

I am for maintaining the Union, and I detest slavery. I am for neutrality, but I lean Union. I am also a practical business-man dependent on river traffic and the goodwill of my neighbors. I have a family to feed, a farm to maintain, a working packet to run on the rivers and a wharfboat where I have to keep peace between sometimes opposing interests. I do not believe in taking up arms against my neighbors. Until this moment, although I had aired my sympathies quietly among like-minded citizens, I had not publicly declared my position. Now, Henry Dexter confronted me.

"Captain Hawkins, I do not mean to put you in a corner, but your boat is up on the ways, and I need a pilot to take the *Bowen* down to Paducah and Cairo. I doubt there is another pilot in Smithland or Paducah who shares my Union sentiments, but I am sure I can find a qualified man in Mound City or Cairo for the return run to Evansville. If you will pilot the *Bowen* to Cairo, I will pay you well and have you back in Smithland before midnight Thursday. I know our schedule says sooner, but we have had a delay."

My thoughts crystallized in a moment, I nodded my assent, and went to tell Beth and to fetch my baggage.

To double her bad luck, the *Bowen* lost power as we approached the Paducah wharf. Now, I have been on the rivers since I was a boy. I can guide a steamer safely by night or day, highwater or low, snags and bars be damned, but machinery pays heed to no pilot. The pitman on the larboard engine separated from the crosshead, depriving the crank of thrust and throwing the paddlewheel out of balance on its shaft. The machinery came to a groaning halt, but because the engineer was quick enough to prevent damage to the engines, the only harm done was to some replaceable hardware. That is not to mention the Cairo-bound passengers' tempers and the *Bowen*'s reputation, however. We retained only downbound freight and a few passengers who intended to make rail or steamer connections in Cairo.

In spite of some Rebel sympathizers among their men, the Paducah Marine Ways agreed to effect repairs and predicted one day's delay.

Friday, September 6, 1861. Impatient to be under way and in spite of the Thursday-evening hour, Captain Dexter reloaded the downbound freight and rousted the Cairo passengers from their after-dinner cigars at the St. Francis Hotel. He told them they could sleep in comfort in their staterooms on the *Bowen* and awake to make their connections in Cairo Friday morning. Captain Dexter was determined to recapture the punctuality of his schedule.

As we proceeded down, there was not another boat on the river. Even at night, that is unusual for the southern Ohio. There is normally at least some upbound traffic. Its absence was not due to a lack of water. There was 7-1/2 feet on the shoalest bars. Being the only steamer on the river was eerie.

As we approached Mound City, I saw through my glass in the darkness the faint outlines of several large boats lying still in the stream. A light in the distance had captured my attention, but just as I trained my glass upon it, the light disappeared. The

Bowen being upwind, perhaps her sounds had alerted the boats below. I slowed and steered toward the Illinois shore, but not wanting to exceed the channel, I unavoidably remained within hailing distance of what I could now see were five boats. Two did not have the silhouette of typical packets. At that point I realized what I beheld—two gunboats and three steamers. Just as I sent a clerk to summon Captain Dexter to the pilothouse, a commanding voice, altered in tone and volume by a megaphone, fairly exploded across the water's surface:

"This is the *USS Tyler*. Stop and hold your boat where you are."

I pulled the stopping and chestnut bells and ordered the clerk to direct a lantern on the *Bowen*'s Union flag. Quiet hung in the night air for a moment. Then the *Bowen* was illuminated by two lantern beams directed on her from the *Tyler*. Captain Dexter and I shielded our unaccustomed eyes from the light.

"Identify yourself," the voice commanded.

Captain Dexter shouted in reply, "We are the *Charley Bowen*, a Union boat from Evansville bound for Cairo."

Seeing the *Bowen*'s Union banner and hearing Captain Dexter's reply confirming the *Bowen*'s identity must have been enough to satisfy the men aboard the *Tyler*.

"Hold your position. We will launch a yawl and board your vessel," the voice announced.

The *Tyler* lowered the yawl to the stream with five men aboard. Three wore Navy uniforms—one man at each oar and one in the stern. An Army officer and a man in citizen's dress sat facing the bow. The yawl came alongside. The men at the oars remained aboard. The other three men boarded at the *Bowen*'s main deck. The Army officer and the citizen advanced toward Captain Dexter and me as we descended the stairs from the pilothouse. The Navy man stood on the *Bowen*'s main deck beside the yawl. With distinct firmness, the Army officer introduced himself and his citizen companion.

"I am Captain Hillyer and this is General Grant, United States Army."

I am certain the two men saw that Captain Dexter and I were taken aback by a rather small and slight man in citizen's dress being introduced as General Grant. Nevertheless, we removed to the main cabin to council.

General Grant said that he and his men were on a mission whose destination he could not disclose. He asked if we had passengers. With a trace of sheepishness, Captain Dexter allowed that under normal circumstances the *Bowen* would be carrying far more passengers, but two mishaps coming down from Evansville had reduced the passenger count to 12.

"And crew?" General Grant inquired.

"Twenty crew, including those present, plus six roustabouts," Captain Dexter replied.

"All loyal to the Union?" asked General Grant.

"I would not tolerate otherwise, but I cannot vouch for the passengers. Four men boarded in Paducah, and you know as well as I that there is much secession sentiment there," Captain Dexter responded.

General Grant spoke plainly. "We have three transports. One, the *W. B. Terry*, has broken down, and the other two cannot carry the *Terry*'s men. I do not want to commandeer a civilian boat carrying crew, passengers and freight unless I must. We are opposite Mound City where I estimate I can find a steamer and crew. However, I do not want to land at Mound City with one of the able transports or a gunboat. Although it is a Union place, there are spies, and the chance of our mission being exposed is too great. Captains Dexter and Hawkins, this is what I want to do: Captain Hillyer and the Navy men will return to the *Tyler*. I will accompany you into Mound City on the *Bowen*. My citizen's dress will arouse no suspicion there. With your assistance, I will quickly find a suitable boat and crew and return to our flotilla. When I do, the *Bowen* can continue down to Cairo. Tell your crew that when we reach Mound City, no one is to step ashore nor speak a word to anyone at the wharf. Your passengers are to remain in their staterooms. Speaking of your passengers, why have none awakened?"

"I suppose it is the supper and drink they enjoyed in Paducah," I replied.

"I see. Are we agreed then, gentlemen?" General Grant asked.

"Yes, sir," Captain Dexter and I simultaneously replied.

Captain Hillyer returned to the yawl, and it to the *Tyler*. General Grant and I ascended the stairs to the pilothouse, while Captain Dexter went to speak to the crew. I pulled the stopping bell to come ahead full and steered for the dim lights of Mound City, a short way off on the Illinois shore. General Grant stood to my side and slightly to the rear. I felt his eyes observing me.

We were at the wharf and secured within perhaps 10 minutes time. The Federal government having leased Hambleton's Marine Ways and having made Mound City a Naval shipyard, we were met at the wharf by several sailors and an officer. The officer came aboard the *Bowen*, where General Grant took him aside and conversed quietly with him. General Grant then asked me to accompany him, General Grant, ashore and Captain Dexter to remain aboard to see to General Grant's earlier orders regarding the passengers and crew. General Grant made both requests in a most firm but gentlemanly manner.

The hour was about midnight. There were several boats lying idle at the wharf. General Grant allowed that he was not an experienced steamboat man and asked my counsel in choosing a boat. I wondered why me and not the Naval officer but did not pursue the point. As we walked along the wharf, I recognized the *William H. Brown*, a Pittsburg boat that I knew had been sold to the U. S. Quartermaster Department in June. At 200 tons, she was a sturdy boat and adequate to the task. I recommended the *Brown* to General Grant, and he readily accepted. We returned to where the Naval officer stood, and General Grant ordered him to raise a crew immediately.

As we waited, General Grant inquired after my credentials and experience on the rivers. I replied that I was a licensed first-class pilot on the Ohio to Cincinnati, the Cumberland to Nashville and the Tennessee to Florence. I added that I was master of the *George Hawkins No. 8*, a second-generation captain and pilot, and on the rivers since a boy. General Grant allowed that perhaps he was getting better at spotting a good riverman. He said the Union needed men who knew these rivers. He had seen reports of Union boats having run aground because the pilots were not local men and did not know the rivers. He asked if I would serve. At that moment and under those circumstances, whatever hesitation I had about abandoning my position on neutrality and siding with the Union disappeared. I said I would be honored to serve the Union. I had taken my first step in that direction for Captain Dexter. Now, I had fully committed to the Union for General Grant.

General Grant said that the Quartermaster would contact me by wire in Smithland. At that, Captain Duff and the crew of the *Brown* appeared. General Grant bade me farewell and I him. He boarded the *Brown* and I the *Bowen*. I backed the *Bowen* off the wharf as the *Brown* raised steam.

We spent the remainder of the night at the Cairo wharf. The only knowledge at that place about General Grant's mission was that he had gone up the Ohio and that a Captain Foote, arriving from Saint Louis following General Grant's departure, had pursued him upriver. Before General Grant left Cairo, he had closed the Ohio to all upbound packet traffic.

Although we passed two downbound transports as we proceeded up on Friday morning, it was not until we reached Paducah just before noon that we learned that General Grant, the gunboats *Tyler* and *Conestoga*, and a force of 1,800 men aboard the steamers *G. W. Graham*, *Platte Valley* and *William H. Brown*, had seized Paducah for the Union early that morning without firing a shot. General Grant claimed he did so just hours ahead of a 3,800-man Confederate force that was advancing from Columbus with the same purpose in mind. Hearing of the Union's occupation of Paducah, the Southern Army retreated.

5

There was a great commotion at the Paducah wharf. It seemed as if every citizen in that city had hastily packed his belongings, gathered his most favored slaves if a slave holder and descended upon the wharf. Union soldiers there told Captain Dexter that General Grant had left word that the *Charley Bowen*, Captain Dexter's Evansville boat flying the Union ensign, would be along by and by. General Grant's orders were to give the *Bowen* free passage, but all freight and passengers' baggage were to be searched for contraband. Any found was to be confiscated and its owner held in Paducah.

With the possible exception of me when my son, Early, was born, I do not think I have ever seen a man look prouder than Captain Henry Dexter did at that moment.

We, of course, complied with General Grant's order. The soldiers searched the baggage and required eight passengers to remain in Paducah. Their places were quickly filled by others who passed inspection, and we left the Paducah wharf in the early afternoon, going up.

Absent any intent of my own, circumstances had involved me in the war. In opposition to many of my Smithland neighbors, I was now a declared Union man.

September 8, 1861. Word of the Union Army's occupation of Paducah reached Smithland before the *Bowen* yesterday. Captain Dexter having found a pilot in Cairo to take the *Bowen* on to Evansville, only I stepped to the wharfboat in Smithland. None of the passengers or freight we had taken aboard in Paducah was bound for this place.

These facts disappointed several Livingston County residents who, having heard of the Union Army's being in neighboring McCracken County, decided to depart Smithland. They correctly thought that in a short time Union troops would be in Smithland to prevent the Rebels from gaining a foothold and to control river traffic at the confluence.

Unfortunately for these anxious residents, the *Bowen* was full and unable to take aboard deck or cabin passengers or freight. As soon as I stepped on the wharfboat, the *Bowen* was on its way to Evansville.

Later in the day, a small force of Union officers and men came up the Ohio by steamer to guard the mouth of the Cumberland. Some residents in Smithland were more upset by the fact that the Union force came on the Sabbath than they were that the soldiers were there at all. We anticipated that a larger force would follow, but there was no knowing when. With at least 1,800 men 12 miles away in Paducah and no sizable number of Confederate troops in the vicinity, the Union command evidently felt no urgency to occupy Smithland.

There was no point in trying to hide my declaration for the Union from my neighbors, and when word got around, I was the brunt of some hostility. Smithland is divided in its loyalties, but most of those who side with the Rebels see nothing to gain by provoking violence among their neighbors.

September 24, 1861. Today, the large Mississippi steamer *Empress* came up the Ohio and landed about 1,000 Union infantry and cavalry soldiers at Smithland. They were met with some grumbling and protest from a few citizens, but the troops occupied the town without firing or being fired upon.

At 854 tons, the *Empress* is an imposing and impressive sight. Rather than approaching the wharfboat, she touched the bank at the foot of Court Street in the heart of town. A seemingly endless stream of blue-uniformed soldiers marched double quick across her stage and onto the streets. They lined Riverfront Street above and below the landing and both sides of Court Street from the river to beyond the courthouse.

Squads seized the telegraph key in the *Times* office and served notice at the courthouse of the Union Army's occupation of this place. A proclamation was issued informing the citizens of the Army's intent and its expectations of the townspeople. The proclamation was signed by Colonel John McArthur, commanding four companies of the 12th Illinois regiment.

November 1861. The situation has changed substantially since Union troops occupied Smithland two months past. The force has been reduced from about 1,000 to 300. General C. F. Smith inspected the works earlier this month and found them respectable. The men stripped the trees from the verdant hills behind town to open lines of sight and shot for two 32-pounders and one 64-pounder. They constructed abatis around two separate earthworks about a half mile apart. The northern works, called Fort Wright, guard the mouth of the Cumberland and sight up the Ohio. The southern works, called Fort Star, sight down the Ohio. Together, the two earthworks make Fort Smith, named for the inspecting general whom General Grant made first commander at Paducah and Smithland. Fort Smith commands the Ohio and Cumberland confluence, and is manned and armed sufficiently to protect the rivers and repel any attack.

Some citizens whose uncompromising loyalty lay with the Rebels have simply pulled up stakes and moved south. Others who sympathize with the Confederates but are not so firm in their resolve have resigned themselves to a grumbling accommodation of the Federal presence. Still others pay no mind to taking sides. They see economic opportunity. The Northern Army will need food and arms and every manner of supplies. With so many Northern men at war and unable to work farms and factories, Northern civilian markets will need to be supplied. Kentucky, with hundreds of miles of river access to the North, is ideally placed to serve those markets.

Then there are spies and saboteurs. There are no kinder words to describe them. Neither we loyal citizens nor the Federal troops know who the spies and saboteurs among us are, but we know that word of the Federals' status and movements is being passed. A week ago, a coal barge that was tied to the Cumberland bank just above town mysteriously sank.

The Quartermaster employs me and the *George Hawkins* to carry Federal officers and men on official Army business. Our most frequent runs are to Paducah and Cairo. There is the occasional trip upriver to Evansville, Louisville or Cincinnati. Now and then we transport prisoners to detention in Paducah or Cairo.

When Navy gunboats are without pilots who know the rivers in this region, I am asked to pilot tinclads or ironclads. Most often, the missions are up the Cumberland or Tennessee, but sometimes up the Ohio. With commercial packet traffic reduced to a fraction of its former volume, the wharfboat and the *George Hawkins* would sit nearly idle were it not for being in service to the Union.

Thus far, my loyalty and service to the Federal government has met with no more than the resentful stare or remark. I sometimes fear for Beth and Early's safety, but they are well. I also fear that if the war and the Union presence is prolonged, division among the townspeople will deepen, and the danger of reprisals will mount.

While Union men are encamped in Sibley tents at the base of the hills behind Smithland, officers have taken up residence in the homes of citizens who were forced to vacate. That coercion does not sit well with anyone but the soldiers. The Saint Felix Hotel has been established as a headquarters and hostelry. The Army's presence and the increasing traffic in goods and men are deeply felt in both positive and negative ways.

6

February 1862. On my routine runs late in January, I saw that troops, transports and gunboats were massing at Paducah and Cairo as well as Smithland. Something big was afoot but nobody knew what.

The rivers were at flood stage. There were no Rebels up the Ohio, and the Mississippi below Cairo was so swollen as to forbid passage. I speculated that the Army and Navy would proceed up the Cumberland or the Tennessee. There were prizes for the Federals up both rivers, but it would take a hard fight to win them. Fort Donelson was on the west bank of the Cumberland just below Dover, Tennessee. Fort Henry was on the east bank of the Tennessee and Fort Heiman on the opposite bank close to the Kentucky-Tennessee border.

On February 2nd, I received orders from the Quartermaster: Infantry and cavalry troops at Fort Smith, except one infantry regiment, were to be transported to Paducah, some aboard the *George Hawkins* and some aboard the *Belle Memphis.*

Paducah looked like a beehive at the height of the spring bloom. The riverfront above and below the landing and up the Tennessee as far as Clarks River was alive with transports, gunboats, supply barges and troops. Late in the morning of the 3rd, our destination was finally revealed. About two dozen transports, escorted by four ironclad and three timberclad gunboats, would ascend the Tennessee to the Rebel forts. There were 15,000 Federal troops at Paducah but not transports sufficient to take them up all at once. The boats would steam 60 miles up the Tennessee, disembark their troops, return to Paducah and ascend again with the remainder.

As I backed the *George Hawkins* off the bank into the stream, the *New Uncle Sam* came up on my port side. Two men in Army officers' uniforms stood on the hurricane deck forward of the pilothouse. As they turned to look in my direction, I realized they were General Grant and his aide, Captain Rawlins. I asked my second pilot, James Drewry, to take the wheel, and I stepped up to the windows on the port side. As I straightened my stance and raised my right arm in the best military salute that I as a civilian could muster, General Grant returned my tribute.

It could well be that I flatter myself to think that a man with 15,000 soldiers under his command, commencing a mission that could turn the war, remembered a packet pilot from Smithland, but I had the impression that General Grant's gesture came from recognition, not polite reciprocation.

The river was high and carrying a great deal of debris. The big, heavy gunboats led our slow pace. The *George Hawkins* had aboard about 500 of General McClernand's troops, plus wagons and horses. Before sunrise on the 4th, after heavy rain, loud thunderstorms and a long night, we reached Itry Landing above Panther Creek less than two miles below Fort Henry. While General Grant boarded the ironclad *Essex* for a reconnaissance of the forts, we began to disembark troops. After the *Essex* took a shell in an exchange of fire with Fort Henry's guns, General Grant returned to Itry Landing and ordered the troops to re-embark. He wanted the transports to move down to Bailey's Ferry, safer at a full two miles below Fort Henry.

By nightfall, the disembarkation and encampment of General McClernand's troops was complete. General Grant held council aboard the *New Uncle Sam*, his headquarters boat. The transports commenced their return to Paducah to fetch General C. F. Smith's division.

On the 5th, the *George Hawkins* and other transports again ascended the Tennessee. We carried about 500 of General Smith's men plus horses, wagons and artillery. Just above Paducah, as I stood my watch and James slept in the texas, I heard a young male voice at the door behind me.

"Permission to enter the pilothouse please, sir."

I turned over my right shoulder, and without really regarding the soldier in blue, I replied, "Permission granted." He came forward and stood beside me about two arm lengths to my left.

"Name's Private Tom Dodge, 12th Illinois Infantry. Before the *E. J. Gay* went south, I cubbed under Captain John Brooks between Saint Louis and New Orleans."

He spoke earnestly and without hesitation. It was only then that I turned to look at him. I am sure he saw the shock that crossed by face. He looked impossibly young for a soldier. I estimated no more than 16.

"I am Captain Will Hawkins, master of the *George Hawkins*, Smithland, Kentucky."

"Pleased to make your acquaintance, sir," he said, "You have a fine boat." He extended his right hand.

As we shook hands firmly, my only thought was, what is this young lad doing far from home and going to war? With his long limbs, Private Dodge had the look of a colt. His cap struggled to contain a wild thatch of blond hair. His eyes shone a bright cornflower blue. He was a fine-looking boy, completely deferential and unassuming. I had to ask his age.

"Eighteen last fall. I left the *E. J. Gay* at Cairo and enlisted in the 12th," he said matter of factly. He seemed unaware of my concern about his innocence.

"Did your folks want you to stay with them on the farm?" I asked. I could tell by his hands that he was a farm boy.

"My brothers are there," he replied. "My folks were proud to see me cubbing on the Mississippi, and when I wrote that I had enlisted, my father replied that he wished he could do the same."

"Do you fear going into battle?" I ventured.

"I am here for the Union," he affirmed proudly.

We fell into easy conversation about steamboats and the rivers. I said that I had been down the Mississippi to New Orleans only once, years ago with my father. By comparison, Private Dodge was my senior in that respect, I said. Yes, he countered, but the Tennessee, Ohio and Cumberland were unknown to him. My companion was gracious beyond his years.

"At this stage of water, there are no shoals," I said. "Since there are no Rebels firing on us from the banks, the only dangers are debris and the other transports. There is enough river between us and the other boats that I am not concerned. Would you like to stand a watch at the wheel?"

He jumped at the opportunity, and I was happy to sit on the lazy bench for a spell. By and by, James came up from the texas and joined us. It was my turn to rest, but I did not want to leave my young friend. The three of us traded stories and laughter. Private Dodge told a tale that I repeat here as best I can recall:

"My Uncle Bill liked to go coon hunting. He would take me along when I was a young boy because he could not convince anyone else to go. He had a fine coon hound he called Red. Uncle Bill had a fondness for Limburger, which I thought was the foulest smelling thing this side of a corpse. Aunt Mae would not let that cheese in her home, so Uncle Bill always took it coon hunting.

"On one hunt, we were sitting on some downed timber waiting for Red to tree a coon. Uncle Bill was eating his Limburger by lantern light. Red made a running pass by us with his nose to the ground. He suddenly stopped and barked toward Uncle Bill. Bill broke off a piece of the Limburger and tossed it on the ground in front of Red. Red quickly snapped it up and just as quickly spit it out. Then he dropped to the ground, spun around and started licking his rear end.

"That did not change Uncle Bill's taste for Limburger, but it sure squashed any likelihood that I would ever eat it."

With the river at flood stage and full of debris, our progress was slow. Private Dodge, James and I traded time at the wheel, on the lazy bench or resting in the texas. The trip up from Paducah to Fort Henry took about 15 hours.

When we reached Pine Bluff, my orders were to disembark one brigade of General Smith's troops on the west bank of the river. They were to move against the Rebels at Fort Heiman, on the high ground opposite Fort Henry. Private Tom Dodge was in that brigade. James and I bade him farewell, and I felt my heart sink as I watched him march across the stage with the men of the 12th Illinois Infantry and onto the bank of the Tennessee.

Early the morning of the 6th, while a few transports remained at Bailey's Ferry to be on hand to ferry troops, the *George Hawkins* was among those that started down for Paducah. Although I heard the artillery from a great distance, I did not know the outcome until the morning of the 7th when Flag Officer Foote reached Paducah on the *Cincinnati*, accompanied by the *Saint Louis*.

The Union had won the day. General Lloyd Tilghman surrendered Fort Henry after an hourlong battle with the Navy gunboats. Infantry and cavalry on both sides of the river had gotten bogged down in mud and failed to reach either Fort Heiman or Fort Henry before the gunboats attacked and won.

James and I cheered and slapped each other's backs at the news. I knew James was thinking what I was thinking—Tom Dodge is safe. On an impulse, I yanked the clapper cord and rang the *Hawkins'* roof bell three times. The deep tone rolled through the morning air like waves in a still pond. The *Cincinnati* and the *Saint Louis* returned the ring, and in a moment, every steamer at the wharf was clanging its bell to celebrate the Union victory. The *Hawkins'* bell has seen a lot since it was cast in 1837.

Before Flag Officer Foote left Paducah, the Quartermaster told the transport captains that we would ascend the Cumberland to Fort Donelson with troops in a few days—as soon as Foote returned from Cairo following repairs.

Late in the afternoon of Wednesday the 12th, the *George Hawkins*, among at least a dozen heavily laden boats, left Paducah and steamed up the Ohio led by Flag Officer Foote and the gunboats *Saint Louis*, *Pittsburg*, *Louisville* and *Conestoga*. The *Conestoga* brought up the rear, towing a coal barge.

Smithland had already learned that Fort Henry had fallen. As we left the Ohio and entered the Cumberland, the only waves and smiles from the bank came from Hawkins folks. Beth and Early were among them. They knew not to cheer.

Of the three rivers I have known since a boy, my favorite is the beautiful blue Cumberland. I never imagined I would be steaming up it with a boatload of soldiers on their way to battle their countrymen.

No cub appeared in the pilothouse, so James and I traded watches at the wheel. We touched the west bank two miles below Fort Donelson at 11 o'clock on the night of the 13th. We began landing troops at first light.

Whatever the outcome, transports would be needed, so the steamer captains were ordered to move a safe distance below and wait. We received periodic dispatches as the battle progressed. The gunboats did not repeat their Fort Henry success. The armies fought through the 14th and 15th, but on Sunday morning the 16th we heard no battle sounds commence.

General Simon Bolivar Buckner surrendered Fort Donelson to General Ulysses S. Grant. General Grant's denial to yield concessions and his demand for an immediate and unconditional surrender made him a national hero overnight in the North.

Late in the afternoon, the transports moved up to the Dover landings and began to board prisoners and the wounded of both armies. There was barely an intact uniform among the Rebel prisoners. Many looked as if they were dressed in rags. Most prisoners were held on the main decks, while the cabins and staterooms were reserved for the wounded. There was no accurate count of how many would be transported. Estimates ran from 10,000 to 15,000. Whatever the number, it meant the steamers would be crowded—some to the point that the captains were concerned about swamping.

The scene at the landings was anything but orderly. The surrender had been sudden, and there was no plan in place for transportation of prisoners and wounded. Thousands of Rebels massed at the landings waiting to board steamers. Searching them for weapons and contraband caused long delays. Prisoners far outnumbered guards, especially aboard the boats. Some Rebels slogged through ankle-deep mud to reach the steamers' stages. The men were disarmed, but officers were allowed their swords and sidearms. This, combined with the sheer numbers of defeated and sometimes angry men, lent a feeling of uneasiness to the circumstances.

As Union soldiers boarded the Rebels, I helped get the wounded into the *Hawkins'* cabin, staterooms and berths. I was descending the stairs to the main deck when I looked across to the *Neptune*, which was at the bank next to the *Hawkins*. Two Federals carrying a wounded Union soldier on a litter crossed the *Neptune*'s stage. I saw a thatch of blond hair, and I knew the man on the litter was Tom Dodge. I rushed across the *Hawkins'* stage, through the mud and up the *Neptune*'s stage. Tom was conscious and even managed a faint smile. His right leg was a stump that stopped mid-thigh. It was wrapped in dirty, blood-stained bandages.

"Take this man aboard my boat, the *George Hawkins*," I said, gesturing to the boat immediately adjacent.

"Cannot do it, Cap, too much to do," the man in front said.

I followed them to a stateroom off the main cabin on the *Neptune*'s boiler deck and helped Tom into a berth. As he lay motionless, I grasped his shoulder firmly and looked at him square in the face. The eyes that had been such a brilliant blue looked faded and distant. He spoke faintly.

"I reckon I can still stand watch on one leg."

"Sure you can," I said. "And if you want to work the Cumberland, come see me in Smithland as soon as you are ready."

Tom nodded.

"I have to go now, Tom. I will look for you in Cairo," I said. My heart ached, but I did not want to show my low spirits to Tom.

The Federals in Dover and on the transports were under strict orders to treat the defeated Rebels with respect as prisoners of war. There was to be no taunting or jeering. However, a company of German soldiers in Smithland either had not heard that order or disobeyed it. As what seemed like the whole town lined the bank thinking the transports would stop, the Germans, in their thick accents, chided and mocked the Rebels.

"Oh, look at the damn Reppel prisoners—you poor, miserable boys," they whined.

We felt the tension among the townspeople, even as the boats steamed by. The Germans had not helped, and the crowd seemed close to exploding. Thus far in the war, I had not seen the sad consequences up close. At Dover and on the boats, I did, and the horror overwhelmed me.

I looked for Tom in Cairo, but the *Neptune* reached that place ahead of the *George Hawkins*, and no sooner had she done so than Tom was transferred to a hospital boat leaving for Saint Louis. I missed him in Cairo, but I hoped I would see him again.

The news of Donelson's fall spread quickly and within a few days casualty lists were posted at court houses and other public places. On February 20th, word came by wire that Mr. Lincoln's son, Willie, had died at the White House in Washington City.

7

May 1862. After the river forts fell, the Rebels and the war were driven deeper south. The next big task for pilots and steamers working in service to the Union was to transport troops far up the Tennessee River to Pittsburg Landing. The *George Hawkins*, however, was snagged near the mouth of the Tennessee and saved from sinking by quick thought and a tow to the Paducah Marine Ways. I missed the call to carry troops to or from the battle that became known as Shiloh.

With the fighting away from Western Kentucky, my service to the Union has become routine runs between Smithland, Paducah and Cairo. There are also occasional runs up the Cumberland or the Ohio. I have more time to spend at home with Beth and Early.

The Federals continue to restrict river traffic. All goods coming into or leaving Smithland must be approved by the Post Commander. The only ferries crossing the Ohio are at Smithland and Henderson, where the Union controls both sides of the river.

July 1863. The war persists, lasting far longer than anyone expected and taking a terrible toll. In this month alone, the
Union victory at Gettysburg claimed 40,000 lives, the Union
siege of Vicksburg destroyed that river city and took the lives
of a great number of soldiers and citizens, and a futile Union
assault on Battery Wagner in Charleston harbor ended untold
numbers of lives, including those of Negro soldiers of the 54th
Massachusetts Regiment.

April 1864. On the 25th of March, Nathan Bedford Forrest,
the Confederate general whom Union General William Tecumseh
Sherman calls "that devil Forrest," raided Paducah and attacked
Fort Anderson at that place. Union troops and gunboats repelled
Forrest's force, and the Rebels withdrew on the 26th.

Although Smithland was not in danger, Forrest's raid had
consequences for the Hawkins family that none of us could have
foreseen. On the 30th of March, Early came running down the
hayloft stairs in our barn shouting, "Papa, Papa, come see quick!
Come see quick!" He grabbed my hand and pulled me toward
the stairs. Early was so excited I expected to find that one of the
barn cats had dropped a litter of kittens.

I found instead a boy, a Negro boy, perhaps 10 years old. He
trembled with fear as I approached him. His eyes looked bigger
than two full moons. He had cuts and scrapes and bruises all
over every visible part of his body. What was left of his clothing was in shreds. His bare feet were cut and swollen. Where
they were not bleeding, his feet were striped with clotted blood. I
have never seen a being look more frightened than that poor boy.

I approached him slowly and tenderly, trying to calm him
and show him that he was safe, that he had nothing to fear from
me and Early. I spoke to him in a consoling tone and reached out
and touched him gently. He winced and recoiled in pain from my
having touched one of his many wounds.

I asked Early to fetch a horse blanket from the tack room
downstairs. As I waited for Early to come back, I sat beside the
boy and continued to console and assure him. Early returned
and I lay the blanket across the hay bales and motioned for the
boy to lie down. He did not speak, but his eyes welled with tears.
I saw that he was beginning to accept my help. He lay face up on
the blanket, I wrapped it around him and gently picked him up,

cradling him as softly as I could in my arms.

I walked down the loft stairs, out of the barn and toward the house, which sat about 50 yards away. I asked Early to run ahead and tell his mama that I was coming and needed her help.

Beth came through the dogtrot and out onto the porch in a fright, probably thinking I was hurt. She saw the boy wrapped in the blanket, and her expression changed from concern to relief and back to concern. She motioned to me to hurry.

"Bring him to the kitchen. I will heat water to clean him up. Is anything broken?" she asked.

"No," I replied. "But he is badly cut up and bruised. We will need salve and bandages."

As Beth raised the fire in the stove, filled kettles and placed them on the iron top, I laid the boy on the table and began to gently remove the rags that stuck to his wounds. He had not spoken a word since I first saw him in the hayloft. I asked his name. He tried to speak—I watched his lips try to form the word—but nothing came out. I said that was all right, not to try now, the words would come.

Beth and I lifted the boy into the tub and began to cleanse his wounds. Regardless of how tender we were, the boy winced in pain. As Beth heated stew and bread, I lifted the boy from the tub, laid him on the table, gently patted him dry and dabbed salve on his wounds. That seemed to provide some relief.

Early fetched one of Beth's sleeping gowns, we stood the boy up and slipped it over his head. We sat him down and Beth began to spoon feed him stew. He took the spoon and proceeded to devour two bowls full and nearly a whole loaf of Beth's dark bread. Seeing that, I knew the boy would be all right. I wondered how long it would be until he spoke.

Beth made up a bed in Early's room, on the second floor above our bedroom. In families with daughters, that room is theirs— the only entry is up a stairway in the parents' bedroom. In our family, since there are as yet no daughters, that room is Early's. The Negro boy will be safe there.

April 1864. It has been more than two weeks since Early found the Negro boy in the hayloft. He has gained weight, and his wounds are healing, but he is stone silent. I cannot imagine what horrors struck him dumb. I see him try to form words and speak, but no sound passes his lips. He has grown more comfortable being among us. He has lost most of his wariness and has begun to trust.

May 1864. In late afternoon of a fine spring Sunday, my sister, Sally, brother-in-law, Louis, and their young children came to visit. Louis brought his banjo and Sally her fiddle, and the lot of us sat out on the wharfboat afloat on the river. It was a peaceful evening with not a hint of military or private comings and goings.

As Louis and Sally played *Blue Tail Fly*, the Negro boy walked up to Louis, stood directly in front of him and extended both his hands in a gesture that said, "Please give me the banjo." Louis stopped playing, slipped the strap over his head, turned the banjo left to right, and looped the strap over the boy's head. The boy immediately began playing from precisely where Louis had stopped. We all had the same reaction—our jaws dropped in disbelief, and we began to cheer. Beth and Early hugged the boy, but that scarcely slowed him down. He finished *Blue Tail Fly* and, without skipping a beat, moved right into *Turkey in the Straw*. Sally had to concentrate to keep up.

The boy grew more lively with each note, grinning as wide as the horizon. Still, we were not prepared for what came next. The boy finished *Turkey in the Straw* and lit right into *Oh! Susanna*. He played through the tune, and when it came around again, he sang,

> *I come from Alabama with a banjo on my knee*
> *And I'm goin' to Louisiana, my true love for to see*

We cheered and whooped and hollered. The women cried tears of joy. I had to choke back tears myself. The lot of us sang through the song twice in a most cheerful way.

The boy's name is Ben York. He is polite and eager to please, yet there is a dignity about him. He has a noble countenance and a fine form. And he has a talent for music.

July 1864. Although Ben is 10 years old, he has had no schooling. He neither reads nor writes. Early is such an eager learner that, even though he will not start school for more than a year, Beth is teaching the boys together. They are learning their numbers and letters, and I am sure they will both be reading and writing before the first frost.

Early and Ben are quite a pair. Early is a small, slight child, like his mama was at that age. He is very animated, yet he has no problem sitting still for his lessons. He seems to sense their importance. It is almost as if he knows he is making an investment.

Ben moves more deliberately than Early, but he is no less bright. He takes great pride in his growing ability to read and write words. He is a tall boy who towers over Early. Ben looks as if he will be a big, sturdy man one day. He entertains us often, playing the banjo and singing in a fine voice.

September 1864. Ben had been with us and making great progress for about five months when one day a stranger rode in on a black mount, trailing a mule on a lead and asking to speak to Will Hawkins.

"I am Will Hawkins," I said. "What can I do for you?"

"You have some property that belongs to me," he replied, "and I have come to claim it."

"Property, sir?" I asked in a bewildered tone.

"Ben. Ben York. One of my boys," he answered. "They told me at the wharf in Paducah that Hawkins, Captain Will Hawkins, was holding a nigger boy in Smithland. I figured that to be my boy, Ben."

"Your boy?" I wondered.

"My slave. One of my nigger boys," he spat back, off his horse and getting angry now. I met his eyes as we stood face to face.

"You are correct, sir," I said evenly. "I do have a young Negro boy named Ben, but I challenge that he is your property."

"By blazes, he is!" the man cried, almost screaming now because I had not backed down. "And I have the papers to prove it."

He drew from his breast pocket papers that described two adult Negroes and two children, a boy and a girl.

"Where are his parents and his sister?" I asked.

"They are dead—killed," he replied emphatically.

"How?" I asked.

"That is not your business," he shot back. "Now, where is Ben? I am taking him to Paducah."

By very fortunate coincidence, Ben and Early had left about an hour earlier with two fishing poles and one of our ponies to try their luck up the Cumberland on the other side of town. The boys had become a nearly inseparable pair. They went everywhere and did everything together. I was very glad that neither the boys nor Beth were here to witness this ugly event.

"Well, it looks as if he is yours fair and square," I said. "How much do you want for him?"

The man's demeanor changed. He saw the opportunity to come away with one less Negro boy but his purse fuller than when he rode in.

"You know, Mr. Lincoln freed the slaves well over a year ago," I ventured.

"Hogwash!" he fired back. "You know as well as me that slavery's still fit and proper in Kentucky."

I did know that. I was just trying to confuse his mind off his greedy tallying.

"Give me $300," he insisted.

"Now, friend," I said, "you know as well as I do that a 10-year-old Negro boy does not sell for any sum near $300."

It was eating my insides to horse trade for a human being, but I was determined to give this man as little satisfaction as possible.

"Give me those papers, I will give you $100 and be gone with you," I offered.

"One fifty," he countered, with an air of triumph.

"One twenty-five," I replied.

He stood silent, stroked the stubble on his chin, looked down at his boot tops, looked at me and said,

"You just bought yourself a nigger."

I winced. It was a reflex I hoped he did not see.

"Wait here a moment," I instructed.

I turned and walked to the house. I mounted the porch stairs and before opening the door to the front room, glanced back to be sure he had not wandered. I stomped on the porch boards to rouse the dogs from their slumber. The man was in his saddle before the dogs got halfway to him. Inside, I unlocked the safe, removed $125 and, before returning outside, tucked my pistol in my waistband in back where he would not see it. With neither of us saying another word, I handed him the money, he handed me the papers, he kicked his horse, yanked the mule's lead and rode off.

He never offered his name, and I had not asked. It was there on the papers though—Judah York. He had given his surname to his slaves.

I swore at that moment never to tell anyone of this ugly incident. Judah York and I were its only witnesses, and this entry is its only record. In time, I will burn the papers.

8

November 1864. Mr. Lincoln has won re-election despite majorities in Kentucky, Delaware and New Jersey voting for his opponent, General George McClelland.

April 9, 1865. The war amongst ourselves is over. Union troops having taken Richmond in the first few days of this month and having blocked the Rebels' retreat, General Robert E. Lee surrendered unconditionally to General Ulysses S. Grant at Appomattox Courthouse, Virginia, on this day.

April 15, 1865. President Abraham Lincoln is dead by an assassin's bullet. After four years of civil war and the loss of hundreds of thousands of lives, we have lost the man who above all else sought to keep us together and hold us to our ideals.

Lieutenant Colonel J. T. Foster, Commanding Post at Smithland, Kentucky, issued Special Order No. 22:

"In accordance with instructions from Brigadier General S. Meredith Commanding District of Western Kentucky, the Commanding Officer of 13th USCHA will on Monday 17th instant cause a gun to be fired every half hour commencing at Sunrise and ending at Sunset out of respect to the memory of our beloved President so recently assassinated."

April 27, 1865. The boilers on the Mississippi River steamer *Sultana* exploded, and the boat caught fire just above Memphis. Most of the passengers were Union soldiers on their way home after their release from Confederate prisoner-of-war camps. About 2,000 lost their lives.

June 11, 1865. Lieutenant Colonel J. T. Foster, Commanding Post at Smithland, Kentucky, issued Special Order No. 42:

"A meeting will be held at the Methodist Church in this place on Wednesday next at 2 o'clock p.m. for the purpose of appointing a committee to make arrangements for the celebration of the coming anniversary of American Independence. All who rejoice in seeing our flag float over our country in peace after the past four years bathed in fratricidal blood are invited to attend and participate in the Ceremonies of the Day."

July 3, 1865. First Lieutenant A. C. Rogers, Commanding Post at Smithland, Kentucky, issued Special Order No. 2:

"In pursuance of orders seen from Headquarters, District of Western Kentucky, all labor will be suspended at this post Tuesday, July 4, 1865. All places of business will be closed."

July 1865. Beth is pregnant and has taken to bed as she did before Early was born.

October 1865. The troops are all but gone from Smithland. The riverfront has returned to civilian hands. Citizens have made good use of everything the Army and Navy left behind. When spring comes, the hills behind town can begin to regain their growth. Townspeople plan to help things along by planting saplings. The abandoned earthworks have become play places and picnic spots. The unbroken views are a sight to see, but we miss the trees.

December 1865. Mr. Seward announced that the Thirteenth Amendment has been ratified by 27 states and is now part of the Constitution. Slavery and involuntary servitude are illegal in the United States.

On Christmas morning, I went to the kitchen and burned the slave papers I got from Judah York less than two years ago.

April 1866. We have been blessed with a healthy baby girl. We named her Amanda. Both she and her very brave mother are well. Doc Sanders says Beth will be unable to have another child.

The Congress has overidden President Johnson's veto, and Negroes are now full and legal citizens of the United States.

May 1866. The broodmare is in foal, and if everything goes well, we should have a colt or filly for Early's seventh birthday next April.

October 1866. River traffic has come back, and our wharfboat and the *George Hawkins* are busy. Commerce has not returned to its pre-war levels, however. The railroads have taken both passenger and freight traffic away.

February 1867. Early and Ben read *Ragged Dick* aloud to each other and anyone else who will listen. It is a new book by Horatio Alger.

As long as packets carry passengers and freight on the rivers, anything new will reach the river towns before other parts of the country distant from the cities—unless they are on a rail line.

April 1867. Amanda is already a year old, Early is seven, and Ben is 13. Ben is growing faster than cane in summer. He towers over Early and reaches nearly my height. Farm work, mixed with helping the rousters, has made Ben a strong boy.

I have the *George Hawkins No. 9* in the Nashville–Cairo trade. Business is fair. This spring, whenever Ben and Early are not in school, I take them on my runs, or parts of my runs, between Smithland, Nashville and Cairo. The boys already knew many of the boats on the rivers, most of them solely by the sound of their steam whistles. As we travel, they are also getting to know the captains, pilots and crews who do not tie their steamers to our wharfboat.

If the *Hawkins* is steaming up the Cumberland and will not be down in time for Ben and Early's school bell, I send them back on another boat. The boats' masters have come to welcome the boys aboard because they delight the passengers so. Early does not play or sing as Ben does, but he has become quite the step-dancer. The boy has enough energy for three youngsters, and dancing is a good way to burn some of it off.

On one of the boys' first upriver runs on the *Hawkins*, while Ben played banjo and sang, Early danced in such a spirited way that his slouch hat flew off and landed upsidedown at the feet of a group of passengers. Several men immediately tossed coins and even paper money into the hat. The money-making opportunity offered by this accident was not lost on the boys. As neither other masters nor I objected, dropping Early's hat became a regular event during the boys' entertainment. Their excitement over earning their own money tickles me, but Beth and I have had to set some rules on what comes of their money. Most goes into the safe, and the rest cannot all be spent on rock candy.

I had Ben and Early on the *Hawkins* in Canton on my way to Nashville. They had to be back in Smithland long before I would return, so I spoke with Captain McComas, and he took them aboard the *Imperial*. It is a boat about the size of the *Hawkins* and is in the Nashville–Saint Louis trade. Ben and Early would be in Smithland that evening.

When I saw Captain McComas again near the end of the month, he told me a story that Ben and Early had not. With the boys aboard, the *Imperial* had stopped for passengers and freight at Eddyville. A woman dressed entirely in black—from the bow on her bonnet to the laces in her high boots—had come aboard. Two coarse young men who looked to be her sons boarded with her. The three immediately climbed the stairs to two staterooms off the main cabin on the boiler deck. After a few minutes in their staterooms, they came into the cabin, and there stood Ben and Early, watching for passengers to assemble so they could play. The woman was taken aback and glared at Ben. She walked straight up to him and planted herself within a foot of his shirtfront. She tilted her head up to look Ben square in the face. Her eyes grew fiery, her face flushed red, and veins strained against the skin of her temples. She pinched her lips, locked her jaw and glared. When she spoke, she spat out the words in a shrill voice that sounded like chalk screeching on a blackboard.

"The only nigras allowed in this cabin and on this deck are the nigras servin' white folks food, carryin' white folks' baggage and cleanin' white folks' chamber pots. Get your charcoal ass down with the roustabouts where it belongs."

Her sons stood just behind her, sneering. Captain McComas swore he heard them hiss. Before the Captain could step in, Ben, in the most defenseless tone imaginable, said, "I just play the banjo and sing, ma'am."

With a 7-year-old's innocence, Early added, "Ben plays the banjo and sings, ma'am, and I dance some."

At that, Ben took two steps back, looped his banjo strap over his head, picked the strings ever so lightly, and in a voice sweeter than honeysuckle, began to sing.

> *Beautiful dreamer, wake unto me*
> *Starlight and dewdrops are waiting for thee*
> *Sounds of the rude world heard in the day*
> *Lulled by the moonlight have all passed away*

The woman melted like ice on a hot stove. Even her sons softened. In great surprise and wonder, she said,

"Nigra boy, you sing like an angel. I want you to sing and play for me all the way to Saint Louis."

"We are aboard only to Smithland, ma'am," Ben said softly.

"Well then, that will have to do," the woman said in a tone that mixed triumph with resignation.

By the time the *Imperial* reached Smithland, Ben had played and sung every song he knew, some twice. Early had just about danced the soles off his feet. When the *Imperial* tied to the wharfboat and Ben and Early came off, the woman called them back, pulled a $20 gold certificate from her purse, grasped Ben's arm from where it hung by his side, and pressed the bill into his palm. Ben and Early grinned, thanked her and crossed to the wharfboat.

Why I heard this story from Captain McComas and not from Ben and Early, I do not know and have not yet asked.

April 1867. The foal is a colt, born nearly black but with white hairs here and there. I suspect he will be a grey like the stallion that sired him. Early and I helped with the birth. When the cord broke, I cupped the stump with antiseptic. Early dried the colt with clean straw and moved him to the mare's head. She nuzzled her foal for a short time and then stood. The colt struggled to stand with his dam. He was steady on his feet within 30 minutes of his first breath. He found the mare's teats and suckled. Early named him Spirit. On his first day, Spirit did little but sleep and eat. I made a point of having Early handle Spirit from birth, especially his legs and feet. On his second day, Spirit was more active. He stood for long stretches and tested his legs by trying to gallop and buck in his stall. Early fit him with a halter and led him to a grassy corral beside his dam. Early spends all his free time with Spirit. He grooms the colt and leads him to and from pasture every day. The bond growing between the boy and the colt doubled after the dam suddenly died. Hay, grain, fresh grass and milk that Early bottle-feeds Spirit from Louis' mare have Spirit growing fast.

May 1867. I trimmed and leveled Spirit's feet for the first time today. He was a little rambunctious, so I calmed him with a twitch. Early handled it well and is bringing the colt along nicely.

July 1867. Spirit has grown to double his birth size. White hairs have formed goggles around his eyes and are appearing elsewhere on his body.

October 1867. We weaned Spirit from the bottle with help from a gentle billygoat. The colt eats his fill of oats and soybean meal, and it shows in his steady growth. Early is growing too, but he cannot keep up with Spirit. The colt's fall coat has grown in. He will be a handsome dappled gray.

April 1868. Early is eight and Spirit is a yearling. The colt has doubled in size since last summer. Early turns Spirit out daily to gallop with other yearlings in Louis' high pasture. Early has started getting Spirit used to tack. He first lay across the yearling's bare back, then saddled and sat him in his stall. Spirit did not object, so Early moved on to walking him in the barn aisle and around the barnyard. The boy is becoming an excellent horseman.

November 1868. Ulysses S. Grant has won the election. I voted for him, of course. I shake my head in disbelief every time it comes to mind that the man who is President of the United States once stood beside me in the pilothouse of the *Charley Bowen* and recruited me to serve the Union.

April 1869. We gelded Spirit today. He barely noticed the knife, but he will be a week or two in the high pasture before Early rides him again. The boy is the best young horseman I have seen. He has trained his colt well, and they ride with confidence as one. Early shows the pride of having brought a fine young horse along. Spirit has brought Early along too.

May 1869. The Union Pacific met the Central Pacific at Promontory Point, Utah. The railroad now extends from the Atlantic to the Pacific.

January 1870. I announced at our New Year's Day gathering that come April and Early's 10th birthday, I would turn the responsibility of keeping the record over to him. He will be the youngest recorder in five generations of Hawkins men. Ten is a milestone for a boy. Becoming recorder will mark that milestone for Early. He is a good reader, and I expect he will be a good recorder.

My announcement caught Early by surprise. He beamed with pride and graciously accepted his kin's congratulations. My pride probably swelled more than his.

April 1870. Early is taking on two important responsibilities. One I have already mentioned. The second is I have given him his first firearm. It is a Winchester .44 caliber Model 1866 carbine. It is a fair-sized gun for a 10-year-old boy. I told Early that if he can learn to shoot well with a carbine, he will one day be an excellent rifleman with a full-length barrel.

This month, I began teaching Early to shoot. Let me note here that although I taught Ben how to shoot and care for a rifle, I have not given him one of his own because there are still too many people who take it on themselves to stop Negroes from doing what they think Negroes ought not to be doing. Gentle persuasion is not the means they use.

This is my last entry as recorder. My son, Early Hawkins, now continues the record.

9

Early Hawkins. In the early 1950s, I compiled the balance of this story from my journal entries, my memories and my recollection of tales others told. Doing so gave me the luxury of including hindsight.

Having been just past five years old when Union soldiers and tars left Smithland for good, I have only vague memories of men in blue uniforms and military traffic on the rivers. And since I've already included some of Will's journal entries through April 1870, I'll start my record just after that date.

April 1870. Smithland in 1870 was a wonderful place to be a boy. I had family, friends, neighbors, the farm, rivers, woods and a bottomless well of adventures to pursue. When the weather was agreeable and there was no farm work to be done, if I wasn't on the rivers with Will and Ben or running with one of my friends from school, I liked to sit on the point of our front porch in a rush-bottomed rocker with whatever book I was reading at the time. From when I first learned how, I loved to read. Books took me places I suspected I'd never go and introduced me to people I was sure I'd never meet.

When I looked up from the page for a moment and scanned the scene before me, I imagined it could be the setting for one grand story or another. Our homeplace sat just high enough above the bottoms to afford a long view. To the west across our fields was the Kentucky Chute, the foot of Cumberland Island, the Ohio River and the heavily wooded Illinois shore. New Liberty and Hamletsburg were scarcely visible through the trees. Turning slightly north, I could see clear up the Ohio. Most times there were steamers in view heading up or down that stream, or the Cumberland to its right. The Hawkins Wharfboat sat tied at the near bank. If there were any doubts about the boat's purpose, the bold lettering on its side erased them.

Beyond the wharfboat was the long outline of Cumberland Island. Its head and foot were wooded, but a large section in the center had been cleared for planting and pasture. During the war, cattle had grazed that pasture. They were beef for Union soldiers at Fort Smith. After the war, Mrs. Carson's tenant resumed farming there.

Turning farther north, Salt Point came into view across the Cumberland from the center of Smithland. About a half dozen families had homes there in a small community called Westwood. Ferries ran between Smithland and Westwood and between Westwood and Cumberland Island.

Smithland itself sat nestled among the trees that began at the northern edge of our fields and stretched along the Cumberland bank, through town and east to the hills behind. During the war, those hills were nearly stripped of trees to build the abatis that surrounded the forts. With the trees down, there were open lines of sight and clear paths for the big guns that pointed in every direction from the peaks of the hills. With help from citizens who planted young trees across the slopes, the hills had grown greener and thicker every year since the war's end.

If I close my eyes now, I can see that scene as it was some 80 years ago. And I'm sure the only place it still exists is in my memory.

On summer afternoons, Ben and I often swam across to the watermelon patch on Cumberland Island and floated back big, ripe melons. The men on the wharfboat opened and sliced them, and whoever happened to be on hand—passengers waiting for a steamer, men loading freight on or off a dray, clerks from stores across from the wharf, neighbors visiting on the benches that lined the riverfront—all dug in, slurped together and shot seeds into the water.

Late in the day, the air was so thick it seemed to slow the sunset. The western sky across in Illinois took on a lavender-or-ange color. There were mosquitoes aplenty. Purple martins helped keep their numbers down, so we hung hollowed gourds on posts along the riverfront as a place for the martins to nest. Near sunset, they darted about snatching skeeters in flight.

Every tree must have had a hundred cicadas, all screech-saw-ing a bizarre kind of concert. Fireflies scattered sparks in the twilight, and the river flowed, reflecting the violet sky. From across on Salt Point, the faint sound of a lazy harmonica came and went with the breeze.

Unlike some bigger river towns like Nashville, Smithland's streets were not lined with gaslamps. Lanterns hung along Riverfront Street and the wharf, and there was an oil lamp on a post here and there in town, but for the most part, after sundown, the only light on the streets came out from within the hotels, taverns and houses. Some folks did keep a lamp lit on their front porch. Evening strollers walked the length of Riverfront Street from above Gower House down to Hawkins Wharfboat. Sleep never came easy on those hot, humid summer nights.

Outside the town plat, just about the only light on clear nights was star or moonlight, if the moon was up and not near new. Down from town, the warm lights of our homeplace glowed dimly on the rise beyond the bottoms. Generations before, my kin had built a sturdy log cabin at the top of the rise. The cabin became the kitchen behind our lumber-built, two-story main house. A deep porch ran across the front. Benches, straight chairs and rockers sat our family and visitors. A dogtrot ran between the front and back porches. To the left of the dogtrot was Will and Beth's bedroom. Amanda's room was above Will and Beth's and reachable only by a stairway in their room. To the right of the dogtrot was the sitting room. Like Will and Beth's bedroom, it had a stone fireplace at the far end. Just to the rear outside the sitting-room door was a stairway that led to Ben's and my bedroom. From our front window above the porch roof, we had a broad view of the rivers, our fields, the wharfboat and Smithland. It was a pretty scene, especially when the leaves were full and green, or in the fall when they blazed with warm colors.

The barn and the slaughter and smokehouses stood to the left behind the kitchen. Directly to the rear was the washhouse. To the right, was a small cabin with its own front porch. It had a pitched roof, a tall window over the porch roof and a stone fireplace at the far end. Will and Louis built the cabin in '66 just after Amanda was born. It was our library. We had moved hundreds of books out of the main house and onto the shelves that lined the cabin's walls from floor to ceiling. The library had comfortable chairs, two writing desks, and lots of candles and oil lamps. It held books collected over five generations. It also held the tall leatherbound books that contained the family record. I made many of my entries at the writing desk in the library.

Maples, sycamores and sweet gum trees grew among and around the buildings at the top of the rise. I liked climbing the maples. One of them near the library had a long, thin, horizontal branch that I hung from. My weight bent the branch and let it carry me to the ground. When I let go and the branch sprang back up, the broad green leaves made a loud whooshing sound.

Will had started learning Ben and me the rivers when I was still very young. He took us on the *George Hawkins'* runs every chance he got, so our knowing the rivers grew and grew. Ben and I sometimes entertained the passengers. I didn't have Ben's musical gift, but I loved to stepdance to his banjo, fiddle or harmonica.

Shortly after Ben came to us, Beth realized he had never been to school. She started teaching Ben and me our letters and numbers. We were her class of two. Soon we were reading simple things, and Ben and I began taking turns reading aloud to each other. We had our library and there were always newspapers and new books coming to town by steamer, so we never ran out of things to read.

Will gave Ben and me our basic lessons in shooting and rifle care, but it was Uncle Louis who kept us practicing. He drilled us on safety, and he had a strict rule about shooting only what we would dress and eat. We practiced by shooting at cans we set up in a clearing deep in the woods. Louis loved the woods, and we learned a lot from him.

Ben and I were inseparable friends. Even I had to admit we were an odd pair. Not only was Ben six years older and much bigger than I was, he was, of course, a Negro. When Ben was 13, he began to grow very fast. I swear, overnight he became about twice as big as I was.

Will and Beth had taught us to be polite, well-behaved boys and to respect others, especially our elders. We almost never swayed from that. I was a highly energetic, eager boy, always asking questions. Adults generally were flattered by my respect and thirst to know what they could tell me. I became a favorite of my teachers, the shopkeepers, the men at the courthouse, the rousters and just about any grown-up who was in town a lot.

That fact caused other boys, especially the mischievous ones, to dislike me. Since I was small, I was an easy target for bullies—unless I was with Ben. They wouldn't dare mess with Ben. Even a gang of boys knew better than to tangle with him.

Ben and I made a pact. His part was to protect me. And my part, in a way, was to protect him. There were still plenty of mean-spirited people who hated Negroes and felt they had no right to be anything but slaves. People like that called Ben "Early's nigger," mostly behind our backs but sometimes to our faces. When that ugliness came from other boys, it would be from a distance. They would taunt and run. Most often we ignored it. Now and then it came from an adult, sometimes a drunken adult. That's when Ben turned quiet and humble, and if he met his accuser's eyes, it was with the look of a dying calf. He seemed to shrink—he actually looked smaller, even to me. I disarmed the accuser by pretending that Ben *was* my nigger.

"Now mister," I pleaded in my most innocent, little-boy voice, "My boy Ben's a mighty good nigger. He minds me and don't mean nobody no harm, 'specially not you. Why don't you just let him be?"

It always worked, and as soon as the accuser was out of hearing distance, Ben and I laughed ourselves silly mocking the slackjawed look of the man we fooled.

We learned that little two-part play by watching Nothet Edmonds, a rouster who worked on the *George Hawkins*. Nothet was a good friend to Ben and me. We trusted him.

Like the other roustabouts, Nothet had been a slave and was now making his way as a free man. He came to Kentucky from North Carolina. I'd place his age then at about 50. His wife, Eliza, was probably 20 years younger. They had three little daughters. The family lived in what was called Brownsville, a Negro section of town.

Nothet was wide, sturdy and nearly 6 feet tall. His thick black hair was flecked with white. He was proud that he could work as hard and carry as much as the younger rousters. He wasn't an educated man, but he was nobody's fool. He knew just how to handle all kinds of folks, white or Negro, and he had earned the respect of the other rousters. Whenever Ben and I traveled on the *George Hawkins*, we passed some time with Nothet.

One Saturday, we had taken on probably two dozen hogsheads of molasses and had just left the wharfboat, heading below to Paducah and Cairo, when Nothet caught Ben and me looking glum.

"What's troublin' you boys?" he asked.

With about any other grown-up, we would have shrugged the question off, but we knew Nothet was an understanding kind of man, so we opened up to him.

"Ben's worryin' some that he doesn't fit anywhere," I said.

"Fit anywheres?" Nothet asked with a grin. "You mean he's growin' outta his britches?"

"Naw, Nothet, you know that's not what Early means," Ben replied.

"Yeah, I knows. I bin watchin' you boys," Nothet said. "I knows jest what yuh mean. Ben's a Negro boy, but he lifs wit' white folks so's othuh black folks shun him. Then Early an' yaw mama an' daddy loves Ben an' treats him like one o' yaw own, but lots othuh white folks don't. Most white folks likes Ben cuz o' his music, but 'neath dat he's still a nigra boy. I knows all 'bout dat. Ben's got one foot in white folks' worl' an' thutha in Negro folks' worl'. An' 'les he can scrub dat coal offa his skin, dat's da way it's always goin' tuh be.

"I tell yuh what tho' Ben—yuh got a good fam'ly, folks who loves yuh. Yuh be a fool tuh let dat go. An' yaw much bettuh off den you'd be livin' in Brownsville, so stick wit' duh Hawkins. An' when deres trouble wit' duh hatin' kinduh white folks, do what ah do. You seen me. Swalluh dat pride fo' a minit or two. Play dere game and beats dem at it. Dey nevuh be duh wisuh."

Ben and I looked at each other and smiled.

At 10, I was small and slight. Among other boys my age, I was the blond-headed, blue-eyed runt of the litter. I remember looking through newspapers for advertisements for grow pills. I figured there was a tonic or pill for everything else, there must be something that would make me bigger. I watched Ben go overnight from a collection of broomsticks to what looked to me like a big, strong, full-grown man. I wondered if it would ever happen to me.

When I was older, Beth told me that as a boy I was full of energy, always talking and asking questions. The shopkeepers in town knew me because I was in and out of their stores every day. Beth was surprised they didn't tell me to take a float down the river. I was around so much they made me a messenger or a delivery boy. Here, Early, run this sack of potatoes or this bolt of fabric or this tin of crackers up to Mrs. Handlin or Mrs. Duley or Mrs. Shelton. If the customer didn't want to visit, I'd be back before the shopkeeper could blink an eye.

I spent more time at Scyster's Grocery than any other store. It was on Riverfront Street facing the water. From the porch, I could scan the wharf from beyond the Gower House clear past the foot of Cumberland Island. I watched the comings and goings and investigated anything that got me curious.

Jacob Scyster ran the grocery store. I knew him as Captain Jake. Years earlier, he was owner and captain of the *V. K. Stevenson* and half owner of the *Nettie Miller*. Both boats ran in the Paducah–Nashville trade. Captain Jake tired of the river and life away from home, so he became a merchant in Smithland. He gave that up and farmed for a while but then returned to town as a shopkeeper, owner of the Scyster Hotel and wharfmaster on the Hawkins Wharfboat. Captain Jake's wife, Martha, died in 1869, leaving him with a son and a daughter.

Captain Jake was a straight-arrow Methodist—honest, courteous, dignified and always a gentleman. If Ben or I stepped out of line, all it took was a look from Captain Jake to pull us back in.

One afternoon, Ben and I were sucking on rock candy that Captain Jake had given us for running some groceries up to the Hodge place. We sat on barrels and leaned against the posts on the grocery store porch. The leaves in the trees that lined the riverfront rustled in a north breeze. I liked the way the cotton-wood leaves dangled like ornaments on a Christmas tree. The wind made them flip and spin. Scores of silver maple leaves turned together like dancers in a troupe and showed the silver undersides that give them their name. Along the line of trees, I don't think there were two alike. The Judge Elm stood up by the Gower House, then a mulberry, a poplar and an ancient syca-more so sturdy that men tied several barges to it at once. I liked the catalpa's huge leaves and giant seedpods that some people called cigars. There was a locust tree, an ash, a buckeye and even a pine in the line above the water's edge. Below town and our wharfboat, willows crowded the bank and continued downriver.

Inside the line of trees, a wooden railing ran part of the length of the riverfront. Benches sat in the shade and invited neighbors and passersby to visit. One stretch favored by regulars was called Buzzards' Roost. That was where they told stories and lies to each other.

This rock candy afternoon was a busy one. The *Shannon*, a big Ohio River packet, sat tied to one end of the wharfboat, and the *Armada*, a sidewheeler that Ben Egan had in the Paducah–Nashville trade, sat tied to the other end. With no wharfboat space open, the *James Fisk Jr.*, a ragged Cumberland River steamer, and the *Umpire*, a big sternwheeler also in the Paducah–Nashville trade, had dropped their stages to the wharf and were passing freight and passengers.

Just then, the *George Hawkins* came into view up the Cumberland. That was always an exciting sight for Ben and me because it meant that Will, Nothet and Gus Mellon, one of Will's pilots, would be home for at least a little while. As the *Hawkins* passed the foot of Court Street, Ben and I leapt from Captain Jake's porch and ran down Riverfront Street ahead of the *Hawkins*. Gus rounded and paused midstream as the *Shannon* let loose her lines and began upstream. Gus eased the *Hawkins* in to take the *Shannon*'s place. Captain Jake was already outside the wharfboat office helping with the lines and the passengers coming off. The freight started coming off next. Ben and I jumped aboard and greeted Nothet as he passed with a big bundle on his shoulder. We were on our way up the stairs to the pilot house when we heard Nothet shout from the riverbank ramp.

"Cap'n Jake! Cap'n Jake! I believe yaw sto's on fire!"

We turned and, sure enough, smoke was billowing out of Scyster's Grocery. A commotion started the likes of which I've scarcely seen since.

Captain Jake was the first across the ramp to shore—even ahead of Nothet. Nothet and the other rousters dropped their bundles and took off toward the store behind Captain Jake. Ben and I skipped down the stairs two at a time, and behind us came Will and Gus. We were through the wharfboat and across the ramp faster than a bee-stung horse. Captain Jake covered the four short blocks from the wharfboat to his store like the fastest steed in the

Derby. He paid no mind to the smoke or anything else. He dashed
into the store, and before we reached it, he was back out with a
stack of nestled buckets. Shopkeepers rushed out of the store-
fronts. With blocks of wooden buildings, everybody knew how fast
a fire could take down the whole town.

More buckets appeared, and Mr. Grayot, the druggist, and
his clerk ran up with a ladder. Every able body grabbed two
buckets and scrambled down the wharf slope for water. Captain
Jake quickly got everyone in two lines. Full buckets came up one
line, and empty buckets went down the other. Ben and I were
near the top of the water line. Will and Captain Jake were at its
head, rushing in and out of the store and tossing water on the
fire. Nothet and other rousters took positions up the ladder and
on the roof, and buckets of water were passed up to soak it.

The fire was out before it spread to other stores. Captain
Jake's store was damaged, and he lost some goods, but it could
have been a lot worse. There were congratulations all around,
and Captain Jake especially thanked Nothet for the alarm.

To tend to his wharfboat duties, Captain Jake had left the
grocery in the care of David Mantz, his clerk. David left his
lighted cigar too close to some spilled lamp oil while he stepped
out the back door to the privy. He didn't know the store was on
fire until it was well on its way to being doused. Captain Jake
was a forgiving man, but he couldn't excuse David's carelessness, so David had to go looking for a new job.

10

In the 1830s, Henry Shreve had built a wing dam that ran
nearly due north from the head of Cumberland Island into the
Ohio River. Some folks called it Shreve's Dike; others called it
Cumberland Dam. Its purpose was to funnel the flow of the Ohio's
current at its low stages from the Illinois side of Cumberland
Island to the Kentucky side. The channel it aided was called
the Kentucky Chute. Current flowing through the chute helped
remove sandbars blocking the mouth of the Cumberland River
and the Smithland waterfront.

A pilot coming down the Cumberland and turning to starboard toward the Ohio had to know to hug the Kentucky shore,

running between it and a small bar, and then to swing gently to larboard. That kept him in the Kentucky Chute and the channel. And it was the way to avoid running aground on the bar or having the limestone that formed Henry Shreve's wing dam punch a big hole in the bottom of the pilot's boat. It was easy enough to negotiate at low water because from a pilot's lofty perch he could see the bar and the rocks. But if the river was high or a pilot was running at night, or both, that was another situation—especially if the pilot was in water he didn't know.

In mid-May 1870, Will suspended his Cairo-to-Nashville runs and ran the *George Hawkins No. 9* up the Ohio to Cincinnati. He had commissioned James Mack to build the hull of the *George Hawkins No. 10* and Glasscock, of Wheeling, West Virginia, to build the cabin. The new *Hawkins* was scheduled for delivery in early August, and Will went to Cincinnati to see about its progress.

Will returned to Smithland early in the evening on Tuesday, May 16th, tied the *Hawkins No. 9* to the wharfboat and shut her down. It was a pleasant spring evening, the sun had set very pretty behind the Illinois shore, and we had our supper by twilight and coal-oil lamps on the front porch. Will told us about the *10*. It was to be the finest *George Hawkins* ever, and its design represented Will's plans for keeping us in the packet business opposite the ever-spreading railroads.

Like so many boys, I was devouring Horatio Alger's *Luck and Pluck Series* about then. I spent the time between supper and bed buried in dime novels about bootblacks and newsboys who go from rags to riches. At bedtime, Ben and I climbed the stairs to our bunks and were asleep by 10 o'clock. Will shook me awake out of a dream at 2:30 a.m.

"You boys get up and get your britches on. There are two boats aground near the dike, and one of them's likely to sink."

We ran to the barn and haltered three horses. There was no time for bridles, bits or saddles. Spirit looked at me as if to say, "What are you doing here? It's 2:30 in the morning!"

We rode at a full gallop down the hill and across the bottoms on the paths that crisscrossed our fields. It was a short distance from the house to the wharfboat, but we covered it faster on horseback than we could on foot. I heard one boat's whistle and clanging bell signaling distress.

The rousters who slept on the wharfboat stood bleary eyed at its edge staring across the water at the dim lights of two steamboats aground. Sure enough, one of the boats was on the dike and probably sinking. The position of the second boat told us she was aground on the bar.

Will called out to the rousters, "There are oars in those skiffs on the bank. Three men to a boat—two on the oars and one in the stern to keep the course. Let's go men!"

We ran to the yawl on the *Hawkins'* main deck. It was in the water inside of a minute. Will and Ben took the oars, and I sat in the stern. As we moved toward the lights, I saw the boat on the bar back off. It turned to larboard and steamed slowly toward the boat on the dike. Another steamer came out of the Cumberland, rounded Salt Point and moved toward the dike. Seeing help on the way, the sinking boat silenced its whistle and bell. The two steamers, the skiffs and our yawl reached the dike at about the same time.

The *Robert Moore* was on the rocks. As its stern sank, the bow slowly shifted on the boulders it had struck. The *Camelia* was the boat that had struck the bar. Before she backed off, she had sent a yawl to the *Moore*. The *Mallie Ragon* was the boat that came out of the Cumberland.

The passengers got off the *Moore* quickly. They moved to the dry points of the boat, men on the yawls and skiffs took them aboard, and ferried them to the *Camelia* and *Ragon*. Then the men started with the freight. But the crews, rousters and the little armada that had come to help couldn't get the heavier freight off before the river swamped the *Moore's* stern and moved forward of the center stairs. Within a few minutes, the stern was in 15 feet of water and the bow in six. Although most of the cabin and the forward parts of the boat past the pilothouse were dry, much of the cargo on the main deck was lost.

The rakish angle the *Moore* lay at caused her stacks to fall before daybreak. Over the next few days, the sand beneath the *Moore* washed away, and the boat rapidly broke up. Her tobacco cargo was scattered along the river for 20 miles.

In June 1870, word spread that a big race was brewing. First, we read about it in the telegraph news that the Smithland *Times* published. The Paducah and Evansville papers published nearly the same news. Then the crews of boats up from New Orleans repeated the story. Although the captains publicly denied it, Thomas Leathers' steamer *Natchez* was to race John Cannon's *Robert E. Lee.* Both boats were big Mississippi River sidewheelers. At 307 feet and 1,547 tons, the *Natchez* was longer and displaced more than the *Lee* at 286 feet and 1,456 tons. But the *Lee* was the handsomer boat, the *Natchez* having been built rather plain, putting function over style.

The captains were well-known in the river trade, fierce competitors who could not have been more different in appearance and temperament. Captain Leathers was a tall, powerfully built man with a fearsome countenance and a surly demeanor. He wore a Confederate gray suit with ruffled shirtfront and a large cluster diamond pin. Captain Cannon was a smaller man, more slightly built, ever the gentleman, gracious and unfailingly polite. His suit was of handwoven tuckapaw, and he sported a Panama hat. Both captains were Kentucky natives, so the interest in their rivalry, and this race in particular, was high among folks near us.

Both steamers were built in Ohio River shipyards, the *Natchez* in Cincinnati and the *Lee* in New Albany. Although Captain Cannon was a Union man during the War, he named his boat after the Confederate general because he would have his packet in the Lower Mississippi trade. Captain Leathers was a diehard Confederate, never admitting the War's end and never flying the American flag.

As the June days passed, interest in the race grew to a fever pitch. Bets were laid and people looked for a way to travel to the Mississippi to see the race. The notices said the race would commence at the New Orleans wharf at 5 p.m. on June 30th and finish in Saint Louis. With the *George Hawkins* in the Nashville–Cairo trade, Will realized that by adjusting her schedule slightly, he could have the *Hawkins* at Cairo when the *Natchez* and *Lee* were likely to pass. Will placed notices in the Smithland and Paducah newspapers that the *George Hawkins* would carry excursion passengers to Cairo to see the race. The notices read:

SEE THE GREAT RACE
The *George Hawkins* will carry passengers to Cairo from Smithland & Paducah to see the Great Race between the *Natchez* and the *Robert E. Lee.*

> Departure from Smithland will be 11 a.m., Sunday,
> July 3rd and from Paducah at 12:30 p.m. Dinner
> and supper will be served to cabin passengers.
> Entertainment will be provided. Return to Paducah
> & Smithland will be the evening of July 3rd.

Within a few days of the notices' appearance, every available place on the *Hawkins* was subscribed.

The captains' denial that the race would occur did nothing to dampen people's enthusiasm. In fact, the denials—published in New Orleans newspapers—had the opposite effect. They fueled the flames like pine knots shoveled into a steamer's furnace.

Earlier in June, the *Natchez* had gained great fame by besting the *J. M. White*'s longstanding record time between New Orleans and Saint Louis. Will used that time to cipher when the *Natchez* and *Lee* would likely pass Cairo. Then he built in a safety margin and set the *Hawkins'* departure time from Smithland so she would get to Cairo before the *Natchez* and *Lee*.

What Will nor anyone else anticipated was that as the boats raced up the Mississippi, telegraphers would send reports ahead of the steamers' progress. Anybody near a telegraph key had nearly hourly news of the race.

The first word over the wire was that the *Robert E. Lee* backed away from the New Orleans levee at 4:55 and the *Natchez* at 4:59. Each captain fired his boat's cannon opposite Saint Mary's Market to mark his departure. No doubt Captain Leathers wanted to pull one of his favorite tricks. He was known to have left the New Orleans levee a few minutes after a rival boat, only to pass her midstream shortly thereafter. The *Natchez* didn't pass the *Lee* this time, however. By the time Captain Leathers fired the *Natchez*'s cannon, the *Lee* was a good mile ahead.

Captain Cannon had stripped his boat of unnecessary weight, carried no freight and only 75 passengers. Captain Leathers, on the other hand, carried a full load of both freight and passengers, and had not discarded excess weight. The *Lee* already had a slight weight and size advantage, and Captain Cannon's competitive actions increased it.

When it became known that the *Lee* would fuel midstream without stopping but the *Natchez* would stop for coal or wood and to exchange passengers and freight, people began to favor the *Lee*. But at the same time, they wondered whether that ornery Captain Leathers had something up his sleeve. People in Smithland pestered Will for information because they knew our cousin, Johnny Hawkins, owned the bar on the *Natchez* and was a good friend of Captain Leathers. But quizzing Will was for naught because he hadn't been in touch with Johnny and knew no more than anyone else.

At Baton Rouge, about 150 miles above New Orleans, the *Lee* was nine miles ahead of the *Natchez*. But at Proffit's Point on July 1st, the *Lee* burst a steam pipe and, while she sat idle as repairs were made, the *Natchez* came within sight, only three miles behind. It was 4 a.m.

By 10:15 that morning, the *Lee* passed her rival's namesake city, Natchez, Mississippi. She lashed two coal flats alongside midstream, then turned them loose after rousters offloaded the coal. Late in the afternoon, the *Lee* passed Vicksburg. Then, just above, Captain Cannon did something that made many at the telegraph key in Smithland cry foul. He lashed the *Lee* to the *Frank Pargoud* and, as the two boats steamed together up the Mississippi, rousters transferred 100 cords of pine knots from the *Pargoud* to the *Lee*. Some of those with money on Captain Leathers and the *Natchez* called off their bets, saying the *Pargoud* helped power the *Lee*.

The *Natchez* laid by at Helena, Arkansas, more than half an hour to repair a defective cold water pump. By late in the morning of July 2nd when the *Lee* came within sight of Memphis, the half-way point, the *Natchez* was a little more than an hour behind.

The Smithland wharf that morning was a picture of excitement. Hundreds of people from all over Livingston County and across the Ohio in New Liberty and Hamletsburg, Illinois, had gathered at the Smithland riverfront awaiting the *George Hawkins'* departure. Runners darted back and forth between the telegraph key and the wharf with the latest dispatches, calling the race as it progressed. A half-hour before departure time, Dorsey Dunn, clerk to James Drewry, the coal dealer in town, stood atop an upright hogshead and cried, "The *Robert E. Lee* passed Helena, Arkansas, before first light this morning. At dawn, the *Natchez* had not yet been seen at that place."

With that, the musical tooting of a calliope was heard above the buzzing crowd. Like many other captains who saw the railroads drawing passengers from steamers, Will had installed a calliope on the hurricane deck of the *George Hawkins*. The days when packets had only to run reliably from landing to landing to fill with passengers were past. Now, captains had to resort to calliopes, fancy decorations and excursions to keep passengers on the rivers.

If rivermen saw the calliope as a gimmick, Ben saw it as a musical wonder. He stood at the keys smiling and tapping out one lively tune after another. The big bell on the *George Hawkins*' roof signaled it was time to depart for the Mississippi. We boarded the Smithland passengers, who then crowded the guards and upper decks to wave goodbye to friends staying behind. About an hour later, we boarded the remaining passengers in Paducah and were away from the wharf by half past noon.

The steward rang the dinner bell for cabin passengers at 2 p.m. The chefs and waiters put out a sumptuous meal, with fresh fruits and vegetables seen only in summer. Deck passengers spread their picnics in off the guards, out of the hot midday sun.

With dinner finished and the tables cleared and moved forward near the bar, the band began to play, and the cabin passengers, who had dressed in their Sunday best, danced. Cairo was about two hours ahead.

Will knew the *Hawkins* would be many hours en route to and from Cairo, and because this was an excursion rather than a packet trip, he felt he had to provide entertainment for the paying travelers. He had asked Ben to put together a band for the trip. For reasons I didn't understand at the time, Ben went to Signore Petrone for help with the band. Signore Petrone was an Italian gentleman who had been staying in town at the Planters' House since spring. At his suggestion, the band included Ben, two music teachers in Smithland—Miss Barbara Morrison and Miss Henrie Shelton— and Signore Petrone himself. Signore Petrone asked that, for the excursion, the piano be moved from the parlor of his hotel to the *Hawkins*' main cabin. If E. E. Morrison, the hotel keeper, hadn't been Miss Morrison's father, he would never have consented. But with his and Will's approval, Ben, Nothet and several other rousters hauled the piano from the hotel to the *Hawkins*' cabin.

We reached the Mississippi at 5:30 and found many other

boats there. The *Armada*, the *Odd Fellow* and the *Idlewild* were among them. Spectators lined both banks. At this spot, where the Ohio meets the Mississippi and the southernmost point of Illinois stands between Missouri and Kentucky, Will decided to stay close to our home state. He rounded to touch the bank at the site of Fort Holt and lowered the stage for any passengers who wanted to go ashore. We would have a perfect view from the *Hawkins'* larboard side as the *Robert E. Lee* and the *Natchez* rounded Bird's Point and continued up the Mississippi.

With the excitement of the race, and Monday being Independence Day, the atmosphere was festive. American flag bunting hung from the railings of many boats, and fireworks popped from scattered spots on every shore.

Ben left the band in the cabin and took his spot at the calliope on the hurricane deck. *Shoo Fly* drifted on the air, mingled with music from other boats and hovered over the rivers. Children's squeals rose above the hum of excited voices riding the breeze. Word came up from the bank that the *Lee* was about an hour below, and the *Natchez* at least another hour below that.

At nearly half past 6 o'clock, boats some distance below us on the Mississippi began clanging their bells and blowing their steam whistles. We looked downriver above the treeline and saw two columns of black smoke rising to become one and arc south. Cheers rose from the boats and the banks. In a few minutes, a large steamer appeared in the channel, charging hard and strong. We knew it was the *Lee* by her black stacks—the *Natchez's* stacks were red.

Below us, at the head of Island No. 1, Captain Gus Fowler's *Idlewild* moved into the stream and steamed toward us at full speed. Great cheers came from the banks and all the spectating boats. The *Lee* quickly caught the *Idlewild*, came alongside and lashed the smaller boat to her. Forty or 50 men leaped from the *Lee* to the *Idlewild*, each carrying a trunk, a valise or a bird cage. Twenty passengers followed. The *Idlewild* would take them to points up the Ohio. Captain Cannon stood majestically on the *Lee*'s roof. If he gave any commands, they weren't heard above the din of the crowd. Wes Connor was at the wheel. The *Lee*'s bell clanged one mighty ring as the signal to let go. Men jumped to their respective boats, and the *Lee* sprinted ahead like a frightened deer. It was a scene of great grandeur that I lack the words to adequately describe.

When the *Lee* passed us, she looked enormous compared to the *Hawkins* and far more ornate. Everyone cheered wildly. Men waved their hats, and women with parasols gaily bobbed them up and down and side to side. Children jumped and screamed. Passengers on the *Lee* vigorously returned the waves and cheers.

The *Lee* moved to the Missouri shore opposite Cairo Point where two coal flats waited. She took them in tow, and the loading began. An Upper Mississippi pilot boarded the *Lee* from one of the flats. As she receded into the distance, the *Lee* released the flats. She had taken on 1,500 bushels of coal.

As calm returned to the *Hawkins'* passengers, Signore Petrone walked among them urging, "Please, ladies and gentlemen, come to the cabin for an especial program. The *Natchez* will be an hour. Please, come."

People streamed into the cabin, where the waiters had arranged the chairs in rows facing aft. To the left at the rear of the cabin, Signore Petrone sat at the piano. Standing at the right, Miss Morrison held a violin and Miss Shelton a flute. Ben stood smiling in the center. The audience filled every seat, and many stood in the cabin and on the boiler deck outside. Children crowded the floor between the seats and the band.

Signore Petrone nodded to the women, and the three began to play softly. Ben waited through the introductory bars and then, in a high, sweet voice, he sang:

> *I wandered today to the hill, Maggie*
> *To watch the scene below*
> *The creek and the old rusty mill, Maggie*
> *Where we sat in the long, long ago*
> *The green grove is gone from the hill, Maggie*
> *Where first the daisies had sprung*
> *The old rusty mill is now still, Maggie*
> *Since you and I were young*

At the chorus, many in the audience joined in:

> *And now we are aged and gray, Maggie*
> *The trials of life nearly done*

Let's sing of the days that are gone, Maggie
When you and I were young.

Ben sweetly sang four verses, with more in the audience joining in at each chorus. By the last, many eyes welled with tears. The applause was generous and respectful. As it ebbed, the three musicians began an unfamiliar melody. Ben straightened up, raised his chin and took a deep breath. He began to sing in a manner and language I hadn't heard before:

La donna è mobile
Qual piuma al vento
Muta d'accento
E di pensiero
Sempre un amabile
Leggiadro viso
In pianto o in riso
E menzognero

As he continued, the audience, both sitting inside and standing within and without the cabin, fell into a stunned silence. Signore Petrone exchanged appreciative smiles with James and Mary Zanone, a Smithland grocer and his wife, who sat in the first row, beaming.

Ben sang and the musicians played beautifully for several minutes. When they finished, people seated in the audience jumped to their feet, and the whole room erupted in cheers and applause. Ben and the musicians looked pleased and a little surprised as they smiled and bowed.

Later, I learned from Signore Petrone that Ben had sung a passage from *Rigoletto*, an opera by Giuseppe Verdi. Signore Petrone added that if the women in the audience had understood Italian, perhaps they wouldn't have applauded so strongly. As beautiful as the lyrics sounded, they portray women as fickle.

I was especially proud of Ben at that moment and happy to call him my brother. I wasn't at all angry that he had kept a secret from me since spring. Now I knew where he had been all those hours when I couldn't find him—he was with Signore Petrone, learning opera.

At half past 7 o'clock, just as things had quieted down, boats below again began clanging their bells and blowing their whistles. The familiar black smoke billowed into the evening sky south of us. In a few minutes, the *Natchez*'s red stacks appeared. Cheers rose on the boats and the banks. As the *Natchez* approached, men checked their pocket watches. It was 7:40. The *Natchez* was an hour and 10 minutes behind the *Lee*. That was a lot of time to make up in the 180 miles between Cairo and Saint Louis. I stood with Beth and Amanda on the boiler deck. We leaned out over the rail and cheered and waved as the *Natchez* passed. Passengers aboard the *Natchez* returned our waves but seemed to lack the enthusiasm of the earlier passengers aboard the *Lee*. The *Natchez* took coal aboard at Cairo but no pilot. As the crowd aboard the *Hawkins* watched the *Natchez* fade into the distance, I saw hopeless looks on many faces. It looked as if the *Lee* would win The Great Race.

People began to talk about the trip home. Just then, a sharp cry rose above the crowd's hum. To my right, a man plunged through the air, falling from the hurricane deck above and splashing into the Mississippi. He bobbed to the surface and began to frantically paddle *away* from the *Hawkins* rather than back toward it. He encouraged the current to carry him away.

First, the big bell on the roof clanged an alarm. Then I heard Will shout through the megaphone, "Mr. Dunn, launch the yawl!" By the time George Dunn and two deckhands had the yawl off the deck and afloat in the river, Will was down to the main deck and stepping into the boat. He stood at the stern, the deckhands manned the oars, and George Dunn crouched in the bow.

From my spot on the boiler deck, I heard Will guide the oarsmen as the yawl moved into the channel, "Hard on the oars, dead ahead!" The jumper had a good head start, but the yawl was faster. In a few minutes, I saw Will and the other men hauling the jumper out of the river into the yawl.

Back on the *Hawkins*, Will got the jumper into dry clothes and listened to the man's anguished tale. He was a Mr. Carlin who had come to Smithland by ferry from Hamletsburg for the excursion. He had gotten caught up in the excitement of the race and bet his every cent on the *Natchez*. Now he saw he had lost it all and in desperation jumped into the Mississippi. Will, George

Dunn and the deckhands had saved Mr. Carlin's life, but he didn't want to appreciate that.

Will withdrew the stage and backed off the bank as the sun hung low in the Missouri sky. Near sunset on summer evenings, the hot, thick, humid atmosphere turned lavender and seemed to suspend the salmon sun.

Amanda and I shared a cabin in the texas on the way home. Ben stayed up late playing and singing with the band in the main cabin. Amanda and I were asleep long before the *Hawkins* paused at Paducah. Will and Beth didn't wake us when we reached Smithland. We slept soundly in the texas cabin until late morning when the marching band began tuning up beside the wharfboat for the Independence Day parade. Word had just come in by wire that the *Lee* had arrived at Saint Louis at 11:09 a.m., three days, 18 hours and 14 minutes after leaving New Orleans, setting a record that has never been bettered. Its being Independence Day, I imagined the celebrations were highly charged. The *Natchez* made Saint Louis by 5:42 p.m. Since the *Natchez* had lost just over seven hours in stops en route, and the *Lee* made no stops, the debate continued over which was the faster boat.

11

Will and the crew returned from Cincinnati on the new *George Hawkins No. 10* on Sunday morning, August 21, 1870. He had wired ahead and told us to be ready to leave for Paducah and Cairo at noon. The *Hawkins* was to resume in the Cairo–Nashville trade. For this trip, we would run to Cairo on Sunday and then leave for Nashville on Monday morning. Cairo to Nashville was three and a half days, with stops at Mound City, Paducah, Smithland, and more than 30 towns and landings between Smithland and Nashville. While in Nashville, the Steamboat Inspection Service would go over the *Hawkins* with a nit comb. Will knew the *10* would pass as easy as a sunrise.

The *George Hawkins No. 10* was the prettiest thing I ever saw. I wished George Hawkins himself was on hand to see his boat. Mr. Durand, the editor of the Smithland *Times* must have liked the *10* too, because he wrote two whole columns on her for Monday's edition:

THE GEORGE HAWKINS No. 10

Just completed at Cincinnati, the *George Hawkins No. 10* arrived at the Smithland wharf at 10 a.m. yesterday, and left for Paducah and Cairo at noon. She is one of the most perfectly finished and furnished packets of her size and class ever constructed, and her owner merits the gratitude of the people along the Cumberland River for the pains he has taken and the expense incurred to furnish the boat so admirably adapted for the trade.

Her dimensions are as follows: Length 160 feet, 33 feet beam, 32 feet floor, 5 feet guards, 5 feet depth of hold, draft 27 inches light. She displaces 369 tons. She has three double-flued boilers 24 feet long and 38 inches in diameter, two cylinders 16 inches in diameter and 5 feet stroke, driving a water wheel 22 feet in diameter, with 24-foot buckets. The wheel is extra braced and is pronounced the finest job of the kind ever turned out. She is also supplied with a doctor and nigger engines and steam capstan. The hull was built by James Mack, of Cincinnati, and her engines by Dumont, and both are first class jobs.

She has a beautiful and graceful model adapted for speed and buoyancy, her guards are extra wide and roomy, suitable for handling freight readily, with a spacious engine room. The stairs leading to the boiler deck are of the most approved style, after the fashion of the Louisville and Cairo packets, with extra room for receiving furniture and a piano.

Her cabin is exceedingly tasteful and elegant, being full length, with recess, laundry and water closets aft. The cabin is painted beautifully white, with two gold bands on the tops of the half columns, and green panels over the bulkhead between the stateroom doors. Her office is in front and is roomy, convenient, and in excellent taste. Her pantry is large and conveniently arranged, and supplied with an outfit that would do credit to the *Robert E. Lee* or *Richmond*, both in quantity and quality. The carpets, from John Shillito's, are rich and beautiful, and furniture, by Baily & Cox, is elegant and substantial. The chandeliers are neat and correspond well with the balance of the cabin outfit. A fine marble-top stand in the ladies' cabin is ornamented with a magnificent silver water cooler, goblets and water bowl, presented by Beth Hawkins, wife of the owner. They constitute a fitting and beautiful present. The staterooms are large and well-ventilated, furnished with the best spring mattresses and coverings, all having the boat's name interwoven.

The cabin contains 27 staterooms and a post office room; and there are two staterooms in the recess aft of the cabin, for the accommodation of colored female passengers. A splendid mirror ornaments the after bulkhead of the cabin. The boat was furnished by the Young Men's Bible Society of Cincinnati with two elegant Bibles of medium size convenient for use. The cabin was built by Glasscock, of Wheeling, West Virginia, and is a very substantial job. On the larboard side of the gangway is a roomy barber shop and washroom. The bar is on the starboard forward, is neat and roomy, and is ornamented with the pleasant countenance of Barney Bliss, who will always have a ready "smile" for his friends.

The office outfit—books, stationery, &c—is from the *Times* Bindery, Job Office, and Stationery Room, and defies competition. Her books we commend to the careful inspection of steamboat clerks everywhere. Her upper guards are spacious and roomy, and, with her forward boiler deck, are admirably adapted to the Cumberland trade for which she was built. An iron foot guard runs around her railing, and her stairs are covered with iron plates for their preservation. Her smokestacks are models of beauty, with elaborately ornamented tops, including tall leaves. A martin box is strung between them, and martins have already taken up occupancy. Her texas will afford ample room for her officers and crew. Her texas and pilothouse are well proportioned, and the boat, in all respects,

presents as graceful and elegant appearance as any
we have seen.

The following are her roster of officers: Captain,
Will Hawkins; mate, Nate Drew; clerks, George
Dunn, Pete Conant and Andy Vickers; barkeeper,
Barney Bliss; steward, John Connor; engineers, P. M.
John and Jessee Paterson; pilots, Gus Mellon and Bill
Burton. As we remarked at the outset, a more perfect or better appointed sternwheel steamboat never
touched at this wharf. She is well worthy of her owner
and builders, and of the gallant officers who will command her. She returns from Cairo at 3 p.m. today and
leaves for Nashville at 4. Freight is taken on and passengers board at the Hawkins Wharfboat.

Any boat that made the Cumberland its regular run had to
be shallow draft. Harpeth Shoals was the main obstacle. River
News items from Nashville in the *Times* always gave the stage
of water at Harpeth Shoals. On Monday, August 22nd, the
Nashville item read, "River falling, six feet on Harpeth Shoals.
Weather fair and warm. Arrived—*Burksville* and *Alpha*, from
Cairo. Departed—*Alpha* and *Burksville* to Cairo."

The *Alpha* was Captain Thomas Ryman's boat. She was a
regular in the Nashville–Cairo and the Nashville–Evansville
trades. The *Alpha* was 150 feet long—only 10 feet shorter than
the *10*—but she drew a scant 12 inches when light. She could
run up the Cumberland to the head of navigation at Burnside at
almost any stage of water. The *Burksville* was a small, low-wa-
ter boat that usually ran only in the upper river above Nashville.
No *George Hawkins* had ever gone above Nashville, which was
at the 187-mile mark.

Runs on the Cumberland were my favorite. The water was
cobalt blue, and the valley was very pretty, especially at sunrise and sunset. Some stretches were heavily forested, others
were lined with bluffs, and still others were fields and pastures.
Cattle in the water on an especially hot day were a regular sight,
as were whitetail deer swimming the river.

This was a special trip on the *10* because the five of us—
Will, Beth, Amanda, Ben and I—were along. Will's work as a

packet captain and pilot kept him away from home a lot. Beth was almost always busy with Amanda and household chores. Ben and I were together most all the time, but our whole family being together was rare. As many times as I had stood proudly beside Will at the wheel in the pilothouse high above the river, it still gave me a big thrill.

Will was my father, so I'm sure my view of him is positive biased, but he was a remarkable man. He had a natural air of certainty and authority about him. I don't think I ever saw him do anything awkwardly. He was able to master unfamiliar things quickly and carry them off like an expert. Other men respected him and deferred to him. Even men who didn't know Will or his reputation quickly came to show respect. And it came about not because Will forced it. Authority that commanded respect just seemed to surround him like a halo. If I could honestly say I've been half the man Will was, I would feel I had spent my time well.

The Cumberland is a tributary river. It's narrower and shallower than the Ohio, the river it feeds, just as the Ohio is not as grand as the Mississippi, the river it feeds. Any Cumberland packet had to be built with that river's features and habits foremost in mind. It principally meant boats had to be shallow draft. To achieve a shallow draft, a Cumberland steamer had to be smaller than one built for the Ohio or one meant for the Mississippi. No *George Hawkins* ever exceeded 160 feet. The *10* was exactly 160 feet long and displaced 369 tons. The *Robert E. Lee*, which regularly ran the Mississippi and was known for running aground in the Ohio, was 286 feet and displaced 1,456 tons. What the *10* lacked in size, however, she made up for with grace, beauty and speed. I hoped one day to own a boat just like her.

By the time the *10* was in the stream above Smithland and on her way to Nashville, the news of a grand new boat had already gotten around. In truth, word about the new *George Hawkins* had spread even before she was launched. People were "Waitin' to see the *10*," as they called her.

Nearly half the staterooms were taken and the deck loaded with freight and excursion passengers when we left Smithland. We were hailed at every town and landing as we steamed up. Will and the crew had a grand old time of it. Whether the pilot was Will, Gus Mellon or Bill Burton, he made liberal use of the steam whistle to announce the *10*'s approach. The new whistle had a distinctive throaty, melodic tone. The bell had its own sound too, but that wasn't new. The *10* was the seventh *George Hawkins* to clang the same bell. The captains had passed it from one *George Hawkins* to the next, like a tradition or family heirloom.

Ben did his part to let folks know the *10* was nearby. He was at the calliope keyboard every time we touched a bank or tied to a wharfboat. If the steam whistle and big bell weren't enough to capture attention, the calliope was.

When we came to the landing at Eddyville early Tuesday morning, one of the cabin passengers who came aboard was an odd-looking little man in a plaid suit. I had never seen a plaid suit before. Will wore a dark blue captain's suit and cap when at work on the *10*. Men who wore suits always wore black, some with long coats. Country farmers wore homespun, and rousters wore blousy shirts with floppy pants that didn't quite reach their feet. So the man in the plaid suit and little round hat stood out in the crowd. And he didn't try to make himself invisible either. He was jolly and talkative, happy to start conversations with strangers in the cabin or on the upper guards. To the adults, and especially the women, he said, "Call me Harry, no need for formality." Most people were a little taken aback by Harry's forward manner. It was plain too that some people were wary of him.

Harry gave his card to anyone who would take it. I picked one up from the deck. It read, "H. S. Manning, Proprietor, Louisville, Kentucky." It didn't say what H. S. Manning was proprietor of, nor did it give an address. Harry spotted Ben's banjo, touched him on the shoulder and said, "I want to hear you play later on." He tugged the brim of my hat and said, "Hey, big man." He greeted Will with a smile and a salute. Everybody knew Harry was on the boat.

Harry's stateroom was forward in the cabin, near the bar. No sooner had he stowed his baggage and watched the *10* back away from the Eddyville wharf than he was circulating among the men at the bar, talking cheerily. By the time the stewards and waiters served dinner, Harry had made a dozen friends. By suppertime, between the Tennessee state line and Tobaccoport, his collection of friends had at least doubled. Before we reached Jackson Landing at about 9:00 p.m., four men had reported their billfolds missing. Will told them no one was getting off the boat until morning and promised that before they reached their destinations their billfolds would be found and the culprit caught.

Any passenger who wanted to get to bed early on Tuesday night had his plans quickly changed when, just as we left Jackson Landing, the entire boat was jolted to attention by a woman's piercing shrieks and screams. Andy Vickers and one of the stewards, running to the stateroom the screams came from, captured Harry rapidly exiting the room, his plaid jacket under his arm, his shirttail out and his plaid britches unbuttoned and drooping. Pockets in the lining of his jacket were found to hold six men's billfolds. Apparently, two gentlemen had been too embarrassed to report their loss.

Will had Andy collect Harry's fare to Dover. Then he locked Harry in his stateroom and posted a rouster at each door. Many passengers thought Will would turn Harry over to the constable in Dover, but Will had other plans.

About two miles above the Dover wharf, Dover Island lies midriver. Gus nosed the *10* into the bank there, and the deckhands dropped the stage. To the cheers of hundreds gathered for the sight, Will appeared on deck at the stage in the lantern light with Harry in tow. With a strong, swift movement, Will grabbed Harry by the seat of his britches and the back of his jacket collar and ran him across the stage to the island. Pete Conant followed close behind. Will and Pete stood by sternly with their hands on their hips as Harry stripped to his underclothes. Will and Pete gathered the shorn shoes and clothes and came back aboard the *10*. The stage came up, and the *10* backed off the island into the stream.

Harry, standing stripped and without baggage on the island, looked ashamed and forlorn as the *10* moved ahead. The passengers cheered and jeered, the steam whistle blew, the big bell clanged, and Ben tooted *Jack o'Diamonds* on the calliope. If Harry Manning had even a small slice of decency in him, he never got over the humiliation of that scene.

12

There was more than four feet of water at Harpeth Shoals when we reached the rivermouth at about 9 p.m. Wednesday. As we approached going up, the *Ella Hughes* approached coming down. She was a little sternwheel packet from Paducah. Captain Billy Dix was her master. Gus slowed the *10* and let the *Ella Hughes* pass the shoals first. She cleared easily without even having to test the bottom with her sounding pole. As the *Ella Hughes* passed us, I was struck by the contrast between her and the *10*. Although she was built in '67, the *Ella Hughes* was an old style boat—complete utility, nothing fancy about her, a dowdy girl. Her owners had not even seen fit to provide staterooms for cabin passengers. Their berths were nothing more than shelves lining the cabin bulkheads, with only hanging curtains providing the barest minimum of privacy. By contrast, Will had built the *10* to the standards of the finest Mississippi steamers. On her first trip, she looked every bit the belle of the ball.

We had a full register of passengers but were light on freight. The river was falling, but with more than four feet of water over the shoals, we passed easily.

The *10* dropped her stage at the Nashville wharf just before half past 9 on Thursday morning, August 25. Even in a big, sophisticated city like Nashville, the *10* drew a lot of attention. The mate, Nate Drew, and the clerks, Pete Conant and George Dunn, had barely begun to disembark passengers and unload freight when drays with freight bound down and passengers going downriver crowded the wharf waiting to board.

Normally, the crew would want to make the exchange quickly and get the boat on her way within hours of her arrival, but the Steamboat Inspection Service had to examine an empty boat.

Pete Conant stood forward on the hurricane deck near the jackstaff, raised the megaphone to his mouth and called for attention.

"Ladies and gentlemen," he said twice above the din. When people and movement had quieted down some, and eyes and ears had turned to him, Pete continued.

"Ladies and gentlemen. The captain and crew of the *George Hawkins No. 10* are very pleased to see your eager faces this fine morning. We want to accommodate you all, but before we can board any passengers or freight, we have to first empty the boat of its Nashville-bound cargo and passengers so the gentlemen of the Steamboat Inspection Service can examine the *10* from stem to stern. Once the *10* has passed its inspection and received its certificate of approval, and we are certain she will,

then we will board downbound passengers and freight. We antic-
ipate boarding to commence by noon. However, the *10* will not
leave the wharf until 9 a.m. tomorrow. Mr. Dunn and I will be
available to book passengers and write bills of lading as soon
as Nashville-bound passengers have disembarked and freight is
unloaded. We will be available until 6 p.m. today and again at
7 a.m. tomorrow. Downbound passengers may take supper and
spend the night aboard or return in the morning."

I had never heard Pete sound so formal, so much like an officer. I think the fancy new *10* had pushed him up in rank.

Ed Jones, Inspector of Hulls, and Sam Harrison, Inspector of
Boilers with the Steamboat Inspection Service came aboard at
half past 10. They wore dark blue suits and captain's caps like
Will's, and carried leather slipcases. Will and the crew met them
on the main deck at the top of the stage. Mr. Jones began in the
hold, and Mr. Harrison in the boiler room. Three quarters of
an hour later, they sat down at a table in the cabin where each
man withdrew a printed parchment certificate from his slipcase.
George Dunn provided pens and inkwells, the inspectors dated
the certificates, wrote in the name *George Hawkins No. 10* and
signed their approval. They stood, shook hands with Will and
the crew, tucked their leather cases under their arms and left.
George slipped the certificates into their frames and hung them
side by side on the bulkhead in the office.

Will could have had the *10* going down by mid-afternoon,
but he had decided this was a special occasion, and the Hawkins
family would spend the night in Nashville at the new Maxwell
House. It was a grand hotel, just completed the year before. It
boasted 240 steam-heated rooms, an elevator, and a bath and
water closet on every floor. Of course, nobody needed steam
heat in August, but the hack drivers at the wharf announced it
anyway, I guess because they thought it would impress out-of-
town visitors.

After dinner, we had the afternoon to explore Nashville in a
surrey before registering at the Maxwell House. Beth had dressed
Amanda in a long, white cotton dress and broad-brimmed hat
with a lavender ribbon flowing down her back. Her blond curls
refused to be contained by her hat and burst from beneath its
crown. I don't think I ever saw Amanda look so clean as she did

that afternoon in Nashville. At home, she was always into something getting her dress soiled and her face dirty.

Beth was never one for cinched waists and hoop skirts. At
home, she often wore men's trousers when working in the kitchen
or garden. She rarely wore a dress but preferred a simple blouse
and long, full skirt. In Nashville, she wore a white pleated long
sleeve blouse with ruffles at the neck and wrists, and a long dark
skirt. She carried no parasol but wore a broad-brimmed hat to
protect her from the summer sun.

Beth didn't make Ben or me wear city clothes, but we did
wear shoes. As usual, I wore my slouch hat. I never liked straw
hats. They don't hold water for a dog or horse, and you can't
really shape them to fit your head. And they scratch places your
hair doesn't cover. I like a nice felt hat. Summertime wear for
me was my slouch hat, a loose, blousy cotton shirt, knee pants
and bare feet. My feet would get so tough and calloused that I
didn't really need shoes. Bare feet were much more comfortable
anyway. But that afternoon in Nashville, leather shoes replaced
my comfort.

While the crew restocked the *10* at the boat store, we rode
through the city in the surrey. We agreed that Smithland could
fit within a few square blocks of Nashville. We intersected with
the horse-drawn railroad twice. Its rail cars went throughout
the city and took passengers to or near every corner.

A short distance above town we stopped in a pleasant grove
of sycamores beside the Cumberland. Amanda and I ran in the
ankle-high grass while Ben sat leaning against a tree playing
his harmonica, and Will and Beth strolled idly along the bank.

We drove up to the Maxwell House at about 6 o'clock. Porters
took our baggage from the surrey as we entered the lobby. A
man in a suit and high, tight collar greeted us at the desk. Ben,
Amanda and I stood back as Will and Beth spoke with the man at
the desk. He looked over Will's shoulder at us as he spoke, shift-
ing his eyes to Will and back to us. Will turned to me and said,
"Early, please run out front and ask Jim to wait with the surrey."

I did, and the whole family soon followed with the porters
and our baggage. We boarded the surrey without a word from
Will or Beth. Will spoke only to the driver,

"Jim, please take us to the wharf."

As we got under way, Will said, "We will be taking supper and staying the night on the *10*."

That was all. Nothing else was said. Ben and I looked at each other, knowing what had happened.

After supper, I stood on the boiler deck and watched lamp-lighters light the gaslamps that lined the streets near the wharf. Martins darted about snatching insects in midair. They very deftly slipped in and out of the nests in the box strung between the *10*'s stacks.

At precisely 9 a.m., Bill Burton backed the *10* off the wharf into the stream. The warm morning light made the *10*'s white paint gleam in the places where the dew still lingered.

We touched the landing at Clee's Ferry just as the *Umpire* backed into the stream going up. She was another Paducah boat. Captain G. J. Grammar was her master. She was a sternwheeler a bit bigger than the *Ella Hughes* but not as big as the *10*.

The word by wire was that the river had fallen to 3-1/2 feet at Harpeth Shoals during the night. Going down, the *10*'s stateroom and deck registers were full, and she already carried nearly her 600-ton freight capacity. After a dozen stops for landings and hails, we reached the shoals at half past 8 that evening. Nate Drew poled the bottom from the yawl ahead and showed a scant three feet. Fully loaded, the *10*'s draft was nearly six feet. With no lighters running, we had no choice but to unload half the freight on the bank above the shoals before continuing down. In the pilothouse, Gus inched ahead with the paddlewheel turning in opposition to the current, and the bow touched the first bar. Even with half the cargo, Will had to give the order to set the spars. In the yawl, Nate and two oarsmen poled the bottom and directed our course as we grasshoppered over one bar after another. We unloaded the remaining freight on the bank below the shoals and went up to retrieve what we had left above. The shoals weren't too bad a struggle, but passing them took better than two hours.

Will woke us at quarter past 1 o'clock on Monday morning to get off at Smithland. A horse and wagon were waiting at the wharfboat to carry us and our baggage up to the homeplace. Will continued on to Cairo. He was eager to regain his schedule and was trying to reach Cairo early so he could leave before noon.

13

In the fall, after the harvest work was done and the corn was husked, my school in Smithland challenged Dierhill School to a spell-down. Dierhill was across the Cumberland, north of Smithland about six or seven miles. The center of the community was above Rappolee's Landing at the horseshoe bend in the river. Although Dierhill School was smaller than Smithland School, because its students had already spelled down other schools in the county, Smithland was the challenger and the underdog. Between the Negro children's school and the white children's school in Smithland, we had seven teachers. Dierhill School had one.

Will brought nearly the whole Dierhill community down from Rappolee's on the *10*. There were grammas and grampas, mamas and daddies and children of all ages. There were 14 spellers and the teacher, Miss Margaret Shaw.

We matched their number of spellers with 14 of our own. All the white Smithland teachers were there, but only Miss Sturges, Miss Dunn and Miss Conant helped with the spell down. Miss Sturges had come to Smithland from Michigan, while Miss Dunn and Miss Conant were sisters of clerks on the *10*.

The *10* tied to the wharfboat with its Dierhill passengers late on a Friday afternoon. I was in a group of Smithland students who met them at the river. We walked the few blocks through town to the school, which was near the southeast corner of Adair and Walnut streets. The day was chilly, and as we walked I noticed smoke from pot belly stoves rising above the chimneys of stores and houses in town.

Smithland had challenged Dierhill about two weeks prior, so there was plenty of time for everybody to get worked up into a frenzy. The whole town turned out, and there was a great deal of excitement.

Beth had been drilling me so much at home that I had *McGuffey's Eclectic Spelling Book* nearly memorized front to back. I had always read a lot, so I had seen many of the *McGuffey's* words spelled right in other books. Even though I didn't know what all of them meant, I knew what they looked like, so I knew how to spell them.

We had a potluck supper and after the tables were cleared and everything put away, we moved over to the schoolhouse to start the spell-down. We had spent the better part of the day cleaning up the school, so it was spotless and everything was in fine order when people came in.

The spellers lined up across the front of the room and down the sides, the Smithland spellers on one side and the Dierhill spellers on the other. As many people as could fit in the scholars' seats and in the rear of the room did, while the rest stood outside the door and looking in the windows. Oil lamps and candles brightened the room, and a potbelly stove warmed it.

As the spellers fidgeted and whispered to one another, two adults' names, one from each town, written on slips of paper, were drawn from hats. Wash Beverly was drawn for Smithland and Thomas Nelson for Dierhill. Mr. Beverly would give out the words to the Dierhill spellers, and Mr. Nelson to the Smithland spellers. Miss Shaw randomly opened *McGuffey's*, and Mr. Beverly and Mr. Nelson guessed the page. Mr. Beverly's guess was closer, so he gave out the first word. Spellers' names were chosen one slip of paper at a time. Mr. Beverly chose Ellen Robinson's name first. She was 10, like me. She was a cute, brown-haired girl with pretty eyes and an impish grin. At that moment, though, she looked very serious as Mr. Beverly, in his deep, resonant voice, gave out her word.

"Annihilate. The gulls will annihilate the grasshoppers. Annihilate," he said.

I knew that word and wished it was my turn. Ellen Robinson knew it too, so it was Mr. Nelson's turn to choose a name. He picked Charley Mayhugh and gave out "abstemious." Charley made me a little nervous because he looked puzzled at first, but then he spelled it right and remained standing.

Several more words were given out before, finally, Jimmy Overstreet, on our side, missed "kaleidoscope" and sat down. I was very lucky because I would have missed "succinct" had it been given out to me. As it was, I knew every word I was given, and in the end, Ginny Daniels, a 12-year-old Dierhill girl, and I were the only spellers left standing. Choosing at random, Mr. Beverly gave Ginny "manikin." She put a "q" and "u" in it and had to sit down. If I got my next word right, Smithland School would win. Mr. Nelson reached into the word-slips hat and chose "eleemosynary." People in the room gasped, but I grinned because I knew the word and, before I spelled it, I knew that we had won the spell-down. When I correctly spelled what every-one thought was a mighty strange word, the Smithland people broke into boisterous cheering and applause. As the last speller standing, my prize was *Belden: The White Chief*, a book that had become popular that year. It was a true story by George Belden, a boy who had run away from home to live with Plains Indians.

After a short recess, several Dierhill and Smithland students recited literary pieces, and two played violin solos. I could tell who the kin of the speakers and players were. They beamed the brightest during and clapped the loudest after.

I went on the *10* when Will took our visitors back to Rappolee's Landing. If they were dispirited at losing the spell-down, they didn't show it.

One of the drummers who came to town late that fall had a bicycle among the goods on his wagon. At that time, the bicycle was still new in America and hadn't yet become commonplace. In fact, they weren't called bicycles at first. They were called velocipedes.

This drummer's bicycle didn't look like today's. There was no chain, and a system of pedals and cranks transferred the rider's power to the front wheel, which was bigger than the back one.

The drummer had been carrying the bicycle for months and had learned to ride it. Of course, no one in Smithland knew how. Those facts produced a scene of great hilarity along Riverfront Street one Saturday afternoon. The drummer mounted the bicy-cle and happily rode up and down the street, weaving through the onlookers and waving as he went.

Then he offered the bicycle to anyone who wanted to give it a try. One man or boy after another tried and fell. Each started out boasting he could ride like the drummer. And each tipped over, embarrassed and laughing—mostly.

Uncle Louis took great interest in the workings of the bicy-cle, and, much to the drummer's and everyone else's surprise, ordered three. The drummer wired the order, and about two weeks later the bicycles arrived at the wharfboat aboard the *Mary Miller*. They had come from Pittsburg by way of Evansville.

It was only then that Louis' purpose became known.

Louis' farm was up on the high ground that lay down from town and across the Paducah road. That put his land east and a little south of the knoll where our house stood. Louis had a fine spread that never flooded, a problem we often had with our land in the bottoms. Louis had two large barns. One he hardly used because the other was adequate to his needs. That winter, the idle barn became Louis's boat-building workshop.

Louis talked with Will quite a lot about the boat's design and in drawing up the plans, but when it came to the actual building, Louis did most of the work himself. Ben proved skillful at cutting and sawing and caulking, but as a 10-year-old boy, I hadn't yet mastered tools or techniques. I did my best to carry out whatever tasks Louis gave me, but they weren't the kind that required much skill.

What emerged before the first planting in the early spring was a pedal-powered sternwheeler. While leaving one bicycle whole for riding, Louis had adapted the mechanism of the other two and built a yawl powered by two pedalers sitting amidships and pedaling to turn the buckets of the wheel churning behind them.

Louis had set up the mechanism as a miniature version of the devices that drive a steamboat, the difference being, of course, the size and the fact that on Louis' boat, people provided the power.

Jim Clark brought a double dray and four mules up to Louis' barn on launch day. The men ran the pedal boat on greased skids up into the dray. We rode alongside on horseback as Jim guided the mules down to the river. The few people we passed on the way stopped and gaped at a boat the likes of which they had never seen before. As the men slid the boat into the river below the wharf-boat, Louis told me to peel back the sack cloths he had used to conceal the boat's name. In the ornate Mississippi riverboat style, Louis had lettered *Hilltop* on both sides below the gunwales.

The *Hilltop* slid into the water easily. Louis asked Ben to join him for the maiden voyage. I held the *Hilltop* close to shore as Ben and Louis settled into the seats at the pedals. Louis took the rudder tiller, and they eased into the stream. They were quite relaxed, pedaling easily going down, looking like two men going fishing for the afternoon, but in a strange vessel. When they

reached Cumberland towhead and rounded to oppose the current, their relaxation quickly disappeared. Both grabbed hard
to the bar that crossed in front of their seats and bore down to
pedal quite furiously and make headway against the mid-river
current. The buckets threw up a wake like any steamer, only
much smaller. Louis steered close to the bank where the current
was weakest, they eased up on the pedaling and moved nicely
back to us. We cheered and waved as Ben and Louis, especially
Louis, smiled broadly.

Several pairs of pedalers tried the *Hilltop*—I went with Jim
Clark—and all returned smiling and praising Louis. He kept the
Hilltop at the wharfboat, where it drew a lot of attention and
plenty of advice from armchair rivermen.

14

Ben and I found that unless the Cumberland was high and
the current especially swift, we could make good headway in
the *Hilltop* going up as long as we hugged the bank, where the
slower current let us oppose it. Our pedaling wasn't easy, but it
wasn't furious either.

About the middle of March, we pedaled the *Hilltop* up just
above town to near where the lumber mill sat in the bottoms. We
knew catfish liked that spot. We gigged frogs for bait, got lucky
and pulled in a big old blue catfish. Later, we proudly presented
it to Beth as the centerpiece for that evening's meal.

Will was with us for supper. He had sent the *10* on to Cairo
with his mate, Nate Drew, in charge. Will being home, I took the
opportunity to make an announcement.

"I've been reading about the Plains Indian tribes," I said. "In
some tribes, when a boy is ready to become a man, he goes off by
himself into the wilderness. It's a test of his survival ability. If
he succeeds, the members of his tribe look upon him as a man."

The family listened closely. I saw Beth and Will trade glances.

"I found an Indian arrowhead," Amanda said, with a dose of
pride on her voice.

"Yes, you did, dear," Beth said encouragingly.

"Are you impressed by what the Indian boys do?" Will asked.

"Yes, I am," I said, "and I'd like to do it."

"I admire your idea and your courage," Will said, "but those Indian boys are 13, 14, 15 years old, and you're only 10."

"I'll be 11 next month," I said. "I've learned a lot about the wilderness from Louis. I think I'm ready for my survival test."

"I'd be afraid for you in the woods at night by yourself, Early," Beth said, looking at me and seeing a boy who was probably talking too big for his britches.

"Son, I know you've spent a lot of time in the woods with Louis, and he tells me you've done real well, but I think maybe you're a colt who's fixed on being a horse a little too soon," Will said. "How about taking Ben along with you?"

Will didn't see that I caught him winking ever so slightly at Ben.

"Naw, I want to go by myself," I insisted.

"I'll tell you what, then," Will said after a long pause. "In one week, when I'm back, and Nate takes the *10* on to Cairo, you and I will take two horses and a mule and spend a couple days in the woods together. We'll see how you do."

I tried to hold my independent ground, but I think my eagerness in accepting Will's offer was probably plain for all to see. Sly little smiles of relief and appreciation for Will's diplomacy sneaked across Beth's and Ben's faces. Amanda was more focused on her rag doll than anything else.

I spent my spare moments that week boning up on everything I'd read and everything Louis had taught me. I practiced with my Winchester by shooting at tin cans. I was determined to impress Will with my knowledge of the woods and with my shooting ability. I was sure he would let me go out on my own if I could show him that I could take care of myself.

There was heavy dew on the ground the morning Will and I saddled up to leave. Two weeks earlier, it would have been frost. Even though the almanac said it was spring, the nights and mornings were still chilly.

I saddled Spirit. We knew each other so well, I barely had to think a command for Spirit to do it. I slipped his bridle and bit on and saddled him by stepping up on a stool. It was the only way I could reach his head with the bridle or throw my saddle across his back. He was true to his name that morning—he seemed eager to get going.

Will saddled May Belle, his chestnut mare. We packed Grady, one of our field mules, with a tent, provisions and gear. We headed southeast on Iuka Road and then onto Dover Road. Will said he had no place in particular in mind and wasn't in a hurry to get there. We'd ride maybe till mid-afternoon, down between the rivers. We'd choose our camp and see if we could hunt up our supper. As we rode two abreast, leading Grady behind us, Will gestured to our right and asked,

"Early, see that big tree yonder? I know it's hard to tell a tree before it grows its leaves, but what do you suppose that one is?"

"Most folks call it tulip poplar," I said. "Some just call it tulip tree, and some call it yellow poplar. It's not a true poplar though. Its scientific name is *Liriodendron tulipifera*. Usually in May, it puts out greenish yellow and orange flowers that look like tulips. It's the tallest hardwood tree in North America—some can grow to 200 feet with a straight trunk that might be 80 to 100 feet to the lowest limb. It likes deep, rich, well-drained soil in coves or a valley like the one we're in now. The pioneers thought tulip poplars told of good soil. Termites don't eat the wood, so it's especially good for construction. It's easy to work and has lots of uses. Indians used it for dugout canoes, and early explorers followed the Indians' lead and used the wood for pirogues."

I didn't realize I knew that much about tulip poplars and surprised myself by talking on so long about them. I must have sounded as if I was reading from a book. I turned toward Will and saw that he had a stunned look on his face.

"Do you know as much about all the trees as you do about tulip poplars?" he asked.

"I wouldn't say all, but most," I replied. "Which ones do you want to know about?"

"Let's just let that rest for a while," he said.

We stopped for our noon meal in a clearing off the Tennessee River side of the road. There was a cabin and plowed fields at one time, but they were long since abandoned, and only a few hand-hewn logs remained to tell the tale.

We ate bread and sardines, and soon continued on our journey. Will said we'd make our camp by mid-afternoon near Hillman's Ferry. We passed through Nickell Station on the ridge that separates the rivers. At the Narrows' thinnest point, the

Tennessee and the Cumberland are barely two miles apart. As we rode and the neck broadened, Will cautioned me.

"Early, here in the Land Between the Rivers, folks have good reason to be very proud of their whiskey. They keep their ways and the design of their stills secret. Stay well clear of any rock furnace built near a creek. You don't want to surprise whiskey makers at their stills. They have rifles, and they're quick to shoot."

Will was silent for a moment, then he continued.

"When we're together, whether it's on the *10*, on the farm or in the woods, I lead and instruct, and you follow. As part of the proof that you're ready to spend days alone in the woods, I want to remain mostly silent, and I want you to lead and show me your knowledge and ability. I'll stop you only if you lead us astray. So please select our camp and explain your choice."

Will laid down the rules, and I eagerly took them up.

"We need a level place with wood for our fire, grass for the beasts and water for us all," I said. "And if we want enough time to hunt for fresh meat, we should make camp soon."

No sooner had I gotten those very mature-sounding words out of my mouth than we came on just such a place. We unsaddled, watered the beasts and picketed them in the grass. I chose to pitch our tent, arrange our baggage and make up a fire ring before hunting. I thought our chances would be better in the later afternoon hours when the animals come out to feed and water.

Will asked what I thought we should hunt. With confidence, I said a deer or even a turkey would be too much meat. I said I thought we should look for small game—rabbits and squirrels. Will didn't object, so we took up our Winchesters and walked away from camp into the woods. We came to a cove of the river where catfish were wallowing in the muddy shallows. That gave me second thoughts about my small-game choice. It didn't matter though, we had no fishing gear.

We were very lucky to spot two fat cottontail rabbits in a grassy area between the water's edge and the woods. We crept close, and I motioned to Will that I would take the one on the right, and he the one on the left. On one knee, I shot the head clean off my target. Standing, Will hit his in the body. He complimented me on my shot. We gutted and skinned our quarry on the spot, wrapped them in muslin we carried, and packed them in Will's haversack.

We retraced our route and were back at our camp within a few minutes. Will reminded me that I was in charge, and he wanted to know what to do. I said that if he would kindle a fire, start a kettle of water boiling and bone the rabbits, I would walk to gather greens and roots and seasonings for a stew.

I left the campsite carrying an empty sack and returned with it bulging about 20 minutes later. Will asked what I had gathered. I emptied the sack and spread its contents on the grassy ground.

"I have onions and garlic and leeks for flavor, spring beauty tubers to use like potatoes, cattails for their root sprouts and cores, and evening primrose for sliced roots. A few primrose and beauty leaves will spice things up a little too," I said.

"Early, you're a good woodsman, you've learned a lot," Will said. "The rabbits are boned and simmering in the kettle. Let's prepare what you've brought and get it in the pot."

In about three-quarters of an hour, we sat spooning into our bellies what we strongly agreed was the best rabbit stew ever made.

After cleaning up, I shinnied up to stretch a taut rope above the ground between two sycamores. I fastened the lid on the kettle with a length of rawhide and, with a boost from Will, suspended it from the rope. That kept raccoons or whatever else happened by out of our breakfast.

We passed a peaceful night and awoke with the songbirds at first light. The sun rose on a tranquil scene of our beasts at pasture, our camp beside a little creek, the smell of woodsmoke, and Will and me spooning rabbit stew.

Will didn't have to be in Smithland to catch the *10* on her way up from Cairo to Nashville until late Monday afternoon. But I was due in school early that morning, so we wouldn't be camping another night in the woods. We would be back at the homeplace by nightfall Sunday.

After clearing our campsite, we followed paths through the woods, moving farther into the Land Between the Rivers. When we came to the Dover Road, we turned toward home.

As we rode, Will said he was positively impressed with what I knew and did in the woods. He didn't need any more convincing and would let me go off on my own.

"When do you want to go and where?" he asked.

"In May, after we finish the spring planting," I replied. "I can ask Miss Sturges about getting ahead in my schoolwork. I think she'll excuse me for a week. I want to go to Mantle Rock. I got the idea about going into the wilderness alone by reading about Indians. Maybe some Cherokee spirits still live at Mantle Rock."

"The Rock's a good choice," Will said. "I leave for Nashville on Monday afternoons. If you ride out on a Monday morning, can I help you pack up?"

"Sure you can," I eagerly replied, probably betraying the confidence I was trying to show.

15

The weeks before that Monday morning went by slower than a snail climbing a post. If I wasn't planning the trip or rambling on about it to Beth and Ben and Amanda, I was daydreaming about the adventures I would have and how I'd meet every challenge and vanquish any foe.

As my departure day drew near, I wrote up a list of everything I would take and started gathering the items. Soon I had more baggage than a dozen people would need for a month. I started thinning out the collection almost as eagerly as I had gathered it. By the Sunday before, I had whittled my goods down to about as much as a mule can carry.

Everyone was up to see me off just after sunrise. Will helped pack Grady, and he insisted I take two dogs along. I thought they could help me hunt, keep me warm at night and scare off any wild beasts that might approach, so I agreed.

Ben stood by looking on with a mixture of pride, fear and envy. Beth tucked a wax-sealed jar of blackberry jam and two loaves of fresh-baked bread in among my baggage. She looked at me with moist, worried eyes. Will saw her concern and said, "Early will be all right. Don't you worry now, Beth."

Amanda hugged me around the waist and whispered, "Watch out for ghosts, Early."

I mounted Spirit and whistled for the dogs. Will handed me Grady's halter rope, and I started out. As I turned in the saddle to look back and tug my hat, I saw the prettiest sight. Will, Beth, Ben and Amanda stood arm in arm in the open area in front of the porch watching me go. Our home stood behind them, and the barn farther back to the left. The tall trees that in summer cast large shadows were green with new leaves. Through the trees, the rising sun was just above the distant hills. It was a sight that grabbed my heart and has stayed with me till this day.

I rode down through our newly furrowed and planted fields on past the wharfboat and up Riverfront Street to the ferry landing. Sheriff Piles and the constable, Mr. Hurley, were on the ferry over to the Point. The sheriff looked over my set-up and asked,

"You wouldn't be running away from home, would you Early? I'd have to let your mama know if you was."

He knew darn well I wasn't running away—he was just teasing me.

"Yup, I reckon I am," I said, "I'm headin' west. I hear there's gold and silver out Colorado way."

Mr. Hurley chuckled—not so much at what I said—more that I was funning with the sheriff.

As I crossed the ramp onto the bank at the Point, Mr. Hastings, the ferryman, wished me luck and asked me to bring him back a big, shiny nugget.

I struck out on the road to Oak Ridge, whistling to keep the dogs close, patting Spirit, trailing Grady and rejoicing in my freedom. I figured I'd be to Berry's Ferry across from Golconda and then on to Mantle Rock by early afternoon.

Golconda was a busy river town on the Illinois side of the Ohio. Berry's Ferry constantly worked back and forth between Kentucky and Illinois. I didn't stay longer than to water the animals and then turned onto the Darlington Road. Before long, I was at the trail up to Mantle Rock. It was just as Louis had described it. There was a large, open field going up the slope. It was green with fresh spring grass and strewn with wildflowers of many colors. I dismounted, tied Grady to Spirit and let them graze. Spirit never wandered far and came to my whistle. I lay on my back in the grass, gazing up at huge billowy white clouds in the blue spring sky. A dog lay panting on each side of me. I dozed off and awoke to one of the hounds pushing my slouch hat back with his snout and slobbering over my face with his long, wet tongue. I stood and whistled for Spirit. I mounted, soon gained the ridge and entered the woods, through which lay Mantle Rock.

Once we were in the woods, Mantle Rock was just a short distance in and to the right of the trail. I stopped and gazed at the arch for a few moments. I judged it to be maybe 200 feet long and 30 high. On a sunny day, with new leaves on the trees, the woods were thick enough to dim the light and give the arch and cliff behind it a somber, brooding look.

The recent rains had left the forest floor damp and spongey. I looked for a rise and chose a low mound near the arch and a branch of McGilligan Creek. I found a stump to stand on to get the saddle off Spirit and the packs off Grady. I tied a picket line between two sugar maples for the beasts and brought them some young cottonwood branches to gnaw on.

I rolled out my gum blanket and pitched my tent atop it. Being on a rise, I saw no need to dig a trench around my tent. I tied the dogs, picked up my Winchester and set out to get some squirrels and maybe a turkey. I move quieter without dogs. They scare the game away.

I walked down along the creek branch, scanning the ground but keeping my eye high in the trees too, looking for squirrels. Before long, I saw some scampering in the branches above. I stood with my back to a large oak and waited for a shot. One came momentarily, and I got a squirrel and then quickly a second. I knew I wouldn't see another here after the shots, so I moved on.

As the ground rose out of the ravine where I walked, the woods opened up some. The higher ground had thinner soil and less water to grow trees. A tall, thin sycamore on the slope had toppled some time before and fallen toward the creek branch. Rather than crashing to the ground, it had lodged in the crook of a big old oak. The sycamore, the oak and the sloped ground outlined a triangle. A thicket had grown beneath the fallen sycamore's trunk, enclosing its now dead branches. I saw that if I climbed the slope to the base of the fallen sycamore, I could scramble up its trunk to a high perch where it met the oak. From there, I would have a bird's eye view of a large area of forest. I stored that idea away for the moment. My sooner need was a turkey.

A ways farther on, I found turkey spoor—tracks toward the creek branch where the wet ground was bare, droppings and, off to the side, feathers where there must have been a scuffle. If this was where the birds came to water late in the day, they would be along soon. I pulled a handful of dried corn kernels from my coat pocket and scattered them along the track line. I moved away several paces, concealed myself among the trees and waited.

Sitting still and quiet let me watch and listen to the woods. I heard squirrels scampering but didn't dare a shot because it would warn the turkeys away. An old hickory stood a few paces from me. A cavity had developed where one of its low branches had sheared off at the trunk. I watched a pair of Carolina wrens fly in and out of the hole again and again, and heard their clear, rolling melody as they came and went. They brought food for their hungry brood on each incoming flight. They worked tirelessly to feed the spring clutch, which lay unseen in the hollow.

By and by, the turkeys came, a flock of about a dozen, toms and hens. They found the corn and pecked it off the ground as they walked. I picked one of the dowdier-looking toms, remembering what Louis had told me: If you have a choice, leave the finer birds to make more fine birds—take only the weaker ones.

My tom turned and gave me a straight shot at his breast. I hit him dead center where his neck broadened into his chest. He dropped in his tracks and breathed his last. The other birds took to wing in a flurry, moving quickly away from their fallen mate. I picked up my prize by the feet, lopped his head off at the base of the neck and held him upsidedown to let his blood drain onto the forest floor. The tom and the squirrels would keep me and the dogs in meat for a couple of days.

At my camp, I boned the squirrels for the dogs, gave Spirit and Grady some of the oats the mule had carried out, and gutted and plucked the tom. I turned him on a spit over coals and low flames and enjoyed a drumstick just after dark. Having brought a stave bucket with a handle and tight lid for just this purpose, I cut up the remains of the tom, wrapped them in muslin, packed them in the bucket, applied the lid and hung it from the picket line between the beasts.

May weather in Western Kentucky is downright unpredictable. It can be sunny and warm one hour, and chilly and pouring rain the next. My first night was warm and dry, so I left the dogs outside the tent and crawled into my bedroll feeling content and right proud of myself so far.

I awoke from a deep sleep at I don't know what hour to the sound of the tent flaps beating and snapping like a flag in a stiff wind. The dogs were restless and seemed not to know whether to growl or whimper. They sounded spooked—as if they couldn't make sense of whatever was going on. I stuck my head out between the flaps to see. A few paces away I saw a gossamer figure that seemed to glow and come and go. I wasn't sure if it was real or just the waning moon casting its light through the swaying treetops. I shook my head and rubbed some of the sleep from my eyes. I focused, and again the figure was there, looking like a bluish-white wisp. It was an Indian in ceremonial dress. He stood erect and proud before me and spoke.

"I am the spirit of the Cherokee. Young brave, you sleep on my grave."

I was awestruck and dumbfounded. I knelt on all fours with everything but my head inside the tent. My chin about hit the ground from two feet up, and my eyes must have looked as big as a cow's. In a moment, the figure was gone, the wind was still, and the dogs lay curled and quiet. To this day, I don't know if it was a dream or a ghost. At first light, I struck my tent and moved it off the rise and over closer to the arch.

After feeding the beasts, the dogs and myself, I started down the creek branch toward the fallen sycamore. I wanted to climb to that high perch to see what I could see. No sooner had I reached the tree's base than I heard a terrible ruckus coming from the direction of my camp. The dogs barked wildly, Spirit snorted and whinnied loudly in alarm, and Grady bayed as mules do. I ran as fast as I could in the uneven creek branch bottom. As I got within sight, I could see the dogs jumping and pulling on their cords, spinning and barking with much force and anger. Spirit and Grady bucked and strained on their picket line in great agitation. I reached camp and looked in the direction the dogs were pulling—toward the arch. Sitting erect midway atop the span as calm as could be, surveying the scene below and licking his chops, was a huge panther. I had never seen a panther before. I was struck by the fact that he looked like an enormous barn cat. I stood for a few moments amid the angry dogs and frightened beasts just staring back at the cat. I felt no need to shoot him—I just wanted him gone. I raised my Winchester to my shoulder and sighted on the lip of limestone below him and to the right. My aim was true. The shot rang loudly as it chipped off a piece of rock. The cat quickly rose, turned, leaped away and was gone.

It took some doing to calm the animals. When I had, I led them up the trail to the grassy field past the edge of the woods. I drove four picket stakes and tied the animals far out in the clearing where I was sure the panther wouldn't show himself if my shot hadn't already chased him off. Where there was a panther, there were deer, and I'd rather they were his prey than my animals.

Feeling my companions were safe, I returned to the woods and headed for the fallen sycamore. I climbed its trunk to the perch where it crossed the oak. I rested there, enjoying the birdsongs and the gentle, refreshing breeze. Sitting just below the forest canopy, I could see a long way, clear down the cradle that held the creek branch and up the slopes on both sides.

Presently, a lone whitetail doe descended the slope and entered the thicket beneath me. There was an opening directly below, like a window behind which the doe stood, unaware of my watching. She remained motionless for a moment, then a quiver ran through her body. She extended her head slightly and began to gently push her tongue out and pull it in, as if she was savoring something that had stuck to her lips. She spread her hind legs and squatted slightly, like a bitch urinating. She seemed to brace herself with her fore legs. She strained and waited. In a few moments, a tiny hoof appeared high between her hind legs just beneath her tail. Then another hoof appeared. She strained. And two thin legs covered in a milky white veil emerged and lengthened. Then came the nose, the head and the shoulders. Soon a spotted, bay-red fawn lay on the leafy floor of the thicket, having broken the navel cord as it bumped to the ground. The doe licked the fawn intensely, removing all traces of the covering membrane. She consumed the afterbirth and everything else that might leave a scent.

The doe lay down on her side, enclosing her fawn between her fore and hind limbs. The fawn could have nursed but did not. Several minutes passed and the doe stood. She nudged the fawn, which then struggled mightily to stand. It stood and collapsed, and stood and collapsed again. On the third try, the fawn succeeded and stood with its legs splayed to steady itself and ensure it wouldn't topple. The fawn sought and found its mother's teat, and it suckled. The fawn wagged its tail as it drew milk. The doe turned and licked the fawn beneath its tail. The fawn released urine and droppings, which the doe quickly ate. The fawn continued to suckle.

Not much more than an hour had passed since the fawn's birth. The doe and the fawn left the thicket together, a little wary at first. They walked steadily up the slope on a diagonal line, gained the ridge and disappeared from sight.

I had seen mares foal, cows calve, bitches whelp pups and cats birth kittens. I had seen sows yield piglets and chicks peck their way out of eggshells. But this was different. This was bigger. This was a wild creature continuing her line against all odds. The scene made a deep impression on me. I never again raised my rifle on a wild thing without thinking of that doe and her fawn.

I descended the sycamore and then the little branch that led to the main stream of McGilligan Creek. I wanted to gather greens and roots to go with turkey for my supper. I soon reached the fork and turned downstream. My footsteps rousted a great blue heron from the creekbed. It crouched slightly and sprang gracefully aloft, fanning its wings in long, slow arcs and carrying itself away from the intruder. Its wingtips seemed to almost touch the branches that stretched across the creek from each bank.

As the heron glided out of sight, I turned my gaze to the edges of the creek and the slopes up both sides of the ravine. Watercress, wild celery and spring beauty tubers were easy to find and served my purpose.

The dogs were especially glad to see me return to the field, but Spirit and Grady would have been content to stay at their picket stakes and continue to eat the sweet spring grass. Dogs have more need for human companionship than do horses and mules.

Our second night at Mantle Rock was quiet and uneventful save for the hooting of the owls. I passed the night in the comfort of my tent with the dogs lying quietly nearby outside and the beasts secured to the picket line.

After breakfast in the morning, between the dogs and me, the turkey was almost gone. I still had one loaf of the bread that Beth gave me, and I could collect greens and roots, but I needed game or fish. I wondered if I followed the main stream of

McGilligan Creek farther down, whether I might find a pool and some good-sized fish.

I picketed the beasts in the field again but not the dogs. They were eager to run. I packed the remaining turkey and some bread in my haversack, took up my Winchester, my cane pole and net, and proceeded with the dogs down the branch.

As it descended toward the Ohio, McGilligan Creek at least doubled the width of the branch. The dogs ran ahead to make sure I didn't see any squirrels or rabbits. They ran up and away from the creek bed and didn't scare the fish. More than once as I rounded a bend, I surprised a fish lounging in a shallow pool before it detected me and darted off to its hideout. The fish were too quick for me to identify, but I could see they were good-sized.

I came to a pleasant spot where a sycamore shaded a bench just above the bank. A ledge in the creek formed a pool behind a small cascade. A glance told me this was my place for a while. I netted a crawdad and baited my hook. In 10 minutes, I had a longear sunfish. In another 15, I had a pan-size largemouth bass. In an hour and a half, I had three of each and enough to feed us until the next night. Considering how easily I got bait and fish, I figured this creek wasn't fished much.

I ate turkey and bread and dozed off, leaning against the sycamore's trunk. The returning dogs roused me from my slumber. They slurped water from the creek, then lay panting on its bank. Their tongues hung from the sides of their mouths like limp cords. They looked well exercised and content. They spied my line of fish and looked expectant. The dogs and I had done this before, and they knew what was coming for supper.

At my camp, I cleaned the fish and pan-fried enough for the dogs and me. I kept the rest in a sealed bucket that I set in the cool water of the branch.

It felt like rain when I went up to bring in the beasts. I picketed them beneath one end of the arch and moved my gear and fire beneath the other. If it rained, the arch would give some shelter.

It did rain Wednesday night and all day Thursday. It was a steady rain, punctuated with a downpour now and then. There was enough water to bring the branch up considerably.

The sun had returned by Friday morning. I hiked to the lower end of McGilligan Creek again and brought back two channel catfish. They held us until Sunday morning, when I packed up and rode toward Smithland, arriving there late in the afternoon. Amanda was on the porch and saw me coming up the rise out of the fields. She squealed, "Early's home," and ran inside to tell Beth. Ben came from the smokehouse, Will from the barn and Beth and Amanda from the house. As much as I liked the test of being on my own in the woods, I was very glad to be home. Will and Beth quizzed me and looked me over for damage. Finding none and satisfied with my brief replies, they got the beasts in the barn and me into the kitchen for a home-cooked meal. Amanda looked at me with smiles and admiration, while the others bore looks of relief and pride. Will spoke for the family when he said, "Son, we're very proud of what you've done and glad to have you home."

That evening I sat down to start writing the report that my teacher, Miss Sturges, had asked me to do to excuse a week's absence from school. I looked forward to presenting it to my fellow scholars.

16

With Smithland being the county seat and site of the court house, it was naturally the site of court week. Court week was a special event all year, but it was extra exciting during the summer.

Things in town started to perk up as much as two weeks before. Shopkeepers, liverymen, blacksmiths, and hotel and tavern owners began sprucing up their establishments and laying in stores of goods and whatever else visitors might need. Wharfboat business grew as the incoming freight volume multiplied. As court week drew near, passenger traffic to Smithland grew greater. In town, lawyers touched up their signs and ran cards in the *Times*, making sure folks knew what services were at hand.

One week before, the sheriff and his deputies rode from one corner of the county to another serving subpoenas on witnesses, summoning jurors and demanding under penalty of law that all be present in court at the appointed time.

Chambermaids cleaned, re-cleaned and dusted the best room at the Gower House. It was reserved for the circuit judge, who would arrive by steamer and check in Sunday evening before Monday's first court session.

The Market House, at Adair and Court streets in the center of town, was open on Thursdays and Fridays. Farmers from around the county came into Smithland to wholesale their produce, smoked hams, honey, preserves and whatever else their families' labors created. Some stocked up and returned to their farms, while others stayed for business or pleasure during court week. Lots of folks came simply because they knew lots of other folks would be coming too. Some took rooms at the hotels, but most made camps wherever there was open space.

Summer was also when wealthy planters and their wives came to Smithland to escape the extreme heat and humidity of the Deep South. That struck me as odd because I couldn't imagine a place hotter and more humid than Smithland in the summer. Sometimes the air was so thick it made breathing a chore. Planters in frock coats and top hats, with their wives in hoop skirts and carrying parasols, promenaded Riverfront Street, inspecting vendors' wares and enjoying the views as they strolled.

On Monday morning, a pealing bell announced the first court session. Those with business in the courthouse crowded in. The judge took his seat, the lawyers entered with their briefs and books in green baize bags, and the clerk squared up at his desk. The sheriff stood at the door and in a loud, piercing voice cried, "Oyez, oyez, the court of common pleas is in session."

Outside was like a festival. People had cider, fruits, vegetables, jerked meats and baked goods to share. Vendors sold every manner of goods at stands lining the streets. Kids ran foot races, jumped over poles, putted stones and played ring toss. Men discussed the merits of the cases being tried inside. When court recessed for the noon meal and people poured into the streets, an eight-piece brass band wove its way through town playing a Friederich quickstep. Small boys trailed behind mimicking the players.

Late Thursday afternoon, after court had recessed for the day, the Market House had closed its stalls, the planters and their wives had emerged from their hotels to promenade, and the streets were otherwise filled with folks of every stripe, W. P. Bledsoe, a traveling photographer who had happened into town in his horse-drawn darkroom, proposed to make a photograph of the riverfront. Ben obliged by boosting Mr. Bledsoe up into the huge sycamore by the wharfboat and then passing his camera, black hood, wooden box of plates, and tripod up to him.

Mr. Bledsoe set up his equipment, tore a few leaves out of the way, called for the attention of those within earshot and asked everyone to stand still. Word passed back through the crowd until scores of folks on the wharfboat, on Riverfront Street, on the porches of the stores, taverns and hotels, on the steamers, and lining the bank clear up to the Gower House stood riveted, their attention and upturned faces focused on Mr. Bledsoe, or rather on the eye of the camera and the black hood that draped behind it.

From beneath the hood, Mr. Bledsoe called out, "On three, please—one . . . two . . . three." I was close enough to hear the shutter click. Everyone in the crowd relaxed and started breathing again. There was movement beneath the hood, and then Mr. Bledsoe cried, "Again, please." Everyone stiffened, turned toward the camera up in the tree and heard, "One . . . two . . . three." Again, I heard the shutter click. Mr. Bledsoe came out from under the hood, called thanks to the crowd and announced that prints would be available for a dollar apiece the following afternoon.

When I look at the print today, I am struck by several things. First, the faces of the people. Many I didn't know, but many others I did and remember dearly. I'm sure not one among them, save for me, is living today. Next, the hustle-bustle of Smithland, a town I haven't seen in decades, but I know is now a shadow of its former self. Gone is Hawkins Wharfboat, the steamers, most of the shops, hotels and taverns that lined Riverfront Street, and the traditions that made court week.

From today's view, I wonder why so many people dressed in black wool on a hot summer day. I see few people in shirtsleeves and then that's mostly the roustabouts, who seemed to have enough sense to ignore convention and dress for the weather. In the foreground, I see a smiling young boy in a slouch hat, a loose white blouse, suspenders, knee pants and bare feet. I was that boy a very long time ago.

I most looked forward to Saturday for two reasons—the shooting match and the baseball game. The shooters, judges and spectators gathered at the ball field above town on the far side of the Cumberland on Saturday morning. The judges oversaw as volunteers set up the shooting range. They placed barrels on end

about eight feet apart and nailed wooden rails across their tops,
joining them in an arrow-straight line. They banded lengths
of board together to form planks about two feet wide. The men
leaned the planks against the rails so they formed ramps down
to the ground. Six marksmen could take position at once. Each
had a ramp and space between the barrels. The shooting posture
was to kneel on one knee, using the top of the ramp as a rifle
rest and its slope as an arm rest. Spotters tacked printed marks
on posts 50 yards across the field. The wind was calm, so that
wasn't a consideration, but the morning sun was. The judges
had oriented the range so the sun was behind the shooters.

I was the youngest shooter in the 1871 contest. There were
several teenage boys and a lot of young men in their 20s and 30s,
but the numbers fell off quickly as age claimed the keen eyesight
necessary to hit a mark at 50 yards. I had taken fourth place in
the contest the year before. My short experience with a rifle and
my lack of familiarity with the range had handicapped me then.
But in the year between the two contests, I had practiced a lot at
a range Louis and I set up in the woods.

By late morning, the elimination rounds had narrowed the
shooters down to six. I was one of them. All my shots either hit
the mark or touched its outside edge. That got me pitted against
Billy Lyles, a young farm laborer from Carrsville, in the final.
Billy was known in the county as an expert marksman and
small-game hunter.

Billy shot with a Sharps .44 caliber rifle that he had bought
about a month earlier. I thought the fact that Billy had the Sharps
such a short while would disadvantage him, but he must have
mastered it because he had progressed to the final round without
a hitch. I shot with Will's .44 caliber Winchester rather than my
carbine because I wanted a longer barrel. At 24 inches, mine was
two less than Billy's 26, but the carbine's was only 20. I had practiced with Will's Winchester for months and knew it well.

The final round took up just before noon. We each had 10
shots, to be alternated. I won the coin toss and chose to shoot
first. Although Will and Louis stood well to my rear, as were the
rules, I could feel their pride and encouragement. My first shot
was a dead-center bull's eye, exactly as I had hoped. It laid down
the challenge to Billy right at the outset. His shot nicked the

outside edge of the mark. The advantage was mine.

My second shot was within the mark but off center. I kept the advantage through the fifth shot, but then I faltered and Billy drew even. When we had each made nine shots, we were matched. With Billy having the last shot, the pressure was on me to hit the center of the mark. He would have to match my bull's eye to earn a tie. The spectators hushed as I took my aim. As I sighted, I first heard my own breathing and the chirping of birds, but as I focused, allowing for the distance and the particular peculiarities of Will's Winchester, everything fell silent. I saw the mark so clearly it seemed a foot wide and an arm's length away. I squeezed the trigger, and the Winchester's sharp crack pierced the silence.

The spotter walked to the mark to check my shot. The noon sun made his white blouse glow. His walk through the grass looked like a gliding dance and seemed to take forever. He pulled the mark from its post, held it up to the light, turned to us and signaled Dead-Center Bull's Eye. A cheer like a thunderclap rose from the crowd. I was elated, but in the back of my mind I knew it wasn't over yet, and the best I had so far was a tie.

Billy looked a little surprised but fiercely determined nonetheless. I stepped back from the rail and joined Will and Louis. We watched Billy kneel and carefully take his aim. He took a little longer than he had with his earlier shots. The crowd hushed, then the crack of the Sharps broke the stillness. From my view, the spotter moved quickly direct to the mark's post. He checked it, turned to the crowd and signaled On the Mark but Off Center. The crowd's cheer was like thunderclaps over top of cannon fire. I threw my slouch hat high in the air and rose off the ground myself as it sailed. The crowd closed around me and showered me with congratulations. Will and Louis absolutely beamed with pride, clapped each other on the back and just about smothered me in a crushing bear hug. It was the finest moment in my young life. I was 11 years old and the best rifle shot in Livingston County, Kentucky.

The umpire cried "Play ball!" at about 2 o'clock in the afternoon. The visiting Salem Stavers led off against the home team, the Smithland Steamers. The Stavers began with a bang—seven runs in the first inning. The Steamers bounced back with five runs of their own in the bottom of the first. The lead switched back and forth, and when the teams and spectators broke for supper at 5 o'clock after six innings, Salem was ahead 36 to 34.

The food must have hurt the pitching and helped the batting because when play resumed shortly after 6 o'clock, both teams had trouble making outs but great success getting runs. The innings lengthened, the score ballooned, and the game had to be stopped on account of darkness with the score tied at 51 after eight innings of play. Baseball games in the county were more social events than competitions, so everybody went home happy.

On a very hot Sunday in August, Ben and I pedaled the *Hilltop* up the Cumberland to the mouth of McCormick Creek. The river was so low that some of the higher bars were visible. Only the smallest boats with pilots good at finding the channel had a chance of getting through. Cows from pastures above both banks had come into the river to cool off. Ben and I had our poles and, in a wooden bucket, live bait. We were after whatever might bite.

We had just set our anchor, baited our hooks and dropped our lines in the river when we heard faint singing above the south bank. It gradually drew closer and louder, and then a group of about 40 Negro men, women and children came into view. By the time they reached the bank, the rich and rhythmic harmonious singing had risen to a great height. One group called,

> *"Didn't you hear my Lord when he called?"*

And the other responded,

> *"Yes, I heard my Lord call, my Lord callin' in my soul."*

Then,

> *"Didn't you hear them angels moan?"*

And,

> *"Yes, I heard them angels moan, angels moanin' in my soul."*

The call and response went back and forth, back and forth.

As the people sang, some draped several others in white cotton garments. Then they all turned toward one man, the preacher, who began his sermon. His voice was deep and melodic and rose and fell in crescendos and decrescendos. He drew responses from the congregation. Many began to shout, "Amen!" or "Yes, my Lord!" Sometimes the entire group shouted in unison and repeated hails in rhythmic cadence.

As if on cue, two elders left the group and descended the bank into the river. They probed the bottom with long walking sticks until they found a large area about waist deep. The preacher, still talking, walked into the middle of the feverishly singing group. He raised his hand, and the boisterous singing instantly reduced to a beautiful softness.

The preacher left the group, walked into the river and stood with the elders. As the soft singing continued, one of the white-draped members was led into the river to the preacher and the elders. The preacher asked,

"Do you believe in Jesus and in His power to wash away your sins?"

"Yes, I do," came the response.

"I baptize you in the name of The Father, The Son and the Holy Ghost," the preacher said.

At that, he quickly tipped the convert backward into the river and lifted him up again. The convert then seemed seized by some violent, otherworldly force that brought irrepressible shouting. He ran to the bank, where others grabbed him and soon calmed him. The events were repeated until all the white-draped converts had been baptized.

The Hawkins family was not religious, which was unusual in Kentucky in those days. Most folks went to church regularly and had a worshipful regard for the Lord. Will and Beth said they were content to let the mystery be, and they passed that feeling on to me. I watched the baptisms with awe and wonder, if for no other reason, for the great energy and unity.

Ben, of course, hadn't come into the Hawkins family until he was 10. He had never spoken of his life before coming to us—not a word. Usually, any music compelled Ben to join in, but on this day, as we floated side by side in the *Hilltop* with our hooks hanging hopefully in the river, Ben sat completely still and quiet and watched.

17

When school started in the fall, Ben began spending his free time with Maria Rucker. Maria was a schoolmate of Ben's at the Negro children's school. At 17, she was the same age as Ben. Maria lived with her parents, three younger brothers and an older sister on the family's farm northeast of town.

Maria was the color of coffee with cream. She was tall and graceful, and her simple cotton dresses revealed that she was a fully developed woman. She had a sweet, beautiful face and hair that jumped out of her head like thousands of coiled springs.

Maria and Ben made a strikingly handsome couple. Ben looked like a sculpture carved from polished jet. He had high, prominent cheekbones, fine, intelligent eyes and bold, chiseled features. His muscular torso tucked down to a slim waist and narrow hips above long, straight, powerful legs. He was an athlete, strong as a blacksmith and seemingly made to outrun a deer.

Maria and Ben did everything together. They pedaled the *Hilltop*, rode horseback, walked in the hills, strolled to Captain Jake's store for rock candy, skipped stones on the river, and helped with each other's schoolwork and chores. Maria even took Ben to the Negro people's chapel, the inside of which no Hawkins had ever seen.

When Maria and Ben sang together, they carried their listeners to some other place. At first, they sang in school shows and, later, in the main cabin of the *10*. As Ben's family, we attended all the school performances. Will, Beth, Amanda and I were the only white faces in the crowd. I learned how it felt to be the few among the many. As I listened to Maria and Ben sing, I liked to gaze at the faces in the room. Many appeared transfixed, bearing pleasant, gentle looks as if they were awash in warm, sweetly scented breezes.

Maria's voice matched her sweet, beautiful face. She sounded as if she sang from an angel's perch. As Ben got older, he had become a rich baritone. He sang well in the tenor range and

could also summon a sweet falsetto. Maria and Ben had practiced together until they became a polished duo.

With freight and passenger business on the *10* continuing to
fall off, Will was interested in anything that would help. School,
Maria and Ben's busy lives, and the *10's* schedule prevented
them from performing in the main cabin as often as Will would
have liked. When they did, it was usually on the runs between
Smithland and Cairo and back. Will ran cards in the Smithland,
Paducah and Cairo newspapers announcing when Maria and
Ben would be on board. Many citizens who had no other business
aboard the *10* booked passage just to hear Maria and Ben sing.

With Ben busy with Maria, I began spending more time with
my chums from school. Some of the time we spent together was in
the Hawkins family library. At first, it was only my best friend,
Charley Mayhugh, and I, but then several other boys became
envious of our reports, the good marks we made in school and
the favor of our teacher, Miss Dunn, who was especially pretty.
The boys asked if they could use our library too. Will and Beth
set down some rules, and, with Will on the *10* toward Nashville,
it fell to Beth to tell the boys.

On a late September afternoon, Beth sat four 11-year-old
scholars down in a line on the long bench on the library porch.
As was her custom when working in the barn or elsewhere on the
farm, Beth wore trousers, boots, suspenders and a long-sleeved
blouse. To keep her long red hair out of trouble, she put it up in
a bun and tucked it under a slouch hat. If you didn't look closely,
you'd think Beth was a lanky teenage boy. She had been sweeping in the loft and stood straight in front of the boys holding onto
her broom.

The boys sat in stunned silence. Beth had no trouble keeping
their attention—they couldn't take their eyes off her. I suspect
they thought if they didn't listen to the rules and follow them,
Beth would swat them with her broom.

"Boys, some of the books in the Hawkins family library are
over 100 years old," Beth announced. "George Hawkins carried
them into Kentucky through the Cumberland Gap. The library
represents five generations of Hawkins bookhounds, including
your friend, Early. We're happy to have you use the books and

learn from them, but only if you treat them with respect. That means, first, clean hands and no food. Next, no writing in the books, and no tearing or folding pages. Handle the books carefully, and put them back exactly where you found them. Do you understand and agree?" Beth asked.

"Yes, ma'am," the boys responded in unison.

"Any questions?" Beth asked.

"No, ma'am," they replied together.

"All right, then. Early will always be with you in the library. If I hear of any boy violating the rules, he will no longer be welcome. Study well and be good scholars," Beth concluded with a sweet, encouraging smile.

She must have made an impression on the boys because there was never a lick of trouble, and we used the library through the whole school year.

In early October, Will came down from Nashville on the *10* with an unusual group among the passengers. He had given free passage to the Colored Christian Singers in exchange for their performing in the evenings in the main cabin. There were eight singers—four men and four women—and a woman accompanist, Ella Sheppard, who played piano. I say women, but two were really girls, scarcely older than I was. Their leader, a choir director named George White, was taking the singers on a tour of Northern cities, hoping to raise money for Fisk University in Nashville.

They were a very handsome, formal-looking group. The men wore frock-coat suits, and the women wore matching full dresses, with high buttons and clean white collars. The singers and Miss Sheppard were Negroes, but Mr. White's complexion matched his name.

Nate Drew took the *10* on to Cairo, and Will stayed in Smithland. The singers were on their way to Cincinnati and had a layover in Smithland until their Ohio River boat came up. Will said the wharfboat was almost empty of freight and asked Mr. White if the singers might perform there for as many waiting passengers and Smithland townspeople as we could muster on short notice. Mr. White agreed immediately, and Will sent me and Charley Mayhugh to spread the word through town. Ben rode off to find Maria and bring her to the wharfboat.

In less than an hour, about 100 people had come to the wharfboat. Ben was back with Maria, Beth and Amanda were down from the homeplace, and Louis, Sally and their children had come from their farm on the hill. There wasn't much time before the *Idlewild* was due on its way up to Evansville, so Will, Captain Jake, Mr. White and the singers didn't waste a minute getting the wharfboat space and themselves ready.

Mr. White stood in front of the singers, who were grouped at the downriver end of the wharfboat. He raised his hands, and the crowd hushed. There was no piano, so Miss Sheppard blew a note on a pitch pipe to prepare the singers to sing *a cappella*. I expected to hear the kinds of songs that Ben and I heard at the baptism—the kind Negroes sing in church, but that's not what they sang. They sang classical works and a formal hymn. Today, I suppose they did so because they sang mostly for white folks, and that's who the songs had to appeal to.

After the singers had sung three beautiful songs, Will approached Mr. White and talked quietly with him for a moment. Mr. White nodded, and Will motioned for Ben and Maria to come up in front of the crowd. The Colored Christian Singers remained standing behind Ben and Maria, but Will and Mr. White sat down.

Ben turned and spoke quietly to Miss Sheppard. She blew a note on the pitch pipe, and Ben and Maria began. I had never heard them sing anything like the song they sang first. Like the Fisk singers, Ben and Maria almost always sang for white folks, so they chose their songs and sang in a way that pleased whites. I didn't know that Ben and Maria knew any other kinds of songs. Ben sang in his lowest bass voice,

When Israel was in Egypt's Land

Maria replied in her high, pure angel's voice,

Let my people go

Then Ben,

Oppressed so hard they could not stand

Then Maria,

>*Let my people go*

Then both together,

>*Go down, Moses, way down in Egypt's land,*
>*Tell Old Pharaoh, let my people go*

Then, to everyone's surprise, including their own, Ben and the four Fisk men,

>*No more shall they in bondage toil*

Then Maria and the Fisk women,

>*Let my people go*

Then 10 soaring voices that seemed to lift the crowd off its feet,

>*Go down, Moses, way down in Egypt's Land*
>*Tell Old Pharaoh, let my people go!*

The crowd's roar and applause filled the wharfboat and seemed to bounce around the space. The singers beamed.

When the cheering and clapping quieted, Ben and Maria huddled with the Fisk singers and Mr. White. They regrouped, and Miss Sheppard again blew a note on her pitch pipe. In a beautiful blend of hushed voices that ranged from the lowest lows to the highest highs, the singers began,

>*Steal away, steal away to Jesus*
>*Steal away, steal away home*
>*I ain't got long to stay here*
>*My Lord calls me, he calls me by thunder*
>*The trumpet sounds within my soul*
>*I ain't got long to stay here*

The audience's reaction was as hushed as the song—soft, gentle clapping and, here and there, a teary eye.

Mr. White spoke with Ben and Maria, and all three sat down. The singers regrouped, Miss Sheppard blew a note, and the singers began:

> *Swing low sweet chariot*
> *Coming for to carry me home*
> *Swing low sweet chariot*
> *Coming for to carry me home*
> *I looked over Jordan and what did I see*
> *Coming for to carry me home*
> *A band of angels coming after me*
> *Coming for to carry me home*

Ben and Maria rocked and flowed with the music, and joined in on the words. The singers continued with the verses, and soon the whole room joined in on the choruses. Over 100 people sang strongly together,

> *Swing low sweet chariot*
> *Coming for to carry me home*
> *Swing low sweet chariot*
> *Coming for to carry me home*

If the *Idlewild* hadn't blown her whistle long and loud just down from the wharfboat, that whole crowd would have continued singing into the night. The barriers between Negro and white fell that day in Smithland. The Colored Christian Singers and Mr. White boarded the *Idlewild*, and we all waved them goodbye.

In November, a telegram came addressed to Ben from Mr. White in Cincinnati. He said the group's concerts were going well, and that the sacred songs were best received. The group had chosen a new name—The Fisk Jubilee Singers. He invited Ben and Maria to join the group and to become students at Fisk University when they finished school in Smithland the following spring. Mr. White urged them to think about it, to stay in touch with him through the university and to let him know next spring. Ben and Maria were thrilled.

18

The weather was unusually warm, so we had a very large turnout for our yearly family meeting on New Year's Day, 1872. Most of the kinfolk who came stayed in hotels in town. We held the meeting itself in the ballroom of Captain Jake's hotel, the Scyster House.

Will stood on a low platform at the front of the room and called upon family members one at a time to make whatever announcements they had. Folks talked about births and deaths and marriages. They talked about how things were going on their farms and in their jobs and businesses. If one rambled on, another thanked him to hurry it along. When all had spoken, Will said that he had an important announcement.

"You all know that George and Meredith Hawkins established our family in Kentucky almost 100 years ago," Will began. "Early and Amanda are the fifth generation in Kentucky with the Hawkins name. I know that some of you have that many generations in your branches of the family too.

"In 1822, Craig and John Hawkins built the family's first steamboat and named it the *George Hawkins*. The present *George Hawkins* is the 10th and finest boat to carry that name. Since the end of the war and the rise of railroads, the steamboat business has steadily declined. Building the *10* was a try at reviving our business by attracting passengers with the *10*'s first-class accommodations, fine meals, entertainment and scheduled service. In spite of our efforts, I'm afraid the railroads have outdone us. The *10* barely breaks even. The wharfboat, however, continues to do well."

Will sounded as if he was leading up to something.

"Beth and I have talked the situation over," he said after a pause, "and this is what we've decided to do. We'll sell the *10* before spring and not build another boat."

There were gasps and calls of "No!" from the crowd.

"After 10 boats and more than 50 years in the packet business, the Hawkins family is leaving steamboating," Will continued.

There were cries that sounded like grieving.

"We'll keep the wharfboat and the farm, but only for a short time," he went on. "Our branch of the Hawkins family—Beth,

Ben, Early, Amanda and I—will leave Kentucky and remove to Idaho, where we will homestead farmland."

Some people were stunned, turning to each other with expressions of utter surprise. Others dropped their jaws and drew breaths.

"Where in Idaho?" a cousin in the front asked.

"In the Raft River Valley where it meets the Snake River," Will replied.

"Sounds like Smithland," the cousin responded.

"In a way," Will continued, "but steamers can't run on either river. The nearest town is about 20 miles as the crow flies, and the railroad is about 60."

"Will the family be boarding the train for Idaho?" the cousin asked.

"Ben, Early and I will travel by steamer to Kansas City and then by horseback to Idaho on the Oregon Trail," Will responded. "Beth and Amanda will follow later by railroad, once we get settled."

Of us in the family, only Beth knew any of this until that moment. It was news to Ben, Amanda and me. At six years old, Amanda was really too young to understand the meaning of it all. The first thoughts that came to me were of Indians and buffalo.

Will sat with Ben and me afterwards and said he was sorry he couldn't have told us sooner. He didn't want the news known until he was sure, so he kept it between Beth and him. Will told Ben that he knew Ben was about to turn 18, and it was up to him whether he wanted to remove to Idaho with the family or not. He said that he included Ben when he announced the news because he truly wanted him to go. Ben responded that, yes, he supposed he would go.

Will said he wanted to leave Smithland on the first of May. We would take riding horses and, most likely, pack mules. There was a lot to be done in the next four months to prepare for the trip. Will wanted Ben and me to read everything we could find on the West. He mentioned authors from Lewis and Clark to Frémont to emigrants who wrote guides and diaries of their travels on the Oregon Trail. Will wanted us to make notes on what we read. He said to divide the notes into categories. The first category was to be what gear and baggage we would pack for the trip.

Will added that as soon as the winter weather broke, we would ride a trial trip. We would ride down the Land Between the Rivers on the Dover Road to Dover, Tennessee, cross the Cumberland and return on the right bank on the River Road. We would cross back to Livingston County at Ross' Ferry. The trip would take about a week.

At that point, of all things, I wondered about school. I was about half way through my sixth year. Would I finish? I had been looking forward to going to Shelton High School in Smithland. I wondered if there were schools in that town 20 miles from the Raft River Valley. We were leaving Smithland, the rivers, steamboating, Kentucky, the East, our farm and all but our immediate family. I was excited, but at the same time I felt a big hole in my belly.

I didn't ask Will why we were removing to Idaho, probably because I thought to question his and Beth's decision would be disrespectful. I did ask a different question though.

"Will, why *aren't* we going by the railroad?"

"Because I want you and Ben to see Indians before they're all behind a fence, the buffalo before the herds are slaughtered and the Great Plains before every section is broken by the plow. And because I want us to have a grand adventure."

Ben and I started right in on reading. What books we didn't have, we ordered from publishers by letter or wire. Will continued his regular schedule in the Cairo–Nashville trade. He had put the *10* up for sale, and until he had a buyer at the price he wanted, he would be on the rivers. Louis and Sally began spending more time on our farm and the wharfboat. When we left, they would be taking over our family's interests.

Will sold the *10* in late February. She brought $50,000, the cost of building her. A captain, pilot and crew from the Evansville, Cairo and Memphis Steam Packet Company would take the *10* up to Evansville on the first of March.

It seemed that half the town of Smithland gathered at Hawkins Wharfboat early that morning to say goodbye to the *10*. Captain Gus Fowler and his pilots, Wash Phillips and John Newman, came down on the *Idlewild* to fetch the *10*. In the cool light before the rising sun had warmed the day, Will descended the stairs from the pilothouse and stepped from the *10*'s main deck to the wharfboat. The rousters let go the *10*'s lines, and with three long, throaty blasts of her whistles, that beautiful girl steamed away up the Ohio. We watched in silence as her white woodwork and red paddlewheel faded into the distance. We turned to see many forlorn faces and misty eyes looking longingly after the *10*. She was the last steamer with Smithland as home port, and with not a word spoken, everyone knew an era had passed.

We walked slowly along the paths through our fields of lucerne and timothy hay, and winter wheat and rye. We climbed the gentle slope to the homeplace, and there on the front porch in its cast iron frame was the *George Hawkins'* bell. Louis, Nothet Edmonds and two other rousters stood beaming like a sunrise beside it. Nothet tugged the clapper cord and rang the bell three times. The deep, resonant sound that had rung on the rivers for better than three decades vibrated through the morning air in repeating waves. They echoed and lingered and were gone. Will smiled warmly. Tears glistened in the corners of his eyes. He stood in his dark blue captain's suit and cap for the last time, and I saw history resting on his shoulders.

We left for Dover in mid-March, a few days before the equinox. Will rode May Belle, I rode Spirit, and Ben rode Tibbs, a handsome, buckskin gelding he had recently broken to bridle and saddle. We trailed three mules packed with everything Ben and I had devised we needed.

On the Dover Road, other travelers in wagons or carriages looked at us as if we had taken a wrong turn somewhere. It wasn't common then to see trail riders with pack mules in the Land Between the Rivers. Of course, we didn't expect to see Indians or buffalo or sod houses, but riding to Dover and back on two sides of the Cumberland was as close as we could come locally to emigrating on the Oregon Trail.

By our third night, we had ridden about 50 miles. Rain had slowed us some, and we expected to be in Dover the following day. One of the tricks we learned was how to pack the mules so the daily packing and unpacking wasn't such a time-consuming chore. We made notes in our journal about some of the things we should have brought and others we shouldn't.

At our camp, after we had picketed the beasts, pitched our tent and eaten our supper, we sat like three points of a triangle near the fire to take away the chill. The woodsmoke went straight up, telling there was no wind. The night air was crisp, and the sky held so many stars that their light was an unbroken glow across the dome.

Will suggested that each of us should tell a story the others hadn't heard before. Ben and I agreed, and I asked Will to go first.

"In 1854, when I was 22, my father, Craig, and I made a run to Natchez, Mississippi. The Smithland Lumber Mill had chartered the *George Hawkins* to steam down the Mississippi and return with a large load of pine logs. It was spring, so the river was high and didn't require long experience to know her bars. I was second pilot and Amon Price, another steamboatman from Smithland, was first pilot. Amon had brought his 12-year-old son, Amon Jr., along for the trip.

"Craig and the other men had been warned about Natchez-Under-the-Hill and knew to give its notorious thieves and gamblers a wide berth. The crew's plan was to get in, load the logs and get out as quickly as possible. It was strictly a freight trip. The *Hawkins* carried no passengers down or up. As captain, Craig had prohibited the crew from gambling or even looking for entertainment in the taverns and dance halls. Any man who broke that rule would forfeit his pay for the trip.

"This was in slavery times and although there were a few free Negroes working the wharf, most of the rousters were young German and Irish immigrants. They had been loading logs onto the *Hawkins* since early morning, and as the wharf lanterns glowed in the twilight, they were nearly finished. I was standing with Craig on the wharf down from the stage, watching the last of the logs cross to the deck. Amon was in the pilothouse, and his son was standing on the wharf up from the stage. He stood between the line of rousters carrying the logs and a wagon that had just driven up.

"A steamer approaching the wharf from downriver blew its whistle, and Craig and I turned to look. As young Amon told it later, just then, two huge hands grabbed him from behind. One gripped his jacket collar and the other the seat of his pants. Next thing he knew, he was flying through the air and tumbling into the wagon beside him. As soon as he hit the floorboards, a heavy canvas tarpaulin fell over him and two big men who smelled of whiskey lay across the tarp. He couldn't move, and his shouts were muffled by the tarp and men. He heard a whip crack and a man shout. The team lurched ahead, quickly yanking the wagon wheels over the cobblestones that lined the wharf.

"The team had barely gotten started when young Amon heard more shouts, and the wagon came to a sudden halt. The men who lay across Amon atop the tarp scrambled out of the wagon, and he heard their boots running on the cobbles. The wagon shook, and he heard the driver hit the ground and start running.

"All this happened in a few seconds, but it caused enough commotion to catch Craig's and my attention. Craig ran to the wagon, and I ran up the wharf after the fleeing men. As young Amon shouted and struggled to toss the tarp aside, Craig jumped into the wagon after him. I chased the culprits, but they had a good head start and got away.

"One of the rousters, a sturdy young German, had seen Amon tossed into the wagon. He dropped his end of a pine log and grabbed the team's harness at the head, dragging them to a stop before they got fully started. He remained with the horses, gripping the harness in two massive hands.

"Craig jumped down from the wagon and approached the German. I came down the wharf and joined them. The young man spoke almost no English, and we spoke no German. Craig motioned to him to come aboard the *Hawkins*. We would thank him with supper before getting under way.

"Telling the young German thank you was tough, but we got the point across. The two Amons and Craig and I kept saying 'Thank you, thank you,' and he kept saying 'Ya, danke, danke.' We all smiled and laughed because we knew we understood each other. Craig asked the German to say his name and write it out.

'Hine-rick—Hine-rick Schod-de,' he said, with a thick accent. When we saw his name written out, it was easier to understand and repeat.

'Danke, Heinrich Schodde, danke,' Craig said.

Although Heinrich was much bigger and thicker than I was, I sensed that he was younger. I didn't think it disrespectful, so I said, 'In America, Heinrich, you're Henry.'

'Hen-ree,' he said haltingly, 'Hen-ree.'

"Henry enjoyed the finest supper the *Hawkins'* cook could muster. When he crossed the stage to the wharf, Amon Sr. blew the *Hawkins'* whistle and rang her big bell. The crew raised the stage, and Amon backed into the stream. As we started up against the Mississippi's spring current, Henry waved from the wharf, silhouetted in the lantern light. I stood with young Amon at the rail on the hurricane deck and returned Henry's wave. We were both very grateful that he had saved Amon from whatever terrors those wharf rats had in mind."

Will asked if I had a story. I said I did but doubted it was as exciting as his.

"Some kids like dogs, some like cats, and others like horses. My friend, Charley Mayhugh, likes amphibians. He catches frogs and newts and salamanders, keeps them in one pen or another for a while, then releases them and finds more.

"Late last spring, Charley and I crossed the Cumberland on the ferry to Salt Point and walked up the Ohio bank. We each had a wooden bucket. We were hunting for mudpuppies. Charley knew exactly where to look. He wore rough gloves to keep the mudpuppies from slipping through his hands. As we walked, Charley stopped at one spot after another, reached into the shallows and pulled up a mudpuppy. He passed many other spots that looked just the same to me but said, 'Nope, no mudpups there.' I don't know how he knew where the mudpuppies were and where they weren't, but he did. By the time we were back on the ferry to Smithland, we each had a half dozen mudpuppies in river water in our buckets. Charley kept them in a pen he had built on Ferguson Creek. About a week later, he released them back into the Ohio."

Ben had listened very quietly to both stories. Will asked him if he had one to tell. There was a long silence, then Ben began.

"In March 1864, my mama, daddy, baby sister and I lived in a shack alongside the fields and away from Master York's house. At that time, the Union Army occupied Paducah, and the Union Navy controlled the rivers. The soldiers' stronghold was Fort Anderson at the edge of town and close to the Ohio River. The Army had been in Paducah since Grant seized the town in September 1861. The soldiers had built abatis and placed batteries around the perimeter. The town was protected on every side, whether land or water.

"Nathan Bedford Forrest was the only Confederate general either brave or reckless enough to challenge the Union Army at Fort Anderson. After battling the Federals but failing to take the stronghold, Forrest's men retreated. Many were wild with rage and looking for revenge. Forrest had a deep hatred of Negroes. He felt we were property, not people. He encouraged that same hatred in his men.

"As the Confederates retreated, three dragoons rode into Master York's cornfield, where my daddy was walking a plow behind a mule. I had been beside him but had gone into the woods nearby to relieve myself. I was squatting in the brush with my britches around my ankles. I watched wide-eyed and afraid as two of the horsemen pulled Daddy away from the plow. They unhitched the mule and stood the plow upright, forcing its blade into the broken ground. They tied Daddy at his hands and feet and bound him standing to the plow. The third horseman had remained mounted at a distance across the field. The two who had tied Daddy remounted their horses and moved away from him, leaving him unable to free himself or even fall to the side. I wanted to run from the woods and help him, but I knew there was nothing I could do against three Rebel soldiers.

"Across the field, the third horseman suddenly let a out a blood-curdling yell and charged my daddy at a full gallop. He drew his sword, circled it over his head and with another yell cut my daddy's head clean off his body at the neck. It fell to the ground a few feet away. His body and the plow remained standing. The horsemen laughed raucously among themselves and congratulated each other, then they rode off, taking the mule.

"I waited in the woods until they were out of sight, then I ran to our shack. I found my mama's bloody body lying run through, skewered, just outside our door. I found my sister's body lying crushed at the base of a nearby tree. They had held her by the feet and smashed her against the trunk, leaving it bloody and sticky with her flesh.

"I ran in terror and panic, thinking they would return or others would come. I hid in the woods until dark and then found my way to the Tennessee River. I crossed and kept moving all night. I hid and slept by day. Daddy had told me if there was ever killing or wild talk of lynching, to cross the river to Livingston

County and head for Smithland. He said to look for the barn just before town with a big, white H on the hayloft door. He had drawn an H mark in the dirt with a stick. He told me there was a skiff at the river close by waiting to cross to Illinois. I got as far as the hayloft, where I fell asleep, exhausted and hungry."

Will and I sat speechless staring at Ben's emotionless face in the flickering glow of the campfire. After a long silence, Will leaned forward and said, "Ben, son, it was a long time ago. It was a horrible tragedy with no reason or excuse. I can only say that we are sorry and ashamed that your mama, daddy and sister were so brutally murdered. I wish there was something we could do to bring them back, to make it right, but there isn't. You must have re-lived that day a thousand times to be able to talk it out without breaking down, without falling apart. You're in our family now, and we love you like one of our own. That's the way it's been since the day Early found you in the hayloft, and that's the way it will always be."

Ben's eyes were locked on Will's. As he began to speak, he turned to me and then back to Will.

"I've decided to go to Idaho with you. Maria has accepted Mr. White's offer and will be going to Fisk University in Nashville," Ben said.

"I'm very glad to hear that, Ben," Will said, "and I wish Maria the best."

"I'm glad you're going with us too, Ben," I added.

We looked at each other reassuringly, then stood and moved into the tent to sleep.

We rode into Dover the next afternoon and spent the night at the Dover Hotel. Will told us it was where General Buckner surrendered to General Grant 10 years before. The walls couldn't talk, and after three days and nights on the trail, it felt good to have supper, a bath and a bed.

In the morning, we stirred the curiosity of some folks in Dover. They were used to seeing Will, and sometimes Ben and me, on a *George Hawkins* steamer, so the sight of us dressed as trail riders and leading a string of mules unsettled them a little.

We crossed by ferry to the right bank and started down toward Tobacco Port on the River Road. Before we got far, Tibbs threw a shoe, so we were obliged to stop, unpack a mule and find the farrier's tools. Will put on the chaps and picked out a shoe he knew to be the right size.

Tibbs, being a young horse, hadn't gotten used to standing on three legs while a man held up the fourth, picked at the hoof, filed it and hammered it with nails. Will lifted the left hind leg, straddled the cannon bone and braced the hoof across his knee and thigh. Tibbs immediately turned his head, stretched his reins and knocked Will off his feet. We all had a good laugh, but when Tibbs kept making trouble, Will started getting annoyed.

"Tibbs, if you keep this up, I'm going to have to tie you," Will warned.

Tibbs did keep it up, and Will did tie him. He rigged a Scotch hobble. He looped a rope around Tibbs' neck, drew the line back and tied the hoof up a little off the ground. He knotted the rope so it worked like a pulley. He could raise or lower Tibbs' leg by pulling on the rope's loose end. Standing on three legs while the fourth dangled by a rope, Tibbs couldn't do much *but* cooperate. Even at that, though, he struggled. Will got eight nails in and clipped their points flush with the hoof, but he pronounced the shoeing a poor job that wouldn't last long. The clipped nails ran in an uneven line like a pencil drawing of hills and valleys.

"This'll come off easy," Will said, "the nail line should be an even arc, showing the nails were driven at a high angle and are well-seated."

As we mounted and rode on, Will spoke playfully to Ben about Tibbs.

"Ben, you know, you've got a fine horse there. You've broken him to bridle and saddle well, and except for his nerves about getting a shoe, he behaves as a young horse should.

"Now, I'm not usually a betting man," Will went on, "but I'll bet you can't teach Tibbs a trick I taught May Belle."

"What trick is that?" Ben asked, knowing he had taken the bait.

"Well, if I kick my heels into her belly, she'll take off," Will said as he kicked her, and she took off. He reined her back to a walk and went on.

"But if I dig my heels firmly into her belly, she'll stop dead and not move an inch," he said as he dug his heels in and May Belle stopped in her tracks.

"Well, Will, I'll just bet you I *can* teach Tibbs that trick, and while I'm at it, I'll see if I can dance him backwards," Ben countered.

"You're on, Ben," Will said. "What's the bet?"

"If I can teach Tibbs that trick by April 15th," Ben challenged, "you'll muck out the stable and care for the horses until we leave for Idaho. If I can't, I'll be the only barn boy."

"That's a bet, Ben, and Early is our witness," Will said as he smiled and extended his right hand to shake Ben's.

As we moved farther down the Cumberland, we stirred the same curiosity at almost every town and landing as we had in Dover. What are Will Hawkins and his boys doing trail riding? Where's the *10*? I supposed the word of the *10*'s sale and the Hawkins family quitting steamboating hadn't gotten around. Or maybe it had, but folks just didn't believe it.

On the third day, we reached Ross' Ferry and crossed back to the left bank. We rode through Frenchtown and then the last few miles into Smithland. We agreed that our week on the trail was probably tame compared to what we'd face between Kansas and Idaho. But at least we got a taste of what lay ahead and wouldn't be starting off completely green.

Try as he did, Ben was not able to teach Tibbs to stop in his tracks when he felt Ben's heels tight in his belly. Tibbs either bucked or took off running. I guessed he just had a different temperament than May Belle. Ben took losing the bet like a good sport and excused everybody else from any duties they had in the barn.

With school, spring planting, keeping up with our reading about the West and preparing for the trip, we had plenty to keep us busy until the first of May.

19

There was but a faint glow of light in the eastern sky when we awoke on Wednesday morning, May 1, 1872. We had spent the day before in last-minute preparation. Our boat for Cairo, the *Arkansas Belle*, was due at the wharfboat at 9 o'clock.

Beth had the kitchen fire up and oil lamps lit when Will, Ben and I came in for breakfast. The three of us came across from the barn, and the warmth in the kitchen took away the morning chill.

"So, this is the day when my men will leave me," Beth teased as we sat down around the long wooden table.

"Yup, but only for a short while," Will responded, continuing her teasing tone. "You'll be together with your men again in a few months."

Beth had fruit, biscuits, grits and eggs for us. The smell of frying eggs mixed with the aroma of fresh-baked biscuits and strong coffee. Beth moved about in the kitchen in her simple cotton blouse, long, pleated skirt and apron. She had pinned her red hair up in a bun. Curly wisps escaped here and there and hung like delicate ribbons. She was all mother that morning. Her men were leaving her caring eye, and she wanted to be sure we were well-fed and prepared to look after ourselves.

"I packed new boar-bristle toothbrushes for you," she reminded, "and I want you to use them vigorously with salt every day. I don't want to see any teeth missing when we join you in Idaho."

We lingered over breakfast much longer than it took to get the food into our bellies. We knew this was the last we'd see of Beth for some time, and we wanted to hold onto her presence.

Our trail ride to Dover had convinced Will that he wanted pack mules rather than horses for the trip to Idaho. In April, he and Louis had gone up the Ohio on the *Idlewild* to Crittenden County and bought two matched pairs of 15-hand mules from a breeder there. They were geldings and well-broke to pack, ride and drive. All four were out of Norman mares and sired by Andalusian jacks. Will and Louis agreed that finer mules could not be found anywhere. They joked that our riding horses might get jealous.

I had abandoned my bare feet and knee-length britches for boots and long trousers. But my loose cotton blouse, suspenders and slouch hat remained. Although we were different in size and bearing, Will, Ben and I were dressed alike. As we stood from the table, Will spoke to Ben and me as he would for the length of the trip.

"Men, it's time to saddle the horses, pack the mules and get under way."

Beth smiled knowingly. I guessed the others saw me swell with pride.

We saddled the horses in their stalls. As I slipped the bridle over Spirit's head, I wondered if he had any idea what was in store for him. Will figured if we rode about 20 miles a day, we wouldn't wear ourselves and the beasts out, and we'd all have strength left once we reached Idaho. Will expected we'd be to the Raft River by the middle of August. That meant three and a half months on the trail.

We led our mounts out to the hitching rail beside the house and returned to the barn for the mules. We led them to the front porch where we had gathered our baggage. It struck me that a person doesn't realize how much he has conveniently at hand until he tries to collect it and take it somewhere.

We packed the baggage evenly over the four mules so they were well under their weight limit. Each pack saddle and harness looked like a spider in its web. Leather straps led out from the saddle and surrounded the mule. Actually, they were simple rigs that let the mules carry their burdens in something like comfort. If a man could even lift the weight a mule carries, he'd barely be able to walk a few steps.

Standing out among our baggage were two padded wooden cases Ben made to carry his fiddle and banjo. Will had replaced my carbine with a Winchester rifle and had bought another for Ben. All told, we had three Winchesters, a Sharps buffalo rifle and three Colt pistols. Will figured those arms would do us well for hunting game and protecting ourselves.

We didn't want to delay the *Arkansas Belle*, and we knew there would be a crowd at the wharfboat to send us off, so we moved down to the river long before the steamer was due. Beth and Amanda, and Louis and Sally followed in wagons.

Only the rousters and some downbound freight were at the wharfboat when we rode up. But one by one, and in pairs and small groups, others came. Captain Jake, Nothet and Gus Mellon were there. Maria came to say goodbye to Ben. They held hands, walked away from the group and spoke quietly, looking into each others eyes. Just before 9 o'clock my sixth-year classmates walked up. They crowded round and wished me luck. Charley Mayhugh made me promise to write and tell him if there were mudpups in the Raft River. Well-wishers were everywhere, and there was much cheerfulness, but I saw sadness in more than one unguarded eye.

I had packed a new ledger book to continue the record. The rest of the books stayed behind. They would follow once we were settled in Idaho. I had read in the record that about 70 years earlier, two Hawkins families had bought wilderness land here at the edge of town, cleared it and started to farm. They had founded a heritage in Smithland that this day in May was starting to move toward its end.

The *Arkansas Belle* came in sight up the Ohio at about 8:45. She pointed her bow into the Kentucky Chute, came around the head of Cumberland Island, then rounded and tied to the wharf-boat at 9 o'clock on the nose. Most goodbyes had been said by the time the steamer landed. Ben led Tibbs and the string of mules across the stage onto the main deck. I held onto Beth and Amanda and Louis and Sally as long as I could. Beth bent to take off my hat and kiss my cheek.

"Take good care, Early, we'll see you in a few months," she whispered. As she rose, I felt her tears on my face.

I led Spirit aboard and turned to see Will embrace Louis, then Sally, then Amanda and, finally, Beth. They stood in each other's arms at the foot of the stage until the steamer's parting bell signaled she was ready to leave. Will kissed Beth tenderly, released her hands and led May Belle across the stage. Will and Beth had been together since Beth was an infant. They knew each other as well as they knew themselves. I have never seen more love, respect and trust between two people as I did between Will and Beth. I don't think they once exchanged an angry word.

The *Arkansas Belle* let go her lines, nosed into the stream and rounded to go down to Paducah. With our backs to our horses and mules, we waved goodbye to family, friends and Smithland. I felt an odd mixture of joy and sadness. We were bound for Idaho!

Will had checked the steamer schedules in the newspapers and booked our passage by wire. If the *Arkansas Belle* was not delayed between Smithland and Cairo, we would be there in time to board the *Belle Memphis* for Saint Louis late in the afternoon. We'd arrive in Saint Louis Thursday afternoon, spend the night in a hotel near the wharf and board the *Emilie La Barge* on Friday for a 5 p.m. departure to Kansas City.

I hadn't been to Paducah for some time, and it struck me that the town was prosperous and growing, while the Smithland we had left an hour before was doing just the opposite. After the war, with the railroad in Paducah but absent in Smithland, many businesses and prominent families had left our town and removed to Paducah. Now, with the railroads taking freight and passengers away from steamers, and steamers gone from Smithland, our town seemed doomed.

We exchanged passengers and freight at the Paducah wharf and were under way within 30 minutes of landing. Will sat on the hurricane deck with Captain Jack Grammer, the master of the *Arkansas Belle*. Will looked as if he was enjoying being a passenger on another captain's boat. Ben sat with them, picking his banjo. I left them and went about exploring the boat.

The *Arkansas Belle* held the U. S. Mail contract for points between Evansville and Cairo. She was a sidewheeler just over 200 feet long. Although she showed a good amount of jigsaw work and had a comfortable main cabin, the *Arkansas Belle* was a dowdy girl compared to the *10*. She had tall stacks, and her pilothouse sat atop a very long texas, but the bell mounted forward on her hurricane deck was puny next to the *10*'s, the bell we had left behind on the homeplace porch. The *Arkansas Belle* did have one feature that made her a favorite of brides. Two of her staterooms—Arkansas and Tennessee, opposite each other across the main cabin—were bridal chambers. Their beds were built high, requiring the brides to climb short ladders to reach them.

When the dinner bell rang, Will, Ben and I sat at the captain's table. The conversation was about Ohio River packets. I asked Captain Grammer how it was that a boat named *Arkansas Belle* was in the Ohio River trade.

"Well, young man," he replied, "she was built to run up the Arkansas River from Memphis, but the Evansville, Cairo and Memphis Steam Packet Company bought her and entered her in the Evansville–Cairo trade."

By 1872, packets on the Cumberland below Nashville had lost or were losing the freight business in cotton, iron, tobacco and grain to the railroads. As one Cumberland pilot put it to Will, "Hell had really busted loose, and it was time to quit sittin' 'round and wonderin' what would happen next. Damn, if it didn't look like the railroads were slow poisonin' us by puttin' out the fire under our boilers while we sat in the pilothouse blowin' a toot or two on the whistle."

But the railroads hadn't yet extended their web from lower

Ohio River towns to Saint Louis. So packets like the *Arkansas Belle* that ran from places like Evansville down to Cairo still earned a profit. From Cairo, people and goods moved up or down the Mississippi on big, ornate steamers or straight up Illinois to Chicago by rail on the Illinois Central line.

We made only two way-landings in the 45 miles or so between Paducah and Cairo. As we neared the mouth of the Ohio, we saw a line of steamers tied at the Cairo wharfboats and others coming or going in the stream. Illinois Central rail cars ran atop the levee that ringed the city and protected it from Ohio and Mississippi floods. The *Arkansas Belle* rounded and tied to a wharfboat just above the *Belle Memphis*. Will checked his pocket watch. It was 4 p.m. We had an hour to move ourselves and the beasts aboard the boat to Saint Louis.

Passengers crossed to the wharfboat first, then the livestock. We led our animals off the *Arkansas Belle* and aboard the *Belle Memphis*. Ben stayed with them while Will and I went to see about feed. We walked up the levee to 10th Street, where we found corn, oats and hay at a merchant's, and hired a man with a dray to haul us and the feed back to the *Belle Memphis*. As we drove, the drayman asked about our supper plans.

"Yo' got feed fuh yo' hosses, how 'bout yo'selves?" he drawled, and gave Will a handbill. On it was a drawing of a little man standing in an outline map of Kentucky. In big, bold letters, it said "The Little Kentuckian" and below that in smaller type, it said:

No. 53 Ohio levee is the place where they keep the freshest fish and game, and the finest wines, liquors and cigars to be found in the city. Dinner only 25 cents. Open day and night at all hours.
—J. E. Park, Proprietor

Will read the handbill and said, "Why, thank you, sir. It's tempting to have our last taste of Kentucky, but we'll be taking our supper on the Mississippi aboard the *Belle Memphis* bound for Saint Louis."

We boarded the steamer, saw to the animals, checked in with the first clerk and went to our stateroom—Kansas—entering from the main cabin. As a mature white man, a young Negro man and a young white boy traveling together, we drew the usual stares from some. And, as usual, we ignored them.

20

The *Belle Memphis* rang her last bell a few minutes before 5 p.m. and, after taking on some late-arriving passengers, backed into the stream, rounded and steamed toward the mouth of the Ohio. We went all the way forward to the boiler deck rail. When the boat came around the point into the Mississippi and started up against the current, Will, Ben and I were in new territory. None of us had been above Cairo on the Mississippi before. The supper bell rang at 6 o'clock, just as we entered Abel's Bend.

Before packets left the rivers altogether, there were two steamers named *Belle Memphis* and another named *Memphis* that for some reason people called *Belle Memphis*. The *Belle Memphis* that took us from Cairo to Saint Louis was built at the Howard Ship Yards in Jeffersonville, Indiana, in 1866. She was one of at least a dozen packets owned and operated on the Mississippi at that time by the Memphis & Saint Louis Packet Company. Most steamboats lasted only about five years. They either blew up, got snagged and sank, burned, or, on the upper rivers, got crushed in an ice jam. The *Belle Memphis* ran on the Mississippi for 14 years and suffered no such fate. She was dismantled in 1880.

She was a large, graceful girl, a sidewheeler 260 feet long, 40 wide and seven deep. She displaced 919 tons. On this trip between Cairo and Saint Louis, she carried a heavy load, with almost no freeboard showing and the river licking her guards. When we left Cairo, reports were that the Mississippi was falling fast at Saint Louis, and there was hardly nine feet of water over the shoalest bars. Some old hands aboard wondered if we'd be striking bottom before nightfall.

The stewards and waiters had set fine tables for supper. The main cabin was so long that if you stood at one end and looked clear down to the other, you couldn't recognize your own relation standing there. We sat with a young family at a large oblong table and introduced ourselves all around. Mr. and Mrs. Howard Reed and their daughter, Sara, were traveling from Memphis to Saint Louis for Mrs. Reed's sister's wedding.

Mr. Reed was a talkative, outgoing man. His wife and daughter were quiet, simply nodding in agreement with everything he said. His first notice was that supper would barely be started before we came upon the wreck of the *Oceanus*. It would be sitting midstream in Dog Tooth Bend near Brook's Point about 20 miles above Cairo. Mr. Reed knew all the particulars of the disaster. The *Oceanus* was small for a Mississippi steamer. She was upbound for Saint Louis from Shreveport on April 11th when, at 4 o'clock in the morning, her boilers exploded and she burned. Thirty-four lost their lives, including the captain, two pilots, and the first and second mates, a father and son.

Some of James Robinson's Circus were aboard, and four lions and their trainer were among those lost. Bloated, decomposing bodies were still being found weeks later. The lion tamer, F. M. Sleight, was one, found 2-1/2 miles below the wreck and identified by dispatches found on his person.

Young Sara Reed winced, and Mrs. Reed spoke for the first time.

"Mr. Reed, please, this is hardly a subject for supper conversation," she said quietly, almost under her breath.

"Uh, yes, missus, I am sorry," Mr. Reed apologized. "I became caught up in the moment."

Just as the waiters cleared the appetizers and began to serve the main course, the *Belle Memphis* blew three long blasts of her whistle, accompanied by an equal number of strong strikes of her bell. A long pause dwelled between each ring.

"We're saluting the *Oceanus*," a man at the next table said.

Will, Ben and I quickly turned one way, then the other, looking at each other. As if on an agreed signal, we stood, excused ourselves, dropped our lap napkins on our seats and exited the cabin to view the wreck.

We stood at the boiler deck rail on the larboard side as the *Belle Memphis* passed, mindful of the channel, close by the wreck's Illinois side. The sun was setting beyond the Missouri bank, casting an eerie red glow across the charcoal hulk. The *Oceanus* lay listing and half submerged, looking sad and helpless, the victim of what carelessness or neglect we didn't know.

Returning to our table, we found supper at our places. Mr. Reed learned of Will's connection with the river trade and turned the conversation to the just-announced agreement between the Illinois Central and Jackson & Mississippi Central railroads. The latter was to extend its line from Humboldt, Tennessee, to the Kentucky shore opposite Cairo. The track laying would take seven months. The Illinois Central would build a bridge from Cairo across to Kentucky. That would take two years. In the meantime, a steam ferry would connect the rails from the south to those from the north. Thus, Mr. Reed announced, the Gulf at New Orleans would be linked by rail with the Great Lakes at Chicago.

"So, Mr. Hawkins," Mr. Reed asked, "do you think this sounds the death knell for steamboats on the Mississippi?"

Ben and I looked at each other, and I knew we were thinking the same thing. It was the first time we had ever heard anyone address Will as "Mr. Hawkins." It had been only "Captain Hawkins" and always spoken in a tone of great respect.

Will paused for a moment between listening and speaking.

"I suppose the rail connection will have an effect," he said. "I saw in the *Cairo Daily Bulletin* that there were 466 landings and 463 departures at Cairo in April. That sounds like a lot, but I don't know if the numbers are up or down. Then, also in April, 15 large tows of coal passed Cairo from above on the Ohio. That's about 2,500,000 bushels. It would take 10,000 rail cars to carry that volume. Perhaps the steamboat business isn't dying. Maybe it's just changing."

The talk had taken us through dessert. As we rose from the table, Mr. Reed's final reminder was that the Republican Convention had begun in Cincinnati, and the presidential election season was heating up. Would President Grant be returned for a second term? Mr. Reed wondered aloud. Or would the scandals that plagued his administration relegate him to heroic status only in the dustbin of military history?

Will looked as if he was straining to be patient and polite. He excused us from the company of the Reeds, and we went below to check on the horses and mules.

A touch of deep violet lingered in the western sky, and, except for the lanterns of the *Belle Memphis*, the only light was the stars. I realized there would be nothing to see along the Mississippi banks but a dim landing light flickering here and there. I retired to our Kansas stateroom and made notes in the record. I read a little and drifted off to sleep, planning to awake at first light to see the day on the Mississippi.

When I woke, there was barely a hint of light behind the Illinois shore. I dressed quietly to not wake Will and Ben. Mindful of Beth, I took my toothbrush and a spoonful of salt in the hollow of my hand when I went to the wheelhouse washroom. When I returned, the cook and the stewards were lighting the kitchen lamps.

I went to the main deck and spread lucerne for the horses and mules. We must have offloaded a lot of heavy freight during the night because the river was no longer licking the undersides of the guards, and we were showing probably a foot of freeboard. I guessed we were 100 miles above Cairo. That would put us above Tower Rock but well below Sainte Genevieve. I stood between the stages far forward on the bow of the main deck. With my back to the jackstaff, I watched the eastern sky brighten. Silhouettes of birds appeared in the young willows that lined the Illinois shore. Birdsongs rose above the sounds of the *Belle Memphis'* bow cutting the current, her 'scape pipes exhaling steam and her buckets churning the muddy water. Little by little, the brightening sky extinguished the stars.

Captain White stopped by our breakfast table to say good morning. J. M. White was usually master of the *Katie*, another Mississippi packet in the New Orleans–Saint Louis trade. But the *Katie* was up on the ways for repairs, so Captain White had come over to the *Belle Memphis*. He said the river was holding steady at nine feet over the shoalest bars. He expected no delays and said we'd be at the Saint Louis wharf by the middle of the afternoon. He turned to Ben.

"Ben, I heard you playing your fiddle in the cabin last evening. Do you play calliope?"

"Yes, sir, I do. I used to play the calliope on our boat, the *George Hawkins*."

"Well, the *Belle Memphis* has an especially fine calliope, and I'd certainly like to hear you play it. And speaking for the passengers and the people at the landings, I'm sure they would enjoy it too."

"I'll go up to the calliope directly from breakfast," Ben said.

As long as steamers had been on the Mississippi and with all the boats that had passed this way, the arrival of a packet at a small river town still created great excitement. When we came within sight of Sainte Genevieve, we saw small boys running to the wharf. Teams drew wagons and drays, empty and full, toward the river. The *Belle Memphis'* whistle announced our approach, and the calliope enlivened an already lively scene. Doors opened in the buildings above the wharf, and people stepped out. Others appeared on the upper galleries on many buildings. From the river, Sainte Genevieve looked as if it had come alive, as if the *Belle Memphis* had turned a switch, and all the parts of the river town started working at once.

Landing at Sainte Genevieve was little different from making so many of our landings on the Cumberland. The motion and sounds stood out most. The *Belle Memphis* was a big, imposing presence as she moved to the bank and lowered her stage. People and drays and wagons moved down and across the wharf. Friendly greetings were exchanged. Ben tooted lively tunes on the calliope. Passengers and freight crossed from the boat to the wharf, then the upbound freight came aboard. There were dozens of hogsheads of tobacco, 200 sides of hog meat, 100 stands of lard, 50 coops of chickens, 50 cases of eggs, hundreds of hides, barrel after barrel of molasses and at least 200 head of livestock. The goods moved quickly across the stage and a ramp that stretched from the wharf to the aft deck. The clerk rushed about tallying the goods and writing bills of lading. Last, we took on a dozen or so upbound passengers and coal for the fires beneath the boilers.

About 45 minutes after touching the wharf, the *Belle Memphis* raised her stage, backed into the stream and continued up toward Saint Louis. The city lay about 50 miles above.

21

The Saint Louis wharf must have been at least a mile long. It was lined with steamers, some tied at wharfboats and others with their stages dropped directly to the cobblestones. Near the upper end of the riverfront, piers for a bridge under construction stood at the bank, mid-river and on the eastern shore. A rail line ran the length of the wharf at its top. The street behind the rails was lined with warehouses and other commercial buildings, most built of brick. Cathedral spires and the courthouse dome and cupola rose far above the height of the other structures and dominated the skyline. The whole city looked as if it was smothering under a cloud of black coal smoke.

As the *Belle Memphis* tied to the Memphis & Saint Louis Packet Company's wharfboat, Will asked Captain White to recommend a hotel. He replied that the Planters' House was a fine hotel and easy to find—just head for the courthouse dome. The hotel is right there across the street.

We waited as passengers crossed to the wharfboat, then we followed, walking the animals in a single line. We mounted on the wharfboat and led the mules down the ramp to the cobblestones. The animals had been standing in one place so long, they seemed eager to move.

The wharf was busy with everything that could be mounted on wheels—wagons, drays, carts, carriages and hacks. Freight was stacked everywhere in barrels, crates and sacks, some in the open and some under tarps. Logs, lumber, pig iron, livestock and every manner of goods was either on the wharf, going aboard the steamers or coming off. I turned to see the wharfboats boldly labeled on the shore side to show their boats' destinations—Cairo, Memphis, Vicksburg, New Orleans, Mobile and Way-Landings. The big painted signs made things easy, even for nervous travelers.

We rode straight to the Planters' House, passing the post office and telegraph office along the way. Will said after we got settled, we'd send a wire to Beth and Amanda. The Planters' House was the biggest hotel we had ever seen. It was 4-1/2 stories tall and took up the whole block between Pine and Chestnut Streets on the west side of Fourth. We asked for directions to the nearest livery, proceeded there, saw to the beasts, secured our baggage and returned to the hotel on foot, carrying only our necessaries.

Saint Louis was like nothing we had seen before. Nashville was a town by comparison and Smithland a crossroads. The 1870 census counted fewer than 2,000 people in Smithland. Saint Louis had 310,000. There was lots of hustle-bustle. Teams and wagons, carriages, horse-drawn streetcars, open markets, block after block of buildings, and people were everywhere.

The desk clerk at the Planters' House didn't give Ben a second look. Maybe that's the way things were in a big city. We had a room on the third floor, looking out over Fourth Street.

Supper service started at 6 p.m., half an hour before sunset. We had time, so we walked to the telegraph office a few blocks away. Will wired Beth, saying we were safely in Saint Louis and the next day would be on our way to Kansas City. Will asked Beth to wire us back no later than Friday afternoon with news. We returned to the Planters' House and entered the dining room. As soon as we had been seated, a well-dressed, white-haired man joined us.

"Good evening, gentleman, name's Prentiss," he said, "mind if I join you? The wife and I used to sup here before she passed away. I still like to come here, but I have no one to sit with."

"No, don't mind at all," Will said. "Please, sit, be our guest. I am Will Hawkins, and these young men are my sons, Ben and Early." Will nodded first in Ben's direction and then mine as he said our names.

"Fine, gentlemen, fine," the man said. "I'm Prentiss, Max Prentiss. I was in the foundry business here before I got too old. Now, all my friends are old and sick, or gone to their final reward. I'm the only old bird left flying," he said, mixing pride with regret. "What's your line, Mr. Hawkins? You gentlemen aren't dressed like city folks."

"Mr. Prentiss, I was master and pilot of a steamer out of Smithland, Kentucky," Will said. "My son, Ben, here, is a fine singer and musician, and my son Early is a scholar, a voracious reader and the best rifle shot in Livingston County, Kentucky." There was pride in Will's voice. "We are on our way to Idaho."

"Idaho, eh," Mr. Prentiss said, "are you traveling by rail car then?"

"No," Will replied, "we're on horseback and trailing mules."

"How many animals do you have?" Mr. Prentiss asked.

"Seven in all," Will replied.

"Hmm, better check the grass," Mr. Prentiss said.

"Check the grass?" Will asked, turning toward Ben and me. "Do you men know about checking the grass?"

"I do," Ben said as he nodded. "Emigrants sometimes had to wait on this side of the Plains for the grass to grow so they could graze their beasts as they moved west."

"Mr. Prentiss," Will asked, "what is the condition of the grass?"

"I regret to say I don't know," Mr. Prentiss said. "And I doubt you'll find anyone in Saint Louis who does. They'll know in Kansas City though," he added.

"Mr. Prentiss," I said, "we saw a bridge being built toward the north end of the wharf. Do you know anything about it?"

"Why, yes," he replied, "that's the Eads Bridge, being built by the same man who built the ironclads for the North during the War. And it's steel, not iron," he added.

"When will it be finished?" Ben asked.

"Mr. Eads expects in two years more," Mr. Prentiss replied.

Waiters came and went as we talked, bringing full plates and removing empties.

"It'll be the first rails to cross the Mississippi," Mr. Prentiss continued. "I'm afraid the steamboats' days are numbered."

"Why is there so much coal smoke about the city?" Will asked.

"That's due to a combination of causes," Mr. Prentiss replied. "We mine iron downriver. Coal fires the furnaces to remove it from the ore. And coal fires the steamers and rail cars that bring it here. Then coal fires the foundries that form the iron into everything a man can imagine. And coal fires the other industries in the city. Then coal heats our buildings and homes in winter. And it's all dirty coal this side of the Mississippi."

Will had asked the right man about coal smoke.

"Yes, we're under a cloud here," Mr. Prentiss continued. "The women are often heard complaining that they hang their clean wash out to dry, and by the time it *is* dry, the soot has made it dirty again. I suppose it's not too healthy for breathing either," he added. Then Mr. Prentiss changed the subject.

"Mr. Hawkins," he said with some hesitation, "I'm not a man to question another man's habits, but I have a curious thought. You introduced your companions as your sons. Yet one is black and the other is white, while you yourself are white. Can you explain that?"

"Certainly, Mr. Prentiss," Will replied. "Ben is my adopted son and as dear to me as Early, my natural son."

"You're fortunate to have such fine sons," Mr. Prentiss said. "And you're fortunate that since Emancipation and the War, the strict black codes that once applied to the behavior of both freedmen and slaves in this city have been relaxed, especially here at the Planters' House. It wasn't but a short time ago that Negroes were not permitted to eat or sleep in this hotel. They could work here, but they couldn't stay here."

It seemed that Mr. Prentiss was ashamed of the codes and glad they were gone.

"These changes do not come easily to a city where there was much pro-slavery sentiment. Saint Louis was under martial law through most of the War," he explained.

"Mr. Prentiss," Will said, "our boat is not until 5 p.m. tomorrow. What can we do with the day?"

"Do you need provisions?" Mr. Prentiss asked.

"We'll be aboard the *Emilie La Barge* of the Star Line for several days," Will replied, "so we'll be provided for."

"I'd like to buy a new book," I said.

"Well, then, young man," Mr. Prentiss said, "you're here on Fourth Street, if you head for the 300 block north, you'll find a large stock of books at the Saint Louis Book and News Company. I buy my *Missouri Republican* there every day."

"What else can you recommend to us?" Will asked.

"The courthouse across the street is a sight inside and out," Mr. Prentiss replied. "Maybe you know the Dred Scott case. That courthouse is where it was tried—twice—before the Supreme Court took it up and led us to the War. Then, I'd say hire a hack, and have the driver show you the city. See if you can find a driver named Johnnie Mack. He knows the city better than I know my own house."

After the pie, we excused ourselves, thanking Mr. Prentiss for his company. Will asked him if he would like to tour the city with us, but he declined, saying that on Fridays he always visited his wife's grave.

Come morning, we had a big breakfast and then crossed Chestnut Street to the courthouse. There was no guided tour, just a lot of people going about their business. We walked through the building, laughing a little at the fact that it sure took a lot longer than walking through the courthouse in Smithland.

As Mr. Prentiss suggested, we hunted up Johnnie Mack. We found him on Market Street, coming up from the wharf bound for the Southern Hotel with four passengers. Will asked if he could give us the grand tour of the city. He told us to wait right where we were. He would take his passengers to their destination and come right back for us.

Johnnie Mack was a short, round, jolly Negro man. He wore overalls, black boots and a big straw hat. As we climbed into his hack and got comfortably seated, Will told him we wanted to go by the telegraph office, the bookstore Mr. Prentiss had recommended, the livery to look in on the beasts, and the Star Line wharfboat to confirm our boat's schedule and our passage. Otherwise, we were his until 3 o'clock in the afternoon when we would have to start readying for our trip. Johnnie Mack replied that he would be happy to oblige.

We had a telegram from Beth and Amanda. We were all pleased. They said they missed us, everything was fine and please send wires and letters as often as possible, if not more often.

At the bookstore, I bought *Roughing It* by Mark Twain, a new book that had become a favorite. Ben bought a songbook for piano. He would spend his spare time transposing the tunes to fiddle, banjo or mouth harp. Will's choice was a surprise—*Origin of Species* by Charles Darwin. Will said he had started reading it about 10 years before, but the War interfered and then his copy disappeared from the *George Hawkins* on a trip down from Nashville.

Will also bought a *Missouri Republican* newspaper. The Liberal Republicans had nominated Horace Greeley, the New York newspaperman, and his running mate was to be Benjamin Gratz Brown. The Republican Convention wouldn't be until early June, but the editor assumed its nominee would be Ulysses S. Grant, the current president. The editor wrote that Grant's term had been plagued with scandals and corruption, and he predicted a down-and-dirty campaign.

We had a sunny day for our tour and a favorable west wind that blew the coal smoke across to Illinois. Johnnie Mack was just as Mr. Prentiss had said, an encyclopedia of information about Saint Louis. He knew everything that had ever happened and everybody who made it happen. As he drove, he talked on about the buildings we passed, the buildings that were there before, the good and the bad citizens, and all kinds of events in Saint Louis history.

"On your left here . . . on your right there . . . straight ahead a ways . . ." he went on. Every so often, he'd stop and ask, "Now, y'all got any questions 'bout dat?" We rarely did because he supplied all the answers beforehand and left no questions to ask.

Johnnie drove to the bridge site and told us about Mr. Eads and the bridge he started building in 1867. Then we drove on to the Saint Louis, Kansas City & Northern Railroad depot and, after that, the Water Works. Next was Bellefontaine Cemetery and then back around to the large and beautifully kept fairgrounds. Johnnie especially liked to point out the parks. We saw Washington Park, Missouri Park and the extra large and lovely Lafayette Park. But even Lafayette Park was small compared to another that was Johnnie's favorite. A wealthy man named Henry Shaw had donated his large botanical garden to Saint Louis years earlier. Then a few years later, he donated an even larger adjoining tract that became Tower Grove Park. Together, the two tracts formed an L and were well over 300 acres in size.

As we had asked, Johnnie had us to the livery by 3 o'clock. I bet we had seen and learned more about Saint Louis in a few hours than other visitors do in a month. We saddled our horses, packed up the mules and were to the Star Line wharfboat and aboard the *Emilie La Barge* by shortly after 4 o'clock. We saw to the animals' feed, secured our baggage and went to the office to ask about our stateroom. The clerk introduced himself as James Gunsolis and said he proudly shared ownership of the boat with its master, Captain David Silver. Learning we were from Kentucky, Mr. Gunsolis assigned us to that stateroom and wished us a pleasant trip to Kansas City.

"Kentucky" was a three-berth stateroom with a door on one end that opened onto the main cabin and another at the opposite end that opened onto the boiler deck gallery. The *Emilie La Barge* was a smaller, shallower packet than the *Belle Memphis*. She was built for the Missouri River trade, and those boats tended to be designed more for utility than the fancier and larger Mississippi River steamers. Not that *Emilie* was a dowdy girl, she just didn't dress up as pretty as the Mississippi belles. The five-pointed star strung between her stacks said that she saw herself as a hardworking but comely maiden.

As we settled into our stateroom, Will turned to me and said, "Early, there are a few things I want to talk to Ben about. Why don't you go on up to the pilothouse? I expect we'll be backing into the stream presently, and maybe they need some help up there." That sounded like a fine idea to me, so I was quickly out of the stateroom and bounding up the stairs to the pilothouse.

There was only one man there, and he was sitting on the lazy bench. He was a young man with fair skin and thick blond hair. Not being a shy boy, I stepped right up and introduced myself, assuming the man was the pilot.

"Good afternoon, sir. I'm Early Hawkins from Smithland, Kentucky, here with my papa, Will, and my brother, Ben, on our way to Kansas City. They're taking care of some business in our stateroom, and my papa said I should come up to the pilothouse and see if I could help."

"Well . . . Hawkins . . . Smithland. Now, that sounds familiar to me. I'm Tom Dodge, one of the pilots on the *Emilie La Barge*. And, yes, there is something you can do to help."

With that, he took hold of his right leg with both hands and stretched it straight out in front of him. He leaned forward, grabbed the bottom of his pants leg and rolled it up, making quick, neat tucks as he went. He revealed a finely carved and polished wooden limb, hinged at the knee.

"My leg's gotten a little crooked here. I have to loosen the straps, turn the leg and reset the straps. Maybe you can help me by tightening the straps the way I instruct you."

I was taken aback at first when Mr. Dodge revealed his wooden leg. I hesitated a second but then said, sure, I'll help. He loosened the straps, adjusted the position of the leg, and then had me reset and tighten the straps in an exact way.

He thanked me and as we stood, a rather short, sturdy man in a dark blue suit and vest opened the door and came into the pilothouse. He held his head down momentarily, watching his step. He had steel gray hair and a full beard. When he raised his head and I met his face, my own face awakened in great surprise and I fell back half a step.

"Why, Gen, why, Prez, why, Mister Grant!" I exclaimed. The man chuckled and smiled kindly.

"Oh, mais non, mon jeune homme. Je ne suis pas Général ou Président ou Monsieur Grant. Je regrette, mais il est vrai. Je suis Capitaine Joseph La Barge. Je voyage à Saint Charles. Et vous, monsieur?"

Of course, I hadn't understood a word he said, and I was stunned into silence. I thought I was face to face with Ulysses S. Grant, and the man started speaking a mysterious language I had never heard before. The man chuckled and smiled again.

"I'm sorry, son, I was just having some fun with you. I'm Captain Joseph La Barge. People take me for U. S. Grant all the time, so I turn it into an amusement for me and, I hope, the mistaken party."

I probably looked a little relieved, but I took a minute to recover.

"I built this boat and named it for my daughter about three years back. Then about a year ago I sold it to these fellas. I'm visiting in Saint Charles tomorrow, and when I travel there, I always go by steamer. And you, young man, where are you bound?"

"I'm Early Hawkins, and my papa, brother and I are going to Kansas City on the *Emilie La Barge*, and then on horseback on the old Oregon Trail."

"On the Oregon Trail and not the railroad?!" he exclaimed. Now, that sounds like a fine idea. If I were a younger man, I'd do it myself. Where are your companions?"

"They're in our stateroom below, Captain. I expect they'll be here any minute, but if they're not, I'll go fetch them."

"Oh, there's no need for that if they're coming up by and by," he said.

Captain La Barge and Mr. Dodge exchanged friendly hellos and started talking about the conditions on the rivers. Freshets above had reached the lower Missouri, and the river was running high and strong. The *Emilie* will be working hard going up, they said.

At that, the door opened behind Captain La Barge, and Will and Ben stepped in. I saw Will do a quick double take when Captain La Barge turned around, but he seemed to quickly realize this was not President Grant who stood before him.

Will introduced himself and Ben to Captain La Barge, and then he turned to Mr. Dodge. A look of great surprise and happiness burst upon his face.

"Why, Tom Dodge!" he exclaimed loudly and almost leaped in Mr. Dodge's direction. Mr. Dodge had an equally excited reaction, and the two men quickly embraced and clapped each other on the back.

"Isn't this a coincidence to beat all coincidences?" Will asked. "How have you been, Tom?"

"I suppose it's been near 10 years, Captain Hawkins," Mr. Dodge said.

"Yes, that's right, Tom," Will replied. "Where have you been in those 10 years?"

"Mostly here in Saint Louis when I'm not on the rivers. My wife and two boys are here. I was married in the city before the War was through. I've been piloting, and I hope to buy a boat with a partner before long. What about you, Captain Hawkins?" Mr. Dodge asked.

"My sons and I will be crossing the Plains to Idaho. We plan to homestead where the Raft River meets the Snake," Will replied. "I have a question that maybe you or Captain La Barge can answer."

"I'll try," said Mr. Dodge, "but can you hold on for a few minutes while I get the *Emilie La Barge* under way?"

"Sure," Will replied, "I'll be happy to watch a good pilot at work."

Mr. Dodge stepped to the starboard side of the wheel and yanked the backing-bell pull for the larboard engine, and the backing-bell rope for the starboard engine. He bent to the speaking tube and said, "Back full, please, Mr. Dugan."

Mr. Dodge backed into the stream, then yanked the stopping-bell pull and rope twice—the first to signal stop, the second, to come ahead, full. He bent to the speaking tube and said, "Come ahead, full, nicely, please, Mr. Dugan."

Mr. Dodge steered into his course and then said, "And now, about that question, Captain Hawkins."

Hearing Will addressed as "Captain Hawkins" felt right.

"Last evening at supper at the Planters' House, a Mr. Prentiss suggested that we should ask after the condition of the grass on the Plains."

"Leaving Saint Louis early this evening," Mr. Dodge said, "you'll be in Kansas City Wednesday next. From what I've heard and by my calculations, that will make you about three weeks past or three weeks before good grass. Spring was late this year. Then there were several large droves of stock coming to Kansas City from the west. Unless you go some miles off the trail, you'll have no grass for your animals. How are you traveling?"

"Three horses and four mules," Will replied.

"You'll need grass," Mr. Dodge said. "You can't pack feed. You'll want the beaten path of the trail, and you can't turn the clock back to the first growth of grass, so the only choice you have is to bide your time until the end of the month and the return of the grass."

"I hadn't heard about this spring," Captain La Barge said, "but that's what thousands of emigrants did years ago. They waited for the grass."

"I'll have to think on this some before I decide what to do," Will said. A moment later, he asked, "Didn't Nathan and Daniel Boone build a stone house west of Saint Charles along the river?"

"Yes, they did," Mr. Dodge and Captain La Barge replied in chorus. With a nod, Mr. Dodge deferred to Captain La Barge.

"Some years before he died in 1820, Daniel Boone helped his son, Nathan, build a sturdy home of Missouri limestone on Femme Osage Creek some distance up from the river, near where Schulersburg is today. I visited Nathan at the house before he sold it. He died in the middle 1850s. I don't know if the house remained in the family."

Turning to Ben and me, Will said, "Men, this is what I propose to do rather than loafing around Kansas City waiting three weeks for the grass. We'll disembark from the *Emilie La Barge* at the landing nearest Schulersburg, we'll visit with the Boones if there are any Boones at the limestone house, then we'll proceed overland along the river to Kansas City. It being about 400 miles from Saint Louis by river, and our having covered some of that distance by steamer, at a gentle speed we should reach Kansas City within a few days of when the prairies will be tall and green with fresh grass."

Of course, Ben and I agreed immediately. We respected Will's judgment without question.

"Captain Hawkins," said Captain La Barge, "yours is an excellent plan. The timing is correct, and there's some beautiful country along the Missouri this side of Kansas City."

"As much as I dislike seeing you get off the boat," Mr. Dodge said, "I think riding across Missouri beats the dust out of lolling around Kansas City for three weeks."

"It's unanimous, then," Will said with a smile. "We'll be with you on the *Emilie La Barge* until the landing nearest Schulersburg, then we'll give our beasts a chance to walk a little across the Missouri countryside."

22

We reached the mouth of the Missouri at sunset. As we had heard, the river was running high and strong. Whole trees floated on its current. I wondered how Captains Lewis and Clark and the Corps of Discovery made headway against the torrent without steam power. It seemed impossible for a keelboat or pirogues to oppose that current.

Mr. Dodge turned from the Mississippi into the Missouri, proceeded up a mile or two in the gathering twilight, then tied to the north bank to await sunrise. Navigating the Missouri at night, especially in flood conditions, was too dangerous.

We were under way before 5 a.m., when there was just enough light to see the river surface. Our first landing was at Saint Charles, about 20 miles above the Missouri's mouth. We had sat for breakfast with Captain La Barge. He reminded us with some pride that it was at Saint Charles in May 1804 that Captain Lewis met Captain Clark and the expedition began. We bade Captain La Barge goodbye at the wharf. He turned, smiled his warm smile and waved before climbing into a waiting hack.

"Au revoir, mes amis," he called. "Bonne chance!"

We offloaded very little freight at Saint Charles, but we took on probably 100 barrels marked "Spring Brewery." Big men rolled the barrels one by one across the stage and stood them on end on the main deck. They were likely bound for various places above, but passengers on board joked that all the beer was intended for the state legislators in Jefferson City.

After exchanging hearty goodbyes with Mr. Dodge, Will, Ben and I disembarked at the third landing above Saint Charles. Captain Silver called it Missouriton. It was on the north bank, opposite Port Royal and Saint Albans. The only freight offloaded was one of the beer barrels. A deckhand rolled it across the stage just behind us and our beasts. That drew some good-natured ribbing from a line of passengers at the rail. We laughed as loudly as they did. We waved from the bank as the *Emilie La Barge* backed into the stream and continued up.

A young man, alone in a wagon drawn by a handsome chestnut gelding, drove up to the landing. He climbed down and tied his horse to a willow. He pulled a long plank from the wagon bed and set it up as a ramp from the tail to the ground behind. He walked to the edge of the bank, heading for the Spring Brewery barrel. He tipped it onto its round side and rolled it toward the wagon. The gelding flicked his ears and pawed the ground as the young man rolled the barrel by. He reached the ramp, turned the barrel, rolled it up and stood it on end in the wagon bed. He walked down the ramp, loaded it, walked to untie the gelding, climbed into the seat and reached for the reins, all without so much as a glance toward us. Will approached him just as he was about to slap the horse's quarters with leather.

"We're passing through on our way from Kentucky to Kansas City. We're looking for the stone house that Nathan and Daniel Boone built."

The young man hesitated. There was a long, awkward silence. Finally, he said, "I live in that house. It's about five miles up the creek road." He turned in his seat and pointed to the road. He spoke with a slight foreign accent that I didn't know.

"I'm Will Hawkins and these fellows are my sons, Early and Ben," Will said, nodding to us in turn.

The young man hesitated again.

"I am Henry Buenger. My stepfather is Ludwig Paul. He owns the stone house. His wife is my mother, Elizabeth. No Boones about, though, haven't been for years."

"May we ride with you to the house?" Will asked. "We'd like to see it."

Henry Buenger paused. "Ya, mount up and follow me."

He turned his wagon and headed toward the creek road. We fell in behind. Will and Ben each trailed two mules, and I brought up the rear. We didn't talk much among ourselves or with Henry as we rode. I switched between coming up to ride beside Will and Ben, and falling to the rear behind the mules. I think Spirit liked being off the boat and back on solid ground.

The stone house sat west of the road, with its rear to us. Its front faced a broad meadow. Large trees surrounded the house. There was a huge barn and several outbuildings, including a springhouse. Fields of young corn and grain stretched north, south and west.

We crossed a stone-and-plank bridge to the property. I expected to see dogs, but instead saw several peacocks and hens walking the ground. Henry called to them, "Hallo, birds! Hallo, birds!" He stopped at the springhouse to unload the beer barrel. He motioned to the barn.

"There's a hitching rail on the near side beyond those low trees. I'll be there as soon as I store this barrel."

We tied our animals and checked the cinches and packs. In a few minutes, Henry drove into the barn. He saw to his horse and then came to us.

"What's in the two hard cases you haff tied to the mule?" he asked.

"The smaller one's a fiddle, and the other's a banjo," Ben replied.

"I play accordion," Henry said, with a hint of a boast in his tone.

"I've never played an accordion," Ben said, "but I'd like to try."

"Why don't we go to the house. You can meet my mother," Henry said. "My stepfather is in the fields and vill be along soon."

We met Henry's mother, Elizabeth. She was a large woman with a big, generous smile and huge teeth. Her long braids were wrapped in a spiral around a bun on the crown of her head. She spoke with an accent like Henry's, but thicker.

"You can stay den for zupper and dancing?" she asked. "Vee haff a party tonight."

"That's very kind of you," Will replied, "we would love to."

"Good, then, Ludvig vill be along soon. He finishes early today," she said. "Henry, help our guests with their animals. Remove their saddles and make them comfortable in the barn."

"Ya, come," Henry said as he turned and walked toward the barn. We led the animals inside, removed the packs and saddles and walked the beasts into stalls. Henry pitched lucerne down from the loft and saw to getting oats and water.

As we returned to the house, we saw a man and wagon in the distance, coming from the south. He stood at the front of the wagon with his feet set wide apart. He held the reins for a team of big work horses. We walked and watched as the man slowly approached on a path across the field. Standing in the wagon in the softening afternoon light, he looked like a king in a lonely procession across his rural realm. As they drew closer, the figures got bigger and bigger until the horses, driver and wagon stopped before us, looking massive and strong. Henry grabbed the harness, and the man jumped down to greet us.

"Hello. I am Ludvig, Ludvig Paul. Velcom to our home."

He spoke with the same thick accent as his wife. Will stepped forward, shook Ludwig Paul's hand, thanked him for his hospitality and made introductions all around. Ben showed no unusual signs, but I was stunned. I had never seen such size in a man, horses, or a wagon, for that matter. I judged Mr. Paul to be about 70, but age hadn't slowed him a bit.

"Ya, ya, please, please, stay for zupper and dancing. Our neighbors vill be here later," Mr. Paul urged. We accepted, of course, and as Henry led the team to the barn, Mr. Paul swept us into the house.

"Elsebein, my Anna Maria Elsebein," Mr. Paul called, "you have met our guests, Hawkins, ya?"

"Ya, Ludvig, I have," she replied, "they stay for zupper and dancing."

"Das good," Mr. Paul exclaimed. "We have vunderbar time."

A long kitchen and dining room ran the length of the front of the house. Its floor was stone. There were huge, rough-hewn walnut beams overhead. Oak and walnut made up the window and door frames, mantelpieces and other woodwork. The blue limestone walls were two or 2-1/2 feet thick, depending on whether they were at the back and front of the house, or at the ends, where the fireplaces were. Everything about the house looked strong and manly. There was barely a woman's delicate touch anywhere.

While Mrs. Paul worked at the stove, hearth and table, Mr. Paul sat us in the dining area and offered beer or spring water. We chose water, he had beer.

"What brings you to Missouri?" he asked.

"We're on our way to Kansas City and then on the Oregon Trail to homestead in Idaho," Will replied.

Mr. Paul paused for a moment and then asked the question we had heard many times before and would hear many times after.

"Why don't you go by railroad?" he asked, almost in a roar. He made big gestures and a had voice like a bullhorn. He had already drunk a whole mug of beer.

Will explained our reasons. His manner seemed almost soft and retiring compared to Mr. Paul's.

"May we camp in your meadow tonight?" Will asked.

"Nein!" Mr. Paul bellowed. "You vill sleep comfortable and warm in our house!"

Henry came up from the barn and helped his mother spread the supper on the table in front of us.

"Henry, have beer," Mr. Paul roared.

"Nein, danke, Papa," Henry replied, almost sheepishly. He turned to Will and asked, "Mr. Hawkins, why did you want to see the Boone house?"

"We had heard that Daniel Boone helped his son, Nathan, build this house and that Daniel had died here," Will replied. "Our ancestor, George Hawkins, helped Daniel Boone cut the Wilderness Trail into Kentucky in 1775. We couldn't pass this place without paying a visit and our respects."

"Vunderbar!" Mr. Paul roared before either Henry or Mrs. Paul had a chance to speak.

We ate a hearty meal, and when we finished, Ben and I offered to help Mrs. Paul, just as we did with Beth at home.

"Ya, sure, danke," she accepted.

Mr. Paul offered Will a pipe, which he politely declined, not being a smoker. Mr. Paul had barely lit and drawn on his pipe when the peacocks announced that the first neighbors had arrived.

We met the Diederich family—Jacob and Dina Diederich and their five children. They had come from about a mile up the road, where they had a farm and log home on the other side of the creek. Mr. Diederich was a jovial man. He carried a small barrel on his shoulder. He announced he had brought a keg of his best honey beer, and he needed help pounding the spigot in. Ludwig Paul said he would help do that up in the dance hall when they put a spigot in the Spring Brewery barrel.

Mrs. Diederich carried a large platter covered with muslin cloth. Charles and Anna, the eldest children, each carried a covered bowl.

"Come, come," Mrs. Paul urged, "bring your things up to the dance hall. Put the dishes on the tables there."

The whole Diederich family followed Mrs. Paul up the hall stairs. A moment later, two more wagons drove up outside, joined by a chorus of peacock screams. Henry opened the big walnut door, and the Langemann and Niemeier families came in. Mr. Conrad Langemann carried a string instrument he called a zither, and Mr. Andrew Niemeier had a fiddle. Mrs. Mena Langemann and the two eldest of five children carried large, covered platters. Mr. Niemeier and his wife, Caroline, were older than the Diederichs and the Langemanns. Two of their four children, August and Catherine, were young adults. August had an accordion, while Caroline, one of the younger children, and their mother carried covered bowls and a large glass jar of frothy amber liquid. Mrs. Paul came down the stairs, greeted the new arrivals and urged them up to the dance hall.

The last family to come was the Staakes. Mr. Charles Staake carried an infant boy in a small, handwoven cradle. The Staakes brought no instruments, but Mrs. Elizabeth Staake and the older children had platters of food. We and the Pauls had just finished supper, and if the arriving families had too, I wondered what would become of all the food the neighbors brought.

The third-floor dance hall ran the full length of the house. It had a polished walnut floor and, at each end, a stone fireplace and hearth. Two long, narrow tables sat at the south end, and straight-back chairs lined the walls nearly all the way around. There were about 30 people all told, and everyone was in high spirits, happy to be among friends and ready for a good time after a week of farm work.

Henry asked August to help bring the beer barrel from the springhouse. When they returned, Mr. Diederich helped them knock wooden spigots into the Spring Brewery and honey beer barrels.

As the musicians got ready to play, Ben went to the barn and came back with his banjo and fiddle cases. Earlier, when we met the neighbors downstairs, I had heard one of the men mutter "Schwarze." I didn't know what the word meant. Will told me that the Pauls and their neighbors were from Germany and *Schwarze* was the German word for Negro. The neighbor had commented to himself about Ben. But in the dance hall, when Ben opened his cases and took out his banjo and fiddle, I heard only "Ya, ya, ya" from many who gathered around.

The musicians started playing music that was new to me. The neighbors and the Pauls immediately joined hands and formed a large ring. They motioned for Will and me to join the dance. Ben stood with the musicians, listened to their playing for a few moments and then played along. Some time back, I had stopped being amazed at Ben's ability. I just took it in stride. He played and sang as easily as I breathed.

The beer flowed freely, and there was lots of laughing and cheering. The dancing changed when the music changed. Mrs. Paul bounded up to me, extended both her hands and said, "Mein Schatzie, dance vith me." I didn't have a choice. We reeled around the room, dancing what she said was a polka. She urged me to ask one of the girls to dance, now that I knew how. I guessed Anna Diederich was about my age, so I asked her. She was a tall girl with long brown hair and brown eyes. She had a pretty smile. We danced the polka, and Anna did more leading than I did. Between dances, I asked her what the foods spread across the tables were. She quickly pointed to one after another.

"Bratwurst, Sauerkraut, Knockwurst, potato salad, Sommerwurst, Limburger, venison, turkey and Pumpernickel bread." When she mentioned the bread, she grimaced and held her belly, although I didn't know why.

"My papa lets me sip beer at dance parties," Anna said. "Does yours?"

"Uh, I don't know, Anna," I answered. "I'll ask."

Will stood with large a mug of beer in his hand, talking with Mr. Staake. The music and crowd had become so loud that he had to bend down and put his ear to my mouth to hear me.

"Anna says her papa lets her sip beer at dance parties," I said. "May I?"

Will straightened up, turned to Mr. Staake and winked, and then turned back to me, smiling a big, broad smile.

"Why, I suppose," he said, nodding in case I couldn't hear him above the din. "A few sips will be fine."

I took a mug from the table and filled it about a quarter way up from the Spring Brewery barrel. I didn't much like the taste, but I didn't want to look foolish in front of Anna. She sipped freely from her mug, and I matched her sip for sip. A few minutes later I felt a lot more like dancing, and Anna and I stepped very lively as we wheeled around the room. I heard myself singing nonsense words out loud, and I didn't give a hoot what anybody thought. Actually, anybody who noticed just clapped and cheered me on.

"Come, let's dance a schottische with the other children," Anna urged as the music tempo changed. The children gathered in the center of the room, joined hands and formed a circle. As we danced, the circle turned and turned like a paddlewheel lying on its side. We laughed and sang as the circle spun. The adults sang, clapped, tapped their feet and cheered us on.

When the schottische tune ended, Mr. Paul walked to the center of the room, raised his hands over his head and called for quiet in his big, bellowing voice.

"Please, please, everyone, shhhhh, quiet, please. It is time for our songbird, Dina Diederich, to sing for us," he said.

Mrs. Diederich blushed a little but smiled gracefully and walked to a place just in front of the musicians. She gripped her skirt at both sides and curtsied delicately. She turned and nodded to Mr. Langemann. He plucked the zither strings gently with his fingertips, making a beautiful, light, tinkling sound. The room hushed, Mrs. Diederich took a deep breath and began singing a lilting German ballad.

> *Muss ich denn, muss ich denn*
> *Zum Städtele hinaus*
> *Zum Städtele hinaus*
> *Und du mein Schatz bleibst hier*

She sang several verses in a sweet, high voice that perfectly matched the song and the zither.

"That's my mama," Anna whispered.

"What's she saying?" I whispered.

"It's about a soldier who must go away. He promises his girl that he'll come back to her," she whispered.

When Mrs. Diederich finished, everyone applauded warmly. "That was beautiful, Dina, danke schön," several people said.

Mrs. Diederich returned to her seat, and with the room still quiet, Ben stepped out in front of the musicians. All heads turned toward him. He raised his fiddle to his chin, bowed one high note and dropped his arms to his sides. In a pure, high voice that filled the room, he sang,

> *Beautiful dreamer, wake unto me*
> *Starlight and dewdrops are waiting for thee . . .*

He sang the Stephen Foster song all the way through, and I saw his singing have the effect it often did. People seemed to be carried away. Tears welled in at least the women's eyes.

When Ben finished, and as everyone applauded, he motioned to Will and me to join him. If we hadn't been drinking beer, I doubt we would have done what Ben asked us to do. We stood one on each side and slightly behind him. He raised his fiddle, bowed one long, low note, dropped his arms to his sides and sang,

Swing low, sweet chariot

Will and I joined in at the second line.

Comin' for to carry me home
Swing low, sweet chariot
Comin' for to carry me home
I looked over Jordan and what did I see
Comin' for to carry me home
A band of angels comin' after me
Comin' for to carry me home

We continued with the verses, and the neighbors joined in on the choruses. Every voice in the room sang as loudly and richly as it could. All swayed to the music as they sang. Smiles filled every face as we closed, and tears left trails across many cheeks.

We sang, danced, ate and drank late into the night. When the neighbors left for home, it was a good thing the horses knew the way.

23

We got a late start that Sunday morning after the party. Everybody was moving very slowly, even after strong coffee. We said goodbye to the Paul family and over the next few days fell into a traveling rhythm that we would follow, more or less, for the next three months or so. That meant starting early every day, unless it was pouring rain. We stopped for rest and food at about noon, depending on where we found water, grass and wood. We went into camp for the day late in the afternoon. Again, the time varied some, depending on where the water, grass and wood were. We made about 20 miles a day.

Toward the end of the third day away from the Boone home, we had crossed into Callaway County. The river road was some distance up from the Missouri bottoms, and the country was hilly. Each valley we crossed had a creek, and most were muddy. But Little Tavern Creek had a gravel bottom, and the water was clear. The creek was lined with sycamores, some with low branches running out across the water. There must have been ledges or a cliff face nearby because cliff swallows darted to and fro, snatching insects as they flew. The air was rich with birdsongs and bug noises.

The bank was low and the water shallow at the crossing. The animals' hoofs stirred the bottom and sent light clouds of silt downstream. Up the slope on the west side of the creek was a flat, grassy area and a grove of trees. Will rode up to take a look, then waved to us to follow.

Hardwoods and conifers stood side by side in the grove, and green grass grew tall in the open areas. A rock fire ring filled with fresh coals and ashes said that others had found this a good place to camp.

We unsaddled the horses first. Will asked Ben and me to walk them to the creek for water while he unpacked the mules. Ben and I haltered the horses and led them down the slope to the crossing. We walked upstream a short way to a point where the bank was a little higher. It was shady and cool in the creek bed beneath the sycamores. The horses bent to the water and drank.

I told Ben I had to take care of some business in the brush at the top of the bank. I climbed straight up, leaving Ben with the three horses. I squatted in the brush and a few moments later heard a big commotion down near Ben. It sounded like several riders in a hurry, crossing the creek from the east. They stopped short, with water splashing, horses neighing and a gruff voice shouting, "There's the nigger! Get him!"

The next voice I heard was Ben's. "Early! Get Will!" The three words electrified me. I stood, pulled my britches up and looked in Ben's direction. I couldn't see him through the brush.

I ran up the slope toward camp faster than I knew I could run. I saw from a distance that Will had one mule unpacked and had started on the second.

"Will, Will, some men have Ben!" I screamed. By the time I reached Will, he had grabbed two Winchesters and a pistol, and was on the mule's back reaching down to grab my hand and yank me up.

"Tell me exactly where Ben is," Will shouted as we rode.

"He's in the creek just up from the crossing."

"I'll ride to that spot, dismount and sight Ben from the bank. You crouch on the bank just up from my spot. Shoot only if I yell 'Shoot.'"

We jumped off the mule and ran a few steps to the bank. Will spotted Ben and motioned to me to move a little upstream. I looked through the brush and trees, and saw two men mounted and three standing. They had Ben up on one of our horses. There was a noose around Ben's neck. The rope draped over a syca-more branch above him. His hands were bound behind his back.

"He's on May Belle, and he's digging in his heels," Will said to me. "Don't shoot."

Will shot into a boulder on the opposite bank. The bullet rang and ricocheted. May Belle stood still as a statue. The other horses moved nervously but didn't run.

"Take the noose off his neck, or you're all dead men," Will shouted.

One man raised his rifle, and Will shot him in the foot. That stopped them all.

"Take the noose off and back away from his horse. Dismount and drop your guns," Will shouted.

I had one man in my sights. My heart was beating fast and hard up into my throat. The men did as Will said.

"OK, Early, we'll show ourselves. Move down the bank as I do, but keep apart from me. Stay ready to shoot." We moved slowly down the bank with our rifles ready.

"Kick your guns into the water," Will commanded. The men did as he said. I saw they weren't outlaws, but they *were* vigilan-tes. They looked like farmers and tradesmen.

"Walk backwards across the creek," Will said. They did. "Early, keep your gun on them. And don't you men get any ideas about my boy. You're looking at the best shot in the county back home." Leave it to Will to make me feel 10 feet tall.

Will reached up and slit the rope off Ben's wrists. Ben jumped down, and Will handed him the rifle. Will took the pistol from his belt and spoke to the men.

"Now, just suppose you men tell me what's going on," Will said.

"A nigger stole horses east of Bluffton and headed west. Them's horses and that's a nigger. We want him." The biggest man spat out the words.

"Those are my horses, and these are my sons," Will said.

"You got a nigger son?" the man sneered.

"I said these are my sons," Will repeated, then spoke to me.

"Early, quickly tie their horses and ours. Tie them where they stand."

I scampered about grabbing horses and tying them. Will and Ben kept their guns on the men. When I finished, Will spoke to the men again.

"I want you men to strip to your underclothes. Be quick about it! Move!" he shouted. The men looked at each other and hesitated. Will shouted again, angry. "Move!"

The men scrambled to get their boots and shirts off.

"Everything!" Will shouted when they slowed at their britches. In a minute, five men stood in their underdrawers at the edge of the creek.

"Start walking east," Will said. The man with the shot foot moved slower than the others. It looked as if Will's bullet had taken a toe off.

"Your horses, clothes and guns will be here tomorrow. If we see you back here before then, we'll shoot to kill on sight," Will said.

They grumbled as they moved up the bank. We crossed and followed them. We watched from the top of the east bank, making sure they kept going. The last thing we saw was five sets of underdrawers walking up a long grade on the road. All moved tenderly in stocking feet. One man was limping.

"Early, stay here and watch them until Ben and I gather the guns, clothes and horses and move up the other bank," Will said. When they had, I crossed back, joined them, and we walked on to our camp. We unsaddled their horses and picketed them with ours, spread out across the grass. We unpacked the other mules, picketed them and set up camp, all the while keeping one eye out for the men. We didn't say much until we sat to cook and eat. Ben spoke first.

"That was close. I thought I had sung my last song."

"As soon as I saw your heels in May Belle's sides, I knew we had them licked," Will said.

"I thought my heart was gonna beat right out of my throat," I said. "I never had a man in my rifle sights before."

We looked at each other and smiled big, satisfied smiles.

"We'll have to take turns and keep watch till dawn," Will said. Ben and I nodded and yupped in agreement.

"They'll get back home, find out they were wrong and come back tomorrow for their horses and guns," Will said.

"And we'll be halfway to Cedar City," Ben said, looking at our map.

In the 20 or so years that Will had been a riverboat pilot and then captain, I'm sure he handled a lot of desperate characters and tense situations. A captain is responsible for hundreds of passengers, a boatload of freight, the crew and the steamer itself. The job requires the man who holds it to be commanding and courageous, but temperate. I had seen Will act as a captain must when he deposited the thief Harry Manning on an island in the Cumberland, when he helped rescue scores of passengers as the *Robert Moore* sank at the head of Cumberland Island, and when he saved a *George Hawkins* passenger from drowning in the Mississippi. But until five vigilantes tried to lynch Ben at Little Tavern Creek, I hadn't seen Will be the man he was that day. Before that afternoon, I had held Will in high respect. After it, my respect rose a hundred notches.

At twilight, two of the horses farthest down the slope toward the road whinnied and tugged on their ropes. They looked like shadows dancing in the fading light. We leapt up, grabbed our rifles and jumped out in front of the fire.

"Who's there?" Will shouted.

"My wagon's thrown a wheel down at the road. Can you help me?" a voice called back.

"Show yourself," Will shouted. "Come this way." A clothed man in a wide-brimmed hat appeared among the horses and mules.

"Come ahead," Will shouted. We relaxed some but held our rifles ready. The man walked up to within about 30 feet of us, stopped and pushed his hat back, up and away from his forehead.

"Name's John Snyder," he said. "I'm driving east. I thought I could make Bluffton for the night. I have friends there. But my wagon's thrown a wheel, and I can't lift the wagon and the wheel at the same time. Can you help me?"

"Not tonight, we can't," Will said. "In the morning, yes, but not tonight. If you want to unhitch your horse and bring your gear, you're welcome to stay the night in camp with us. I'm Will Hawkins and these are my sons Ben and Early."

"Yessir," Mr. Snyder said. "I'll do that. Much obliged."

He disappeared down the hill and returned in a few minutes, leading his horse. It had a large canvas sack draped across its back. He dropped the sack to the ground, opened a leather strap near one end and pulled a picket stake and mallet out from inside. He led his horse out into the grass, drove the stake, tied the horse, removed its harness and returned.

"We've already had our supper, but there's some left, and you're welcome to it," Will offered. Will had relaxed, but Ben and I still eyed the stranger warily.

"Yessir," Mr. Snyder said, "I'd like to eat, much obliged."

Ben spooned stew into a bowl for him. It was only when he sat by the fire, removed his hat and began eating that I got a good look at him. He was a young man with a kind, open face. There was an earnestness about him. If he was armed, his gun must have been tucked away in his canvas sack.

"I'm from Saint Charles," he said, "but lately I've had a farm near Mechanicsville. I do some surveying there too. I'm thinking about a farm out here in Callaway sooner or later. Been here looking the past few days. How about you fellows?"

"We're on our way to Kansas City and from there, across the Plains," Will replied.

"Need a wagon?" Mr. Snyder asked. "My cousin's a wagon-maker in Independence. You'll pass through there. Was here in Callaway. Used to visit him summers when I was a kid. Name's Henry Crump. Makes a good wagon, even if one might throw a wheel now and again."

"No," Will replied, "we won't need a wagon, but thanks for the information."

"Going to Oregon?" Mr. Snyder asked.

"Idaho," Will replied.

Then, of course, Mr. Snyder asked what we would come to call "*The* Question."

"Why don't you take the train?"

I spoke up and explained why. I thought maybe Will was getting weary of answering.

"That's a ride I'd like to make some day," Mr. Snyder said. "Where did you camp east of here?"

"This is our third night camping along the river road," Will said. "We spent Saturday night at the Boone house on Femme Osage Creek."

"The stone house?" Mr. Snyder asked.

"Yes, that's the one," Will replied.

"I know that house," Mr. Snyder said. "Some of my kin built it. I'm a Boone on my mother's side. Daniel Boone was my great-great-grandfather."

Ben and I exchanged surprised glances.

"Well, then, we're connected, in a way," Will said. "My great-grandfather blazed the Wilderness Trail with Daniel Boone."

"Well, I'll be!" Mr. Snyder exclaimed and slapped his knee. "Maybe I ought to cross the Plains with you. It's like keeping a tradition." He looked pleased at his own recognition. "But I don't suppose I'll leave Missouri. I have my eye on a place right here in Callaway. You know, this county was named for a Boone, my grandfather, Captain James Callaway, son of Daniel's daughter, Jemima. If you want to meet Boones, you've come to the right place."

After a while, we bedded down. John Snyder fell right off to sleep. We didn't tell him about standing watch for vigilantes. In the morning, all but Mr. Snyder were a little groggy. We had each stood our watches, the vigilantes hadn't returned, and Mr. Snyder was the only one who had slept through the night.

After breakfast, Ben stayed at camp with a rifle as Mr. Snyder, Will and I started down the slope toward the road. We stopped among the beasts scattered at their pickets. Mr. Snyder harnessed his horse and pulled its picket. He remarked that we had a lot of horses for only three of us on the trail. Will explained that five of the horses belonged to some visitors who would be back for them that day.

"Are the mules yours?" Mr. Snyder asked.

"Yes, they are," Will replied. "They're Kentucky mules."

"They're fine looking mules," Mr. Snyder said. "Callaway folks will admire them. Folks here raise mules for cane and cotton far south. I have to give you a friendly warning, though. Some small-minded people in these parts haven't gotten over the War. They were Rebels then, and they're Rebels now. Not everyone, mind you. Most folks are decent, but a few will object to your Negro trail mate."

"We've already learned about those objections," Will said. "We'll have to be careful. Thanks for the warning."

We reached the wagon, which sat lopsided on three wheels at the side of the road. The thrown wheel lay flat nearby. The three of us hoisted the wagon and braced it with a fallen tree limb we had yanked out of the brush. We lifted the wheel and rolled it into place. Mr. Snyder set a new axle pin with his mallet.

"I think that'll do her," he said. "Much obliged, gentlemen, and happy to make your acquaintance. Good luck on your trip west."

"Always willing to help a neighbor or fellow traveler," Will said. "We wanted to meet a Boone here in Missouri, and we're glad we did."

"If you want to meet another, look Henry Crump up in Independence, even if you don't want a wagon," Mr. Snyder added with a grin.

Will and I shook Mr. Snyder's hand, he climbed up onto his wagon seat and headed east. He turned, took off his hat and waved it as his horse gained its pace. We returned the goodbye with waves of our hats.

Will and I walked back up the slope to our camp, where Ben had pulled the horses' pickets and saddled all three. We packed the mules, and before we mounted to ride west, re-picketed the vigilantes' horses in fresh grass. We piled their tack, rifles and clothes near the fire ring. We supposed they'd be by later in the day, and we hoped they wouldn't follow us west. We took all their cartridges.

It was slow going early in the day, as the road stayed up in the hills and out of the Missouri bottoms. By the time we reached Portland, about four long miles from our previous night's camp, we were all but sure the vigilantes weren't on our tail. Even so, when I scouted ahead for eats, we made sure I was always west of Will and Ben. After three days of dried beans, rice and jerked venison, we were ready for greens, game and whatever other fresh foods we could find.

In the two miles or so until we got out of the hills and into the Missouri bottoms at Logan Creek, I found watercress at a spring up from the road and then picked a sackful of riverside grape leaves and cleavers. I also bagged a squirrel.

We went into camp up from the road just past where Mud Creek joined Logan Creek. Ben got a rabbit, and I found wild garlic and fairy spuds. We had everything we needed for a fine pot of stew. The sunset blazed red, then a crescent moon cut the purple twilight. In the stillness, a Pacific Railroad locomotive whistle drifted across the bottoms from the far side of the river. The sound had echoed off the bluffs at the south bank where the tracks ran.

In the morning, our pace across the bottoms was quicker than the day before in the hills. We moved through the flat country fairly quickly. The fields were planted in grain, corn and beans, from the road clear down to the river. From bluff to bluff, I judged the valley to be about two miles wide.

We reached Saint Aubert well before noon. The town was clustered near the steamboat landing. It was probably 10 times the size of Portland. A man named Sam Nichols ran a ferry across to the rail line near Medora on the south side. We watered our animals in town and bought a sack of fresh coffee beans at the grocery. Just as Mr. Snyder had said, several men there admired our mules. We caught some chatter about Robert Kemp, a murderer who owed his life to slick lawyers. Three local men were angered enough to still be talking about a verdict that was about two weeks old.

We passed through Côte sans dessein, a town not quite so big as Saint Aubert, in mid-afternoon. Ben said it was along this stretch of river that the returning Corps of Discovery rejoiced at their first sight of cows, knowing it meant they had reached civilization. Our aim was to make Cedar City, opposite Jefferson City, by nightfall. We had tempted ourselves with the thought of hotel meals on china dishes and a good sleep in soft beds.

The air grew thicker as the day got older. By late afternoon, dark clouds had gathered in the west. A north wind raced freely across the bottoms, rustling young wheat and corn, and flipping the leaves of bean plants that sat in long lines above the furrows.

The rain started just as we caught sight of the Capitol, high on the bluff across the river. The building's columned front faced downstream, and its dome rose far above anything else in view. Having seen the Capitol, we knew Cedar City was just ahead and didn't bother to stop and put on our slickers.

The rain came and went, as did the sun, one minute lighting the rain drops, the next disappearing behind a curtain of clouds. I turned in my saddle to see a full arc rainbow stretching the width of the valley. Will and Ben were in front, with their hat brims pulled down and their heads held low against the rain. I called to them to look. When they turned, I watched their eyes widen and their grim faces break into ear-to-ear grins. Of course, the beasts paid no mind at all. They just plodded on, getting wetter with every step.

The rain clouds passed over, and we rode into town with about an hour of fresh sunshine left in the day. The Cedar City Hotel's sign said "Absolem Hughes, Proprietor." There was a livery adjacent. Things couldn't have been more convenient.

The Chicago & Alton Railroad line ended at Cedar City. When the last train of the day reached town, its engineer ran the locomotive onto a turntable above the depot. Passengers came off the cars, grabbed handles and pushed to turn the engine around. It would rest there till morning, when the engineer backed it down to South Cedar Station, picked up passengers, freight and mail, and headed north toward Fulton.

We enjoyed a generous supper in the hotel dining room and then walked to the landing. There would be no riverboats till morning. The steam ferry that ran across to Jefferson City finished its last crossing of the day and shut down for the night. The freshet we had seen when we first entered the Missouri had long since gone, and the river's flow had returned to its steady serenity. Purple martins darted about, nabbing insects in the last light of day. Red-winged blackbirds clung to tall marsh reeds at the mouth of Cedar Creek and bobbed back and forth, looking like metronomes. It struck me that although the river was wider and stronger, so far the natural world in the Missouri Valley wasn't much different from that of the Cumberland or Ohio valleys.

We had a good sleep in comfortable beds that night and a satisfying breakfast in the morning. When we walked the beasts out of the livery, even they looked refreshed and content.

We crossed on the steam ferry. Our only business in Jefferson City was to locate the telegraph office. We found it at Jefferson Landing near the Lohman Building and the Union Hotel. We were at the base of the bluff below the Capitol and the governor's mansion. Will wired Beth, telling her we were traveling overland and would be in Kansas City before month's end. For safety, we rode with very little cash. Will told Beth he would telegraph again from Kansas City and ask her to wire us money there.

24

The Pacific Railroad tracks and the public road ran side by side for about four miles above Jefferson City. At Upper Jefferson, the tracks turned straight west. The public road ran northwest along the river but, for the most part, well up from the bank. The country was lush rolling hills. Woods mixed with open prairie and planted fields. Where the prairie was fenced, cattle and horses grazed in fresh grass. The fields were planted mostly to corn and wheat. A steady southwest wind kept the sycamores and cottonwoods busy.

We came to the river at Marion at about noon. It was a way-landing, but there were no steamers at the bank. The town was about midway along a big, gentle bend in the river. The banks were low on both sides and thickly lined with trees—mostly tall, straight cottonwoods. Whole drift trees lay on both banks, some freshly carried from above by the river and others having lodged long enough ago to now be completely stripped of bark and small branches. There were few people about. We found some graze for the beasts, watered them, had our meal and got under way.

The road stayed close to the river, crossed Little Moniteau Creek and led to Sandy Hook, another quiet way-landing. Then the road turned sharply west away from the river and up into high, gently rolling prairie. We went into camp alongside a little creek our map didn't name. We unpacked and picketed the animals, set up our camp, and walked out with rifles and sacks to see what we could hunt and gather for supper and Saturday's breakfast.

Along the road, our idea was to halt at each way-landing and scheduled steamer stop. We thought we might get recent word on the state of the prairie grass west of Kansas City from a boat going down. If we heard there was graze enough for our beasts along the Oregon Trail, we might catch a steamer going up to Kansas City and, thus, quicken our pace.

But since the railroad had reached Kansas City some years earlier, and now ran clear to the Pacific, steamer traffic on the Missouri had dropped to just a few boats. There were no steamers or even word of them at Marion and Sandy Hook. At Boonville, where a Pacific Railroad spur line ran up from the south, and a Kansas City & Northern Railroad bridge crossed the river, there were no boats due, going up or down.

Arrow Rock was the next landing before the road turned west to shortcut a huge north bend in the river. Just below town, we scared off two turkey vultures feeding on a box turtle a wheel had crushed in the road. We came into Arrow Rock shortly before noon on Monday the 13th. Word at the landing had the *Mountaineer* due, coming down from Wyandotte, Kansas City and other points above. We decided to wait for her.

"We'll see a thunderstorm late this afternoon," Will said as we stood at the landing, "so we ought to find the livery and hotel." How he knew a storm was coming, I don't know. We rode up from the landing and hitched the animals at the rail in front of the Arrow Rock Hotel. The sign read "Richard Horn, Proprietor."

"We had no trouble at the Cedar City Hotel," Will said, "but now we're on the south side of the river. They call this area 'Little Dixie.' Things might be different here. We ought to make sure we can get a room before we put the beasts in the livery."

The three of us walked into the hotel lobby. Will went to the desk and rang the bell. Ben and I stood a few steps back. A man I supposed by his age was the owner came through a doorway behind the desk. He looked first at Will, then at Ben and me. He seemed uneasy. Will drew the man's eyes and held him in a hard stare.

"We have seven animals for the livery, and my sons and I need a room for the night." By his tone, you couldn't mistake Will's meaning, and the man didn't. He looked down at the desk and fidgeted with the page corners of the register. He weighed his choices. Will grabbed the register and quickly turned it to face him. He jerked the pen out of the inkwell and wrote on the register page. He reached into his pocket and nearly slammed his money down on the desk.

"If people here treat my son Ben with the respect he's due for being a man, and if they ask him real nice, he might just play and sing in the tavern this evening." As Will spun sharply around and walked away from the desk, he gave us a sly smile and a quick wink.

We put the animals in Crockett's Livery, secured our packed gear and carried our baggage up to our room. Will said he wanted to sit on the hotel porch with his Darwin. He suggested Ben and I go on down to the landing. If he heard the *Mountaineer*'s whistle or landing bell, he'd join us, he said. He cautioned us to watch for signs of the storm so we could get out of it before it got us.

Ben and I walked one block over from Main to Van Buren and then down the curved slope to the landing. The hollows coming up from the river were thick with trees and brush. There were a few men and wagons at the warehouses but no boats. The river flowed about twice as fast as I could walk. It was a rich brown flow about 200 yards wide. A ferry sat on the opposite bank. It was the link to the Boone's Lick country. A blue heron stood motionless in the shallows upstream. Just down from the landing, a lone fisherman sat in a chair on the grassy bank. We walked over to say hello.

"What are you trying for?" Ben asked.

"Anything that's out there," the fisherman replied.

"What's out there?" I asked.

"Oh, I might get me a blue cat or a croaker," he replied.

He was a short, squat old man with a wrinkled jaw and no fringe of hair below his hat brim. He had huge ears and what looked like little bushes growing out of them. He had three lines in the water, stretched out from poles standing upright in braces jammed into the bank. He sat in a wicker chair that he must have brought with him.

"I suppose those cats and croakers smell the bait, cause they're sure not going to see it in this water," Ben said.

"They smells it all right," the old man said. He kept an eye on his lines, ready to grab a pole that showed the right motion. "See how I got my britches bottoms tucked into my boots?" he asked. "If you boys are gonna be here in the grass, you better tuck yours.

Chiggers. You boys got chiggers where you come from?"

"Oh, yeah, we have chiggers," I replied. "My mama has me dust my legs with sulphur powder and perfumed talc to keep the chiggers away." Ben and I tucked our britches into our boots.

"If they gets ya," the man said, "you'll itch like the blazes, and you'll have red spots for a year. Them's mean, long-lasting bugs, them chiggers."

"We're from Kentucky, heading to Kansas City and then across to Idaho," I said.

"My family was on our way to Oregon in '42. This is as far as we got. Used to farm, can't no more," he said.

"I'm Ben and this is Early," Ben said.

"Marshall, Richard Marshall. Wish I could catch a fish," he said.

"We hear the *Mountaineer*'s due," I said.

"Probably not till 8 or 9 o'clock tonight," he said. "She'll be comin' in by torch light. I won't be here to meet her. I'll be asleep in my bed."

"What's a flood like here?" Ben asked.

"I've seen 20 feet of water where you're standing," the old man replied.

He had a forked stick leaning against the side of his chair. I thought maybe he had been whittling, but I didn't see a knife or shavings.

"We usually fish from a small boat on the Cumberland," Ben said.

"Ain't got no boat," the old man said. "That far line is probably 100 yards out in the deep channel. That's where them cats are. Got cut gizzard shad on my hooks."

He suddenly grabbed the forked stick, stood up and walked out into the grass behind his chair. We didn't follow. He jammed the fork into the grass, bent down and came back up holding a two-foot snake behind its head.

"Got 'em! It's a garter, and he smells foul already," he said. "One of you boys be a good feller and carry this garter back to the bluff away from my bait."

I walked over, took the snake from him and carried it to the edge of the grass. A line of trees grew at the base of the bluff. I put the garter down and watched him slither away. A flash of orange caught my eye up in a sycamore. It was an oriole bouncing about, getting insects. I walked back to the chair. Ben and the old man stood staring upriver. Dark gray, almost black clouds grew up far above the distant treetops.

"My daughter will be down to fetch me. You boys go on ahead," the old man said.

We said goodbye and headed back to town. The sky got darker by the second. A strong north wind swept the leaves and made the branches sway. Will had been right about the storm. We found him sitting on the hotel porch with his book. We were no sooner under the roof than the first big, fat raindrops plopped into the street and sent up little dust clouds. The dust didn't last long. In the next few minutes, a punishing rain turned the street to mud. The whole sky turned near black. Lightning flashed, with loud, cracking thunderclaps right on its heels. We were in the center of a storm that was moving quickly north to south. At places, the rain ran off the roof in unbroken sheets.

"I wonder how the *Mountaineer* will take this storm," Will said. "I guess we'll know shortly."

"Not till 8 or 9 o'clock tonight a man at the river said," Ben added.

"That late, eh?" Will said. "Well, that'll give us time for a good supper—under a roof."

Our hotel was a large, two-story, fired-brick structure built by slaves in the Federal style in the 1830s. The dining room and saloon were in separate rooms on opposite sides of the lobby. We had our supper in the dining room, where our waiter proudly acquainted us with the history of the building. Toward the end of the meal, he spoke for his boss.

"Mr. Horn says you play and sing," he said to Ben. "The *Mountaineer*'s not due till about 9 o'clock. Do you think you might wanna do some entertainin' in the saloon?"

"Yes, I think I'd like that," Ben replied. "I haven't had a chance to play in a few days, and I'm beginning to get a little itchy." Ben smiled his bright, much-obliged smile. He had learned years earlier how to handle himself in the white man's world. He went up to our room and came back with his fiddle and banjo.

We walked across to the saloon and took a table next to an open area at the far end of the bar. Ben started with his fiddle and his choice of Stephen Foster songs. He stuck with the toe-tappers and avoided the ballads. The place got lively pretty quick. Several men left and returned a few minutes later with their wives. They pushed tables and chairs back to open an area for dancing. People who didn't dance stood and clapped and tapped their feet.

When Ben paused for a breather, a young bartender came out from behind the bar, spoke to him and motioned to the banjo at our table. The voices in the room were so loud, I couldn't hear what the barkeep said. He stepped up to our table and had to nearly shout for us to hear.

"Name's Sam Crew. Ben says I can join him on the banjo."

"If it's all right with Ben, it's all right with us," Will said.

Ben and Sam went on playing lively tunes one after another. Word must have gotten around, because the saloon filled with people—dancing, clapping, toe-tapping, smoking and drinking. I was moved to demonstrate my step dancing, and Will was on his feet clapping and tapping along with everybody else.

In the excitement, I lost track of the time, but it must have been close to 9 o'clock when a boy came into the saloon with a hand bell and a megaphone. He stood on a chair, rang the bell and shouted through the megaphone, "Boat's in!"

The room nearly cleared out. Almost everybody, including us, streamed out of the saloon and headed for the landing—on foot, on horseback, in wagons, in buggies, by every means available.

The *Mountaineer* had already lowered her stage to the bank when we got there. She had two basket torches blazing light from her bow, and men quickly brought other torches from the warehouses. The whole landing and the *Mountaineer* glowed orange in the flickering light. She was a sidewheeler about 200 feet long with a very shallow draft. If she was true to her name and went all the way up to Fort Benton, she'd need a shallow draft.

There was a flurry of activity around the warehouses, and between them and the boat. Freight came off and freight went on. There was no railroad at Arrow Rock, so the few boats still on the river were the town's main link to the outside world.

When there was a break in the traffic across the stage, we boarded and found the captain. He was a man older than Will, I guessed about 60. As we approached, and before Will could greet him and introduce us, the captain pointed to Will and said, "You're a steamboat man. I can spot 'em a hull's length away."

"Yes, I am," Will replied, with as much excitement as the captain. "And thank you, sir, for the compliment!"

"The mates and my other men can take care of all this business," the captain said. "What can I do for you gentlemen?"

"I'm Will Hawkins, and these are my sons, Ben and Early."

"I'm Robert Wright, master of the *Mountaineer*. Welcome aboard. Are you men going down? Can I offer you passage?"

The captain wore white shirtsleeves and dark blue cap, vest and trousers. He had removed his jacket in a nod to the warm spring weather. He spoke with great exuberance, as if he was thrilled to meet other rivermen.

"No, but thank you, we're going up," Will replied.

"Up?" Captain Wright asked, as he arched his eyebrows, seeking details without saying so.

"Yes, Kansas City and then west," Will said. "We thought you might have word about the grass on the prairie."

"Let's go inside and sit comfortably in the cabin," Captain Wright suggested, without commenting on the grass. We followed him inside and sat at the large, oval captain's table forward in the room. He motioned a waiter over.

"I'll have coffee, and bring my companions anything they'd like," he directed. Ben and I asked for sarsaparilla, and Will asked for coffee.

"So, the grass," Captain Wright began. "Yes, we had a man on board between Wyandotte and Lexington who had just come across from Denver. He talked about the grass, said it was clipped low, big droves of cattle earlier had taken it off. It'll probably be the end of the month before it's fully back. Course, you could always travel away from the trail if you have to go sooner."

"That's the same as we heard below," Will said. "We don't know the country west of Kansas City, so I think we best stay close to the trail."

"There's always the train," Captain Wright said. He sounded reluctant but obligated to suggest it.

"No, we're on horseback, trailing pack mules," Will said. "We're riding to Idaho."

"I see," Captain Wright said. "I suppose you'll have to wait for the grass then." He paused, then asked, "Where did you do your steamboatin'?" He seemed eager to switch to a brighter topic.

"Mostly on the Cumberland," Will replied.

"Mostly on the Missouri for me," Captain Wright said. "Steamboatin's almost all gone now. I miss the early days. One of my proudest moments was in '56. Gates McGarrah and I were pilots on the *James Lucas*. We took down the time of the *Polar Star* between Saint Louis and Saint Joe. Made the run up in just under 61 hours. The horns later hung in the Lee Line wharfboat at Memphis. The *Lucas* was dismantled in '61. Her machinery went to the *G. W. Graham*."

"The *Graham*?" Will asked, surprised. "I know the *Graham*. She was one of the transports that carried Union troops to seize Paducah in September '61."

"That's her," Captain Wright confirmed.

"I met General Grant then on the Ohio before he took Paducah," Will said.

"Grant," Captain Wright said, sounding dismayed, "looks like Greeley and Brown might take him come November."

"It's probably too early to tell," Will said.

Just then, the mud clerk came into the cabin.

"We're ready, sir," he said.

"Thank you, Jimmy," Captain Wright said. "Well, gentlemen, it's time for the *Mountaineer* to continue down. Happy to make your acquaintance, and good luck on the trail."

We stood, said our thank-yous and goodbyes, shook hands all around and filed out of the cabin. We knew then we'd continue overland to Kansas City, take it slow and still probably have to wait in Westport for the grass.

25

Above Arrow Rock, the Missouri followed its big north bend. The public road turned west and carried us farther from the river than we had been. For three days, the country was mostly open prairie. I came to a clearer understanding of why in so many Oregon Trail diaries the writers concentrated on three things—wood, water and grass. They needed wood for cooking fires, water for themselves and their animals, and grass for their herds and either the mules or oxen that pulled their wagons. When the trail turned away from the river, or when there were long stretches between streams, finding wood, water and grass became crucial. And as they moved farther west into drier country, it sometimes became a matter of life or death.

On our first night out of Arrow Rock, we went into camp near a salt spring west of Marshall. We spent the second night among the apple orchards just past Waverly. A traveler there told us that captains Lewis and Clark and the Corps of Discovery had spent three days nearby felling trees and shaping oars. By the third night away from Arrow Rock, we were back at the river in Lexington.

A local man there pointed out a Civil War cannonball lodged near the top of a courthouse pillar. It had struck and stuck there in September '61, during the Battle of Lexington. The man also told us the streamer *Saluda* had exploded her boilers just off the Lexington landing in '51, killing at least 200 people. Families in town had adopted orphaned children. I told him my mama was orphaned in the *Moselle* disaster in '38, and that's how she came into the Hawkins family. He looked at me sidelong, as if he thought I was telling a tall tale.

Lexington was the county seat of Lafayette County and looked like a prosperous town. When railroads displaced Missouri steamers, many river towns that the rails bypassed shrank to shadows or disappeared altogether. A Pacific Railroad spur line helped keep Lexington alive.

We went into camp the next night about halfway between Lexington and Independence. We were near Fort Osage, which decades before had been the westernmost U. S. Government outpost. After studying our map, Will made a suggestion.

"We'll be in Independence tomorrow afternoon. Since we have plenty of time, why don't we say hello to John Snyder's cousin, the wagonmaker, Henry Crump?" Ben and I looked at each other, shrugged and said, "Sure."

We rode into Independence about midday on Friday the 17th. With help from a boy at the square, we found Henry Crump's wagon shop. About two-thirds of the building looked like a large low barn. It had big wooden doors that slid to open and close at the front, back and one end. The other third of the building was two stories high, had tall windows above and below, and looked like a house. There was a large, fenced yard in the rear. Several sheds—some small, others large, some enclosed and others open—stood in the yard. We dismounted, hitched the animals and stepped through the big, open front doorway. Will addressed the first man we saw.

"Good afternoon, sir, we're looking for Henry Crump."

"Hello, gentlemen," the man replied, "Mr. Crump has gone to Spring Street to deliver a wagon. He should be back shortly. Is there anything I can do for you?"

"We met a cousin of Mr. Crump's who suggested we stop and say hello," Will said.

"Are you looking to buy a wagon?" the man asked.

"No," Will replied, "it's a social call."

With that, the man walked between us, out the door and looked up the street.

"Here comes Mr. Crump now," he said.

About two blocks distant, we saw a man astride one horse with another horse alongside. As he drew closer, we saw it was a team in harness with no wagon behind. Mr. Crump rode bareback. He reined in at the door where we stood, dismounted, handed the reins to the man who greeted us and turned our way.

"Good afternoon, gentlemen, I'm Henry Crump. What can I do for you?"

He was about Will's age, maybe a little older. He was tall and sturdily built. He had thick, bushy hair and a full, neatly trimmed mustache but no beard. He wore tradesman's clothes, with broad suspenders holding his britches up. He had a ready smile and a pleasant, outgoing manner. Will stepped forward, shook Mr. Crump's hand and introduced us.

"I'm Will Hawkins and these young men are my sons Ben and Early," nodding to us in turn. Ben and I instinctively touched the brims of our hats in greeting.

"We met your cousin, John Snyder, in Callaway County. He suggested we look you up in Independence," Will said.

"Johnny?" Mr. Crump exclaimed. "Why, I haven't seen Johnny since he visited us summers in Nine Mile Prairie. That must have been 15, almost 20 years ago. How is Johnny? What's he doing?"

"He was in a bit of a jam when we met—his wagon had thrown a wheel in Callaway near the Montgomery County line. We helped him re-mount the wheel, and he was on his way. He lives near Mechanicsburg. He farms and does some surveying. He's a Mason in the lodge there. He was in Callaway looking for a farm to buy."

"I knew Johnny had become a Mason. I'm in the lodge here. How did you happen to run into him?" Mr. Crump asked.

"Solely by chance," Will replied. "It was a good coincidence because he needed help with his wagon, and we were hoping to meet kin of Daniel Boone."

"Why's that?" Mr. Crump asked.

"An ancestor of ours, George Hawkins, helped Boone blaze the Wilderness Trail, and we thought it would be fitting to make a connection several generations removed," Will replied.

"I'm kin of Boone myself, and so's my wife, Celia. I'm a great-great-grandson through Daniel's daughter, Susannah. Celia's a great-granddaughter through Daniel's daughter, Levina. Celia and I have four children, and there's not a bleeder among them," Mr. Crump said. At the time, I don't think we knew what he meant by that.

"What brings you to Independence?" he asked.

"Passing through on our way to Idaho," Will replied.

"Do you need a sturdy wagon?" Mr. Crump asked.

"No, but thank you, sir," Will replied. "We're on horseback trailing these pack mules here."

"I bet you're waiting a week or two for the grass," Mr. Crump said.

"That's right," Will said.

"Where are you putting up for the night?" Mr. Crump asked.

"We'll either camp outside town or register at a hotel here before moving on to Kansas City and Westport," Will replied.

"I'll tell you what then," Mr. Crump said, "why don't you spend a day or two with us? You can stable your animals here on the shop property and stay at the house with Celia, the children and me. We have plenty of extra room at home."

"That's mighty kind of you," Will replied as he turned to Ben and me. "What do you men think?"

"Sure," Ben and I said as one.

"Let's lead your beasts around to the stable, get them unpacked and comfortable, and then I'll show you around the shop," Mr. Crump said.

"Sounds fine to us," Will said.

After stabling the animals, Mr. Crump gave us a tour of his wagon shop.

"Here in the yard, we store our logs and mill them with a steam-powered saw in the large shed back yonder. We usually have hickory, oak and yellow poplar on hand. There, just outside the main building, we have our forge and blacksmith shop," he said. A man wearing a thick apron turned a piece of white-hot iron on an anvil as he pounded it with a mallet. We walked through the big, open doorway onto the floor of the main building.

"On the floor here, we have our paint shop enclosed on the south end, then our wheelrights, woodworkers and assemblers," Mr. Crump said. A man nearby worked a wheel hub with an auger. Two others turned a dowel on a pedal-powered lathe.

"We make all kinds of wagons—freight, express, delivery, farm, ranch, buckboards, buggies and even surreys, but no coaches. We leave that to the men in Concord. Our storage area is above us in the loft, and the offices and harness stock, hardware and accessories are in the two-story building adjacent on the north end," Mr. Crump said.

"It's a fine factory, Mr. Crump," Will said. "How long have you been making wagons?"

"I started in Callaway," Mr. Crump replied, "and we came to Independence about '56. There was much more demand here. Independence was a greater crossroads. Since then, the railroads, cattle and grain have shifted a lot of people and business to Kansas City, but that's close by, and we still have plenty to keep us busy."

Mr. Crump paused for a moment.

"We slide the doors shut here at half past 5 o'clock," he continued. "If you can wait till then, we'll go by two-seater to our house on North Main."

"Sure," Will said, "we can use the time to curry and brush our animals."

While Mr. Crump went about his business, Will, Ben and I spent the next few hours caring for the animals, and straightening out our packs and personal baggage. When Mr. Crump and his men shut down for the day, we were ready for the wagon ride. It was a fine-looking rig with upholstered seats front and rear. The box sat on elliptical springs above the axles. I sat up front with Mr. Crump, while Will and Ben sat behind.

"I sent the office boy to tell Mrs. Crump we'd be having guests," Mr. Crump said as we got under way. "She loves company, and she and the help have had the afternoon to get everything ready."

"We don't want to impose," Will said.

"Nonsense," Mr. Crump quickly replied. "We want you to stay and make yourselves at home. Henry Jr. is about Ben's age and my daughter, Lucy, is about Early's age, so there will be plenty of companionship." He spoke with great cheer.

We turned onto Main and passed the courthouse at the square. The business district gave way to large, two- and three-story houses, some constructed of bricks, some of quarried stone and others of wood. All were handsome and well-kept. Mr. Crump turned into the drive of an especially fine carpenter-gothic house. It had a covered porch across the width of the first floor. Two more floors rose above that. A round room with a steep, cone-shaped roof sat high at the corner away from the drive. Mr. Crump drove into a carriage house at the rear. A young Negro boy was there to take charge of the horses and wagon.

"Sam, I'd like you to meet some friends of mine," Mr. Crump said as we climbed down. "This is Mr. Will Hawkins, and these are his sons, Early and Ben. Gentlemen, this is Sam, the best stable boy in Independence, Missouri."

"Happy to meet you, suh," Sam said as he greeted Will and me first.

"And we're happy to meet you, Sam," Will replied. Ben had stepped down from the far side, and Sam looked a little surprised when he came around the back of the wagon for the introduction.

We walked back up the drive and mounted the stairs to the front door. Mr. Crump proudly welcomed us to his home. He opened the tall door and held it, motioning for us to enter ahead of him. A well-dressed woman and four children stood smiling in the entryway. I say children, but the oldest was actually a young man.

"Celia, I'd like you to meet Will Hawkins and his sons Early and Ben. Gentlemen, this is my wife, Mrs. Celia Crump, my sons Henry Jr. and Jesse, and my daughters, Lucy and Josie," Mr. Crump said.

Several "Pleased to make your acquaintance" declarations passed back and forth. Even the little ones, Jesse and Josie, politely said theirs.

"Shall we sit for supper as soon as you get settled?" Mrs. Crump asked. "You're in the large room at the top of the stairs if

you want to stow your baggage and wash up. Supper is ready in
the dining room as soon as you are."

"Thank you, ma'am," the three of us said, our words overlapping each other. I could see that Will and Ben were just as taken
aback by the reception as I was.

Mr. Crump sat at one end of the large oval dining table, and
Mrs. Crump sat at the opposite end, close to the kitchen. The
four Crump children sat on one side of the oval, and we sat on
the other. Henry Jr. was nearest his father, Lucy was next to
Henry Jr., then Jesse, then nearest to Mrs. Crump, Josie, who I
guessed to be about two. She sat on a fashioned box that rested on
her chair and brought her up to table height. Full place-settings
sat in front of each of us. The day was nearing sunset, and the
room was softly lit with oil lamps and candles.

Sam, the stable boy, and a Negro woman brought serving
bowls and platters of food in from the adjacent kitchen.

"This is Minnie, our cook and housekeeper, and Sam, her
son," Mrs. Crump said. "Minnie and Sam are an enormous help
to us. I don't know what we would do without them. Is John
home yet, Minnie?"

"No, ma'am, he must be working right past sundown. I expect
we'll see him in about an hour or so," Minnie replied.

"Minnie's husband, Sam's father, is a stonemason," Mr. Crump
said. "The family lives in rooms above the carriage house."

"And it's right comfy," Sam pitched in. Everybody smiled and
laughed, appreciating Sam's honest statement. I saw Minnie
and Ben exchange glances. I knew she was wondering. Having
put the food on the table, Minnie and Sam disappeared into the
kitchen.

With nine mouths to feed, the table was full of bowls and platters from one end to the other, but nobody moved. We seemed to
be waiting for a cue. Finally, Mr. Crump broke the silence.

"Thank you, Lord, for these gifts we are about to receive from
thy bounty. Bless our family and our guests." All the Crumps said
"Amen" in unison, as if by habit. The end of grace caught our side
of the table by surprise, so our "Amens" came a little late.

"Serve yourselves, please, and pass to your right," Mrs. Crump
said. When each bowl and platter had made the circuit of the
table, the eating and conversation began.

"Celia, the Hawkins men are on their way to Idaho," Mr. Crump said.

"And the Hawkins women?" Mrs. Crump asked.

"My wife and daughter will join us once we've settled and built a home," Will replied.

"Where in Idaho, Will?" Mr. Crump asked.

"We want to homestead where the Raft River meets the Snake," Will said. "It's flat bottomland and ideal for farming."

"I believe I've heard of that country," Mr. Crump said. "How far are you from a rail line?"

"The transcontinental line is about 60 miles south," Will replied.

"I'll tell you what, then," Mr. Crump continued. "Once you're settled, you'll need a wagon, maybe two or three. If you wire me what you need, I'll ship by rail, and you can wire back the payment. Unless you need something fancy or unusual, I can probably fill your order from stock. Otherwise, give me a week or two, and I'll have your wagon on a rail car on its way west."

"I don't see how I can refuse an offer like that," Will said, "and having seen your shop and stock, I know I'd be buying the best wagons available."

"Why, thank you, Will," Mr. Crump said. "I appreciate your confidence."

Mr. Crump changed the subject and the attention to Henry Jr.

"Henry has been spending time in Kansas City, looking for opportunities. Why don't you tell us what you've seen there, son?"

"Well, of course, since the Hannibal Bridge opened across the Missouri about three years back, Kansas City's population has boomed," Henry said. "There are about 35,000 people now. The rail connection to the East makes the city the shipping point for beef up from Texas and grain from this whole region. The meat-packing industry is growing fast, as is any business related to grain. Everything's up to date in Kansas City. They've gone about as far as they can go. I'm looking at opportunities, but I haven't made any decisions yet."

Mr. Crump picked up his son's line of thought.

"With the War's end, the telegraph and railroads have had a great impact on people's lives. Abolition changed how farmers farm. It changed what they grow and how much land they work. The railroads make distant markets available to farmers and ranchers. And that works both ways—the East is a market for the West, and the West is a market for the East. The rails put everyone within days of almost anyplace on the continent, and the telegraph within minutes."

"With that in mind, Henry," Mrs. Crump said, "when will we make that visit to Callaway and on to Saint Charles and Saint Louis?"

"Well, my dear, it's funny you should ask," Mr. Crump replied. "Will, Ben and Early met our cousin, John Snyder, in Callaway."

"My word, you don't say!" Mrs. Crump exclaimed, "What a coincidence!"

"Not so much a coincidence, Celia," Mr. Crump said, "Johnny asked Will and his boys to look us up here in Independence."

"Nevertheless," Mrs. Crump said, "that settles it. We haven't seen Johnny since he was a boy. We all ought to go back to visit this summer."

"Consider it decided, then, my dear," Mr. Crump said, "we will go before fall."

Mr. Crump changed the subject again, and this time turned the attention to Will.

"The Hawkins family has a connection to Daniel Boone. Will you tell Celia the history of that, Will?"

"My great-grandfather, George Hawkins, helped Boone blaze the Wilderness Trail into Kentucky in 1775," Will said.

"I suppose Henry has told you of our lines to Daniel Boone," Mrs. Crump said.

"Yes, he has," Will replied.

"You are from Kentucky, then?" Mrs. Crump asked.

"Yes, Smithland, where the Cumberland meets the Ohio," Will replied.

"Did you farm there?" Henry Jr. asked.

"Yes, we did, and we were 50 years in the packet business," Will replied.

"That's another thing railroads changed," Mr. Crump added.

"Yes, changed is the right word," Will said. "Packets have been cut way back. Steamers on the Mississippi and the smaller streams have gone to big tows—products like coal and bulk grain that move cheaper by water than rail."

"When I first started building wagons in Independence in '56 or '57," Mr. Crump said, "most of my orders were for big freighters. Now it's rare we build a freighter unless it ships west by rail. The tracks east of here are a thick web, and they'll soon be that west of here."

This time it was Mrs. Crump who changed the subject.

"What will we all do tomorrow?" she asked.

"I would suppose that Jesse and Josie will be here with you, my dear," Mr. Crump said, "and I can see that our Lucy is itching to get out of that dress and into her tomboy clothes. Maybe she can take Early to some of her favorite spots. And perhaps Henry will show Ben around Kansas City. Will, if you'd like, I can give you a closer look at how we make wagons in our shop."

"Papa, may I go to Kansas City with Henry and Ben?" Jesse asked.

"It's fine with me if it meets with your mama's approval, and if two young men like Henry and Ben want a 4-year-old boy tagging along."

"Oh, I won't be no trouble," Jesse said.

"You mean you won't be *any* trouble, Jesse," Mrs. Crump said. "Don't use a double negative, dear."

"I won't be *any* trouble, Henry, I promise," Jesse said, "can I go with you and Ben?"

Henry and Ben looked at each other.

"Sure, Jesse," Henry said, "You can tag along with us."

"I can run faster and throw a baseball farther than any boy my age in Independence," Lucy suddenly blurted, as if she had been containing herself till then.

"Well, Early's a fine horseman and the best rifle shot in Livingston County, Kentucky, so I guess you two will get on just fine," Ben said with a smile.

"Oh, Ben, stop bragging on me," I said, feeling embarrassed.

"It sounds as if they *will* get on fine," Mr. Crump said. Mrs. Crump, on the other hand, looked a little doubtful.

"Where's your horse, Early?" Lucy asked.

"He's in your papa's stable down at the wagon shop," I replied.

"Well, then, can we go there in the morning and ride him?" she asked.

"Sure, I suppose we can do that," I said.

"Is that all right?" I asked Will.

"Fine with me," he replied.

"Sounds fine to me too," Mr. Crump said. "We can drop Henry, Ben and Jesse at the depot for the train to Kansas City, and Lucy, Early, Will and I can continue on to the shop. Celia, will you and Josie be all right at home without us all day?" Mr. Crump asked his wife.

"Henry, I assure you, I will survive the peace and quiet," Mrs. Crump replied with a gentle smile. "Supper will be at 6 o'clock. And on Sunday, we will all attend service."

26

At 8 o'clock on Saturday morning, Sam had the team in harness and the two-seater wagon in the drive, facing the street and ready to go. Lucy, with her short blond hair, blue eyes and tomboy's clothes, looked more like my brother than a girl I hardly knew. Jesse was excited to be going by train to Kansas City, and Henry Jr. and Ben were doing their best to be patient. On Saturdays, Mr. Crump opened his shop at 8:30, so it was first to the depot to drop the big-city boys off and then to the shop.

I showed Lucy our mules and horses, then put a halter on Spirit and led him out of the stable into the morning sun. It was a warm spring day. Since I had curried and brushed him the afternoon before, Spirit looked especially fine.

"Why did you name him Spirit?" Lucy asked.

"His mare died soon after she foaled, then her colt had to struggle to survive. He was very brave and determined to live, so I called him Spirit. He was born when I was 7, so he's 5 now. We grew up together. My Uncle Louis' mare foaled just after Spirit's mare, but she wouldn't let Spirit suckle, so I milked her every-day and bottle-fed Spirit. When he was a young colt, he thought I was his mother. Sometimes, I think he still does."

"Can we both ride him bareback?" Lucy asked.

"I do, so I suppose we both can," I replied. Where do you want to go?"

"It's a secret," Lucy said. "I'll ask Papa if we can go."

We asked both Mr. Crump and Will, and neither objected.

"Be careful riding double bareback in town when there are so many wagons and buggies about," Mr. Crump said. "If you'll be gone long, stop at the grocery and have Mrs. Wilkes pack you something to eat. Tell her I'll pick up the bill before the end of the day. Be back here by 4 o'clock to take care of Spirit before we go home for supper."

Lucy had a look of delight and excitement about her. We'd ride Spirit with only halter and reins. I had gotten big enough that if I gripped his mane just above the withers, I could leap and get my right leg high enough on his back that I could squirm the rest of the way up. I couldn't do that if he was saddled.

I leapt on Spirit's back, reached down, grabbed Lucy's hand and pulled as she climbed up behind me. She wrapped her arms around my waist and locked her hands together over my belly.

"Which way?" I asked.

"First up to Wilkes Grocery the way we came from home and then straight east out of town," Lucy replied.

We tied two sacks of food with a cord and slung them between us across Spirit's back like saddlebags. As we turned on the road east, I asked Lucy where we were going.

"I'll tell you when we get out of town," she said, mysteriously. I didn't know if she was teasing my curiosity or what. When we were away from town and out among the grain fields, I asked her again.

"Can you keep a secret?" she asked.

"Yes, I can," I replied.

"The Little Blue River," she said.

"The Little Blue River!" I exclaimed. "That's no secret. We crossed it on the way to Independence."

"I'm not talkin' 'bout the part near the road, Early," she said, with as much exasperation in her voice as I had had in mine.

"See this next crossroad coming up ahead?" she asked.

"Yes," I replied. "It's kind of hard to miss, don't you think?"

"OK, smarty pants," she said, "at the crossroads, turn half to the north and ride straight across the prairie. It's a shortcut," she said.

"Are you sure you know where we're going?" I asked.

"I'm sure, and you better not ever tell anybody this secret," she replied. She had a mischievous tone in her voice.

"How do you know about this place so far from home?" I asked.

"It's only about five miles," she replied. "Jamie, a girl in my class at school used to live out this way. We were exploring and found it."

"What is it?" I asked.

"You'll see once we get there," she replied. "Just enjoy the ride and the pretty spring day. Do you know nature, Early?"

"I know it if it's the same as at home," I replied.

"Those white flowers with the yellow middles are prairie larkspurs," she said, "and the pale purple ones are coneflowers. The blue stems and blazing stars won't bloom till about July or August. That high-pitched chirping is an indigo bunting, and the louder, more-drawn-out whistle is a meadowlark. The rolling trill is a summer tanager."

She sounded like me when Will tested my tree knowledge.

"Miss Larson takes our class on nature walks and teaches us the plants and animals," Lucy continued. "My friend, Jamie, and I take turns imitating bird calls and then guessing what the other's is."

"I know a lot about trees," I said, "and I've read about which plants you can eat. Actually, my Uncle Louis taught me more than I read. How much farther is it to the Little Blue?" I asked.

"I suppose we've gone about half the way since we turned off the road," she replied.

"Let's get down for a while and let Spirit graze in the fresh green grass," I suggested. Lucy agreed, so we crossed our legs over and slid off Spirit's back. "He won't wander far with us in sight, so we don't have to picket him," I added. I let his reins fall, knowing that kept him close, and let him graze. He immediately bent his head and ripped the grass.

Lucy lay on her back and gazed at the sky. I lay beside her and did the same. The tall grass formed a wall around us. The sky was purely blue, dotted here and there with pillow-like white clouds. A light breeze blew from the northeast, just strong enough to gently sway the tallest grass.

"This is awfully nice, isn't it, Early?" Lucy asked.

"It sure is," I replied.

"It's a lot better than wearing a dress and having a tea party," she said.

"I don't know about dresses and tea parties, Lucy," I said.

"Course not," she laughed.

I whistled for Spirit, and he came to where we lay. Lucy asked if she could try to leap up on his back as I had done at the stable.

"Sure," I said. "Steady, Spirit."

She grabbed his mane and leapt up on his back on her first try. I felt a little odd about that. She leaned down, extended her hand and yanked me aboard behind her. I wrapped my arms around her waist and locked my hands together over her belly.

I saw a decline and tree line far ahead and figured that had to be the Little Blue. When we reached it, we followed the stream north toward the Missouri. In a few minutes, we came to a glade where the water ran swiftly down a rapid and then broadened into a pool before it narrowed again some distance farther down. On the east side, a limestone bluff rose above the pool. There was a narrow shelf about half way up. Shadowed recesses cut into the wall behind the shelf. The rock face was uneven above the water line and looked as if you could find handholds to climb up. The bank on our side was low and smooth. Sycamores, cotton-woods, maples, and willows lined both banks, interrupted only by the limestone outcropping on the opposite side.

We slid off Spirit's back, and he bent to drink from the stream. I found a stake in the litter below the trees, walked Spirit out into the grass, drove the stake with a rock and gave him a long lead to graze. I walked back to the creek bank and found Lucy sitting and gazing across the pool to the bluff. I sat beside her and looked across too.

"Are those caves above the shelf?" I asked.

"Are you sure you can keep a secret?" Lucy asked.

"Yes, I promise," I replied, a little impatiently.

"Two secrets?" she asked in a teasing way.

"Yes, two secrets," I replied.

With that, she laughed a mischievous laugh, reached down and pulled her boots and socks off.

"Come on!" she urged.

I pulled my boots and socks off. She stood, unbuckled her belt, dropped her britches to the ground and stepped out of them. I hesitated.

"Come on!" she urged again. "Don't be scared."

I dropped my britches and stepped out of them. She crossed her arms in front, grabbed the hem of her shirt and in one swift motion, pulled it over her head and dropped it to the ground. I did the same with mine. With not a moment's pause, she slipped out of her underclothes. So did I. I was 12, she was 11, but we stood on the bank innocent as the day we were born. Neither of us had reached puberty. We were two skinny kids that a stiff wind could have blown over. Lucy stepped forward and dove into the pool. I followed. The water was chilly, so we quickly paddled to the bluff on the other side. Lucy found a hand hold and then another farther up. I followed, and in a moment we stood on the narrow shelf we had seen from the west side.

"This way," Lucy said as she motioned to me to follow her downstream. It was slow walking in bare feet on the rocky ledge. We came to a deep depression in the bluff face. Lucy turned, crouched a little to avoid the rock above and entered the depression. I followed. It was nearing midday, and the sun was high enough to cast some light into what I now realized was a cave. Lucy's white skin and the water droplets that clung to it reflected enough light that she was easy to see and follow. We walked maybe 20 feet until she stopped, turned to her right and pointed. I let my eyes adjust to the now dimmer light against the cave wall.

I was stunned by what I saw, and Lucy was delighted to see my surprise. It was a man's skeleton, dressed in a tattered Union-blue uniform. His rusted pistol was holstered at his waist. He lay flat on his back with his head propped up slightly against the cave wall. His rusty musket rested on its stock leaning against the wall beside his head. I turned to face Lucy in amazement. Tears welled up in my eyes.

"How did you find this?" I asked.

"Jamie and I were exploring one day last summer," she replied.

We stood facing each other in the dim light of the cave. Her eyes glistened with tears, as I'm sure mine did. We were naked, but there was no shame, no embarrassment. I was touched that she had shared her secrets with me. I felt an odd feeling rushing through me. It was like nothing I had ever felt before. I didn't know if it meant I should do something or not do something. Without thinking, I raised my hand and touched Lucy's cheek. She raised her hand and held mine against her face. It was cool in the cave out of the sun, and we had both begun to shiver. Goose bumps rose on our quivering arms.

"We should go out in the sun where it's warm," I said softly.

"Yes," she replied.

I turned and led the way out. We climbed back down the bluff face and swam to the opposite bank. We gathered our clothes and walked out from under the shade of the trees into the sun. We stood and shook the water off like wet dogs. Lucy walked around me and patted my chest and back dry with her shirt. I did the same for her. We dressed and sat down in the prairie grass to eat the food we had brought from Wilkes Grocery.

"Was there a battle near here?" I asked.

"The Battle of the Little Blue," she replied.

"Thank you for sharing your secrets with me," I said. She said nothing. She just smiled. Maybe she didn't want me to think so, but she looked very pretty. I've kept Lucy's secrets for better than 80 years, and I don't think I'm betraying her trust to tell them here.

About the Sunday service, I remember only that we went as a courtesy to Mrs. Crump. I made no notes in the record about the church, the sermon or the congregation, so I have nothing to write. We spent the remainder of the day in the garden, which Mrs. Crump kept in a nice way. Will read his Darwin, Ben transposed piano tunes to banjo and fiddle, and I caught up with writing the record.

On Monday morning, we said goodbye to Mrs. Crump, the children and Minnie and Sam. Lucy and I were still waving as Mr. Crump left the drive. We went to the wagon shop, where we packed the mules, saddled the horses, said our thank yous and goodbyes, and were on our way. Will assured Mr. Crump that he'd get wagon orders from us once we reached Idaho.

27

Will had to wire Beth, and he was certain there was a key in Kansas City, so we rode there rather than to Westport and the head of the trail. It was an easy, level ride on a well-used road. We came to the wharf early in the afternoon. We registered at the Gilliss House and stabled the beasts at the O. H. Short Livery.

While Will and Ben were in the telegraph office, I waited at the train depot. I hoped to see an incoming train. I checked the schedule and, sure enough, if the afternoon train from the east was on time, it would reach the Kansas City station before Will and Ben were through.

First, I heard the locomotive's whistle from a distance, then saw the plume of smoke. I'll always be partial to steamboats, but a huge iron engine pulling into a depot trailing a long line of freight and passenger cars is a grand thing to see.

There was a good crowd of people waiting either to meet passengers or to board going west. As the train settled in, the people moved to the stairways at the passenger cars. At one stairway, a mother and a boy I guessed to be about 15 waited for the porter to place the stool. The boy was dressed like a railroad engineer. I was struck that he was too old to be imitating an engineer's dress as a novelty. He clung to his mother and made jerky, awkward movements. She was dressed in the fashion of a well-to-do man's wife. She wore her long hair up beneath a stylish hat. Her bodice was high at the neck, flared at the breasts and narrow at the waist. The skirt was trim in front but gathered in a bustle at the rear. Her fashions were deep purple, trimmed in white and bore a soft sheen.

The porter placed the stool, and the boy moved to step down at his mother's gentle urging. It was plain that he was having trouble making the step. Two waiting passengers, a man and a woman, quickly stepped forward and extended a hand to help the boy down. Even with help, he stepped to the stool and then the platform with difficulty. His mother followed, thanked the two boarding passengers and slowly walked toward a bench with her son. He didn't walk well. His mother firmly held his arm at the elbow and helped him along.

I sat on a bench against the depot wall, while they sat on a corner bench, facing the sun. The mother looked, searching for whoever was to meet them. Although she had a parasol, she didn't open it. Instead, she held her hand like the bill of a cap to shield her eyes from the sun. The boy sat very close to her. There was a feeling of communion between them. He held his head tilted down toward the brick sidewalk. The bill of his cap hid his face. As mother and son spoke quietly, she turned toward him and spotted a speck of lint on his far shoulder. She reached behind and around him and delicately picked it off. As they continued speaking, the boy raised both hands to his shoulders, bending them at the elbows. His hands looked poorly formed and awkward. He shook them, as if flicking water off.

Will and Ben came for me before whoever was to meet the mother and boy. As we walked away, Will said it would probably be tomorrow before Beth's wire came with the pocket money we needed to move on. We walked along the wharf on the way to the Gilliss House. There were two mountain packets nosed into the bank. It would be a long time before I'd see a steamboat again.

In the morning, we were surprised to find a wire from Beth already waiting for us at the telegraph office. Will read the message first. The corners of his mouth turned up in a gentle smile, and he began to chuckle.

"Beth says if we want this money to go farther, we should stop staying in hotels. I guess that settles it, men. Unless we can find a kind citizen to put us up for free, we'll have to do our waiting in camp out on the prairie."

We returned to the Gilliss House, picked up our necessaries and proceeded to the livery. We were packed, mounted and on our way to Westport by mid-morning. We rode on Main Street and then through Market Square. A restaurant sign near Marble Hall advertised fresh oysters. I wondered how they could still be fresh so far from the Gulf. The square was full of wagons, buggies, horses and men lolling about and swapping stories. Despite Hannibal Bridge over the Missouri and booming industries and population, Kansas City was about a 10th the size of Saint Louis. The streets were mud, most buildings were wood, as were the sidewalks, and the atmosphere was wide open.

We shared the Westport Road with wagons, buggies, riders and a horsecar rail line, although the cars we saw were drawn by mules. We stopped in Westport just long enough to stock up on supplies and provisions. Between Mr. Rucker's and Captain Wachsmann's side-by-side stores, we got what we needed. We expected our next supply stop to be Lawrence, on the Kansas River.

We made inquiries in Westport and learned that we had better take the public road to Olathe if we hoped to reach Elm Grove camp before sunset. The road followed the Olathe Cutoff route, which was shorter than the Santa Fe-Oregon Trail. That trail lay farther south and looped below Olathe, adding eight or 10 miles to the ride.

We had ridden across short stretches of prairie in Missouri, but now we were in Kansas on the far side of both great rivers. We were on *the* prairie at the edge of the Great Plains, beyond the eastern forests.

I reined Spirit from a walk to a halt, leaned forward, patted him on the neck and spoke in his ear. "Still, Spirit." I pulled my boots from the stirrups and stood on my saddle. I slowly turned a full circle by inches. The space was immense. It seemed infinite. Here and there between me and the horizon, the expanse was broken by a line of brush or trees marking the passage of a creek. Scattered widely across the plain were cabins, farmhouses and barns. The horizon seemed an unreachable distance away. I heard Ben call my name from ahead.

"Early, catch up with us. What are you doing lagging behind? We want to reach Elm Grove camp before dark. Come on ahead."

I settled back down into my saddle and said, "OK, Spirit, let's go." We galloped on and joined Ben and Will. As it turned out, Elm Grove was too far, so we spent the night at Indian Creek.

Wednesday, May 22nd was our first full day on the Kansas prairie. The previous day's clouds had cleared, and the morning was bright, warm and sunny. The breeze was in our faces as we rode west. About mid-morning, we overtook a covered wagon drawn by four mules. Two lanky boys rode horseback behind. Our pace was faster than the wagon's by almost half, depending on the ground. We came up alongside the driver, tipped our hats and said good morning.

"Where you folks headed?" Will asked.

The driver took a moment to push a plug of tobacco aside with his tongue. A woman and a young girl sat in the bed of the wagon beneath the canvas.

"California," the driver replied. "You?"

"Idaho," Will said. "Where did you spend the night?"

"'Bout halfway between here and Indian Creek," was the reply.

"We'll probably make Elm Grove south of Olathe by noon," Will said.

"That's our next rest," the driver said. "Be there 'fore sundown, I 'spect."

"We'll see you there," Will said. We regained our pace and pulled ahead of the wagon. Before the transcontinental railroad, there were probably scores if not hundreds of emigrant wagons on this road in spring. Today, there was an occasional farm wagon, buggy or rider, but only one emigrant wagon heading west.

We crossed the Kansas City & Santa Fe tracks at Olathe and, with no need to stop in town, continued about two miles to Elm Grove camp on Cedar Creek. After unpacking and setting up our camp, Will led the beasts to the creek, while Ben and I took our Winchesters and walked along the bank with two purposes in mind—gathering wood for a cooking fire and bagging a rabbit or two. As we found windfall wood, we tossed it up onto clear ground away from the bank so we could pick it up on the way back.

We heard rustling in a thicket just ahead and, to our great surprise, a young whitetail buck darted out and straight across our path. I hesitated and didn't raise my rifle. Quickly, like a reflex, Ben fell to one knee, raised his rifle, braced it, drew a bead on the buck and dropped it with a perfect chest shot. The deer was likely dead before it hit the ground and certainly was by the time we ran the 40 yards to where it fell. We knelt by the buck, and I congratulated Ben.

"Nice clean shot, Ben." I didn't look at him though. I didn't want him to see the tears in my eyes.

Ben gutted the buck where it lay and left the entrails for the buzzards, coyotes or whatever other scavengers happened along. He slit the deer's throat, and we hung it from a branch to bleed. We'd take it down on our way back.

Will was pleased to see Ben with the buck and me with two arms full of wood.

"If those California folks rest here, there's five of them and three of us. The deer should do fine for a few meals," he said.

The wagon drove up about a half hour before sunset. They quickly went about setting up their camp about 50 yards below ours. Will asked me to walk over and invite them to join us for supper. I did and they accepted right away.

"Name's Oliver Bidwell, this is my wife, Sarah, my young daughter, Priscilla, and my boys John and Joe," the driver said as he walked up with his family gathered around him. Will introduced us and said that about two hours before, Ben had gotten the deer they saw on a spit over the fire. Mrs. Bidwell offered a cast iron pot of greens and tubers they had bought in Olathe. All together, we had the makings of a fine meal.

As we arranged ourselves around the fire, Joe stood, pointed first to the west, then to the east and said, "Look! There and there!" As a fiery sun slowly sank to the horizon, a huge yellow moon rose into full sight at the opposite edge of the plain. For a moment, they hung there, balanced like two big balls on the ends of a seesaw, with us in the middle, wide-eyed.

We settled into the meal, and the conversation began.

"This breeze'll keep the skeeters away," Mr. Bidwell said.

"If it keeps blowing in one direction and we arrange ourselves just right, it'll keep the woodsmoke out of our eyes," Ben said.

"Will yuh folks be on your way in the morning?" Mr. Bidwell asked.

"We're not sure," Will replied. "We've been told we should wait till month's end for the grass."

"That's 'bout right," Mr. Bidwell said. "Ah went 'cross to California in '49. If yuh get to the short-grass prairie too early, there won't be enough graze for your animals day after day."

"Even with only seven?" Will asked.

"Ah'll tell yuh what," Mr. Bidwell said, "we're in the tall grass prairie right here, the grass is only 'bout four or five inches high, and there's cowpies all 'round. A couple big droves of stock came through from way up the head of the Platte short time back. They et the grass near the trail right down to the ground. That's just like having hundreds of wagons ahead, with all their stock eatin' the grass 'fore yuh get to it. At our pace with the wagon and six animals, the grass'll be just fine as we go. But without a wagon, you're too fast, and yuh'll get there before the grass." He spoke as if very sure he was right. "I see yuh got two choices. Yuh could move real slow, or yuh can wait and ride at regluh speed."

"How long would you say we should wait?" Will asked.

"I'd say set right here at least till the first of June," Mr. Bidwell said. "Yuh've got grass, yuh've got water, if yuh need anythin', Olathe's only 'bout two mile and for 'musement, the railroad tracks are just over yonder. Yuh can go over and wave at the trains."

That brought laughter all around.

The twilight deepened from purple to black, and the sky filled with a dazzling blanket of stars everywhere but near the moon. The Bidwells thanked us and excused themselves after a while. We slept to the music of bugs and frogs nearby, and yips and howls of coyotes in the distance. The Bidwells joined us for breakfast and were on their way early. The bright full moon still hung high in the western sky.

We stayed at Elm Grove camp nine days, clear through to the end of May. Ben and I rode into Olathe twice for fresh vegetables and fruits, leaving Will in camp. Some days we hunted cottontails and prairie chickens. One emigrant wagon passed by, and another stopped to camp. They came at sunset and left at first light, having rested some distance from us and not stopping to talk. Occasionally, a rider paused to water himself and his horse. We exchanged a few words, and the riders moved on. I read Twain and got the record all caught up. Will read Darwin, and Ben finished transposing the tunes in his piano book.

One morning I sat by the creek and counted the different birdsongs. There were seven. I knew the Eastern Meadowlark by its whistle. I saw one as it sang. But then I saw another that had a tumbling, flutelike call. I judged that was a Western Meadowlark, like the one in my Audubon book at home. I figured we must be where their ranges overlapped.

During our time at Elm Grove camp, we had light showers two days and late afternoon or evening thunderstorms four days. I must have counted 50 or even 75 kinds of wildflowers on the prairie.

Our beasts had taken down the grass near camp, so we hobbled them and let them roam, bringing them back before sunset each day. By the time the first of June came around, we were itching to go.

28

The Olathe Cutoff ran southwest from Elm Grove about four miles to its junction with the Santa Fe-Oregon Trail. The other route was a public road running northwest from Olathe to Lexington and Eudora, and then east through Franklin to Lawrence. The public road probably would have been faster, but we chose to follow the cutoff and then the trail. Just past the point the Oregon and Santa Fe trails split, the way to Oregon turned sharply north. We found water at Captain Creek and went into camp about mid-afternoon.

We left Captain Creek shortly after dawn, taking no time to scale Observation Bluff, which lay just west of our camp. Will felt we'd have a thunderstorm in the afternoon, and if we wanted to cross the Wakarusa River ahead of the freshet the storm would bring, we couldn't waste time sightseeing.

As it turned out, we did some sightseeing anyway. May Belle threw a shoe as we reached Blue Mound, so we had to stop, unpack the mule that carried the farrier's tools and put a new shoe on the mare. While Will shoed his horse, Ben and I found the binoculars and climbed Blue Mound.

On the softly rolling plain, the long oval hump called Blue Mound stood out and was visible from miles away. On top, we had a full-circle horizon view. Red-tailed hawks soared on the updrafts and drifted with the wind. In the distance to the west, turkey vultures glided over the rolls of the prairie. Their wide spans, the slight V of their wings and the way they tilted to steer made it easy to tell they weren't hawks, even from a great distance.

By mid-afternoon, dark clouds grew above the western horizon. As they rose, we saw heavy rain curtains. We reached the Wakarusa under a clear sky, but the rain to the west had already quickened the river's flow and raised its level. Crossing was out of the question. It would be a race to unpack the mules and pitch our tents before the rain was upon us.

We found level ground south of the crossing in the lee of a hill. A grove of nearby trees was a good place for a picket line and some protection for the beasts. We quickly unpacked and set up two tents, one for the gear and supplies, and one for us. The first big, fat raindrops came just as we tied the last mule to the picket line. We raced back to the tents, checked to be sure the canvas was staked as tight as we could make it and dove inside.

The storm was furious. There was thunder, lightning, whipping wind and punishing rain. We were dry inside, but the animals got drenched, trees or not. We wondered if the ground would absorb the rain quickly enough to stop a lake from forming around us and flooding our tents. The worst of the storm passed in about 20 minutes. When it let up some, we burst from the tent with shovels and worked feverishly to dig trenches and build mounds to keep the water away from the canvas. For the most part, we succeeded. We got wet but our change of clothes and almost all our gear and provisions stayed dry. It was our first big plains storm, and we learned a good lesson.

A clearing sky spotted with showers and an especially bright yellow sun followed as the cloud canopy moved east. A double arc rainbow stretched north to south, and the birdsongs returned as the storm receded. We changed to dry clothes and ran a line to hang our wet things.

I walked to the base of the hill and found a clear, sweetwater spring flowing from the rocks. I gulped several handfuls, then returned to our camp for a pitcher and tub. Back at the spring, I used the pitcher to fill the tub and was about to tote it back to camp when two young Indian boys appeared nearby on a pony. Where they came from I don't know. As far as I could tell, they didn't see me at first. They each crossed one leg over and slid down from the pony's back. They sat on a flat rock up from a big puddle the rain had left in a buffalo wallow. The boys removed their moccasins, squatted at the water's edge and began playfully floating the moccasins like little boats.

When I picked up my tub and pitcher to return to camp, metal banged on metal and attracted the boys' attention. They quickly pulled their moccasins from the water, stood, dropped the moccasins to the ground, slid their feet in one-by-one and ran in my direction. They pulled up short right in front of me, and each extended an upturned palm. They were begging. Neither said a word. Straight, thick, jet-black hair framed their deep red faces. They gazed at me with expectant eyes, their mouths slightly agape. I dug into my britches pockets and produced two 3-cent pieces and one mother-of-pearl button. Their intense black eyes widened as I placed a coin in each boy's hand and then held up the button as if to ask, who gets this? They stared at the gleaming button for a moment, then the boy on my right grabbed it. They broke into broad smiles, laughed gleefully, turned and ran back to their pony. One boy crouched alongside the beast. The other boy stepped first on the crouching boy's knee, then on his shoulder, grabbed the pony's mane and pulled himself aboard. Still gripping the mane, the mounted boy reached down, grabbed the other boy's outstretched hand, and with a leap and a yank, the second boy was aboard. The boy in front gathered the rawhide reins, both boys kicked their heels into the pony's ribs, yelled "Haah!" and they galloped off toward the Wakarusa. I stood still, amazed by it all. I carried the springwater back to camp and didn't see the boys again.

Will was gathering rocks for a fire ring. He said Ben was in the grove with the beasts and asked me to go over and give him a hand. We led them up into the grass, strapped on their hobbles and turned them out to graze. We returned to the grove and moved the picket line out to the edge of the trees. We would tie the beasts there at nightfall.

We heard a rustling high to our left and walked over to see four turkey vultures perched high up in the stripped branches of a long-dead elm. They held their naked red heads low between hunched shoulders. All four stared intently in the same direction. We walked to the spot where their gaze met the ground. A litter of five black puppies lay partly hidden in the grass. Four were dead, and the fifth was about a breath away. We knelt and touched the nearly lifeless pup. He tried to respond, but life left him. Ben and I silently looked at each other, stood, and then turned our gaze up to the vultures. They unclenched and re-clenched their feet and slightly raised their wings. The setting sun gave their black feathers a rosy tinge. We stepped away from the pups, turned and started back to camp. Behind us, we heard loud rustles, creaking branches and then thumps as the birds hit the ground. We looked straight ahead, where, maybe 100 yards away, we saw two white canvas tents and out front, Will tending to our supper at the fire.

Ben and I brought the beasts in and tied them to the picket line at the edge of the trees. We sat for supper. The rain had cleared the air and left us with a crisp night lit by a thick blanket of stars. The waning moon would not be up till well past midnight. A hooting owl added a new rhythm to the usual night sounds. We followed the hoots and saw, silhouetted in the starlight, a great horned owl perched on the highest branch of a tall oak. His head and chest thrusted up and forward with each hoot, pushing the sound into the night. Seeing us, he glided away and out of sight. We returned to our tent to sleep.

There was no rush to get under way in the morning. At dawn, the river was still running too high and fast to cross safely. By mid-morning, it had dropped and slowed some. Will took his boots off, rolled his cuffs up, mounted May Belle and rode her through the cut on the south bank and into the stream. He called out that the bottom was rock. The water swirled around May Belle's legs and reached her belly. Half way across, it covered Will's thighs but got no higher than his hips before he started up the opposite bank. The far side was low and muddy. Will hesitated, looked up and downstream, and found a way out that supported his and May Belle's weight. He surveyed the crossing from the north side and returned along the same line he had taken going over.

"If we pack the mules high and light, and make two trips," Will said, "we can cross safely and keep everything dry. If you don't want to fill your boots with water, go barefoot as I did."

The packings, crossings and re-packings took about two hours. By the time we were on the trail on the north side, we were nearly ready for our noon rest. We delayed that a little so we could get some ground behind us. We were in the Wakarusa Valley just a few miles from Lawrence. Being that close to town, almost all the land was cultivated. There were acres and acres of young corn and wheat. Farmhouses and barns dotted the plain. If there was perfect farming country, this was it.

We were surprised Lawrence was such a big town. Will guessed 8,000 or maybe 10,000 people. We expected a lonely outpost on the prairie, but found a bustling town on the Kansas River's south bank. There was even a university under construction on Mount Oread overlooking the town and river.

We had several things to do in Lawrence, and we wanted to get to our night's camp at Coon Creek west of town before sundown, so we split up, hoping things would go faster that way. Will took the mules and headed for the telegraph office. He wanted to wire Beth and ask her to send money to Topeka, where we'd be the next day. He'd also find a blacksmith and buy muleshoes and horseshoes.

One of Ben's boots was coming apart, so we'd either have to find a shoemaker who could fix it quickly or buy a new pair. I needed ink powder and a new pen nib. Before he rode off, Will pointed out Berger's Grocery and said he'd meet us there as soon as he could.

We found a shoemaker named Alex Gregg. He was a Negro man, probably 10 years or so older than Will. He told Ben there would be no need to buy new boots, he could fix this one. He invited us to wait or come back in about half an hour. Ben pulled his other boot off, left the pair and his stockings with Mr. Gregg, and we rode on to Marsh & Ross' Books and Stationers, with Ben going barefoot.

I got my ink powder and nib, and when we came out of the store, there was a photographer in the street setting up his tripod, camera and black hood, getting ready to photograph the storefront. I suppose he found the sight of a tall, strapping, barefoot Negro man and a skinny kid in a slouch hat and baggy britches curious because he stopped us and asked if he could take our picture.

"Pardon me gentlemen, I'm Lamon, W. H. Lamon," he said, "and I would be much obliged if you would allow me to make a photograph of you."

Ben and I looked at each other and hesitated.

"If you're staying here in town, I would be happy to give you a print tomorrow, and if not, I will send it to you by U. S. Mail," he said.

"We don't have an address as yet," Ben said, "can you send it to our mama in Kentucky?"

"Why, certainly, I would be happy to," he said, looking a bit puzzled.

"All right, then, take our photograph," I said.

Mr. Lamon moved his camera in place, made some adjustments and ducked under the black hood.

"Steady, boys," he called out. The shutter clicked, Mr. Lamon threw the black hood up over the camera, came up on the plank sidewalk where we stood, pulled a notebook from his pocket and asked for the name and address.

"Beth Hawkins, Smithland, Kentucky," I said.

"That's simple enough," he said. "I'll have a print in the U. S. Mail to your mama tomorrow. Much obliged, gentlemen."

As Ben and I rode off toward the shoemaker's, we wondered what Beth would make of a photograph of Ben, barefoot, with me but no Will standing in front of a bookstore in Lawrence, Kansas. We thought we better explain in our next telegram from Topeka.

When we picked up Ben's stockings and boots, Mr. Gregg asked if we knew anything about the history of Lawrence. We said we didn't. He mentioned Quantrill and the murders he and his raiders committed in '63.

"Things here in Lawrence are a whole lot different now for folks like you and me," Mr. Gregg said, looking directly at Ben.

"I lived my first 10 years in Paducah, Kentucky, starting in '54," Ben replied, "and I know what you mean."

Ben sat on a bench out front and pulled his stockings and boots on. He paced back and forth and announced his satisfaction to Mr. Gregg with a big smile. The repair was much cheaper than new boots.

We rode on to Berger's Grocery, where we found Will waiting. He had already bought our groceries and was passing a sack of oats among the beasts. He had rolled the top of the sack down and held it open for each animal in turn.

"How did you men do?" he asked.

"We got everything we needed plus a surprise for Beth," Ben replied.

"What's that?" he asked.

"A man made a photograph of Ben and me, and he's sending a copy to Beth by U. S. Mail," I replied.

"Well, that's a nice surprise," Will said. "I'm sure your mama will be pleased."

29

We left Lawrence on the public road. Coon Creek lay about 14 miles ahead, near Lecompton. We reached it about half an hour before sundown and went into camp.

The sky was so wide at Coon Creek and the plain so broad that the sun looked small as it set. The night sky glowed from edge to edge with more stars than anyone could ever count.

Dawn lit wheat and corn fields. The wheat was just tall enough to bend with the breeze. The corn stood straight and trembled faintly.

We had bought fresh, sweet strawberries at Berger's in Lawrence. Getting them from town to breakfast at Coon Creek without crushing them was a neat trick. We made it a little easier by eating a good share the afternoon before.

Where people hadn't taken the timber, there were elms, black walnuts, oaks, hickories and other trees in the bottoms. Cottonwood fluff floated lazily on the breeze. Birdsongs were plenty, insects too.

The turned ground along our way was a rich, dark loam. There probably wasn't better cropland anywhere. The prairie seemed to roll on forever in all directions. Sunflowers lined our route, and here and there clusters of lavender thistles stood. Where the land wasn't worked, prairie grasses and wildflowers flourished.

Will guessed Topeka to be half, maybe two-thirds the size of Lawrence. A telegram and cash from Beth were waiting for us at Western Union. We wired back to say everything was OK and to tell her to watch the mail for a picture of Ben and me taken when Ben's boots were getting fixed in Lawrence. We crossed the Kansas River on an iron toll bridge and made our next camp on the north bank up from North Topeka.

Over the next days, our route ran overland, mostly west alongside the Kansas Pacific Railroad. We passed Silver Lake and met the public road at Rossville. At Saint Mary's Catholic Mission, the tracks continued west, while our road turned northwest and then, near Louisville and the Red Vermillion River, more north. Scott Spring, Westmoreland, the Black Vermillion River, the Big Blue River, the town of Blue Rapids, the Little Blue River and the Hollenberg Ranch lay ahead in Kansas before we crossed into Nebraska. At each night's camp, we found wood for our cooking fire, water and plenty of grass for the beasts.

On June 7th, as we neared Scott Spring outside Westmoreland, we overtook a peddler's wagon. It was a big, enclosed rig painted bright yellow, red and blue. There were cabinet doors and drawers all around the outside. Lanterns, washtubs and pots and pans hung from hooks at the roofline. A short, chubby man in a plaid suit and domed hat held the reins to a two-mule team. They walked very slowly, tugging a heavy load. The peddler sang loudly as he drove, interrupting his song now and then to talk to his mules. With his singing and the loud clatter of the hanging wares, he didn't know we were alongside until we were even with his seat. We didn't intend to, but we startled him. He jumped a little.

"Hal-lo friends, hal-lo neighbors," he shouted, "mighty glad to see ya this fine and dandy afternoon. Happy to see ya, happy."

We tipped our hats and said good afternoon.

"I'm camping at Scott Spring, just ahead," he called. "Will I see you there?"

"Yes, you will," Will replied. "That's our camp for the night."

"Capital, captain," the peddler said. "Fine and dandy. See you at Scott's."

Even at a walk, we easily passed the wagon and drew into the road ahead of his team. We reached the spring, found a level spot and had begun to unpack the mules when the peddler drove up, singing and clanging. He jumped down, told his team to stand still and walked over to us.

"O'Malley, Jimmy O'Malley, pleased to make your acquaintance," he said. We introduced ourselves.

"With the weight you're hauling," Will said, "you might do better adding another team."

"That's what the girls keep tellin' me," Mr. O'Malley said, "but I tell 'em I have faith in them, I know their strength."

"That's a sturdy-looking wagon," Ben said. "Where are you from?"

"Well, I came in the cars from Saint Louis to Jeff City and then on to Independence," he replied. "I thought there was opportunity out here in Kansas and Nebraska, so I had this wagon built and loaded it with goods."

"Who built your wagon?" Will asked.

"Man named Crump, Henry Crump, in Independence, a good man," Mr. O'Malley replied.

"We know Henry Crump," Will said. "We met him and stayed with his family in Independence."

"It's a small world and gettin' smaller all the time," Mr. O'Malley said.

"Will you join us for supper?" Will asked.

"Why, certainly," Mr. O'Malley said, "if you'll join me in a glass of fine Missouri Valley wine. I'm carryin' the best vintage and will be happy to bring it to your table."

"I'm afraid we have no table," Will said, "but, yes, we'd be happy to taste your fine wine."

Mr. O'Malley grabbed his team's harness and led them to the

spot where he wanted to set his wagon for the night. He picketed his mules in the thick grass nearby as we did the same with our animals. Mr. O'Malley had no tent to pitch. He slept in his wagon. He started a cooking fire as we pitched our tents.

We made up supper from provisions we had bought that morning in Louisville. Mr. O'Malley brought two bottles of wine and four glasses.

"One glass among the three of us will be fine," Will said, "but don't let that stop you, Mr. O'Malley. Have your fill of food and wine."

Mr. O'Malley took Will at his word. He ate an enormous platter of food, took seconds and swallowed one glass of wine after another. He talked even more than he ate.

"I do much better away from the rail lines," he said. "Folks in towns on the tracks get everything they need shipped in by rail. But when I get up to towns like Louisville and Westmoreland and Merrimac, away from the Kansas Pacific and the Central Branch Union Pacific, then I sell, sell, sell. But I sometimes have trouble out this way crossing creeks with no bridges."

"Freshets in the creeks have slowed us some too," I said.

"Now, I see you boys have some books in your tent there. Maybe I can interest you in a *Webster's Unabridged* or a *Zell's Encyclopedia*."

Without pausing to take a breath, let alone wait for an answer, Mr. O'Malley continued.

"Now, you know, *Webster's Unabridged*, well, it's a whole library in one volume. Ten thousand words and meanings not in other dictionaries, 3,000 engravings, I tell you, 1,840 pages quarto, my good friends. It's a necessity for every intelligent family. What library is complete without the best English dictionary?" he asked.

"Well, Mr. O'Malley, perhaps if we were settled in . . ." Will began to say.

"Yes, of course, I understand, Mr. Hawkins," Mr. O'Malley continued. "Well, then, I have *Zell's Popular Encyclopedia*, the best, cheapest and latest work of its kind published in America. I tell you, it's the only encyclopedia written since the war and, consequently, the only one giving a complete history of same— its great battles and who fought them. It's complete in history, biography, geography, science, the arts and languages. Every family should have one."

"Well, Mr. O'Malley, maybe if we . . ." Will began to say.

"Yes, of course, I understand Mr. Hawkins," he continued. "Well, then, gentlemen, I have the Greeley hats. They're handsome hats. They're tall, white hats of the stovepipe persuasion, with brown bands and trimmings. Just imagine—you can announce your support of Mr. Greeley and look dapper at once."

"Well, Mr. O'Malley, I'm not sure we want to announce for Greeley or look dapper," Will said.

"Yes, of course, I understand, Mr. Hawkins. I'll tell you what then. I know every man wants to keep his own natural teeth, and I'm willing to wager that Mrs. Hawkins insists that her men clean their teeth at least twice each day. Am I right?" Mr. O'Malley asked.

Will, Ben and I looked at each other. I knew they were thinking what I was thinking. They looked a little sheepish.

"You see?" Mr. O'Malley said, "I know you gentlemen want to keep your teeth, and I know Mrs. Hawkins insists you clean them, so I have just the thing for you. Wait a moment, and I'll demonstrate."

Mr. O'Malley jumped up and quickstepped to his wagon. He came back with a cup of water, a bone-and-bristle toothbrush and a small, white can with dark blue lettering on it. He held the can up for us to see.

"Here it is, gentlemen," he said, "Sozodont, the world's best tooth powder. It renders the teeth pearly white, gives the breath a fragrant odor. It extinguishes the ill humors that usually flow from a bad and neglected set of teeth. Sozodont is convenient and produces a sensation at once so delightful it's a pleasure to use. Allow me to demonstrate, gentlemen."

As he continued talking, he sprinkled powder from the can into his cupped left palm.

"Now, my friends, I just ate a delicious supper with garlic and onions, and I drank wine. Am I right, gentlemen?" he asked.

"Yes, we'll testify to that," Ben said.

"You bet I did," Mr. O'Malley said. "Observe, please."

He dipped the toothbrush into his water cup, then pressed it into the powder in his left palm. He vigorously brushed his teeth, up, down and all around. He threw his head back and gargled. He turned aside, spit and then repeated the process. He took a mouthful of water, flushed it around his mouth and spit again. He turned to us, grinning like a horse having his teeth shown.

"Now, I ask you, my friends, are my teeth pearly white and sparkling?"

We hesitated. "Yup, it looks like they are," I said.

"Thank you, young man," he said. "Now, if you'll permit me." He leaned over to me and blew his breath in my face. I was a little startled.

"Now, I ask you, does my breath smell fresh and clean? No onions, no garlic, no wine?" he asked.

"Yup, I suppose it does," I said.

"Well, there you have it, my friends—Sozodont, the gem of the toilet. And a mere 50 cents for a new, sealed can. Can I interest you?" he asked.

Ben and I looked at Will.

"Sold, Mr. O'Malley," Will said. "We'll buy two cans."

"Excellent, Mr. Hawkins," he said. "You've made a choice you'll not regret."

Mr. O'Malley gathered his brush, cup and can, again quick-stepped to his wagon and came back with two cans of Sozodont.

"Thank you, sir," Mr. O'Malley said as he and Will made the exchange. Will nodded.

That night and the next morning, as Mr. O'Malley smiled approvingly, Will, Ben and I brushed with Sozodont. If nothing else, it was invigorating.

In the morning, as we made ready to leave camp and enter the road, we paused to say goodbye to Mr. O'Malley.

"Westmoreland's just ahead," he said. "I'll stop there and sell maybe half the contents of my wagon."

"We'll stop for a few provisions and be on our way," Will said.

"Have you seen Indians yet? Buffalo?" he asked.

"I saw two Indian boys at Wakarusa Crossing," I said, "but none other."

"Haven't seen buffalo yet," Ben said.

"Chances are you'll see both soon," Mr. O'Malley said. "Good luck, gentlemen."

"Good luck to you too," we said, almost together.

We led the way, soon gaining distance on the slow-moving wagon. Mr. O'Malley's singing trailed off as we moved ahead.

We left the public road a day past Scott Spring at Merrimac and crossed the Black Vermillion River on a rickety, one-way, wooden bridge. We made our camp in the bottoms on the far side.

Rain kept us in camp till almost noon the next day. With the sky clearing, we followed the Central Branch Union Pacific tracks and crossed the Big Blue River on the trestle, stopping first to listen and be sure a locomotive wasn't near. The next town was Irving, on the rail line in the valley of the Big Blue. Will telegraphed Beth, asking her to wire money to Blue Rapids, which was about three miles distant and the next station stop. We made our camp in a small clearing in the timber that lined the river past Irving. We heard the westbound train at the edge of the bottoms just past sunset. Mars and Mercury were bright points in the twilight.

We needed provisions and expected we'd get them in Blue Rapids the next day while we waited for Beth's return wire. Our next supply stop and telegraph office was probably about five days past Blue Rapids at the Union Pacific tracks and the Platte River in Nebraska.

We woke at first light. Venus shone brightly at dawn. It was Monday, June 10th. We rode between the tracks and the river toward Blue Rapids. Springs flowed from the limestone bluffs at several places along the way. An eastbound passenger train passed at about half past 6 o'clock. One of the cars was a fine new coach.

We reached town just before 7 o'clock and were surprised to find the place already bustling. A dozen or so farm wagons waited at the depot. Several merchants were out in front of their stores, either sweeping or setting goods out on display. Carriages, saddle riders, wagons and people on foot were out and about on the streets. We dismounted and tied to the hitching rail at the depot. Will doubted that Beth's wire would be in yet, but he went inside to check.

Next to Ben and me, a farmer unloaded a sack of potatoes from his wagon and added it to maybe two dozen he had stacked on the depot platform. No sooner was Will inside than we heard a locomotive whistle in the distance to the west. The toots grew louder until, finally, the train steamed into the station in grand style. A bell behind the stack clanged in a slow rhythm. The cowcatcher was bigger than any I'd seen. I figured it was for buffalo. The locomotive and coal car were freshly painted and clean, trailing a short line of box and flat cars. As the freight was quickly exchanged, the engine took on water from an overhead tank alongside the tracks.

The farmer who had shipped the potatoes came back with a small barrel on one shoulder.

"Honey," he said as he lowered the barrel into his wagon. "My missus uses it in her baked goods—strawberry pie a short time back. Did you fellas get any sweet strawberries?"

"Yup, we did," I replied. "We bought strawberries at a grocer's in Lawrence."

"Where yuh headed?" the farmer asked. "Is it just the two of yuh?"

"Idaho—our papa's inside for a telegram," Ben said. The farmer paused. He looked a little puzzled.

" 'Bout the first of the month, a thousand head of cattle passed this way headin' for Idaho," the farmer said.

"Going *to* Idaho?" Ben and I asked together in the same amazed voices.

"We heard the droves of cattle passed *east*," Ben said.

"That was earlier this spring, and much more than a thousand," the farmer said.

"Will there be grass along the trail ahead?" I asked.

"Sure, plenty of grass," he replied. "You fellas have seen the prairies 'round here. There's a carpet of grass over 'em. Even with the emigrant trains passin', there's plenty of grass."

"I'm glad to hear that," Will said as he walked up. "Our beasts need grass. And I see you've met my men." The farmer brightened and straightened up as he turned to meet Will.

"Yep, I have," he said, "they're fine men. They say you're bound for Idaho. All the way on the trail, is it?"

"As far as the Raft River," Will replied. "But for the time being, we're waiting on a wire from home."

"How long do yuh 'spect it'll be?" the farmer asked.

"Don't know for sure," Will replied. "It's coming from Kentucky."

"Give it a day, maybe two from east of Saint Louis. We're on a back-end line here in Blue Rapids." He paused for a moment. "My name's Robertson, Robert Robertson. I have a wife and three kids on 200 acres 'bout two miles north of here."

"I'm Will Hawkins and these are my sons, Early and Ben," Will said. There was that touch of pride in his voice I was always glad to hear.

"Happy to meet you fellas," Mr. Robertson said. "I'll be in town for a short time before headin' back to the farm. If yuh want to ride with me and don't mind the bunkhouse, you're welcome to stay with us till your wire comes. My missus and I would be happy to have yuh."

"That's very kind of you, Mr. Robertson," Will said. He turned to Ben and me and asked, "Men?"

Ben and I nodded, saying, "Sure."

"We need supplies, but we should get them just before we leave town," Will said. "I can ride in this afternoon and check on the wire."

"I'll be a few minutes," Mr. Robertson said, climbing onto his wagon bench. He had a fine pair of bay geldings in harness. He was gentle with them. He was a big man, but graceful. Broad suspenders held his britches up, and he wore a wide-brimmed hat. "I have just one stop—at the bank on the way out of town."

Mr. Robertson led the way.

30

The Big Blue ran generally south from up in Nebraska down to the Kansas River. But at Blue Rapids, the Big Blue turned a loop and took an east line for well over a mile. That put Mr. Robertson's farm north of the bend and the town south. Blue Rapids was a small town, barely three years old but already looking prosperous. The site lay between the rails and the Big Blue, about two or three miles below the mouth of the Little Blue.

We tied our string of mules behind Mr. Robertson's wagon and rode on both sides of it, up by the bench where he sat. A double tubular arch, wrought-iron bridge spanned the river just up from big limestone buildings that sat on both banks. As we crossed, I saw a big turtle struggling with the current below.

"The bridge is only 'bout a year old," Mr. Robertson said. "Makes crossin' to town from our place a lot easier, 'specially when the river's high like this past week."

"It sure is a pretty valley," Ben said. The sun's low angle lit the dew on the grass, making it glisten. Little cottonball clouds floated in a deep blue sky. Small birds darted back and forth between the prairie and the timber that lined the river. It was barely 8 o'clock.

"Blue Rapids looks as if it has a bright future," Will said.

"The first settlers came from Genesee County, New York, during the '69 to '70 winter," Mr. Robertson said. "There are about 12 hundred or so in the township now. Mary, the kids and I came with the first 50 families in '69."

"The town's grown a lot in less than three years," Will said.

"The railroads bring the growth," Mr. Robertson said. "Marshall County has the Union Pacific and the Saint Joseph–Denver City lines running parallel east and west. Surveyin' is under way to link Beatrice, Nebraska, north of us, to Manhattan, Kansas, south of us, straight through Marshall County. That'll open a line from Duluth to Texas.

"We've got a gypsum mine and mill, a brick-makin' plant that runs 15 hours a day, a flourin' mill and a woolen mill. The woolen mill has new wagons and machinery due this week by rail. Everythin' comes and goes in the cars. You saw the hustle-bustle in town this mornin' for the eastbound 7:30 freight. Passengers traveled on the eastbound 6:16. The railroads have developed so much in Marshall County in three years that in three more, I wonder if I'll know the place."

"That's the conflict," Will said. "It's a blessing and a curse. Do we want the calm of the old ways or the commotion and convenience of the new?"

Our road topped a rise, and beyond it, Mr. Robertson pointed out his farm. It spread down the decline, across and up the next rise. A steady southwest breeze swept acres of ripening wheat. Hip-high corn stood in long, neat rows, and newly cut lucerne lay scattered, waiting to be raked, gathered and stored. Young fruit orchards showed bright green leaves at the base of the far rise. A silo stood beside the barn across from the house. Both house and barn were built of limestone, with split-shingle curb roofs. A long, narrow pond lay beyond a stretch of wheat, between us and the farmhouse. Under a wide, deep blue sky and bright morning sun, the Robertsons' place was a pretty sight.

"It's 'bout half past 8 o'clock," Mr. Robertson said. "My boys should have the cows milked and long since out to pasture. I 'spect we'll find the boys workin' in the orchard."

Our road skirted the wheat and came around to the house and barn. As we rode up, a woman and a young girl came out to greet us.

"Did you bring my honey, dear?" the woman asked. She had her hair pulled back into a bun and wore an apron over her blouse and skirt. She was simply dressed, as I guess any working farm wife would be. The girl skipped up to Mr. Robertson as he climbed down from the wagon seat.

"Hello, Papa!" she said in a merry, excited voice.

"Hello, dear one," Mr. Robertson replied as he bent on one knee and embraced his daughter.

"And, yes, Mary dear, I have your honey. I'll bring it in presently, but first, please meet my friends."

Mr. Robertson introduced us to his wife, Mary, and his daughter, Irene. He told them of our telegram in town and said he had invited us to stay the night.

"Well, I'm sorry it's only the bunkhouse," Mrs. Robertson said. "With Robert and me and the three children, our house is full up."

"The bunkhouse will be fine, ma'am," Will said. "It will seem like a fine hotel compared to the tent we've been sleeping in."

"We're happy to have you," Mrs. Robertson said. "Please make yourselves at home. Dinner's at noon, supper's at 6 o'clock, and we're up before the sun."

Mr. Robertson lifted the honey barrel from his wagon, hoisted it to his shoulder and walked toward the house.

"Are the boys in the orchard?" he asked his wife.

"I believe they are," she replied. Mr. Robertson turned to us.

"Let me deliver this honey, then we'll tend to the animals and walk out to the orchard," he said.

We took care of our animals while Mr. Robertson unhitched his team and removed their harness. We turned the beasts into a corral behind the barn and walked off toward the orchard. Two boys, one nearly full grown and the other about my age, were pulling weeds and cleaning up beneath the young trees. Although small, the trees would bear fruit come fall—peaches, pears and apples. Mr. Robertson introduced us to his sons, George and Lafayette.

"We named our first boy after Washington and our second after the Frenchman who was such a friend durin' our Revolution," Mr. Robertson explained.

"Those are good American names," Will said.

Lafayette was the younger boy. He asked me to explain my name, which I did. Strangers often eyed Ben suspiciously, but not so the Robertsons. I felt comfortable with the family. I think Will and Ben did too. We walked to the top of the rise past the orchard with Mr. Robertson.

"Our 200 acres run from the river down yonder," he said, pointing west, "and up this swale between the two low ridges to that mound yuh see east of us. There's a trickle of a creek that fills and drains our pond. There's just enough slope that the rain neither rushes nor pools. This year we have wheat, corn and potatoes. I shipped some Early Rose potatoes this mornin'. The winter wheat is almost ripe, and we'll be cuttin' and threshin' in a week or so. We've had oats, rye and barley, but this year we'll sow wheat again. The alfalfa you see dryin' there is for our horses and dairy cows."

"What you call alfalfa, we call lucerne. You've done a lot here in less than three years," Will said. "It's a farm to admire."

"Thank you, Will," Mr. Robertson said. "We came as a colony of 50 families. It was neighbor helping neighbor. The Robertsons could never have done what you see here on our own."

"Still," Will said, "it's a proud accomplishment."

"Mary and I had been married nearly 20 years when we left New York for Kansas," Mr. Robertson said. "This farm is our second start, and we're happy it's workin' out well."

"Robert," Will said, "your family has done here in Kansas what our family wants to do in Idaho."

"Why all the way to Idaho, Will?" Mr. Robertson asked. "There's plenty of good land right here in Marshall County, and yuh can see the growth and prosperity all around yuh."

"Robert, you were the first man to break the soil in this little valley," Will said. "Mary was the first to cook a meal, to keep a house, to nurture a family here. Your family is the first to draw sustenance from this land. That's what our family wants to do in Idaho. We want to be pioneers."

That was the only time I heard Will say "We want to be pioneers." About six months earlier, he had said the family would remove to Idaho to homestead and farm, but the reasons he gave were that the steamboat business had all but died, and our wharfboat business was dying too. In talking to Mr. Robertson in Kansas, Will revealed a deeper drive. Our move wasn't only a business decision. There was more to it. I didn't fully understand the meaning of Will's words that morning in Kansas, but they lodged in the back of my mind, and as I worked beside him in Idaho over the years, the meaning of "We want to be pioneers" became clear.

Mr. Robertson looked toward his lucerne field.

"It's past 9 o'clock, it's 80 degrees and the dew is gone. I'd wager that with your help we can have that alfalfa raked by noon," he said, "then we can gather it after dinner."

"Count us in," Will said.

Mr. Robertson was right. We had finished raking the lucerne into windrows just before Mrs. Robertson rang the dinner bell. We washed up at a pump in the yard and sat with the family for the noon meal.

"Did you see any wagon trains on the trail, Mr. Hawkins?" Lafayette asked when Irene finished grace.

"No, I'm afraid we didn't," Will replied. "We saw only one emigrant wagon and one peddler wagon, and then carriages, farm wagons and horsemen."

"Well, there's a train ahead of you, and I'd wager another behind you," George said. "At this time of year, we see about one train a week campin' at the grove near the bridge and takin' on supplies in town and at Olmstead's flourin' mill."

"Will," Mr. Robertson said, "my guess is you'd want to avoid the trains—too much dust and commotion, too many people and too many animals."

"You guessed right," Will replied. "We travel faster and easier on our own."

"I'd suggest then, Will," Mr. Robertson continued, "when yuh ride out of town, stay west of the Big Blue. Cross the Little Blue just up from the mouth, then follow a line northwest, keeping the Big Blue on your right. Yuh'll reach the trail east of the junction with the road from Saint Joe. Yuh'll get out ahead of the wagon train that left Blue Rapids on Saturday. From here, they usually follow the public road to Marysville, then cross the Big Blue just west of town. If you're lucky, yuh'll be ahead of the trains from Saint Joe. If not, yuh'll overtake them in a day or two."

"Sounds like a good idea to me," Will said.

"Wolves ate our pigs last Christmas," Irene said.

"Prairie wolves or gray wolves?" I asked.

"Don't know, didn't see 'em," Irene replied. "Just heard the pigs squealin', and when we run out, three wuz gone."

"*Ran* out and three *were* gone, dear," Mrs. Robertson said.

"Yes, Mama," Irene said, looking a little sheepish but annoyed.

"I'd wager they were coyotes—prairie wolves," George said. "We don't see gray wolves in these parts since the buffalo and elk are gone."

"The peddler we met said we'd see buffalo up this way," Ben said.

"Naw, not anymore," George replied. "Yuh'll have to go north to the Platte and the Union Pacific line to see a herd. Yuh might see some stragglers down this way, but the herds are north."

"There's a buffalo hunting party leavin' Irving in a few days," Mr. Robertson said. "I hear they're goin' north to the Platte. Yuh know, first it was the professional hunters killin' buffalo for meat for railroad workers. Now, they kill 'em by the thousands for the hides. It's wholesale slaughter. They take the hides and leave the carcasses rottin' on the plains. The Government's behind it too. They control the Indians by destroyin' the buffalo."

"We had a cornstalk over 19 feet last year," Lafayette said.

"That's about three times as tall as Will or me," Ben said with a grin.

"How do you feel about living out on the prairie, Mrs. Robertson?" Will asked.

"When we first came, it was difficult," she replied, "but we're only two miles from town, and since the bridge, we never have to wait to cross the river. And we have so many modern conveniences now," she added. "We have the railroad, steamers on the Missouri, gas in the larger towns, friction matches, the telegraph, expresses and, for us ladies, sewing machines and my pride and joy, my Charter Oak cooking stove. I love to bake, you know."

"Where do you suggest we go in town for groceries and supplies?" Will asked.

"Gosh, now you have to choose, I suppose," she replied. "T. G. Morris' General Store has groceries. Then there's Hinkston and

Scott's, and Loban and Sweetland's. If it's just groceries you need, it's Loban, but if you want dry goods too, it's Morris or Hinkston."

"Thank you, ma'am," Will said.

"Certainly," Mrs. Robertson replied.

"Our Blue Rapids Club is playin' the Irving Pioneers come Saturday," George said, "should be a good game. Waterville whupped Irving last Wednesday afternoon, 28–26."

"Some of those Blue Rapids boys are gettin' a little too excited 'bout baseball," Mr. Robertson said. "Ora Douglass was out front of his store in town Tuesday and was hit severely by a ball from a bat. He went inside, sat on his counter and fainted. He fell to the floor and suffered quite a bruisin'."

"Good Lord," Mrs. Robertson said, "those boys ought to be more careful."

"Yes, dear, they should," Mr. Robertson said. "Either that or Ora should learn to duck." That remark drew chuckles all around.

"I'll be riding into town this afternoon to see about our wire," Will said. "Is there anything you need?"

"I don't," Mrs. Robertson said, "but Lafayette and Irene will be your loyal friends forever if you fetch them some rock candy."

"Yes!" the two youngest Robertsons screamed together.

"All right, children," Mrs. Robertson reminded, "that's a little too loud for the dinner table." She smiled and asked, "Now, who's ready for pie?"

All replied with one or another version of "I am."

"I talked with Mr. Tibbits at the *Times*," Mr. Robertson said. "In Thursday's number, he'll endorse Mr. Grant for President and Mr. Wilson for Vice President."

"If I were home to vote in Kentucky," Will said, "they'd have my vote."

"Yup, mine too," Mr. Robertson said. "I'm not a Greeley man, no matter how many white stovepipe hats appear on the streets."

"I won't be able to vote in Idaho until the territory becomes a state," Will added.

"From what I've heard of the Raft River country," Mr. Robertson said, "even if yuh could vote, yuh'd have a devil of a time findin' a pollin' place."

"Yes," Will said, "it would probably take some doing."

After dinner, we gathered wagonloads of lucerne and stored

them in the hay mow. Late in the afternoon, Will rode into town
to check on Beth's wire. It hadn't come yet, but the telegrapher
was sure he'd have it by morning. Telegram or no telegram, Mrs.
Robertson said, we were welcome to stay till we were ready to
leave. Will brought rock candy for us kids. Lafayette, Irene and
I were delighted.

The Robertsons had an upright piano in their front room.
After the supper dishes were cleared, Ben brought his banjo and
fiddle in from the packs. Mrs. Robertson and Irene took turns at
the piano. We all sang, although some not too loudly.

Mr. Robertson and his neighbors had built a bunkhouse for
hired hands and friends who came for planting and harvest.
That's where we slept—and quite comfortably too.

We rose with the sun, had breakfast in Mrs. Robertson's
kitchen and went to the barn to saddle and pack. Irene and Mrs.
Robertson came out with loaves of fresh-baked bread and a sack of
biscuits. The Robertsons couldn't have been more hospitable. As we
mounted, Ben said what I'm sure he knew Will and I were thinking.

"We sure thank you folks," Ben said, "you make it mighty
hard to leave."

We said our goodbyes and when we reached the top of the
rise on the way to town, we turned to wave. The Robertsons were
where we had left them, returning our waves. They cast long
shadows in the early morning sun.

As it had been the morning before, Blue Rapids was bustling.
The passenger train had come and gone, and the 7:30 freight
was due. I went into the depot with Will, while Ben waited with
the beasts. As the telegrapher had thought, Beth's wire was in.
After Will had settled the cash, the telegrapher turned to me.

"You look like a boy who likes books," he said.

"Well, yes, I do," I said, surprised. "How did you know?"

"Oh, I can tell," he said, "I don't know how. A British gentleman was through town about a fortnight back, and he left a book
he had finished. He wanted me to take it myself or pass it on to
a reader I chose. Well, it's a book I've already read, so would you
like to have it?"

He handed me *Beyond the Mississippi* by Albert Richardson.
"Sure," I said, "I'd like to have it, much obliged."

I had finished my Twain book and thought I would pass it

on to Ben. I had left a copy of Richardson's book in Smithland, mostly unread, so to get a later edition in Kansas was a treat.

Morris' was a big general store for such a small town. They had penny postcards and little pictures of the town square on the counter next to a bottle of Kehoe's mucilage, an inkwell and a pen. I picked up one of the pictures to take a closer look. Colonial Hall and the LaBelle House took up most of the picture. There was a circle of young trees in front.

"Go ahead," the clerk said, "spread some glue on back of the picture, stick it on the card, write your mama's name and address on front, sign your love, and drop it over yonder at the post office." He raised his hand and pointed vaguely out the door. "In a few days, your mama will be right pleased to get a picture post card from her boy."

I don't know how they did it, but the telegrapher and the grocery clerk had me figured out. I glued and stuck and wrote as the clerk said, and after we bought and packed our supplies, I ran the card over to the post office and pushed it through the slot.

We rode out of town and followed the big loop of the river, staying on the west side as Mr. Robertson had suggested. We crossed the gravel bottom of the Little Blue about two miles out of town, followed a diagonal course west of the Big Blue and came to the Oregon Trail after about six miles more. We didn't see another rider or wagon until we reached the junction with the Saint Joe road. There, we moved ahead of a six-wagon train and went into camp at Cottonwood Creek. The train caught up and camped there too.

We passed Hollenberg Ranch early next morning and crossed the state line into Nebraska at about noon. That night's camp would be on Rock Creek. It was Wednesday, June 12th. The train was somewhere behind.

31

We reached Rock Creek late in the afternoon. I had read that the station was a stage stop, a Pony Express station, and a camp along the Oregon Trail. Now, with the transcontinental railroad in place and the Saint Joe & Denver tracks running up the valley of the Little Blue, stations like Rock Creek were falling out of use.

We were ahead of June's emigrant wagons and figured the travelers we'd meet on the trail or in camps would be local or short-trip people. As it was, we were alone in camp at Rock Creek that afternoon. Judging by the look of things, somebody lived in the log buildings nearby, but no one was about.

As we finished setting up camp near the cottonwoods and cedars along the creek, a large freight wagon drawn by two yoke of oxen drove up. It came from the direction of Kansas. A man and a young boy sat on the bench. The box was loaded rail to rail with saplings in wooden tubs. The rig looked like a rolling tree nursery. After they had found a level spot to camp and turned their oxen out to graze, the man and boy approached our site.

"Hallo," the man called from some distance as he raised his hand and waved. I thought the space was a precaution.

"Good afternoon," Will called back in greeting.

"My boy and I have been to Marysville to pick up trees," the man said. "The new railroad won't unload heavy freight up Fairbury way till the depot's finished. That'll be in a week or two."

"Do you need help hauling water for the trees?" Will asked.

"Don't think so, but much obliged," the man replied. "We wet 'em down back a ways when we crossed the Little Blue. Folks up Fairbury way say they miss the trees they had back East, so Thomas & Champlin ordered 'em and sent me down to pick 'em up. They came in on the longest train I've ever seen—38 cars were haulin' nuthin' but iron and ties to build the road out past Fairbury."

"We heard the train but didn't see it," Will said.

"Name's Gibson, John Gibson, and this here's my boy, Nate," the man said. Nate tipped his hat. He was probably a year or two younger than I was. Will introduced us all around.

"Would you like to sit for supper with us?" Will asked. "We have rabbit and some fresh greens."

"Sure, much obliged," Mr. Gibson said.

As we sat around the fire with our supper plates on our laps, Mr. Gibson talked about Nebraska.

"My wife, my boy and I have been here about a year now, came from Ohio. We have a quarter section on Brawner Creek this side of Fairbury. We'll prove up, and it'll be ours. Not many neighbors yet though. I s'pose there's only 'bout a thousand folks in all of Jeff County. Now that the Saint Joe & Denver's comin' through, that'll be changin' pretty quick, I'd say. The rails is past Fairbury and headin' on toward Juniata. They say they're goin' clear to Kearney Junction. That's where the Burlington & Missouri is goin' to meet the Union Pacific on the other side of the Platte. I don't know, we'll see. There's a lot of empty country out there."

"Any Indians or buffalo?" Ben asked.

"The Union Pacific has pretty much split the buffalo range. You might see a small herd south of the Platte headin' north this time of year. And where the buffs go, the Injuns go. We haven't seen neither in these parts, but you might catch sight of some if you're headin' as far as the Platte."

"We are," Will said. "We're following the trail all the way to Idaho. We plan to reach the Raft River by middle August."

"Seems 'bout right," Mr. Gibson said. "Bein' here in middle June'll have you in Idaho by middle August if'n you hold your pace."

"Have you seen any wagon trains this year?" I asked.

"Not as yet," Mr. Gibson replied. "My guess is they're right on your heels. Give 'em a day or two, and they'll be comin' through for a week or more. They know if they're headin' for California or Oregon, they have to be to Independence Rock by middle July, or they'll get snowed under in the mountains."

"Does somebody live here in the station buildings?" I asked.

"Best I know, there's a family livin' here but where they are now's anybody's guess. Their animals is gone too," Mr. Gibson said. "They can't be away too long cuz somebody's been waterin' them narcissus flowers there by the ol' post office buildin'.

"This spot goes back to fur tradin' days, you know, then the trail and the Pony Express. Fact, that buildin' yonder's where Hickok kilt his first men. Claimed self-defense and went scot free. Sounded like an ambush to me."

"You mean Wild Bill Hickok?" I asked.

"That's him," Mr. Gibson replied with a tone of disdain in his voice.

We turned in early but were awakened in the night by a fierce windstorm. We tied our tents down tighter, pulled the pickets that kept the beasts close and walked them down into a hollow. The wind about picked me up and took me with it. Mr. Gibson's wagon was too heavy to tip, and his saplings were protected by the high, staked sides. But I saw a gust knock Nate over backwards when he and his father walked out to fetch their oxen.

The wind backed off and calmed by dawn. It had broken limbs off the timber along the creek, felled several trees and scattered litter all around. None of us was hurt.

We broke camp and left Rock Creek about an hour past sunrise. Our quicker pace kept us ahead of the Gibsons and got us to Fairbury before their wagon.

Fairbury was rearranging itself according to the new Saint Joe & Denver tracks. A handsome new depot was going up and didn't show any damage from the night's wind. But the blacksmith shop had been blown off its foundation. Several men with teams were busy setting it right.

There was a Saturday paper in town, the Fairbury *Gazette*. The tidy-looking Star Hotel sat on the east side of the square. Merchants had a lot of farm implements for sale. One store had a rotating 12-horse thresher set up out front. The merchants must have been anticipating a wave of settlers now that the railroad was running up the valley.

It would be a long stretch before our next town stop, so we bought more than our usual amount of supplies at T. J. Kirk's store. Will telegraphed Beth and asked her to wire triple the usual amount of money to North Platte, where we expected to be in about 10 days.

That night we went into camp on the Little Blue past Big Sandy Station. It was a clear, warm, still night on the Nebraska prairie. We saw flashes of lightning far off and heard low rumbling thunder. Ben played a slow, mournful fiddle tune from the book he had bought in Saint Louis. It was the first time I felt homesick for Smithland. I missed Beth and Amanda and Louis. I missed the rivers and the green hills.

Over the next several days, we worked our way up the valley of the Little Blue, at first in the bottoms and then on a plateau between the Little Blue and the Platte. The only timber was what lined the river and creeks. It was mostly elm, cottonwood and oak, with some maple and walnut mixed in.

We caught our first glimpse of the Platte on Tuesday the 18th. It was like the Kaw—wide, shallow and muddy, only more so. The only timber was on the high islands in the stream. The low islands had been scoured by the spring floods. Thickets of brush lined the banks.

The abandoned Fort Kearny was on the south side of the river, but past it, the town of Kearney Junction was up away from the bank on the north side. The Platte was probably a mile wide at that point, and there was no bridge. A telegraph line came across the river there and ran west. We stayed on the south side and, after the night's camp, rode toward North Platte, which was about 100 miles farther on.

The country was upland prairie, almost completely flat, treeless and without streams coming from the south toward the Platte. The grass was short, due to Nature, not eating. What few farms there were drew water from wells pumped by windmills.

Every so often, there was a wide, shallow draw. Stopping at the edge of one of these and looking ahead a great distance, I spied a line of animals moving north toward the river. A look through the binoculars proved they were pronghorns, the first we had seen. They were too far off to pursue, and with their well-known swiftness, we were sure they would stay far off.

If the pronghorns were impossible to catch, prairie dogs were impossible to avoid. We came upon a very large town and found them highly amusing. They posted sentries that sat upright on their haunches, watching. One of the sentries spotted a hawk and barked a warning cry that sent every prairie dog scurrying underground. They were gone before the hawk had a chance to tuck its wings and dive.

Near the end of our second day riding along the Platte, we spied another column in the distance moving north. But these weren't pronghorns. They were mounted Indians, dragging travois and leaving a dust trail. Even their dogs towed travois. The sun was behind the column, making them silhouettes. If they saw us, they paid no mind. We expected they would wait till morning to cross the river, and if we continued west before going into camp, our overnight spot would be too close to theirs for comfort. We turned toward the river where we were and went into camp.

Early the next day, we came to the Indians' trail and investigated their camp and crossing. The ashes from their cooking fires were still warm.

The Union Pacific and the towns it spawned were on the north side of the Platte. We were on the lonely south side. We followed the line of the bank, riding from plateaus to swales, surrounded by seemingly endless prairie. Small sunflowers dotted the ground, and here and there what we supposed were badger holes. They seemed too big for the jackrabbits that darted about. We moved to the river and the shade of the thicket for our noon rest.

The afternoon brought huge, billowy clouds that rose high above the horizon, encircling us and everything in sight. Turkey vultures on the lookout for a meal floated among cottony clouds in the deep overhead. I imagined how we looked to them, seven curious figures moving slowly through an immense landscape, obviously alive.

The west wind carried volley after volley of distant rifle fire to our ears. It sounded more like a battle than a hunt. Will told us to wait and hold the mules while he rode ahead to look. He galloped across a wide swale, then stopped and dismounted before he came to the top of the next rise. He belly-crawled to the top, looked over for a minute, stayed low and backed down. He mounted May Belle, rode part way back and waved us ahead. By the time we reached him, the shooting had stopped.

"Half a dozen hunters slaughtering buffalo they caught crossing the river at the next swale. There must be more than 50 carcasses bleeding on the ground," Will said with pity in his tone. "Outfits of skinners are already pulling the hides. Two of the shooters are pursuing the herd across the river. The others will probably follow."

We moved ahead slowly. The slaughter dampened our eagerness to see buffalo. We had hoped to see live herds. We surveyed the scene from the top of the rise. The animals were strewn across the swale, mostly up toward the river. A few that had either fallen behind or turned in a vain effort to escape the killing lay dead closer to us. From the look of the wallows, this must have been a crossing for a very long time.

Three men with long rifles had reached the north side. They waited for three others who were midstream. The remainder of the herd was beyond the brush that lined the river. The buffalo moved slowly north, not seeming to know they were about to die.

We watched the skinners from our saddles for a while. They moved quickly from carcass to carcass, working in pairs. With long knives, they circled the animal's neck and lower legs, slit the belly and limbs, and took the hide off in one piece. Skinning each buffalo took little more than five minutes. Two men in a wagon moved about the swale, loading the skins.

Any thought that Will had of using the Sharps to kill a buffalo left him. "You men ready to go?" he asked. Neither Ben nor I said a word. We just kicked our horses and moved on.

We rode a bit farther than our usual distance to reach Fort McPherson by late afternoon on Saturday the 22nd. Our trail and the telegraph line that we had seen cross the Platte near Kearney Junction led straight to the fort. The fort was near the base of the bluffs and the mouth of Cottonwood Canyon. It was a lot bigger than we expected. It was like a town, not even surrounded by a stockade. What at first looked like warehouses at the edge of the parade ground turned out to be barracks.

Before going into camp at the river, we talked to several soldiers at the fort. They said they had seen a few riders and freight or farm wagons but no emigrant wagons as yet. They advised hunting for turkeys in the brush up a ways along the river. They asked our destination and said our next stop would probably be North Platte, which was less than a day's ride ahead. They reported no hostile Indian activity between there and Fort Laramie.

After we had unburdened the beasts and picketed them in the grass along the river, Will sent Ben and me out to shoot a turkey while he set up our camp. We hadn't walked too far upriver when I got a fat tom with a clean chest shot. We found some wild greens, and were set with fresh food for two or three meals. That was a welcome relief after living mostly on beans and dried meat we had bought in Fairbury.

By the middle of Sunday afternoon, we reached the iron bridge that crossed the south fork of the river and led to North Platte, a railroad town. It was on the Union Pacific line between the two forks of the river. The railroad had built a roundhouse and machine shops there for the purpose of repairing locomotives and cars. Will thought with that solid foundation, the town was bound to grow.

There was scarcely a tree to be seen anywhere in town. We learned the reason was cattle. The railroad being at North Platte made it the shipping point for longhorns driven up from Texas and bound for markets in the East. Any sprout or sapling a citizen might encourage was quickly trampled under the herds' hoofs.

Beth's wire was waiting for us at the telegraph office. Will wired back to tell her we were near the point where the trail and the rails, and therefore the telegraph lines, split. The only line to Fort Laramie was a government wire, operated by the Signal Corps. He asked her to wire extra money to Kelton, Utah, where we would be in middle August. He added that we loved and missed her and Amanda, that we would be all right and not to worry. He neglected to say that for the next seven or eight weeks we would be in Indian country, where white settlements were few and far between.

We stocked supplies at a grocery we were fortunate to find open on Sunday afternoon and rode to camp near the bank of the Platte's north fork. We would follow that stream and meet the trail where it crossed from the south some miles ahead.

After four days in the North Platte bottoms, we rejoined the trail at Ash Hollow on Thursday, June 27th. We hadn't seen rain, except for light thunder showers, since Kansas. Every day brought a wide, clear blue sky and highs in the 80s or 90s. We had gotten into hilly country with canyons and washes, junipers and beavertail cactus. The air was dry, the grass was short, and there were thistles and sunflowers everywhere. Big, fat grasshoppers outjumped the cottontails and jackrabbits. Where bluffs lined the river, cliff swallows darted about, catching insects in flight. We heard the soft cooing of mourning doves at every noon rest and night's camp.

32

The North Platte was our lifeline in the week between Ash Hollow and Fort Laramie. We drank its water, our beasts chopped the grass along its banks, and we hunted in the wide swath of brush that greened its bottoms.

The sun shone brightly every day from rise to set. There wasn't a drop of rain. Daytime temperatures got into the low 90s. At night, the mercury dropped about 25 degrees. Our noon rests were a welcome relief. We sought the shade of bluffs or brush along the river. The beasts knew our clock and eagerly walked to water.

We passed the great landmarks we had read about in emigrants' and writers' accounts. From a distance across the flat plain, we saw Courthouse and Jail Rocks and Chimney Rock. Then, nearing the Wyoming border, the trail nearly touched the base of Scotts Bluff, an imposing sight. We left our camp and found our way up the bluff for a view that seemed to stretch to the end of the Earth. Junipers and ponderosa pines dotted the heights. After a magnificent sunset, we scrambled down to reach our camp before twilight turned to starlight.

Under way in the morning, we saw a cable ferry sitting idle on the far side of the North Platte. Our map told us it was at the Red Cloud Indian Agency just inside the Wyoming Territory line. We had left the States behind.

Fort Laramie was bigger than Fort McPherson. The clear, swift Laramie River curved around its east and south boundaries. We met the post commander, Colonel John Eugene Smith, and two Pawnee scouts who were with him. The scouts mounted and galloped off as we talked with the colonel. He welcomed us to his post and said he was sorry we missed the Independence Day celebration on the parade grounds earlier. We expressed our regrets and said that we had staged our own celebration during our noon rest.

We asked what we should expect farther west. He said the buffalo had been driven either far south or to the high plains north of the Union Pacific line. There had been no Indian troubles. In fact, Colonel Smith said, not one white man had died across the Department of the Platte by an Indian's hand so far in 1872, and he intended to keep it that way. Evidently, the Sioux were satisfied with the Great Sioux Reservation ceded them in the 1868 treaty and with their freedom to hunt in the unceded territory north and west of the fort.

Colonel Smith added that, except for emergencies, the post telegraph was for government use only. He said it was built and maintained by the Signal Corps. But if we wanted to post a letter, he offered, the mails were open to the public. Before leaving the fort, we wrote to Beth and Amanda, each of us adding several lines and assuring our loved ones of our safety. Our letter would go on the next day's coach to the rail line in Cheyenne.

We decided to make our camp on the Laramie River near the

point where it met the North Platte. As we rode in that direction, one of the Pawnee scouts we had met at the fort galloped up.

"Hawk One," he said, addressing Will, "the Man of Five Legs want meet you."

"The Man of Five Legs?" Will asked.

"He wait for light there," the Pawnee said, pointing southwest.

If we weren't within shouting distance of a United States Army post, and if we hadn't met the Indian scout with Colonel Smith, I doubt we would have followed him. But under the circumstances, we did. As we turned southwest, Ben caught my eye and silently mouthed the words, "The man of five legs?"

Across the plain leading to the Black Hills and Laramie Peak, we saw a team and wagon. Beside it was a dull-white tent and what looked like a very small black tent. The Pawnee pointed and said, "There." When we said we saw our goal, he rode off toward the fort.

As we drew closer, we saw that a flap of the white tent was turned back to reveal an orange calico lining. From beneath the black tent, five legs stretched to the ground. Two of them were wrapped in leggings and high leather boots, while the other three were triangular wooden braces with their points stuck in the ground. Ben exclaimed, "The man of five legs!" in a tone of wonder. We laughed heartily.

The man was a photographer with a very large camera set on a tripod beneath a black hood. As we came to a halt nearby, there was movement under the hood, then, with both hands outstretched, the man threw the hood up over his head and the camera, and turned toward us, smiling.

"Happy Independence Day, gentlemen, and thank you for coming," he said cheerfully. "I was waiting for just the right afternoon light to capture Laramie Peak and the foreground hills, and I think I've just made a beautiful picture."

"It's an impressive sight," Will said, "worthy of a photograph."

We dismounted and approached the photographer. He extended his hand, first to Will, then to Ben and me.

"I'm Jackson, Bill Jackson, William Henry Jackson by profession, and I know your name is Hawkins," he said.

"That's right," Will said. "I'm Will and these men are my sons, Ben and Early."

"I'm happy to make your acquaintance," Mr. Jackson said. "I understand you're on your way to Idaho on the Oregon Trail."

"Yes, we are," Will replied, "We expect to be to the Raft River by middle August."

"I rode the trail from Nebraska City to the Great Salt Lake as a bullwhacker in '66," Mr. Jackson said, "but this time I'm on my way to Yellowstone."

"The national park, you mean?" Ben asked.

"Yes, that's the one," Mr. Jackson said, "inaugurated by President Grant on March 1st of this year. This is my second photographic expedition to Yellowstone."

"Are you going with that wagon and team?" I asked.

"Oh no, young man," Mr. Jackson replied. "I'm on my way to Ogden by rail. From there, Dr. Hayden, many other men with the geological survey and I will travel overland to Yellowstone. I left the train in Cheyenne and came to photograph the Black Hills and Laramie Peak from this vantage point. My associate, Charley Campbell, is somewhere nearby looking for a creek for our camp. We'll rejoin the train and continue to Ogden in a few days."

"We're making our camp near the mouth of the Laramie," Will said. "Would you like to join us there?"

"Let me see what Charley finds," Mr. Jackson said. "I want to photograph the mountains in early morning light from this spot. I hope to camp nearby, if there's water." At that, we heard the report of a rifle west of us.

"That's Charley," Mr. Jackson said. "Either he's found water or he's killed something." He paused, scanning the sky. "The light's fading. There will be no more photographs today. I might as well close up shop while we're waiting for Charley."

We helped Mr. Jackson strike his tent and put his equipment in the wagon. A few minutes later, a young man appeared, walking from the west. He carried a rifle and had a deer slung behind his neck and across his shoulders.

"There's Charley," Mr. Jackson said as he waved to the man approaching us. "Looks as if he's bringing supper. That's surprising. The soldiers told us there was no game within 50 miles."

Charley strode easily, seemingly unaffected by the deer he carried. He walked straight to the wagon, put his back to the tailgate and dropped the mule deer into the bed.

"He's a young buck," Charley said, "much bigger and I wouldn't have been able to carry him."

Charley was a young man about Ben's age, lean, lanky and more slightly built than Ben. He wore a slouch hat like mine. There were blood stains on the bandana he had draped across his shoulders. Mr. Jackson made introductions all around.

"There are draws nearby," Charley said, "but they're dry."

"Mr. Hawkins," Mr. Jackson said as he turned to Will, "we'll accept your offer of sharing your camp. We'll have to be up early to drive back to this spot to catch the morning light. Will you help us eat the buck?"

"Certainly we will, Mr. Jackson," Will replied.

We formed a little caravan and rode down to near the mouth of the Laramie. Its waters were clear, while the Platte's nearby were muddy.

Mr. Jackson removed his hat as we worked to set up camp. He was a handsome man, I'd guess about 30 years old at the time. He wore a beard with a moustache that turned up at the ends, giving him the look of a dashing adventurer. He had large, doleful eyes that belied his cheerful manner. A pistol hung at his right hip.

As Ben and I gathered driftwood and sagebrush for a fire, Charley skinned and dressed the buck. We skewered its parts and stretched the spit across the fire between two upright forks. Mr. Jackson brought out biscuits and tea he had carried from Cheyenne in a sack. We sat cross-legged around the fire with our tin plates in our laps, soaking up the roasted juices with our biscuits and washing it all down with hot tea. The sun sank behind the mountains and set the sky on fire. It was a fine meal, one of the best in my memory.

We talked with Mr. Jackson and Charley, learning that Charley was the cousin of Mr. Jackson's recently deceased wife. She had died in childbirth, and the baby girl had passed shortly thereafter. It was a painful memory for Mr. Jackson, one he hoped the expedition to Yellowstone would help erase.

In the still morning, when there was barely a hint of light in the east, a bugle sounding reveille drifted down from the fort to our camp. We rose from our rest, ate a venison breakfast and made ready to continue on our way. Mr. Jackson asked if he could make a photograph of us and our beasts when we were packed and ready. We agreed, of course. The sun had just revealed itself, lighting us warmly when Mr. Jackson made the exposure. He suggested we contact him through the U. S. Geological Survey to get a copy. He and Charley packed their gear and turned toward the spot where we had met the afternoon before. We struck out on the trail along the North Platte. We waved to our friends as our paths went separate ways.

33

The trail headed northwest, roughly paralleling the river. Depending on the stream's bends, the flow was sometimes within sight and sometimes not. The Black Hills rose to the west, with Laramie Peak the most prominent at more than 10,000 feet. Our route became hilly, with descents to creeks in the draws and ascents to plateaus that stretched to the next draw. At Register Cliff, the trail had returned to the river bottoms and a narrow space between the bluffs and the bank. Hundreds of names were etched in the soft sandstone, some with dates and addresses or destinations.

We took our noon rest at Warm Springs, which gushed noisily from a limestone ledge into a sandy draw. The clear water was refreshing but not particularly warm.

The afternoon brought thunder showers, the first in more than a week. The air cooled, the crickets chirped louder, and the grasshoppers seemed to multiply. Dark clouds, spectacular lightning bolts and tall, gray sheets of rain passed, mostly west of us. We were the highest points in wide open country, so we took shelter in a draw until the storm moved on.

We went into camp at Bitter Cottonwood Creek, which divided into several streams across a wide, sandy bottom on its descent to the North Platte. Thick groves of tall, straight cottonwoods lined the banks. We picketed the beasts in abundant grass and pitched our tents nearby. Before long, we pulled the pickets and moved the animals farther upstream to avoid the persistent and annoying small black flies they attracted.

I found wild mint growing along the creek. We used it to add greens and spice to the venison we had smoked, dried and packed along from the night before. At dusk, low hoots drew our eyes to the top of a cottonwood, about 50 feet above the stream bed. A great horned owl perched there, turning its head in what seemed like a full circle, looking for prey.

I was first to wake in the morning. As sunlight lit Laramie Peak and crept slowly down its flanks, I rose from my blankets and stepped sleepily outside the tent. Looking upstream, I couldn't believe what I saw. I squinted, rubbed my eyes and looked again. I ran a few steps and looked hard ahead to where we had picketed the horses and mules. I was not mistaken. I turned and yelled as loudly as I could, "Will, Ben, the beasts are gone!"

Will and Ben scrambled to their feet and were beside me in seconds. We ran in stocking feet to the pickets. Seven of them sat scattered across the grass where we had driven them into the earth. The animals were nowhere to be seen. We inspected the ground in the soft light and found two sets of moccasin prints. The tracks led upstream. We followed them at a trot until they headed in two directions. One set led the mules along the south bank, while the other set crossed the stream, leading the horses.

"We can't track them in stocking feet," Will said. "Let's go back for our boots and guns."

At the tents, as we sat to pull our boots on, Will spoke.

"They must have come from the same place, and they must be going back there, so why did they take two paths?" he wondered. "It might be a trick to split us up. But we have to follow both trails in case they don't lead to the same place. Men, I want you each to take a Winchester and a pistol. Early, you're too small to wear the holster and pistol on your hip, so tuck the gun in your belt.

"I'll follow the mule trail," Will continued. "Early, Spirit is the only horse who comes at a whistle. That might be valuable. If you see him, whistle. If he can come, he will, and the others might follow. If you need me, fire two shots in quick order, wait three seconds and fire another. If I need you, I'll fire two then one in the same pattern. To confirm, use the same signal—two quick shots, three seconds, then a third shot."

We stood outside the tents for a moment, looking upstream.

"Check your guns, scan the country, get your bearings." Will said. "Are you ready?"

"Yes, Will, let's go," Ben and I replied.

We ran to the fork where the horse trail crossed the creek.

"The tracks look fresh," Ben said, looking at the horse trail. "If they weren't, the creek water would have seeped in and filled them up."

"I think you're right, Ben," Will said. "Let's go get our beasts. Protect yourselves. Shoot the thieves if you have to."

We took off at a trot. Will traced the mules close to the bank, while the horse track went away from the creek on a diagonal. Ben led the way. After about a mile, the trail topped a ridge. We stopped to look ahead. Spirit stood straight across, maybe a half mile away, at the top of the next ridge. Tibbs and May Belle stood on the same ridge about a half mile to our right. There was a wide draw with gradual slopes on the near and far sides.

"I'm not sure what to make of this," Ben said. "Whistle as loudly as you can, and let's see if Spirit hears you."

I drew the deepest breath I could, stuck my fingers in my mouth and whistled. Spirit didn't react. He was upwind of us.

"I think we should go after Tibbs and May Belle first," Ben said. "If we can get them, we can ride up to Spirit. We should run apart from each other in zigzag lines. If we're fired on, drop to the ground and take whatever cover you can. If we can return fire without hitting the horses, we should. You're a good marksman, Early, let's get them if they try to get us."

We ran zigzag down the decline, holding our rifles across our chests like infantrymen. When we reached the bottom, I heard Spirit whinny above us and to our left. I stopped, but Ben kept on toward the other horses. I whistled, Spirit bobbed his head, but he didn't move toward me. Something held his halter rope fast to the ground. I ran toward him, making a diagonal line up the rise.

When I reached the ridgetop, I was breathing hard from running. Spirit was tied to a stake driven into the ground. I saw no trouble nearby. I reached to pat Spirit on the neck. I had barely touched him when somebody jumped me from behind and knocked me to the ground. I lost my rifle, and when I was down, a hand pulled the pistol from my belt. An Indian stood over me.

"Up!" he commanded.

I stood up and he quickly took my wrists and bound them with rawhide. He was a young brave, big, fierce looking and naked except for a breechcloth and moccasins. He grabbed me under the armpits, picked me up and swung me onto Spirit's back. He yanked the halter rope free of the stake, tucked my pistol in his waist cord and jumped up behind me. He held my rifle in one hand and the halter rope in the other. He wheeled Spirit around, kicked him, and we took off at a run, heading over the ridge and down the decline ahead.

My head was filled with panicked thoughts. Did Ben see us? Would Will come? Where was the Indian taking me? I was captured, but, oddly, the first thing I noticed was how bad the Indian smelled.

We rode hard to the bottom of the draw. I saw a dust trail far to our right. It was Ben on Tibbs riding at a full run up the draw straight toward us. The Indian saw Ben too and hesitated for an instant, as if deciding what to do. He grunted, kicked Spirit again and urged him up the slope ahead.

"Buffalo soldier!" the Indian growled. "No good!"

Without slowing, Ben fired two quick pistol shots, then a third. The reply from Will came back in a few seconds. As if taking the shots as a signal, Spirit suddenly stopped. The Indian kicked him and whooped, but Spirit refused to run. He reared violently. I grabbed his mane in both fists to stay mounted. The Indian lost his hold on the halter rope. He slid off Spirit's back, over his rump and fell to the ground. I kicked Spirit and we ran ahead.

I looked back to see the Indian jump to his feet, grab my rifle, whirl around toward Ben, drop to one knee, level the Winchester and fire. His shot missed. Ben fired two pistol shots that also missed. I rode farther up the slope, pulled Spirit to a halt and dropped to my feet. I worked to untie my wrists.

Ben stopped Tibbs about 100 yards from the Indian, dropped to his feet, smacked Tibbs to make him run off and took cover behind some brush. The Indian fired three shots at Ben. I saw Ben's hat fly off and fall to the ground. I couldn't see if he was OK.

I freed my wrists and smacked Spirit to make him run. I crouched low and made my way back down the slope, gathering rocks as I went. I got within throwing distance of the Indian and started pelting him.

Ben wasn't hit. He ran up the draw toward the Indian, taking cover behind one clump of brush and then another. The Indian ran up the slope to his left. He wanted relief from my rocks and a better line of fire from higher ground. I ran left too and stayed low, trying to stay out of Ben's line of fire.

When Ben ran again, the Indian stood straight up above the brush to fire at him. Ben hit the ground on his belly about 50 yards away and aimed his rifle. I threw a rock and hit the Indian in the head. There were two shots. The Indian fell and lay still. Ben stood and ran toward him. I did the same. I reached the Indian first. He had a wound in the center of his chest. He was dead.

"You OK, Early?" Ben asked excitedly as he ran up.

"Yes, Ben, good shooting," I said.

"Good throwing," he replied.

We stood looking down at the dead Indian. We were both trembling.

"It looks as if the whole point was to capture you," Ben said.

"Without shooting you and Will," I said. "The beasts were just bait."

"Whistle for Spirit, and let's find Tibbs and May Belle," Ben said. "We'll drape the body over May Belle's back and ride to find Will."

From the top of the first ridge we crossed, we saw Will galloping toward us on one of the mules. We met him at the bottom of the draw.

"Are you OK? What happened?" he asked anxiously.

Ben and I told him the story and our thought about the Indians' goal of capturing me.

"It's strange, but I think you're right," Will said. "I wonder where their horses are. And what were two braves doing out on their own? I found the mules tied to a juniper. The moccasin trail continued up the bank and into the creek. I don't know how far he walked up the bed. I didn't follow him and never saw him. I suppose their plan was for him to join the other Indian over this way. They didn't want the mules."

As we turned to ride toward the other mules, Will paused.

"I'm proud of you men," he said. "You did everything right. We'll bury the Indian near our tents. We should be on the lookout for the other brave. We'll report the incident to the post commander ahead at Fort Fetterman. It's probably best we don't tell Beth and Amanda." Ben and I looked at each other and smiled.

The full weight of what had happened didn't hit me until we

lowered the Indian into the grave we had dug near our camp.
Ben had killed a Sioux brave to save me from being kidnapped. I
could see that Ben felt the weight too. Will and Ben stood face to
face before we pushed the earth in on top of the body.

"Ben," Will said, "you killed him defending yourself and Early
from an attack that could have been the death of you both. You
did what had to be done and only a courageous man could do." Ben
looked grateful and relieved.

Two days after leaving our camp on Bitter Cottonwood Creek,
we turned north onto the Bozeman Trail toward Fort Fetterman.
The fort was a lonely outpost on a treeless plateau above the
valleys of LaPrele Creek and the North Platte River. Four companies of the 14th Infantry were under the command of Lieutenant
Colonel George A. Woodward. We met with the lieutenant colonel
and told him about the incident on Bitter Cottonwood Creek.

He explained that when Indians lose a man, they often adopt
a stranger into the tribe and assign him the lost man's role. He
supposed that was why the braves tried to kidnap me. Indians
had captured many white children in the past and adopted them
into their tribes. He guessed that the braves were probably
hunting pronghorn or mule deer in the unceded territory where
Bitter Cottonwood Creek lies, saw an opportunity and tried
to exploit it. He said we were very fortunate that the kidnapping attempt was in a time of peace. Otherwise, Will and Ben
might be scalped and dead, and I would be with the Sioux. Will
replied that when we left Kentucky, one of our intents was to see
Indians, but not this way.

Lieutenant Colonel Woodward was concerned about the
effect the brave's death might have. He wired Fort Laramie,
and reported the circumstances of the death. He suggested that
Colonel Smith notify the Sioux chiefs through the Red Cloud
Indian Agency and advise them where they could find the grave.

Retracing our route, we rejoined the Oregon Trail and went
into camp on LaPrele Creek. There was abundant wood, water
and grass. Box elders and cottonwoods lined the stream. The
beasts enjoyed horsetail plants as fodder. We had spent a day
riding to and from Fort Fetterman, and so decided not to take
the time to see the natural stone bridge that lay several miles
upstream from our camp.

Our next night's camp was at Bessemer Bend, past Casper on the North Platte. We had seen many pronghorns that day. Will killed a curious buck during our noon rest. We dried and smoked the meat over the evening fire, our last on the river's south side.

Will led the way across the North Platte in early morning. As we rode on, we saw masses of exposed granite lying to the north and the Black Hills to the south. We were in open desert country beneath a very big sky. Sagebrush and short grass grew everywhere. Sunflowers and lavender daisies lined the trail, while thistles bloomed in the low places. About midday, huge, billowy clouds built in the west and moved east. Sunlight bleached their tops a brilliant, glowing white, while the blue-gray bottoms reflected the dark earth below. That night's camp was at Fish Creek.

Independence Rock was less than a full day's ride ahead, but we made it our next overnight stop. The rock was an enormous dome of gray granite sitting out by itself and visible from miles back. I guessed its perimeter measured about a mile. Walking it without stopping took nearly a half hour. The top was an easy climb. The Rattlesnake Range lay northeast and Devil's Gate southwest. The Sweetwater River looped around the rock's south side.

Most of the names registered on the rock were roughly written in axle grease, but some were neatly engraved, as if by a stonecutter. J. W. Crosby made a mark worthy of a headstone. H. L. Chapin turned his "n" backwards. C. T. Ross passed by on June 9, 1850 and J. W. Jacobs on June 10, 1862.

We swam in the Sweetwater and let its current carry us downstream. The river water tasted true to its name. There was plenty of grass for the animals and two cottontails for us. The rock was very pretty at sunset, turning purple-gray as the ground around it glowed warm yellow. As night fell, fires from several camps flickered at spots scattered across the desert.

34

We left our camp at Independence Rock just as the sun broke above the eastern horizon. It was Sunday, July 14th. Will and Ben each trailed two mules, and I rode lazily behind, almost asleep in the saddle. Devil's Gate lay about six miles west. We pointed our horses' noses toward a notch in the granite ridge. Our map told us the notch opened to a wide gate that the Sweetwater River flowed through.

After about an hour, Spirit stumbled slightly, causing me to perk up and look ahead. I noticed that Jack, the second mule behind Ben, was favoring his right foreleg. I rode up alongside Will and told him that Jack was limping. We came to a halt and dismounted. Will approached Jack, speaking softly and assuring him. He ran his hand down Jack's leg to the hoof but got no reaction that showed tenderness. He lifted the hoof and examined the shoe and sole. The shoe was fine, but there was a sharp-edged stone lodged in the soft sole. Will pulled his knife from the sheath on his belt and pried the stone out.

"It's good you caught that before it did serious damage, Early," Will said. "But we'll have to get the weight off that foot and give this mule a rest."

We unpacked Jack and spread his burden among the other mules. Will had Ben lead Jack at a walk so he could watch his gait.

"Jack will be OK," Will said, "but it'll take a day or so. Let's go on ahead slowly and stop along the river on the far side of Devil's Gate. It's not far, and there's probably more grass where the granite protects the banks from the wind."

We stopped atop a low saddle that stretched south of the granite tower that formed the near side of Devil's Gate. Below us and ahead, a log ranch house and split-rail corrals nestled in a cove just beyond the gate. It looked as if work had started on getting a barn up. A clump of trees stood behind the house, and past them the river flowed east. Beyond the river, a massive granite hill dotted with junipers rose to the north.

"If the rancher's hospitable," Will said, "this would be a good place to rest." No sooner had we started down the slope toward the house than three dogs came out from under a porch and ran toward us, barking. I knew from their tone and tails that they weren't angry. They were just saying hello.

"The dogs will spook the beasts if they run to us barking," Will said. As if on cue, a man appeared beside the house and yelled something we barely heard. The dogs stopped instantly, hesitated for a moment, sniffed the air in our direction, turned around and ran back toward the house. We rode ahead at a walk.

When we came within hailing distance, Will waved his arm in a big arc and yelled, "Hello!" The man returned the wave but said nothing. As we approached, we saw he was unarmed.

"Bonjour, mes amis, bienvenue," the man said.

"He sounds like Captain LaBarge," Ben said under his breath.

"Good morning," Will said. "We speak English, do you?"

"Sure enough," the man said. "I just wanted to see if you'd be surprised by French in Wyoming. And I can see by your faces that you were."

"You're right, we were," Will replied with a smile.

"Where you boys headed?" the man asked.

"Idaho," Will replied. "But we have a mule with a stone bruise, and he needs a rest for a day or so. Can we stop here?"

"You bet you can," the man said, "happy to have you. My partner's off in Rawlins, and there's been Indians about. Four men's better'n one any day."

As we dismounted and introduced ourselves, the dogs walked around us wagging their tails and sniffing.

"Name's Tom Sun. I'm on this place with my partner, Boney Earnest," the man said. "He rode off to Rawlins three days back to tend to some cattle business. I've slept up in the rocks the past two nights for fear of gettin' surprised by Indians. Have you seen any?"

"Not in more than a week," Will said.

"I've only seen 'em at a distance, south of here. They're probably hunting pronghorn," Mr. Sun said. He paused and looked toward our mules. "Fine looking mules. I saw the one with no pack favoring his right foreleg. Mind if I take a look?"

"Not at all," Will replied. "I'd like to know what you think."

Mr. Sun stepped to Jack's right side, spoke to him reassuringly and ran his hand down the mule's foreleg. He raised the hoof and examined the sole.

"He's got a bruise all right, but it ain't serious," Mr. Sun said. "Let him rest and he'll be good as new by tomorrow. We can put him in the corral and picket the others in the grass upriver a ways if you'd like."

"Sounds good to me," Will replied. We walked to the house, where we unpacked the mules. We took the saddles off the horses and stacked the baggage and tack on the shade porch. We switched out bridles for halters, put Jack in a corral and led the others upriver where grass lay along the bank.

"If you drive your pickets here, we can move 'em in a few hours and then corral your animals with mine for the night," Mr. Sun said. "Mine are hobbled and movin' upriver. I'll send the dogs after 'em later."

Mr. Sun was about Will's size but looked to be maybe 15 years younger. He had dark hair and intense, dark eyes. His face was wide and his jaw square and firm. His full moustache wrapped around the corners of his mouth like brackets.

"How about some breakfast?" Mr. Sun asked.

"Thanks, but we ate before we left camp this morning," Will replied.

"Coffee then?" Mr. Sun asked. "I have a pot on the fire inside."

"Sure," Will replied, turning to Ben and me as if asking. We nodded, and the four of us walked toward the house. It was low, sturdy and looked carefully built. The logs were even and well-chinked. It had a pitched roof and stone chimney. There were doors and windows along the wall at the back of the porch. Inside, the floor was unfinished lumber. There was a native stone fireplace and hearth. A long wooden table and set of bentwood willow chairs sat near the center of the room. Bunks lined the wall to the right of the door. Gunbelts hung on pegs beside it, and several rifles rested there on racks. Mr. Sun poured coffee from a big pot into four tin cups and passed them among us. We stepped outside and sat in a row on a long log.

"How did you choose this spot?" Will asked.

"I used to trap beaver west of here, and I scouted for the Army out of Fort Steele east of Rawlins, so I passed this way many times," Mr. Sun replied. "There's water, the granite protects the site north and east, there's full southern exposure and a good line of sight to every approach. Rawlins and the rail line are about 50 miles south as the crow flies. I figured this to be a good place for a cattle ranch."

"Do you have cattle?" Ben asked.

"We're just starting," Mr. Sun replied. "Boney's in Rawlins now, lookin' into buyin' a few head. We've started on a barn, and we'll take that work up again as soon as we haul more logs and lumber."

"There's plenty of room for cows," I said.

"It's free range, no fences," Mr. Sun said. "Cattle fatten well on the buffalo grass, but it's sparse, so you need a lot of acreage." He paused a moment and asked, "Where you goin' in Idaho?"

"Where the Raft River meets the Snake," Will replied.

"I hear that's cattle country," Mr. Sun said, "You gonna ranch?"

"No, farm," Will replied.

"Well, you'll have water," Mr. Sun said.

"Where did you learn French?" Ben asked.

"My folks in Vermont are French Canadian. My full name is De Beau Soleil," Mr. Sun replied. "I ran away from home when I was about Early's age, but the French stuck with me."

"How did you manage on your own as a boy?" Will asked.

"Most people are kind to children, especially a young boy on his own," Mr. Sun replied. "There was always someone to provide a bed or a meal. I made my way down the Ohio, then up the Mississippi by steamer. A French trapper in Saint Louis took me under his wing. He taught me how to trap and survive in the wilderness."

"We're from Smithland, where the Cumberland meets the Ohio," I said. "Did you stop there?"

"I remember passing Smithland," Mr. Sun replied, "but, no, the steamer didn't stop."

"Do you remember seeing Hawkins Wharfboat?" I asked. "That's ours, and the name's painted big and bright facing the river."

"Nope, sorry, can't say I do," he replied. "That was quite awhile ago, and the details fade." He took a last sip of coffee and tossed the dregs aside. "My only order of business today is to kill a prong-horn or two for meat, but that's later in the day. Maybe you fellas would like to walk along the riverbank and take a close-up look at Devil's Gate."

"I would!" I said, almost jumping up off the log. Will and Ben smiled in bemused agreement. Mr. Sun collected our cups, took them inside and returned, toting a Winchester.

"If you fellas want to grab your rifles, we can walk to the gate," he said.

The dogs ran ahead as we set out on a foot trail. There was a narrow green belt along the south bank of the river. Clumps of willows mixed with stretches of grass and stands of rushes. Up ahead, granite came down to the water's edge.

"How high are the towers?" Ben asked.

"The taller one is near 400 feet," Mr. Sun replied. "And the gap is about 1,500 feet end to end."

"Why is it called Devil's Gate?" I asked.

"There's a group of rocks near the top of the tower that folks say looks like the face of the devil," Mr. Sun replied. "Course, the Indians don't hold with that. I don't know their name for the gap, but their legend says a huge beast cut it with his tusk so he could escape from their arrows."

As Mr. Sun walked, he pointed to a spot on the granite above the north bank of the river.

"See that juniper about 200 feet up with a small branch goin' off on its own to the right?" Mr. Sun asked. We said we did. He stopped, spread his stance, sighted his rifle and fired. The branch fell but dangled, still attached. I set my stance, sighted my rifle and fired. The branch dropped clean away. I had hit it exactly at the connecting point. Will, Ben and Mr. Sun cheered.

"Nice shooting, Early!" Mr. Sun said excitedly. "I know who I want along when I hunt for pronghorn later on."

We walked along the bank to a point where the river met the granite of the south tower. The gap looked like a big, gaping jaw. The river wound its way around boulders that lay at the base of the cliffs.

We turned to go back to the house and had walked only a short way when up ahead we saw the dogs standing rigid and looking south. They were growling a low, muttering growl. Their ears were upright, and the hair on their backs was on end. They looked as if they were about to pounce on a foe. We turned south toward the low ridge we had ridden across earlier. There sat a line of maybe 15 mounted Indians peering down at Mr. Sun's ranch and us.

"Hold on, dogs," Mr. Sun said. "You don't want to go after those fellas. They'd just as soon shoot and eat you as a pronghorn."

"Do you know them, Tom?" Will asked.

"No, I don't," Mr. Sun replied, "but my guess is Arapaho or Sioux. Could be Crow or Shoshoni though."

"We had some trouble with two Sioux braves between Fort Laramie and Fort Fetterman," Will said.

"They have rifles, and they have us outnumbered about four to one," Mr. Sun said. "It's hard to tell from this distance, but they don't seem hostile."

Mr. Sun raised his right arm and opened the palm toward the Indians. One near the center of the line returned the gesture. They began to descend from the ridge in single file. We walked toward the house at a quicker pace than we had taken going out. We kept our eyes glued on the line of Indians. The dogs were jumpy, seeming to want to rush the ponies.

We reached the house before the Indians. We stood facing them, holding our rifles low but ready as they walked their ponies in single file. Their horses were smaller, thinner and more ragged than ours. Some of the Indians rode bareback, some had simple saddles, none had stirrups. They dismounted either by swinging a right leg over the withers and sliding down on their buttocks or over the croup and sliding down on their bellies. Their dress was varied and colorful. One wore a calico shirt and a slouch hat like mine. Another wore a vest, a plaited leather thong around his head and a bead necklace. Still another wore a buckskin tunic with a belt of conchos at the waist. All were barelegged and wore moccasins. Their long, thick black hair was parted in the middle and braided. Their skin was deep red and leathery. Several had scars on their arms, legs or faces. Each had a rifle, and none carried bows or arrows. They had no provisions that we could see, and there were no travois or pack animals. They must have ridden out in the morning from their night's camp, where they would return late in the day.

I don't know how the others felt, but my heart was beating up in my throat. I tried to look stern and strong. I gripped my rifle in clenched fists. My palms were sweating. We were clearly outnumbered, but there seemed to be no threat. One rather small, wiry Indian stepped forward. He made the same arm-and-hand gesture he had made from the ridge, but this time it was less forceful. He said something I didn't understand. Mr. Sun returned the gesture and also said a few words I didn't know. Mr. Sun knew just what to do. He must have dealt with Indians before. The wiry Indian moved a cupped hand to his mouth, as if drinking. Mr. Sun took a short step back, raised his left arm, and drew an arc that ended with pointing to the river at our left. The Indians led their ponies to the riverbank. The ponies dropped their heads to drink. The Indians knelt and scooped up water with one hand while holding the ponies' halter ropes with the

other. Some splashed water on their faces and drew a wet hand
across the backs of their necks. As they returned to the house,
several scanned Mr. Sun's homesite. They took their measure of
the house, the beginnings of a barn and the corrals.

The wiry Indian stood close to Mr. Sun, facing him. He spoke
one word. Mr. Sun replied, just as briefly. The Indians leapt
on their ponies' backs and turned toward the ridge almost in
unison, as if dancing. We watched them go, and a relieved sigh
escaped me. I relaxed the tension in my hands and body.

"Arapaho," Mr. Sun said. "Maybe they were just after water,
but maybe they were lookin' us and the place over, plannin' a
raid. They probably saw your picketed animals from up on the
ridge and surely your mule in the corral from here, but my horses
are too far upstream to see."

"What do you want to do, Tom?" Will asked.

"I need meat," Mr. Sun said. "I want to hunt today."

"We have dried pronghorn meat we can give you," Will said.

"Then you'll have none, and what you'd leave wouldn't last
me till Boney's back," Mr. Sun said. "I'd rather hunt today while
there are four of us here. If you and Ben will stay here to guard
the house and your animals, Early and I will go upstream and
come back with fresh meat and my horses."

"That's OK with me," Will said. "OK with you men?" he
asked, turning to Ben and me. Ben and I agreed.

"Now, where have those dogs got to?" Mr. Sun asked. "They
can find the horses much quicker than I can. Dogs!" he shouted.

The dogs came running up from the river, dripping wet. They
stopped and shook from head to tail, sending big arcs of spray all
around themselves. They ran to us, looking excited. They knew
something was up.

"Horses!" Mr. Sun shouted. The dogs took off, running
upstream along the riverbank. "They'll find the horses and move
'em back this way. We'll meet 'em on the way up and ride from
there. Early, if you'll bring your rifle along, I'll grab a couple
of bridles, a coil of rope, spare ammunition and a sack of dried
meat, and we'll start walkin'." He turned to Will and Ben. "Early
and I should be back by late afternoon. If we hear your rifles,
we'll come runnin'. If you're hungry, help yourself to whatever
you find in the house."

Mr. Sun and I walked for nearly an hour, following the winding course of the river.

"I used to hunt in the Vermont woods with my father," he said. "Course, the plants are much different here. If you get up away from the water, you won't see much more than sage, rabbit brush and buffalo grass. Maybe wildflowers like Indian paintbrush here and there. But down by the river you get grazing grass, willows and cattails. There are pretty bluebells in the spring and haw berries and currants for eatin' too. Then, of course, cockleburs. I'm forever pullin' 'em off the horses. Those stubborn little devils'll hook onto you too if you brush up against 'em. Not many trees down this low. But cottonwoods are spreadin' out from where folks settled."

There was barely a hint of a breeze, and we kept a fast pace in what felt like 90-degree heat. The sweat flowed, and we stopped for water twice. At the second stop, we heard one of the dogs barking and knew they weren't far ahead.

We came upon the dogs and four horses in a deep cove formed by a bend in the river. Mr. Sun had fine-looking horses—a black, a dappled gray and two bays, all geldings. They were hobbled and had to jump ahead like kids in a sack race as the dogs drove them. Mr. Sun took the hobbles off the black and the gray, put the bridles and bits on them, and had me hold their reins while he took the hobbles off the bays.

"Hold 'em tight, Early," he said, then shouted, "Home!" The dogs took off, running the bays downriver ahead of them. Mr. Sun boosted me up on the gray and handed me our rifles, the coiled rope and the meat sack. He leapt up on the black's back, then eased over to me on the gray and asked for the rope and sack. He wrapped the rope around his waist, tied the sack to it and asked for his rifle.

"Not too far ahead," Mr. Sun said, "there's another deep cove like this. Pronghorn like to browse there. We'll leave the horses tied below the cove, walk up and see if we can get us an animal or two." I thought of the doe I had watched give birth near Mantle Rock. I wondered if I could shoot a pronghorn.

We tied the horses in the brush and crept quietly to a pile of rocks at the edge of a large grassy area just up from the riverbank. There were no pronghorn.

"We'll just have to settle in and wait," Mr. Sun whispered. "The wind's weak, and it's comin' down the valley. The pronghorn will come from upstream. We're downwind, so they won't catch our scent."

Mr. Sun opened the meat sack and set out several strips. We ate the meat, then crept to the river one at a time for water. I sat comfortably in the warm sun with my back against a smooth rock. I dozed off. I don't know how much time passed before I felt Mr. Sun gently tapping my shoulder. "Look, Early," he whispered. On the far side of the cove, a small herd of pronghorn walked single file over a little ridge down toward the grass. There was a large buck, four does and six fawns. They spread out in a close cluster and began nibbling at the grass. The buck raised his head often and scanned for danger. They were about 250 feet from us.

"We both have to shoot at exactly the same time," Mr. Sun whispered. "You take the buck, and I'll take whichever doe shows a good shot. If we miss our shots, we won't get another chance. We need the meat, so we can't miss."

I sighted my rifle on the buck's chest just above the shoulder. I tried very hard to put the Mantle Rock deer out of my mind.

"I'm watchin' your buck and my doe," Mr. Sun whispered. "Shoot on three." Seconds passed that seemed like hours. There was sweat on my brow, and I felt my hands trembling slightly. I hoped Mr. Sun didn't see. The buck quickly raised his head and looked straight toward us.

Mr. Sun whispered, "One . . . two . . . three!" Two rifle shots cracked. The buck and a doe dropped like rocks. The others took off up over the ridge. They were gone by the time we stood up. We walked to where the pronghorn lay in the grass. Blood oozed from their chest wounds. They were both dead.

"Good shootin', Early," Mr. Sun said as he knelt and drew his knife from the sheath on his hip.

"Good shootin', Mr. Sun," I replied. The doe's eyes were open. She seemed to be looking at me.

"Early, if you can go for the horses, I'll cut the paunches open and leave the entrails," Mr. Sun said.

I walked downstream and came back with the horses. Mr. Sun had dressed both pronghorn and removed the heads. We bled the bodies and carried them by the legs to the river one at a time. We washed them clean inside and out. Mr. Sun cut two lengths of rope and handed them to me. He draped one pronghorn and then the other across the horses' withers and, taking the ropes from me, tied the hindlegs to the forelegs by passing the rope under the horses' bellies. Mr. Sun boosted me up on the gray.

"You know, Early," he said, "one day I hope to have sons like you."

"Thanks, Mr. Sun," I replied, "thanks for helping me do well." He leapt atop the black, and we rode toward home.

As we neared the house, the dogs ran out to greet us, wagging their tails furiously and jumping about. They rose on their hind feet and sniffed toward the pronghorn meat. Will and Ben had moved our beasts from the grass along the river into the corrals. Mr. Sun's bays were there too. Will was standing watch outside. He said there had been no sign of Indians.

Ben had found cattails that hadn't yet begun to flower. He had stripped away the leaves and set the cores to simmer in a kettle hanging over the fire. Mr. Sun added pronghorn meat to the kettle and went to work cutting the rest into strips to spread on drying racks. He took the bones and worst cuts out to the dogs.

After a supper of pronghorn and cattail stew, we tried to sit outside and listen to Ben play and sing, but swarms of mosquitoes drove us indoors. Ben tried to get us to sing along, but we liked listening to him better. We spent the night in bunks in the ranch house. It was our first sleep under a roof since the Robertsons'. There were no warning barks from the dogs.

At first light, Will and Mr. Sun took a look at Jack's hoof. They put a halter on him and asked me to walk him as they watched. He showed no sign of favoring his right foreleg. A day's rest had done Jack a lot of good. He was ready to carry weight on the trail.

"We'd like to move on, Tom," Will said, "but I'm worried about leaving you on your own."

"Don't let that bother you, Will," Mr. Sun replied. "I expect Boney back later today or tomorrow. And I've spent plenty of lonesome time here before. I've got the dogs, and if things look chancy, I can always sleep up in the rocks. I've dried some meat that I want you to take along."

"That's hospitable of you, and we thank you," Will replied. "I hope you'll come visit us in Idaho."

"If I'm out that way," Mr. Sun said, "you can bet I'll look you up."

We packed the mules, saddled the horses and were riding away from the ranch site in under an hour. I turned in my saddle to wave to Mr. Sun. He stood facing us with his feet about shoulder-width apart and his rifle cradled in his right arm across his body. The log house that he and his partner had built was behind him, and behind that in the near distance, the sun had just broken above the granite that formed Devil's Gate. Mr. Sun raised his left hand, tugged the brim of his hat and cut a broad arc over his head. There was a big, warm smile below his moustache.

35

Over the next four days, we moved up the valley of the Sweetwater, crossing the river eight times. We met travelers going in both directions but no emigrant wagons going west. With no towns or settlements along the route, we relied on the provisions we had bought in Casper and what we could hunt and gather. There was good grass and water, and sagebrush and willows for our cooking fires.

About mid-morning on Friday, July 19th, we reached the Lander Cutoff, just east of South Pass. Our map showed the Lander route to Idaho to be shorter by about 100 miles. It meant saving five days or more.

We dismounted a short way up the cutoff to fix one of the mule's packs. A man approached, walking down from ahead on the trail and leading a pack horse.

"If you're goin' across to Idaho on the Lander, you're headin' for some cold country. I hope you've got your woolens," he said.

"How high up will we be?" Will asked.

"You'll cross the divide 'bout 8,000 feet," he replied. "There'll be snow on peaks above that, but I doubt you'll get any. Your water'll freeze overnight though."

"We want to go over to South Pass City for supplies and then turn back for the trail," Will said.

"If you want to deal with desperate miners and pay highway-robbery prices, South Pass City's your place," the man said.

"I don't know that we have a choice," Will said. "We're running low, and it'll be at least two weeks before we reach the Snake."

"There's plenty of ripe berries and lots of game where you're headed," the man said. "Deer, elk, pronghorn, sage hens, bear, trout, the works. So unless you're hankerin' for biscuits and bacon, I'd say your meals are there for the gettin'."

"Who's ahead of us on the trail?" Will asked.

"There were two small trains, one that started here in Wyoming and another from Nebraska," he replied. "I'd say the most of them is behind you. There are Snake Indians camped at Grass Springs and at the Green River. Nothing to worry over, they're friendly. No road agents, neither."

"What's a road agent?" I asked.

"Bandito, bandit," the man answered with a grin. "They'll steal anything they can carry."

"Is there good grass?" Ben asked.

"Most everywhere," the man replied. "There was a large drove of cattle through weeks ago, but the grass has grown back where they ate it down."

"How long did it take you to come through?" Will asked.

"Two weeks from the Snake River to right here where we stand," the man replied. "Walked all the way."

"Are you heading back to the states?" Ben asked.

"No, Casper. I've got family there," the man said. "They're waitin' on me, so I best be goin.'"

"Much obliged for the information," Will said.

"Aw, it's nothin'," the man replied. "Say, I've got one of Lander's guides if you want it. I've been along here so many times, I don't need it no more."

"We have a map, but I'm sure a guide would help," Will replied. "So, yes, if you don't need it."

The man handed me his lead rope and asked me to hold his horse while he looked for the guide in his packed goods.

"It's a bit beat up, but you can still read it," he said as he found the guide, flipped through its pages and handed it to Will.

"We'll make do. Thanks again," Will said.

I handed the man his lead line, and with a wave and a "Good luck" he continued down the trail. He hadn't offered his name, and we hadn't said ours.

The guide named Long's, Clover and Garnet creeks as those we crossed during the day. Any one would have made a fine camp. They were lined with willows, while pines and aspens bordered the trail. Afternoon found us in rolling country with good bunch grass that the beasts enjoyed.

Pines marked the course of the Sweetwater. After a steep descent to the crossing, we went into camp on the far side. There was good and abundant wood, water and grass.

We didn't have the means to measure our elevation, but the considerable morning chill told us we had ridden up out of the plains. We were getting into country the likes of which we hadn't seen, let alone traveled through. To our right, snow-capped peaks of the Wind River range stretched north. The melting snow kept the creeks running clear and cold. Poor's Creek was the last east of the continental divide. Past the crossing, the trail followed the creek's course for nine or 10 miles.

The first creek west of the divide was the Little Sandy, where we took our noon rest. Trout in the stream bit our black-cricket bait, and to the fishes' surprise, I suppose, they found themselves hooked and pulled up onto the bank. We cleaned them and packed them away for that night's supper.

We crossed the Little Sandy in a wooded dell and four miles farther descended to a large grass plain that the guide called Antelope Meadow. If there were pronghorn, our approach must have frightened them away. Colorful wildflowers helped make the scene pretty.

Not two miles distant we came to the large valley where Big Sandy Creek ran. We made it our night's camp. The beasts grazed on bunch grass, while we had pan-fried mountain trout. I wrote in the record by the light of the full moon. We wore our woolens to bed and used extra blankets to ward off the cold. Water we had left out in pans was solid ice by morning.

The Big Sandy crossing was at the base of a mountain about five miles from our previous night's camp. The descent to the ford was very steep, and the creek was running swift and strong. Crossing was difficult even without the wagon and loose livestock that most emigrants had. We lingered long enough on the far side to catch several trout and gather berries. I gazed at the scenery around us. Pines, aspens and white-capped mountains made it grand. I thought of Mr. Jackson. This was the kind of place where he would like to make photographs.

As we began our ascent out of the valley, Will pointed to large tracks along the trail. They were bear. That big, they could be nothing but grizzly. Will dismounted and switched out the Winchester in his rifle sheath for the more powerful Sharps.

We rode through eight miles of waterless sagebrush desert before reaching our next camp at Grass Spring. We saw both pronghorns and sage hens, but they fled before we could get a shot. Grass Spring was true to its name. Fine grass and water were abundant, but there was no wood. We burned sage for fuel. We prepared an early supper of trout and berries. After we cleaned up, Ben stayed in camp while Will and I rode out looking for game.

We came to several Indian lodges. Women worked outside as children ran and played among them. Several men appeared outside one lodge and waved a welcome as we approached. We dismounted and they spoke to us in broken English. With a combination of gestures and words, we said we were looking for game. They pointed north and urged us to go before the sun set. We followed their suggestion.

As we rode on, Spirit was feeling frisky. Maybe the mountain air invigorated him. With the slightest urging, he charged up a slope toward a ridge, leaving Will and May Belle behind. He gained the ridge and bounded down the far side at such a pitch that my head was behind his. I couldn't see what lay ahead. He suddenly planted his front feet in a panicked attempt to stop. Before I knew what was happening, I was out of the saddle, had turned a somersault in the air and landed flat on my back out in front of Spirit. The fall knocked the wind out of me. As I lay squirming and trying to suck air into my lungs, I opened my eyes to see a huge grizzly towering over me. It let out a ferocious roar, objecting to my invading its berry patch.

I couldn't breathe. I froze in place, terrified. I heard a loud shot and saw the grizzly's head pitch back as blood spurted from its skull. Then another shot and a hole in the bear's chest. It toppled backward out of my view. Next thing I knew, Will was kneeling over me. He grabbed my ankles and pumped my flexed legs up over my chest. I gasped, sucked air and finally began to breathe normally. I was trembling, but I told Will I was OK.

We stood up and looked at the grizzly. Will's first shot was to the bear's left eye. His second had pierced its heart. Those were probably the only shots that could stop a grizzly cold. Will had been smart to trade his Winchester for the Sharps. He put his arm around my shoulders and turned me away from the bear.

"Let's fetch our horses and go tell those Indians there's a dead grizzly up here," he said. "They can make better use of it than we can." As I had seen Will do in so many other situations, he took killing the grizzly and saving my life in stride.

The night was very cold. We bundled up in our woolens and every blanket we had. In the morning, as we crouched around our breakfast fire, two Indians approached on horseback. They gave us a large pouch of dried, smoked bear meat. We thanked them, and they wished us a safe journey.

After watering at the New Fork of the Green River, we decided to continue on and make our night's camp at the Green itself, about six miles farther. That six miles was dry, sandy sagebrush desert. We and the beasts welcomed the sight of the Green. We crossed the main fork and went into camp on the west side, where there was a large encampment of Shoshoni Indians. We chose a site some distance downstream and downwind from their lodges. By good fortune, the breeze and smoke from the Indians' fires kept most of the mosquitoes and flies at bay. As the afternoon aged and the air chilled, even the hardiest bugs disappeared.

We went about picketing the beasts and pitching our tents. Three Indian men and a boy approached on foot. Each wore buckskins and carried a rifle. One held parts of a freshly killed deer. They offered the deer, and we accepted. We, in turn, offered bear meat, and they accepted. We communicated with a mixture of hand gestures and simple English. One Indian took several U. S. coins from a pouch at his waist and showed them in his open, outstretched palm. The men challenged us to a shooting contest. We looked at each other, smiled and accepted.

The boy ran into the nearby pines and returned with a straight branch about six feet long. One of the men chopped one end to a point with his tomahawk and drilled two holes into each side of the other end with a pointed tool that was either a bone or antler. He pounded the branch into the ground and mounted feathers of different lengths in the holes. He stood with his back to the post and paced off about 50 steps. He marked a line in the ground with his tomahawk. The boy handed him his rifle. With four shots, he knocked two of the feathers clean away and notched the other two about midway along the quill. One of the other Indian men mounted four new feathers in the post and gave the two notched feathers to the Indian who had shot first. The Indian men turned to us and motioned it was our turn.

Will turned to Ben and me, winked and walked to the line with his Winchester. He shot three feathers clean away and notched one. The second Indian man matched Will's mark. Ben shot next. Two and two. The third Indian man shot only one clean away and notched three. The Indian men then wanted a last round between Will and the Indian who matched his shooting.

"The boys," Will said. "The boys should shoot."

"Boy not shoot good," one Indian man said.

"My boy shoot good," Will said.

The Indian men hesitated, looking at each other as if they were puzzled. They spoke a few words, nodded, and the boy walked to the post and mounted four feathers. They motioned to me and said, "Boy shoot."

I stepped to the line, raised my Winchester to my shoulder and shot all four feathers clean away, pausing between shots to add a little drama. The Indians looked at each other in amazement after each shot. After the fourth, they stood for a moment in stunned silence. Then, together, they jumped up and let out a long, loud whoop. With an air of great respect, the Indian who had held out the coins presented them to me. I didn't feel right taking them, so, with equal respect, I reached into my britches pocket, pulled out the only two coins I had, placed them in the Indian's palm and curled his fingers closed on them. I nodded toward him and made a slight bow. He accepted my tribute, stepped back, stood erect and made a gesture toward me with both hands. I didn't know what the gesture meant, but it felt friendly and good. The Indians made a motion that seemed to mean farewell, turned and walked back toward their camp.

"Nice shooting, Early," Will and Ben said in unison as we watched the Indians walk away through the valley grass.

36

For the next three days, whether in rocky canyons, grassy valleys or sagebrush deserts, we were always in sight of snow-capped mountains. We reached the Salt River Valley on July 25th. We had seen many pretty places since leaving Kentucky, but this one bettered them all. The valley was a huge green meadow with many creeks and springs. Trout filled the streams, almost begging to be caught. Ripe currants and berries were everywhere. Pine and cedar timber stood thick on the surrounding slopes.

We went into camp not far from a small emigrant train that had been lying by for several days. I wondered why anybody going west would go any farther than this beautiful place. Maybe that's why the train stopped.

As we went about unpacking the mules and setting up our camp, two boys, maybe a year or two older than I was, approached on foot. They said their mama would like us to visit once we got settled. We accepted the invitation and sent our thanks.

We started a smoky fire, hoping it would bother the mosquitoes. There wasn't much we could do about the big horse flies that pestered the beasts. The animals stomped their hoofs, swished their tails and quivered their flesh as they grazed.

When our tents were up and our baggage arranged, we took the last of the bear meat and walked over to the wagon train. The boys' mama was a widow, traveling to California with her sons and young daughter. The father had been a soldier posted to the old fort at Casper. He had brought his young family to Wyoming Territory once he mustered out. Soon after, he was gored by a bull and died. The widow tried to make her way in Casper, but the memories discouraged her, so she left for farther west. The men of the other wagons helped the widow with the heavy tasks she and her children couldn't manage.

She added our bear meat to a kettle of stew she had suspended from a tripod over the fire. She invited us to sit for supper. Of course, we accepted. The boys were John and George, and the girl was Sally. They were very polite. I supposed that, without a father, they were growing up quicker than they would otherwise. The widow was Mrs. Morse. When the sun neared the rim of the mountains, she untied the sash of her bonnet and removed it. Her long auburn hair fell to her shoulders. Her young, pretty face showed a hint of the worry that being on her own with three children must have brought.

When the mountains hid the sun and a chill came to the valley, Mrs. Morse wrapped a shawl around her shoulders and fastened it in front. Only the toes of her shoes showed from beneath the hem of her skirt. Fringe circled her sleeves at the wrists. I wondered how she kept her clothing so clean and herself so fresh. As I watched Mrs. Morse and Sally getting things ready for supper, I thought of Beth and Amanda. How long would it be until they were with us in Idaho?

I asked Will and Mrs. Morse if John, George and I could be excused for a few minutes, promising we would be back before dark for supper. They said yes, as long as we stayed in sight. The boys and I walked out into the meadow and then up the slope a bit. We gathered wildflowers and brought back three bouquets. Mrs. Morse smiled warmly, thanked us and asked Sally to put them in water.

After the bear-meat stew, Mrs. Morse served blancmange. She had made it with milk from their stock, sweetened it with cooked currants and set it with cornstarch. We loved it. It was like being home.

One of the men in the train had a fiddle and another a banjo. Ben fetched his fiddle, and we had a singing and dancing party. I danced with Sally, and Will danced with Mrs. Morse. After a short rest, Ben bowed one note and sang a spiritual that the Colored Christian Singers had sung in Smithland. The emigrant families stood close together in the firelight, swaying slightly to Ben's voice. We were an island of warmth in a chilly valley high in the Rocky Mountains. In a few days, we would be in Idaho, and the folks in the train would be on their way to new lives in California.

In our tent, I put my woolens on, slid under my blankets and brought the record up to date by candlelight. After a good night's rest, we delayed our start till mid-morning, riding north up the valley. The beasts were fat and happy, having eaten their fill of grass one of the men said was mountain timothy. Unlike its name, the Salt River was fresh. It was about 20 feet wide, shallow, easy to cross and full of speckled trout. We caught several and packed them away for later. Up from the bank, we found two marked graves. A woman had died in childbirth. She and her infant were laid to rest side by side.

We came to a salt spring a day and a half past our Salt River Valley camp. There was clear, fresh water and good grass, so we nooned there. Several men were packing salt into sacks and barrels and loading them onto wagons. They hauled the salt on the Lander Cutoff to the Salt Lake–Fort Hall road and then north across the Snake River to the mines and settlements in Montana. They told us we had left Wyoming Territory and entered Idaho Territory about four miles back. We realized we would reach the Raft River in a few days. There were smiles all around.

Past the salt spring, the mountains started getting smaller, farther apart and less timbered. Over the next several days, there were some especially rugged and then dusty sections of trail. A lake called John Gray's was alive with ducks and swans.

At Ross Fork Creek, our route rejoined the Oregon Trail, which came up from Fort Bridger south of us. We came upon travelers going in both directions, some heading west and some returning to the states. From a high point, we caught our first view of the vast Snake River Plain. It couldn't have been more different in appearance from the high mountains, deep canyons and grassy valleys of the Lander Cutoff.

The trail made a descent and met the Salt Lake–Fort Hall road. It was a thoroughfare compared to our route of the past two weeks. There were empty wagons going south to Ogden and Salt Lake, and full wagons heading north to the Snake River ferry and beyond. Farmers in wagons up from Salt Lake sold flour, onions and other produce to travelers.

A big, dusty commotion occurred that sent us and everyone else scurrying off the road to get out of the way. An empty coach drawn by six heavily lathered horses came racing up the road. People guessed that road agents had robbed the stage south of us, spooked the horses and sent them off in a panic. There was nothing anybody could do to stop them. They would have to run themselves out.

Fort Hall itself had been abandoned and taken down. The ferry landing and transfer station stood near the fort's former site. We passed that way and made our camp on a creek up from its mouth at the Snake. There was good grass and plenty of sage for fuel. The only game was jackrabbits. It was Tuesday, August 1st, three months to the day since we left Smithland.

At some points along the Snake, the plain sloped gently to the riverbank. At others, high rocky bluffs formed a wide canyon, with the river at its bottom. At American Falls, the canyon narrowed, squeezed the river and dropped it over a ledge. The rock was volcanic, porous and a dark rusty black. It absorbed the day's heat and stayed warm long after sundown.

There were no trees, and the plain seemed endless. Green grass lined the river, but up from its banks we saw little but sage, rabbit brush and bone-dry grass. Low, rounded mountains rose to the south, and buttes were visible far, far to the north. The creek bottoms were thick with brush. Only the trail made them passable. After a night on Bannack Creek and another on the Snake across from Eagle Rock, we reached the broad, shallow Raft River. Its bottoms were rich, dark and crowded with willows. The trail to Oregon went west here, while the way to California turned south. We crossed a short way up from the mouth. We rode upstream through the bottoms, looking the land over. We heard a commotion ahead and were surprised to find cowboys herding cattle.

One of the cowboys left the herd and rode up to us. He was open and friendly. His name was Nibbs Gamble. Will told him we were looking for farmland to homestead in the valley. He told us the Shirley Company had claimed the bottomland for cattle ranching. He encouraged us to look farther west along the Snake, saying there were creeks running through the sagebrush there. He named Goose Creek. It was beyond the rapids and ran year 'round. He also mentioned Marsh Basin, the settlement at the foot of the mountains, southwest of where we were.

We thanked him, turned and rode north along the Raft River to its mouth at the Snake. If Will was discouraged by cattlemen having claimed the bottomland he planned to homestead, he didn't show it.

"Let's ride west within sight of the Snake and see what we find," he said.

Along that stretch of river, the land on both sides gradually sloped toward the banks. An occasional low bluff ran near the water's edge. There were none of the high cliffs we had seen the past few days east of the Raft River.

Here and there across the plain, a black-rock outcropping jutted up from miles and miles of sagebrush. We were in an enormously wide valley. A long, high butte and lines of round-top mountains rose in the near distance to the south. Behind them was a row of higher, ragged-top mountains. Across the Snake, far, far north, a line of pointed, snow-capped mountains sat like white canvas tents on the horizon.

We went into camp before coming to a creek or rapids. We picketed the beasts on a narrow strip of grass near the river's edge.

37

The morning sun swelled over the horizon into a cloudless sky. I rose from my bedroll, stood and turned a full circle. Save for some low willows along the river, there wasn't a tree in sight. There was sagebrush in every direction as far as I could see. The space was immense.

"Makes you feel kinda small doesn't it?" Ben asked as he stood beside me.

"Yeah, and free too," I replied.

We had slept in the open under the stars, so there wasn't much packing to do before we got under way. We had ridden about an hour when we noticed the ground on the north side begin to change. A berm of black rock lined the river. Behind it, a flat bench extended maybe 100 yards to a low bluff. The bluff emerged from the flat plain and gradually inclined as it ran west, paralleling the river. At its highest point, maybe 12 feet, it turned 90 degrees and ran to the river's edge.

The bluff line formed an L shape, with the crook of the L facing southeast. About midway between the riverbank and the crook stood the only tree in sight, a straight, young cottonwood. There was a gravel bar across a low break in the berm just up from where the bluff met the river. It let water pass through and reach the tree. West of the bluff, the ground descended sharply to river level, leaving a short stretch of cliff facing the water.

The sagebrush at the western end of the bench was so tall and thick it obscured the face of the bluff. The sage wasn't quite so high and dense toward the eastern end.

The berm and bench, the bluff behind them, the cottonwood

and an outcropping of rock on the south side were the only out-
standing features near the river for as far as we could see. They
were so unusual that we stopped opposite the tree to look.

"There's a gentle slope into the river on this side," Will said,
"and that looks like another where the berm breaks on the opposite side. Let's tie the mules and see if we can cross to take a look."

Will and May Belle led the way. It being August, the river
was low and slow. We walked the horses across single file and
up the bank on the far side. We dismounted and tied the beasts
to the giant sage. We wove our way through the sage and were
surprised to discover that it hid a cave in the bluff. The egg-
shaped opening faced south. It was about 10 feet high on the
west end, stayed that height for about 50 feet and then gradually decreased as it stretched east.

Without a torch, we couldn't tell how deep the cave was. The
floor was flat and dry. There was an ash-filled fire ring a few steps
in from the mouth. A heap of broken, dry bones sat off to the side.
Thin, weak shafts of light stretched down from above the ring. We
looked up to see a jagged, partly covered hole in the ceiling. We
walked east in the cave until Will's and Ben's hats brushed the
rock overhead, then we turned and stepped back outside.

"Looks as if people have taken shelter here before," Will said.
"I wonder if they lived in the cave or were just passing through.
Seems it was a long time ago. Let's walk crisscross down this
bench and see how far it goes." As we walked, Will bent to one
knee here and there, picked up a handful of soil, crumbled it and
let it fall through his fingers.

The bench between the berm at the river and the low bluff
behind it was almost completely flat. As it had seemed from the
south side, it stretched more than a mile east to a low, black-rock
ledge. We inspected it through our binoculars. The ledge, the berm
and the declining bluff enclosed a nearly perfect rectangle of bottomland. It was overgrown with sage, other brush and dry grass.

We climbed the low bluff and walked north away from the
bottoms to get a view of the surrounding plain. It seemed to
stretch on forever in all directions. The plain sank down slightly
for a good distance north and then rose gradually as it continued. The sage and other brush in the sink was shorter and less
dense than in the bottoms.

We turned west toward the cave, using the top of the cotton-wood like a compass point. Will again knelt here and there to take up and drop handfuls of soil. When we reached the cave, we found a pile of loose black rocks on its roof. We pushed them away and revealed a clear opening about a foot and a half across. It wasn't natural. Somebody had broken through nearly two feet of rock to make a smoke hole.

We found handholds and inched our way down the bluff face near the cottonwood. Tibbs had pulled his reins loose from the sage and stood nibbling on fallen twigs and leaves beneath the tree. Ben re-tied Tibbs, while I gathered leaves for May Belle and Spirit. Will stood with his hands on his hips, scanning our surroundings. He looked as if he was deciding something.

"The rock is volcanic," Will said. "It's hardened lava. The soil is a mixture of ash, sediment from floods and whatever the wind blew in over thousands of years. This bench and the sink beyond it run across the direction of the lava flow. They're filled channels that must have been carved out by a tremendous rush of water a very long time ago. The sage is bigger and thicker here on the bench because periodic floods left rich silt behind. It holds the moisture a little better. This cottonwood is a freak, but it's a good sign."

"What are you thinking, Will?" Ben asked.

"If we could irrigate this soil with river water, it would be very fertile. We could grow almost anything here," Will replied.

"There's not another soul for miles," Ben said.

"The cowboys at the cattle ranch are east, and there's the settlement at Marsh Basin about 25 miles south," Will said.

"Is there a school there?" I asked.

"I don't know," Will replied.

"How far is the railroad?" I asked.

"That's in Utah, probably 80 miles south," Will replied.

"Should we find Goose Creek?" Ben asked.

"That's a good thought, Ben," Will replied. "We should take a look and compare it to this place. There's a sturdy shelter here—for us and the beasts. We could break through the berm at several spots, build gates and irrigate this flat bench. It's probably about 50 acres. The sink north and east of the bench is lower in elevation than the river. If we blasted trenches from the river to the sink, we could irrigate that entire low plain by gravity. It's easily 100 acres. Clearing the sage would be a big job, but once we had, we'd have a lot of good farm land."

"Do we want to find the rapids and Goose Creek today?" Ben asked.

"Yup, let's try that," Will replied. "We can compare the two places, decide if we like one, or we can keep looking."

We crossed to the south side, watered the mules and continued west. Ben thought out loud.

"We already know our Idaho map isn't very accurate, and there's nobody around to ask, so how will we know Goose Creek?"

"The cowboy said Goose Creek runs year 'round," I replied, "and it's west of the rapids. So I expect we'll first come to rapids. When we reach a wet creek past them, that's Goose Creek."

"Early," Will said smiling, "if our cowboy friend was on the level, I think you're probably right. We'll soon see."

As the sun reached its zenith, the heat of the day was upon us, and the sky and landscape took on a bleached appearance. As far as we could see, the long, high butte and the round-top mountains in the near distance south were treeless. But even without binoculars, we could see dark timber on the slopes of the high mountains in the far distance south. It was patchy at the lower elevations and grew thicker above.

We heard rushing water ahead and soon came to the rapids. They spanned the width of the river. The decline was long and fairly gentle. Here and there, boulders jutted above the surface. At a higher stage, the river would cover the boulders, and they would lurk beneath the surface.

"I doubt a small boat could make it safely through," Will said, "even at high water. There are too many hazards. A boatman couldn't avoid them all."

There was a long southwest bend in the river past the rapids. We rode for another two hours without reaching a creek and then went into camp. The river banks were gentle on both sides, and the bottoms were broad and flat. There was enough grass among the sage to satisfy the beasts. We hobbled them to give them range.

The lower the sun fell, the prettier the landscape became. In the softening light, the east and south mountains grew purple, and the Snake turned a deep, silvery green. The southwest breeze bore the scent of sage. Ben and I took our Winchesters and went looking for rabbits for supper. We walked near the willows and reeds at the river's edge. Small birds we couldn't see called to each other, maybe announcing us. We heard a rush and turned to see a great blue heron rise from the shallows. We walked up from the bank, where we each got a jackrabbit. Ben let me have the first shot.

Flies bit us awake in the morning. The river had fallen during the night and exposed a marshy area along the bank. On it lay several rotting fish covered with flies. Some looked like trout, but the others were unfamiliar. We had pitched our tents that night but left the flaps up to help with the August heat. Flies that had gotten tired of fish feasted on us.

By late morning, we reached a dry creek. We stopped to rest and eat. Soon after we got under way, we came to another dry creek. Then, a little over an hour later, we reached a creek whose waters ran into the Snake. We figured it had to be Goose Creek. It ran from the mountains in the south through a huge, gradually declining sagebrush plain to the low banks of the Snake. Near the mouth, it was lined with willows. Upstream there were other trees too far away to identify.

We dismounted and walked some distance up the creek, crossed and came back on the other side. Will knelt and examined the soil here and there.

"The soil is good," he said, "and would support crops if we could keep it watered. I wonder about the reliability of this creek, though, and there's no easy way to get the Snake's water up here on the land."

"There's no shelter, either," Ben said. "We'd have to build something from scratch."

"There's timber in the south mountains," I said.

"And it wouldn't surprise me to find a sawmill in Marsh Basin," Will added. "If there's a settlement there, unless they're building log cabins, they must be sawing lumber."

"There's more land here than we could possibly want," Ben said.

"And it's on the same side of the river as the railroad down in Utah," Will said. "At the other place, one of the first things we'd have to do is build a ferry."

"We know about boats," I said.

We stood silently for a few moments, turning, looking around and thinking.

"If we're to stay in this area," Will said, "I think our better choice is the other place."

"I agree," Ben said.

"So do I," I said.

"It's unanimous," Will said, smiling. "Let's camp here for the night and start back to the bench tomorrow."

Although it was August, there was a chill at dawn. As we sat with our breakfast and hot coffee, Will told us his plan.

"I've given our situation some thought," he said. "We don't have a day to waste, so here's what I propose we do. I'll take May Belle, one mule and several days' provisions and ride south. I'll see what's at Marsh Basin and what timber's in the mountains near there. I'll continue south to the rail line at Kelton. If I can buy a wagon or two, I will. If not, I'll wire Henry Crump and ask him to ship a light wagon and a heavy wagon as soon as he can. I'll wire Beth with our news and claim the cash she sent. I'll return through Marsh Basin or the Raft River Valley, depending on what I find going south. I expect I'll be gone about a week.

"You men take the other three mules back to the cave at the bench. Make yourselves and the beasts comfortable there. Find grass, hunt rabbits, catch fish. Chop sagebrush for fuel. We'll have to remove every bit of sage from the bench by and by, so grub out as much as you can by the roots." He paused, then asked, "How does that sound? Will you be all right on your own?"

Ben and I turned and looked at each other. He smiled. So did I. He looked as I felt—satisfied and a little proud.

"OK by me, Will," Ben said.

"Me too," I added.

"All right, then," Will said. "Let's divvy up the baggage and be on our way."

Will packed his mule light, taking only the necessaries. Ben tied two mules behind Tibbs and one behind Spirit.

"You men will be fine," Will said as we mounted. I felt no doubt coming from him. He had confidence in Ben and me. We exchanged waves and tipped our hats as Will turned south and we turned east.

Ben and I reached the bench by mid-afternoon. We crossed, unburdened the beasts, hobbled them and turned them out. There were no creeks on the north side, so we figured they wouldn't wander far from the river where there was water and good grass.

We started by cleaning out the cave near the smoke hole and arranging our baggage so we could easily get to the things we needed most. We chopped sage and stacked it off to the side of the fire ring. Pulling the sage up by the roots out of the dry ground proved next to impossible. We decided we'd soak a small area with river water, let it sit for a while and then grub the sage out of the wet ground. We had no bucket, so we sank a ground tarp into the river at the bank. We let it sag like a hammock to catch water in the hollow, carried it by four corners and flooded the sage. When the water had seeped into the ground, we attacked the sage with a grubbing hoe, ax and shovel. It was hard, tedious work. We soaked an area about 50 feet square and let it sit while we picked up our Winchesters and went looking for rabbits.

Cottontails are tastier and more tender than jackrabbits, so they were our first choice, but we found only jacks. We bagged three. We saw signs of sage hens, mule deer, badgers and pronghorn but not the wildlife itself.

Grubbing sage was backbreaking work. We welcomed the close of the day. We fetched the beasts and tied them to a picket line outside the low end of the cave for the night. We piled our clothes on the riverbank and dove in to wash away the dust and sweat. The setting sun turned me gold and put a bronze sheen on Ben's jet black. A stillness came over the land. The river flowed its silent, steady flow. Tiny, whining bugs found my wet ears. Here and there, a fish jumped and plopped back into the water. Bird sounds skated across the river surface from upstream and down. Everything seemed peaceful and in order. When we dressed, we realized our clothes needed washing, but that would have to wait till tomorrow.

As we cleaned the rabbits, Ben suggested scraping and saving the pelts. He thought we could use them when winter came. Rabbit skewered and roasted over a sagebrush fire was our supper that night, our first in the cave.

With Will gone, Ben and I spent the days hunting, fishing and grubbing sage. One noon as I sat on the roof of the cave with binoculars examining the butte south of us and the mountains to its west and south, I saw big dust clouds but couldn't make out what was moving west. I supposed it was one of the trains that came up behind us on the Oregon Trail. I guessed it was about 10 miles away.

Another day, as we hunted rabbits and sage hens beyond the sink north of the river, we were surprised to come across a wagon train. They were even more surprised to see us walking through the sage with our Winchesters. They had spent the night at a spring east of us and continued west following the course of the river. They asked what we were doing on foot miles from nowhere. We said we were homesteading nearby. They wished us luck, and we replied the same.

Near sundown on the ninth day that Will was gone, we heard a shout come from across the river. We had grubbed out the sage in front of the cave, so when we stood in the mouth, there was a clear view to the other side. It was Will on May Belle with the mule behind, and behind the mule, a cow. Ben and I walked to the bank and waited for Will as he crossed.

"It's good to see you men," he said as he came up the bank. "The place looks fine. You've been working hard, haven't you." He dismounted, gave us both claps on the back and big bear hugs.

"Gee, Will, you were gone so long we thought maybe you took the train back to Smithland," I jested.

"Early, I think you've grown an inch or two," he said, smiling. "What have you men been eating?"

"Oh, rabbits, sage hens, dried currants and a snake or two," Ben replied.

"Well, it looks good on you both," Will said. "Is that supper I smell cooking?"

"Yep, we're boiling a stew," Ben replied. "Are you hungry?"

"You bet, but I've got some things to show you first," Will said as he reached for two baskets tied on the mule. One of the baskets had been cheeping, so its contents were an easy guess.

He put the baskets on the ground and opened the quiet one. Up popped two puppies. They struggled to get out, but the sides were too high to climb. Ben and I knelt and boosted the puppies out of the basket and onto the ground. They went into a frenzy of tail wagging and romping about. They were excited and clumsy, as puppies are.

"We'll have to keep them close to the cave until they're bigger," Will said. "They'd be easy pickins for a coyote or even a hawk."

"Keep them away from the river too," Ben added.

"They're mongrel pups, nothing fancy," Will said. "The man in Kelton who gave me the pups said they'd get about thigh high." He knelt and opened the other basket. It was full of baby chicks. Most were cheeping, a few looked bewildered, and a few others were dead.

"We'll have to set up a coop for the chicks and another for the pups. I brought some twisted wire, but the coops can wait till after supper," Will said. "Let's look after the beasts, and then we'll eat."

We picketed the cow in the grass by the river and tied May Belle and the mule to the line at the cave. Then we sat for supper. Ben and I told Will our news, which wasn't much, then Will told us his, which was a lot.

"Kelton's not a built-up town like Smithland or Paducah," he said. "It's ragged, with buildings that don't look permanent and some merchants doing business out of tents. There's a hotel, the Central Pacific depot, warehouses to hold goods like our wharf-boat did, and corrals for the beasts that draw the freight wagons and stagecoaches. The stage and freight lines run diagonally across the bottom of Idaho up to Boise and then to the mines above. There's a station at Oakley Meadows about 40 miles south and another at Rock Creek about 50 miles southwest. As the settlement in Marsh Basin grows, the stages and freight wagons will probably go through there. Kelton itself is about 85 miles by the Raft River route and maybe five or six less by Marsh Basin. The Basin's less than 25 miles. Marsh Creek runs through it and keeps the meadows green."

"Is there a school at Marsh Basin?" I asked.

"No, there aren't enough children for a school, Early, but give it a little time and there will be," Will replied. "You're probably the only 12-year-old boy in Idaho Territory who wants to go to school. I'm proud of you for that. But for the time being, we'll have to make do with books and what Ben and I can teach you.

"There were two telegrams from Beth waiting for us," Will continued. "She had addressed them to 'Captain Will Hawkins' and that name got around, so many people in Kelton called me

'Captain.' Nobody asked captain of what. I collected the money she wired and sent a reply. I asked her to ship us two of Harvey Briggs' plows. If they're good for breaking up sod or prairie land, they ought to work well here too.

"She wired back that she and Amanda are eager to join us and asked if we had found a house. So men, if we want our womenfolk here with us, one of the first things we have to do is get to work building a house.

"Two Scotsmen named George Smith and Alex Morton have a steam sawmill in Marsh Basin. It has a grist mill and shingle machine attached. They'll be here in a few days with two wagons of lumber for a ferry and a door for this cave. I ordered tools, hardware and other parts we'll need when I was in Kelton. They're on their way from Salt Lake. When we've built up rock walls for the house, George and Alex can mill the beams and cut lumber and shingles.

"I also ordered light and heavy wagons from Henry Crump," Will continued. "They'll be brought to Oakley Meadows in about two weeks. I arranged with the merchants there to have whatever we order through the station in Oakley Meadows freighted to that place. If we can't buy mules and oxen from the freighters in Kelton, there's a man who raises them near Ogden. We can bring teams from there by rail.

"East of Kelton, close to Ogden, there's a bigger, older town called Corinne. There's a newspaper there called the *Daily Reporter*. The editor says Grant is out front of Greeley and expected to win in November. I don't know if that will affect us one way or another here in Idaho Territory.

"Have you men seen many rabbits?" he asked.

"More jacks than cottontails," Ben replied.

"There's jackrabbit in the stew," I added.

"When we plant crops in the spring," Will said, "the rabbits might see an opportunity and multiply. I brought dynamite to blast irrigation canals. As we blast, we'll surround the fields with trenches and keep water in them. We can use the blasted rock for the house walls and to build up riprap at the trenches. Maybe water in the trenches, the riprap and the dogs will keep the rabbits out."

"There are emigrants on the trail both south and north of us here," I said. "I saw dust from wagons south through the binoculars, and we surprised some pioneers on the other side of the sink one day when we were hunting."

"We'll probably see more this summer and in summers to come," Will said. "The Hudspeth Cutoff crosses the Raft River south of where we met Nibbs Gamble. I found a wagon train camped at the crossing and cattle miles down the valley.

"We have our work cut out for us," Will continued. "We should have this bench irrigated and ready to plant by spring. We can work until the first deep freeze to clear the sink of sage and extend the irrigation there. When the weather's good during the winter, we can work on the house.

"We're in Alturas County. The seat is Rocky Bar, more than 100 miles northwest as the crow flies, but the land office is in Boise, about 40 miles farther. We should file a homestead claim in Boise—160 acres—but we can't afford to be away. There's too much to be done before winter. The trip to Boise will have to wait."

38

Will laid out a plan for the work we had to do before winter set in, and we got right to it, working every day from sunup to sundown.

We grubbed sage off the bench for several days until George Smith and his partner, Alex Morton, came with the logs and lumber. They had been to Oakley Meadows and picked up the tools, hardware and supplies Will ordered in Kelton. They drove two big lumber wagons drawn by six mules each. Will ordered more lumber and wrote out a list of other things we needed from Kelton. He asked George to leave the list for the mail coach when he was at the Oakley Meadows station. Will also sent word that he wanted the freighter to bring Henry Crump's wagons to Oakley Meadows.

The current ferry we built was a platform mounted on four fir logs running lengthwise. We put rails on the sides and gates at the ends. We stretched a thick rope across the river, anchored it to towers and rock and pulled it taut with a winch. Two rollers rode on the thick rope and were rigged with short ropes to each end of the platform. By angling the ferry's leading end with the current, the force of the flow pushed it across the river. The ferry was big enough for a wagon and team and several people. Will said that as soon as we could get a steel cable, we would replace the rope that spanned the river.

We blasted channels through the rock berm that lined the Snake, spacing them evenly along most of the bench's length. We built gates on the river side of the berm that we could adjust to direct water into a tiered ditch system to irrigate the bench. We dug trenches across the bench to the low bluff at its rear, blasted gaps through to the sink and built culverts. The bluff top would become our east-west road.

We lined the trenches with gravel from the blasting and from bars along the bank. The trenches and sink would stay dry until we needed them. Later, we would build another tiered ditch system to irrigate the sink and riprap barriers to line its borders. As we blasted, we saved the biggest and best rock for the walls, fireplaces and chimneys of the house.

We soaked the ground on the bench where we hadn't grubbed out the brush by hand and dragged it clean with a log and chain drawn by a mule team. In all, we cleared and could irrigate about 20 acres. When the Briggs plows came from Smithland, we broke about 10 acres, smoothed it with a harrow and corrugated it with a drag rake. We sowed lucerne, with winter wheat as a nurse crop.

We built wooden walls that divided the cave into three sections. The west end was our living quarters, the middle section was a workshop and storage area, and the east end, where it was high enough for Will and Ben to stand, was a stable and barn. We built regular inside doors between the sections, but the three outside doors were different.

Will wanted a wide walk-through door in each section between inside and outside, but he also wanted to be able to swing each section's door open from bottom to top. We rigged posts, hinges, pulleys and ropes so each section opened like a pocket flap. We could warm the whole cave or any part of it with the southern sun in winter, shut out the heat of summer, or choose any gap in between.

The leaves on our lonely cottonwood began to turn yellow and drop to the ground in early October. As the days got shorter and colder, almost all the leaves turned color and fell. Some went from green to brown and got brittle but didn't fall. They hung in clusters and rattled when the wind caught them.

By the first hard frost, we had started the walls and fireplaces for the house. We made mortar using a recipe Will had torn from a Nebraska newspaper. We began the house on the roof of the cave, being careful to vent the smoke hole. The cave became the house's cellar. The house was to be low slung and stretched out—one story high, 25 feet deep and 50 long. We would surround it with a raised wooden porch and a shade roof. We wanted an open view in every direction.

We brought lumber from the mill at Marsh Basin. George and Alex hauled fir logs to make support posts in the cave and house, and to build corduroy ramps at the ferry landings. Laying the logs in gravel would keep the ramps from becoming quick-sand or mud bogs.

George and Alex stayed for more than a week to help with the work. With a shingle roof on the house, we could spend the coldest months finishing the inside and building furniture. Will ordered a cast-iron cookstove from Ogden. We wanted to have the house and its comforts as finished as possible so Beth and Amanda could come in the spring.

George told us we might still see Bannack and Shoshoni Indians near our place, although both tribes moved onto the Fort Hall reservation in '68. Before that, the Bannacks were east of us, and the Shoshoni west, for the most part. Their land overlapped across the acreage where we settled. Alex said the Indians never had much need to pass this way because there wasn't a lot here to draw them. The Shoshoni caught salmon far downstream and hunted game north and west of us. The Bannack hunted game in the mountains east and northeast, and caught trout and other fish far upstream. In past springs, both tribes rode to the camas prairie west of us to dig roots. Alex warned that if Indians from either tribe did pass by, they might see us as intruders.

We built up a store of food for winter both by bringing supplies through Oakley Meadows from Kelton and by hunting game and curing the meat. George said that as soon as cold weather set in, more deer would come down from the Sawtooth Mountains north of us to winter on the Snake River Plain. He said if we tired of venison and pronghorn meat, sage grouse made good eating, and there were plenty of fish in the river.

Some nights I was so tired from working I went straight to sleep after supper. Other nights I kept the record up to date or went back to my earlier entries to add details we recalled. We had long since finished reading our books and looked forward to buying new ones in Kelton.

I wrote to Beth and asked her to send whatever books they used in the seventh-year class in Smithland. I told Louis the wildlife where we were in Idaho Territory was little like what we had in Kentucky. I said I doubted Audubon had ever come this way, and I knew that Lewis and Clark had passed far north. I didn't know if any naturalist had ever identified the plants and animals, and I was curious to know what they were called. I named the few I had seen that I could identify. I asked if he knew any way I could learn what all the others were.

On our next trip to Oakley Meadows about three weeks later, letters from Beth and Louis and a box of schoolbooks were there waiting. Beth said she and Amanda missed us and were looking forward to coming in the spring. Louis said he had written to the Smithsonian Institution in Washington, D. C., and asked if they knew how I could learn about the natural world in southern Idaho Territory. He said he hadn't gotten a letter back yet, and he would let me know as soon as he did.

In about six weeks, I got a letter from C. Hart Merriam, a naturalist who said he had been on the same 1872 Hayden Survey as William Henry Jackson, the photographer we met near Fort Laramie. Mr. Merriam wrote that the expedition had come to Cheyenne and then Ogden by train and had passed through Idaho Territory east of us, where he had collected specimens. He said less was known about the natural history of Idaho than any other state or territory in the Union, and he was eager to learn more. He said if I would write him descriptions of the things I wanted to identify, and include sketches if I could, he would try to name the plants and animals for me. Maybe I would find some he didn't know, and if I could send samples, we might be the first to name them. He gave me instructions on key features to describe that would help him make identifications.

I wrote back and described a large, slender, black and white bird I had seen near the homeplace and, for that matter, all the way back to Nebraska. It was about 20 inches long overall and had a wedge-tipped, iridescent greenish-black tail that streamed behind it in flight. The tail alone was about 10 inches long. The bird was a noisy, bold scavenger. I had watched one pick a rabbit carcass clean at the mouth of our cave. Big white patches flashed on its wings when it flew. Its nest was a large, coarse mass of twigs and sticks built high in the big sage.

About three weeks later, I got a letter from Mr. Merriam praising me for my thorough description and identifying the bird as *Pica pica*, a black-billed magpie. He noted that I hadn't mentioned the color of the bird's bill, but he was sure it was black. It was. He mentioned that magpies were first recorded in Idaho by Meriwether Lewis in May 1806. In his letter, "Mr. Merriam" revealed he was 16 years old. Spencer Baird, a biologist and family friend who was assistant secretary of the Smithsonian, had given "Mr. Merriam" my letter. He signed his letter *Hart*.

The evidence in the cave and the ruts of the north side Oregon Trail were the only signs of earlier impact by people for miles around. The Indians and whites who passed through had left few marks. We were living in an almost completely natural corner of the world.

Louis had sparked an interest in nature in me, and I had brought it to Idaho. Circumstances here let it flourish. Farm work and lessons took many hours, but I had no friends nearby to take up my free time. Will and Ben had their work and interests, and we sometimes explored and hunted together, but I still had time on my hands.

I started taking the binoculars and hiking out in the sage and along the river. I saw so many fascinating things I began taking a notebook. With food and water in a haversack, I was sometimes gone for the whole day. Will insisted I take my pistol if I was to be any distance from home.

I often sat for hours in one place, watching, writing and sketching. I might record a dozen plants and as many birds and other animals within a small area. Many times, I lost track of time and was brought back to Earth by the setting sun telling me to get home.

In the evenings, I copied my notes and sketches on loose paper in pen and ink. I collected the copies until our next trip to Oakley Meadows, when I sent them off to Hart via the mail coach. Weeks later, I got them back with his notes and identifications added. Over time, I described scores of plants and animals to Hart Merriam, and he identified them for me.

I suppose Indians had names for every mountain, river,

creek, canyon and valley in Idaho Territory, but the names the white settlers chose stuck. In our first few years, only some of the geography had been named. Of course, we were on the Snake River, the Raft River was east of us, and Goose Creek was west. The Sawtooth Mountains were far to the north. But the mountains south and the rapids west of us had no names we knew of, so we gave them our own.

The rapids were about a mile and a half downstream. We lived closer to them than anybody else, so we called them Hawkins Rapids. There was a high mountain far southeast of us on the east side of the Raft River that, from the house on the roof of the cave, looked almost perfectly symmetrical. It reminded Will of the Sibley tents the Union soldiers had at Fort Smith, so we called it Sibley Peak. Also southeast but much closer and on the west side of the Raft River was a high butte with a sharp ridgeline and steep northern face. We called it Ben Butte. West of it and almost 10 miles south-southwest of the cave were the round-top mountains with two peaks, one behind the other from our view. We called them and the other round-tops to their west the Early Mountains. Behind them was a high, east-west ridgeline that climbed to, then fell from a peak. We called it Will Peak.

Marsh Basin was nestled between the Early Mountains and Will Peak. "Basin" was a good name because the area was a bowl-bottom surrounded by hills and mountains. Marsh Creek and several others drained the mountains and kept the basin well watered and green. With timber nearby on the slopes and in the canyons, the basin was ideal for farming and ranching. It was easy to see why Marsh Basin was one of the first places whites settled in southern Idaho.

Our route to the Basin was across the Snake, south to Cañon Creek between the two sets of Early Mountains, through the wide canyon and into town. People in the Basin called Cañon Creek Marsh Creek. To continue to Kelton, we kept south up a long grade, over a pass, east along a creek, then down the Raft River Valley to the Utah line and on to Kelton. To go to Oakley Meadows, we crossed the river, followed it southwest to Goose Creek and turned south along the creek to the stage and freight station.

By early winter, our work and preparation had taken us to Marsh Basin and Oakley Meadows many times but to Kelton only once. We asked Johnny Wilks and Marty Luther, two young cowboys who worked for Jim Shirley, the cattleman, to stay at the bench while we were away at Kelton.

Kelton was a busy, rowdy place, even in winter. Miners, stockmen, cowboys, settlers, gamblers, prostitutes and you-name-it came and went day and night. There were three eastbound and three westbound Central Pacific trains at the depot every 24 hours. Stagecoaches and freight wagons ran on something close to a regular schedule. Saloons catered to anybody who had money in his pocket and time on his hands. Will told Ben that if he had a mind to come back to Kelton with his fiddle and banjo, those saloons were probably not the kinds of places he would want to play.

Huge warehouses stored all kinds of goods that waited for the rail cars or freighters. Big corrals held oxen, horses and mules that pulled the stages and wagons. There was a small settled population that in one way or another depended on Kelton being a crossroads. We were surprised to find Chinamen operating a grocery, a laundry and a tailor shop. They had stayed after coming to help build the railroad.

We telegraphed Beth first thing and got a quick reply. She wired money and asked that we be in touch more often. We replied that we would write more often but not to expect many telegrams because the key was two or three days' ride from our homeplace.

We stayed at the Kelton Hotel. To say it was a fleabag would be wrong because the vermin that infested it were bed bugs. We weren't in bed for two minutes before we were up and hauling the bedclothes and mattresses outside to shake and beat them until we were satisfied they were free of bugs. We took a stiff broom to every part of the room before we moved back in. Will told the owner, Mr. Rosevear, that unless he guaranteed when we registered that our lodgings were free of bed bugs, we wouldn't stay at his hotel again.

We had a lot of business in Kelton. Word about us and our homestead had gotten around, and everybody called Will "Captain." The merchants were eager to sell to the Captain and his sons.

What business we couldn't do in Kelton, we did by wire to Corinne, Ogden or Salt Lake. We bought six young beeves, six weaned hogs, a bull, and a heifer that would become our second milk cow. We ordered two millstones and three big rolls of Kelly's barbed wire from Salt Lake and had them on the next morning's train. We found that the steel cable Will wanted for the ferry would have to come from Saint Louis. We ordered it by wire.

We scoured the newspapers looking for booksellers and ordered books by telegraph to be sent to Kelton and on to Oakley Meadows. We made note of the booksellers' locations so we could order by mail later on.

It had been my first time in Kelton, and when we crossed into Utah, I remembered that Albert Richardson had written his impressions of first entering Utah in *Beyond the Mississippi*. When we got home, I found that passage in the book and wrote it in the record because I liked it so much. Here it is:

> "We entered Utah when the mountains were glori-fied; and white clouds seemed to rest, not against the dome of the sky, but in front of it, very near us, per-mitting us to gaze under and far beyond them, into its blue depths. One long bank lay peak to peak, like a bridge of ice. The ashen ground of the desert was intersected with long slender streaks of light—the sun shining through narrow crevices in the clouds. The sunset was the finest I ever saw; and the twilight a miracle of gold and purple, pink and pearl, all turn-ing at last to sullen lead."

We had taken three days getting back home. One of us drove the wagon with the hogs and supplies in back while the other two rode horseback and drove the cattle. At our camps, we slept in shifts so one of us was always awake to keep the beasts close. Crossing the Great Plains in summer was much more pleasant than traveling to and from Kelton in winter. Being home at "the Hawkins place," as the cowboys and settlers called it, was better than both.

39

Will's goal was to build a self-sufficient farm. We would use some of the ground on the bench to feed ourselves and, as much as possible, the livestock. The acreage that made up the sink would be for pasture, grains, silage corn, and cash or barter crops.

We built a hen house and hog pen in the far eastern end of the cave where the ceiling was low and only I could stand. The western end of the bench would be a place for corrals and for chickens to run and, near one of the channels we blasted through the berm, a hog wallow. Our kitchen garden would be nearby on the bench, and, later, the barn, barnyard, night pasture and orchard. We would rotate the land east in lucerne and grains. We cut about 10 acres of six-week-old lucerne before the first hard frost, raked it, dried it in the field and stored it in the cave for winter feed.

U. S. Grant was re-elected president on November 5th, and it was a good thing because less than a week later, the other candidate, Horace Greeley, died. We didn't hear of these events until about two weeks after when we drove the big wagon to Oakley Meadows for supplies. Oakley Meadows was a meal station on the stage line. If we happened to be there when a westbound stage stopped, we'd hear news from the East. Eastbound stage passengers brought news from Boise, the mines and farther west. That news usually didn't weigh as heavily as what came from the East.

That November visit to Oakley Meadows was the first time we saw a catalog from Montgomery Ward, a company that sold general merchandise, but rather than having a store, they sent the goods through the mail. The catalog was a large sheet of paper with about 150 items, prices and ordering directions on it. In our time on the Snake River, the Montgomery Ward catalog grew to become our wish book, and we bought lots of things for the farm and house through it.

Although we kept busy, the winter passed slowly. During most days, we worked inside. The house roof was already on, and the windows and shutters were finished before the worst of the cold set in. We put up interior walls, laid the floor and built furniture for the rooms. We chiseled rock away to enlarge the smoke hole, built a stairway down into the cave and covered it with a trap door that flushed with the kitchen floor. When the weather was mild, we worked outside building the porch.

We hauled cord wood from Marsh Basin for the fireplaces and split it for the cookstove. Candles and oil lamps lit the long nights. I spent evenings with my schoolbooks from Smithland, other books we ordered by wire or mail, letters back to Kentucky, and writing in the record. I was keeping up with my seventh-year classmates, and I was learning carpentry, stone masonry, farming, stock tending and the natural world better than I had ever known them before.

That year, the river froze solid by mid-December. We hauled the ferry up the bank on the north side when the ice began to form. After four months of crossing the river on horseback or the ferry, walking back and forth on foot seemed odd. We cut holes in the ice big enough to drop a line and pull fish out, mostly suckers and trout.

The pups grew fast, as pups do, and early in the new year they had six beeves, two milk cows, a bull, three horses and four mules to chase after. Whenever we put the livestock out to graze, we turned the cattle loose but always hobbled the horses and mules because they tended to roam. With no creeks coming down to the Snake on the north side, the beasts kept close to the river and were easy to find. They would sometimes move north with the grass, but they never went far from the low spots along the river where they could get water. Finding them was usually a matter of following the dogs east or west until we came to the hollow or bench near the bank where the beasts had found green grass.

The Idaho winter was colder and drier than in Kentucky. Although there was snow, most often it was dry and powdery, unlike the sodden snowfalls we knew in Smithland. Even a light dusting made tracking mule deer easier, and we never lacked venison.

When we hunted deer, we took a mule along to carry the animals we killed. We always rode out at a walk, usually northwest, until we found fresh tracks. Then we tied the beasts and followed the trail on foot to find the deer. There were so many deer on the Plain in the winter, we never came back empty-handed.

Ben stitched rabbit pelts together to make blankets for our beds. They were warmer than quilts or wool. We bought heavy sheepskin coats, and on the coldest days we added buckskin leggings while working outdoors. The beasts grew extra shaggy winter coats as protection against the cold. They scratched through all but the deepest snow to find grass. I noticed the days beginning to lengthen ever so little in January and began to look forward to spring.

Although Ben often played and sang during winter nights at home, he got itchy for an audience and a roomful of people to sing along. Several times during that first winter, he packed his fiddle, banjo and some dried venison, took his pistol and Winchester, and rode the 50 miles to the home station at Rock Creek. Jim Bascom and John Corder had a store, saloon and hotel there, mostly for stagecoach passengers traveling the road between Kelton and Boise.

Ben could make the ride in a day if he left at first light and rode steady till sundown, with maybe a couple of quick stops for water and rest. When he left home, he looked as if he was off on an Arctic expedition. He took a long bandana, folded it over several times, wrapped it around his head to cover his ears and knotted it high across his forehead. He pushed his hat down tight on his head and tied it under his chin. He wore long johns, britches, buckskin leggings, two pairs of socks and high boots. He wore a muffler around his neck, a heavy wool shirt and his sheepskin coat. He buttoned the coat high and turned the collar up. His gloves had long cuffs that covered his wrists and the ends of his coat sleeves. The only part of him you could see was from his eyebrows to his upper lip. Ben would stay at Rock Creek for a night or two and then ride back. He never had to pay for his meals and lodging, or feed and stabling for Tibbs.

In late January, we looked over our progress with an eye to predicting when Beth and Amanda should come. We settled on middle March, figuring spring would be close, and they would be settled in before the heavy work of clearing, plowing and planting began. We made up a long list of what we had or knew we could get nearby, and what we thought they should bring. We added that they should prepare their minds for a little more isolation than they knew in Smithland. We put that mildly. We didn't want to scare them. We also asked if Louis might be able to come for a week or two. That would mean Sally, the cousins and hired help would have to do some of the important spring work on the farms in Smithland while Louis was away. We felt having him along on the transcontinental train would be safer, and we knew we could use his help at our place. We sent the letter off from Oakley Meadows and had a reply in about two weeks. Not only did Beth and Amanda approve, but Louis would come, and they gave the date and time they would be in Kelton—Monday, March 17th on the 10:57 a.m. express.

We had accomplished a lot by mid-March and looked forward to meeting Louis, Beth and Amanda at the depot in Kelton. We longed to see them and were eager to show Beth and Amanda their new home. Will asked Johnny and Marty to look after our place again when we went to Kelton. We took three horses and both wagons, each drawn by a mule team. We could have pressed the beasts and reached Kelton in two days, but we favored going easy on them and allowed three.

Will, Ben and I spent the night at Mr. and Mrs. Rosevear's hotel, went around to several merchants in the morning and were waiting at the depot when the 10:57 from Ogden pulled in. We hadn't seen Beth, Louis and Amanda in more than 10 months, and to say we waited eagerly would be putting it mildly. I must have looked for smoke down the tracks a dozen times in as many minutes. Will checked his pocket watch far more often than needed to confirm the time. Ben couldn't sit or stand still. He moved around the platform like an antsy child.

We heard a distant whistle from the east before we saw smoke. There was the whistle, then silence, then a closer whistle, then silence, then a closer-still whistle. This had the effect of raising our anticipation to something like a fever. By the time that iron monster smoked, steamed and clanged into the station, we were close to jumping out of our skins.

The women who boarded or came off the train wore fashions that were typical of women at the time. That meant a long, full skirt with a blouse or a long dress covered with a fashioned overcoat or heavy shawl, and topped by a bonnet or fancy hat. We spotted Louis almost immediately but didn't recognize Beth and Amanda. They both wore trousers, boots, warm wool coats and hats like mine. Beth was nothing if not practical. After a moment's puzzlement, we all broke out in big smiles and laughter, and shared bear hugs. Amanda had grown a lot and no longer looked like a baby girl. Beth couldn't get over my appearance.

"Early, my goodness," she said, "look at you! What happened to my little boy? You look like a young man!"

"He's barely 13 and does a man's work," Will said.

I guess I hadn't realized quite how much I had grown and how much the hard work had filled me out. But in my eyes, compared to Will and Ben, I was still a young boy. In Beth's eyes, I had jumped up a step or two.

As we greeted each other and talked, the railroad men loaded and unloaded freight, the engine took on water, and passengers came and went. After a while, the conductor called "All aboard!" and men at each car began to take up the step stools at the stairways. The engineer blew the whistle, the bell clanged, steam shot from the engine's sides and smoke from the stack at top. The long cranks struggled to turn the wheels, the cars jolted, and the train started slowly out of the station. Before it got far, a last-minute man in a dark suit came running from the nearest saloon, ran across the platform and along the tracks until he reached the first stairway, and leapt aboard.

We backed the wagons up to the depot platform and began sorting out and loading the crates and trunks. Louis and Beth knew which were theirs by the markings and separated them from the others. Will, Ben and I didn't bother to ask about the contents; we just got everything into the wagons. When all was ready, Beth went to the telegraph office in the depot and wired Sally that they had arrived in Kelton safely, met us, and we were all on our way to the homeplace.

As we left Kelton, Will drove the big wagon with Beth and Amanda alongside on the seat. Ben drove the smaller wagon with Tibbs walking behind. Louis rode May Belle, and I rode Spirit. We traveled slowly to preserve the beasts and switched drivers and riders now and then as we went. We had two nights in camp in the Raft River Valley and another in Marsh Basin.

Our new arrivals noticed right away that mid-March in Idaho was quite a bit colder than in Kentucky. They were also struck by the openness and expanse of the country. Amanda wondered where the trees had gone. I pointed out the junipers on the hillsides, the aspens in the canyons, and the tall firs and pines on the high mountains.

We reached the farm late in the afternoon of the 20th. The final drive across the Plain from the Early Mountains to the river made a good impression. Big, billowy white clouds floated against a deepening blue sky. The afternoon light softened the vast space and gave the mountains at its edges a hint of purple. The flowing river lent the scene some familiarity for the new arrivals. The house sat proudly atop the cave, and the bench looked like the respectable beginnings of a working farm.

Johnny and Marty came from the cave to the far bank and ran the ferry over to our side. We crossed the wagons one at a time. When we had everything over, we gathered at the head of the ferry ramp and stood for a moment. It was nearing sundown, and everything had taken on a warm, golden glow. Beth turned a slow circle, taking in every detail as she moved. "Oh, my," she said as she extended her arms to touch and embrace her family.

We worked through sundown and into the twilight driving the wagons up the bluff ramp and unloading them onto the shade porch. We moved the steamer trunks inside but left the crates out for the night. Johnny and Marty helped with the hauling, then left for the Raft River. I ferried them across and returned to the bench. Stars seemed to overflow the night sky.

While Will and Louis walked along the bench, Ben and I brought cordwood up from the cave for the fireplaces and split bundles for the cookstove. As we got the fires under way, Beth explored the kitchen and pantry. She added several items she had brought from Smithland. When she donned her apron to begin fixing supper, she asked Amanda to set the table. I touched Ben on the shoulder, and we paused a moment to watch them. We exchanged knowing smiles. We were glad Beth and Amanda had come. They made the house feel like home.

40

Louis, Beth and Amanda's first full day at the Hawkins place was the first day of spring, Saturday, March 21, 1873. I wrote the weather conditions into the record as a way to remember the day. At dawn, the thermometer read 26 degrees. It reached 48 degrees early in the afternoon. The sky was clear to the horizon, and a gentle east-northeast breeze drifted across the Plain.

Ben and I tended to the beasts, then we all sat for a family breakfast. Will said that Louis would be with us for two weeks, and we should make the most of the time. Louis added that he was very impressed with what we had done in the seven months since August. Will said we wouldn't plant until early April, but there was plenty to do beforehand. Louis thought we should start by opening the crates and deciding if there was anything else we would need when he returned to Kelton and then to Smithland.

Louis had made the crates and packed them, so he took charge of breaking them open and unpacking them. He set one aside that he wanted to open last. The crates held everything from household goods to clothing, tools, odds and ends, and the books that held the record back to its beginning. If there was any doubt that our branch of the Hawkins family had made a new home, having the record with us erased it.

Louis passed the hammer and crowbar to Will when the time came to open the last crate. Will banged and pried, and removed the lid. The crate was tightly packed with straw that covered the contents. Will banged and pried some more, and the crate sides fell away. He pulled at the straw and revealed what it hid. It was the *George Hawkins* bell—the bell from the *10*—polished and gleaming, hanging in its frame. Will was taken aback for a moment. He took a quick, deep breath, then grinned from ear to ear.

"Louis, thank you," Will said. "That was a thoughtful thing to do."

"It belongs with you, Captain Hawkins," Louis replied.

Will cleared away the rest of the straw, found the cord that pulled the clapper and yanked it. The familiar deep, rich tone rang out into the immense space that surrounded us. Will looked toward Ben and me, and offered the cord. I nodded to Ben to go first. He rang the bell, and I followed. I felt a deep sense of satisfaction. I think we all did.

We mounted the bell in its frame high at the northeast corner of the porch and knotted a rope to the clapper cord. We rigged pulleys so that yanking the cord straight down caused the clapper to strike the bell horizontally. A row of big knots on the rope's end kept it from slipping through the pulley. To ring the bell, you stood away from it to protect your ears, grabbed the knotted rope and pulled. On the rivers in Kentucky, the *George Hawkins* bell echoed off rock cliffs or buildings, or was softened by woods and mud banks. On the Snake River Plain in Idaho, the bell rang into open space with nothing to reflect or muffle its sound.

Soon after mounting the bell on the shade porch, we developed a system for signaling with it. A series of rings with one- or two-second pauses between the clangs was a call to come home. Of course, the bell couldn't say why. The ringing simply meant come to the homeplace for a meal or whatever business needed tending. Fast ringing with no pauses meant hurry to the homeplace because there was trouble.

Late in the afternoon on the second day of Louis' stay, he and I took our Winchesters and went looking for rabbits. We walked along the north bank of the river as far as the rapids. Louis remarked how different from Kentucky the country was. It would take some getting used to, he said. Learning the plants and animals was almost like starting from scratch. The only plants he recognized were willows and cattails. I pointed out sage, and gray and green rabbit brush, then long-billed curlews and several other birds and plants Hart had identified for me.

Louis paid close attention to the bank just above the rapids. He seemed to be inspecting it with some purpose in mind, but he didn't say what, and I didn't ask. We bagged three jackrabbits and turned for home as the sun neared the horizon.

We sat for supper that evening around the long table that Will had built with help from Ben and me. Heat from the cookstove and fireplace warmed the room, and candle lanterns cast a soft light. Each of us mentioned something we had done that day. Amanda said she had collected eggs in the henhouse. Beth had finished unpacking and arranging the household things she brought from Smithland. Ben said he had fixed one of the water gates along the berm. I had gone with Louis and brought in three rabbits. Louis said he had found a good place to build a grist mill. Will had walked the sink and set markers for how he wanted to portion out the land for different uses.

"With the ranchers along the Raft River, we have a ready market for lucerne and hay," Will said. "Eventually, I'd like to plant those crops and grain on the whole eastern section of the sink. We'll have pasture on the west end and orchards on the bench. I hope apples, pears and maybe cherries will do well. When we take Louis to Kelton, we can buy more seed and whatever we need for orchards and the kitchen garden. I think we ought to plant a very large garden so we'll have plenty to put by. It's a long winter."

"We'll need the proper equipment for putting by," Beth said.

"I'm sure we can find what we need in Corinne. If not there, Ogden or Salt Lake," Will said.

"I think you'll probably want to plant a windbreak, at least along the western edge of the sink," Louis added.

"I'll ask the merchants in Kelton what they recommend," Will said. "George and Alex might have some ideas too."

"About the grist mill," Louis said, "if we build it on this side of the river just above the rapids, there will always be a strong enough flow to turn the wheel no matter the height of the water. We don't need a fall, just a good current."

"Can we build it closer to home?" Will asked.

"The gates you built at the berm will collect water at all but the lowest height," Louis replied. "At extreme low water, you'll need wing dams to direct the flow to the gates. But I don't see how you can rig a mill wheel that will turn at low water here. There are two problems—the height of the berm and the slower speed of the current at the bank. You'd have neither problem above the rapids."

"I'm sure George and Alex can cut the wood, can Jim Richardson fashion the iron?" Will asked.

"Any good blacksmith can forge what I have in mind," Louis replied.

"It looks as if we'll be cutting a wagon road between the sink and the rapids," Will said.

"Papa, take the grain in a steamboat," Amanda said. We all laughed, surprised not only that Amanda was listening but that she understood the conversation.

That evening, Louis drew up the plans for the mill wheel and a small building to house the stones. In the morning, he and I rode to Marsh Basin. George, Alex and Jim said they'd have everything ready in three days. Louis and I returned with the big wagon and hauled the lumber and iron back to the ferry, reaching it at dusk. We began work on the mill the following morning and finished in four days. Hauling and placing the millstones was the toughest part. Louis devised a system that let us raise or lower the mill wheel, depending on the height of the river. When we were through grinding, we could crank the wheel up completely out of the water.

Most nights during Louis' stay, he played banjo, Ben played fiddle, and everybody sang. Louis was a little rusty and didn't know many of the songs in Ben's Saint Louis book, but he got by. Beth had a rule against dogs in the house, so they stayed under the porch near the front-room fireplace. When Ben and Louis played and everybody sang, so did the dogs. We were mostly in tune and on pitch, but they weren't. Their singing had an eerie, howling quality, especially coming up through the floor planks. We took to stopping suddenly and letting the dogs go on alone. We could stop singing, but it was hard to stop laughing.

Louis thought we should have a skiff for the river. He said he didn't have enough time to build one before he returned to Smithland, but he could draw up a plan, buy the wood, and get started. He and Ben took the big wagon to Marsh Basin and came back with the wood they needed. Louis staked out the hull and turned the building over to Ben.

All of us were sorry to see Louis leave. Only Will went with him to Kelton. They took the big wagon and four mules. Will returned with a wagonload of seed, two more mules, a young mare for Beth and a pony for Amanda.

41

About mid-May, as we began the first cutting of the lucerne we had sown in early April, an iron axle part on the mower snapped, disabling it completely. We had no blacksmith shop, so the only solution was a trip to Marsh Basin to see Jim Richardson, the blacksmith who had made parts for the mill. Riding to Marsh Basin, waiting for a new axle to be made and riding back would take almost two days. Will said he and Ben could each put in two full days of work if I rode to Marsh Basin. He asked if I felt up to it. I was 13 years old, feeling my oats, and didn't hesitate a second before saying yes.

Will drew a diagram of the part, complete with measurements for Jim to follow. He said Jim was an experienced man and had probably made a hundred axle parts like ours, so the diagram should be enough. I was to ride to Marsh Basin, go straight to Jim's with the diagram, spend the night at George Smith's place, pick up the axle part the next day and be back home before nightfall.

Early the next morning, Beth packed food for the trail, I saddled Spirit, slid my Winchester into its sheath, and Ben ferried
me across the river. Between our wagons and George and Alex's
going back and forth to Marsh Basin, there was a trail worn
through the sage, across the Oregon Trail and to Cañon Creek
where it came out of the Early Mountains.

It was a clear, crisp spring day under a sky that seemed to go
on forever. I felt excited and proud to be making the ride on my
own. Maybe I made a horse too much like a boy, but I thought
Spirit felt the same. I kept him at a trot most of the way, stopping to water at Cañon Creek before getting into the wide canyon itself. Willows, box elders, cottonwoods and water birches
along the creek were a welcome relief from the endless sage.

Just as Will thought, Jim was an old hand with axle parts.
He said he would have a new one ready for me in the morning.
I rode on to George's place and, when he offered, turned Spirit
out in his lush green pasture. George asked about the grist mill
Louis had built, and Mrs. Smith said there was talk in the Basin
about building a schoolhouse. Their children were getting near
school age, and several other families with children had settled
nearby. I said I liked the idea of going to school, but Marsh Basin
was too far for me and Amanda to go back and forth every day.
Mrs. Smith said maybe Amanda and I could come and stay with
them for at least part of the school term. I said if a school was
built, I would mention her offer to Beth and Will.

I picked up the axle part in the morning and set out for home.
The day was like a copy of the day before. I passed through the
broad canyon and was between the foot of the Early Mountains
and the crossing at the Oregon Trail when I looked east and saw
a long line of figures on the Trail about a half mile away, coming
west. I stopped to get a better look. Sitting a horse, even a boy my
size was high enough for a clear line of sight above the sage. The
figures weren't teams pulling wagons. They were individual riders,
some towing travois. They were Indians. Shoshonis and Bannacks
east of Boise had moved to the Fort Hall Reservation five years
earlier, but this party was far from the reservation. I didn't know
if I was in danger, but I didn't want to stick around to find out.

I brought Spirit up to a trot and as I did, two riders broke
away from the line of Indians and came west at a gallop. I kicked

Spirit up to speed and yelled to him.

"He-ah! Let's get out of here!"

When my trail crossed the Oregon Trail, the Indians turned to their right, riding a diagonal line that, if they were fast enough, would meet mine within shooting or even catching distance. I leaned forward, low behind Spirit's neck and urged him on. I figured I had the advantage. At 100 pounds, I was lighter than the Indian riders, and I had a shorter line to run. Spirit was a strong, fast horse with good stamina, and unless those Indian ponies ran like greased lightning, we would outrun them.

That's exactly what happened. The Indians hit our trail a good distance behind us. I could hear them whooping and yelling. I didn't sit up in the saddle to turn to look. I just raised one elbow and tucked lower to look back between it and my side. One Indian was slightly ahead of the other, and they were both eating our dust. Spirit never let up a bit. In fact, once the Indians fell in behind us, Spirit actually opened the distance. Before long, the Indians pulled up. I let Spirit ease off, then I sat up and looked back. The Indians had come to a halt. They whooped and gave us a kind of one-armed salute. Then they turned and headed back toward their party, first at a walk, then a trot.

I walked Spirit on the trail for a short distance, checked behind us to make sure the Indians weren't bluffing and, satisfied they were gone, turned straight toward the river. Spirit had worked up a good lather, I was thirsty, and I was sure he was too. I patted him firmly on the neck.

"Good run, Spirit," I said. He nodded. I swear he understood.

I kept Spirit at a walk near the south bank until we reached the ferry ramp. Will and Ben were standing on the shade porch. They had seen us coming. They waved to me, and I waved back. Will turned and walked to the bell. He yanked the rope, and two deep, strong rings came across the river. I dismounted and stood holding Spirit's reins as Will and Ben ran the ferry across. They looked strong and commanding, as if they were in complete control of their fates. I remember that moment as if it was yesterday. I swelled with gratitude and pride. Those feelings stick.

In early June, when all the planting was done and we were between lucerne cuttings, Will took the stage from Oakley Meadows to Boise to see about our homestead claim at the land office. The stage trip was about 30 hours each way. All together, he was gone five days. Johnny and Marty stayed with us at the homeplace while Will was away.

Homesteads of 160 acres of public land were available to U. S. citizens or people who intended to become citizens. To qualify, a man or woman also had to be at least 21 years old and head of a household, or had to have served in the U. S. Army or Navy for a certain period during wartime.

To gain title to the claimed land, a settler had to live on it for five years, build a house and make improvements. Meeting those requirements and gaining title was called "proving up." By June 1873, we thought we were well on our way to proving up on 160 acres.

Will returned from Boise with bad news, however. Only government-surveyed land could be homesteaded, and our land hadn't been surveyed yet. The best we had was squatter's rights. To own the land, we would have to wait until it was surveyed and then make a claim, or Congress would have to pass a law allowing homesteading on unsurveyed land. Unless we wanted to remove to surveyed land somewhere or go back to Smithland, we had no choice but to squat. We talked it over around the supper table and decided to stay put.

In September, the Eastern newspapers brought word about what became known as the Panic of 1873. Business went into a terrible slump and stayed there for several years. Louis wrote that river traffic was down. What little wharfboat business had remained was gone, and he had sold the Hawkins Wharfboat to a grain-hauling outfit in Illinois. The hull would become a barge. There would be no more river income for us, and Louis' payments on the farm were almost complete. Soon, we would be on our own in Idaho. We would sink or swim by how things went with our farm.

Will was right about the Raft River cattle ranchers. Beyond what we stored for our own stock, they bought all the corn and lucerne we grew, and they wanted more in the coming year. Marsh Basin continued to draw settlers, and Will thought it wouldn't be long before ranchers ran cattle along Goose Creek and across to the north side of the Snake. If thousands of deer could survive on the river plain, he said, so could cattle. There was plenty of grass, and if ranchers sank wells or lifted water from the river, they could open the whole country to grazing. Will felt we were on solid footing and could count on seeing the area grow.

During the summer, we ordered apple, pear and cherry saplings in from Nebraska and planted the beginnings of an orchard on the bench. We also got poplar saplings for the windbreak Louis had suggested. They were tall, straight, fast-growing trees that we set in a close row. We built the irrigation system, fenced for pasture and sowed Kentucky bluegrass. East of the pasture were timothy hay, corn, wheat and lucerne. We had cleared nearly the whole sink of brush but planted only about half the acreage that wasn't in pasture. We planned to plant it all as the demand for feed grew.

Beth and Amanda were busy drying and putting food by through the summer and into early fall. I helped by chopping wood for the cookstove and hauling water. We stocked the cave with food we had grown in the kitchen garden and put by ourselves, and added canned goods that the freighter brought to Oakley Meadows from Kelton.

In September, what began as a summer day could quickly turn dark, wet and chilly when black clouds and wind came in from the west. We spent the early fall days harvesting and threshing, with plenty of help from Raft River ranch hands and Marsh Basin farmers. The men stayed with us until the work was finished. Beth had many hungry mouths to feed. She worked tirelessly and never complained. Amanda helped however she could. During harvest time, the men moved from farm to farm like a work crew. It was a race against time and weather to finish before the killing frost.

The end of the big harvest meant the beginning of lessons for Amanda and me. Sally sent books from our library in Smithland and school texts, and Beth became our teacher. It wasn't quite like learning with a class in a schoolhouse. In some ways, it was better. Amanda and I got more attention than any student could ever have in a room full of children.

We made our final lucerne cutting in early October before the first hard frost. The frost killed the potato plants in the kitchen garden, so Beth, Amanda and I spent two days digging spuds and hauling them to the cave. It looked to us as if we had enough to last the winter.

George and Alex stayed with us again to help build a stone barn. We set it a short walk from the house on the bench past the kitchen garden. We made it prairie style with a gambrel roof. Lava rock walls rose to the roofline at the sides and ends. We built peaks over both loft doors. We could hoist and lower hay with pulleys and ropes rigged to the peaks. Having already dug a privy and well, the barn was the final piece in a set that made the Hawkins place a self-sufficient farm.

With the barn up, we moved the animals there and made most of the cave a cold cellar. The skiff that Louis had started with Ben was coming together just outside the cave. Ben had postponed building it in favor of farm work, and now he wanted to finish it before ice choked the river. Shaping the oars became my job.

Will had found plans for a hay press and made building it his fall project. When we cut lucerne or had timothy hay and wheat straw again, we would press some of it into bales and tie it with twine for easy transporting. We would store the rest loose in the hay mow.

Toward the end of November, Beth asked Ben and me to bring in game that would make a good Thanksgiving dinner. Finding a turkey wasn't likely, but there were sage hens, mule deer and badgers—anything but more rabbits, Beth insisted. We took our Winchesters and rode northwest, trailing a mule that would carry back whatever we killed.

After an hour, we dismounted, tied the beasts to the big sage and continued on foot. There was no snow to make tracking easier, but we did see signs of deer. We walked northeast into the wind under a clear sky. The only sounds were our footprints, the rush of the wind through the brush and an occasional meadowlark. The Plain rose and fell gently. The low places were thick with brush and grass, while the high points were spare. The view from the ridges was endless. The space was immense.

We walked side by side, separating, then coming together as we dodged brush. We topped a low ridge, looked ahead and instantly froze in place. Neither of us raised a rifle to fire. We just stared. Not 100 feet ahead in the hollow was a magnificent buck, easily seven feet from nose to tail and close to four feet at the shoulder, the biggest we had ever seen. I counted 10 points across the spread of his antlers. His black nose glistened with moisture as he gently browsed the brush.

Ben and I stood so closely together I realized we had both stopped breathing. Ben drew a deep breath and blew a soft whistle. The buck jerked his head up, stared straight at us, and in a split second, turned and fled. We just watched him go.

It was rutting season, so we expected to find groups of deer, with the bucks dueling for the does. In about an hour, we found just that. We kept our distance and circled downwind. We crept closer, and each picked a young buck. I had learned to put the Mantle Rock doe and fawn out of my mind. We shouldered our Winchesters and on Ben's whispered signal, fired. Two shots, two bucks down and the others gone. We checked the deer. They were dead. We gutted them and dragged the entrails a short distance away.

We trotted back to the beasts and returned to the dead bucks. We hoisted them onto the mule's back, tied them down and headed home. Beth was very pleased with our kills and promised a feast we'd remember.

She invited many friends for Thanksgiving, but only Johnny and Marty came. The others either had work that couldn't wait, or they planned to spend the day with their families.

Beth joined several cloths to cover the long table. Amanda and I set a line of candles in holders down the center end to end. Two large plates held pine cones Ben and I had collected in the mountains above Marsh Basin. We set out the food—venison, potatoes, string beans, carrots, peas, squash, butter, milk, cheese and fresh-baked bread—in a mix of bowls, pitchers, and platters.

There were seven neatly arranged place settings. Will sat at the head of the table, Beth at the foot. Ben, Amanda and I sat along one side, and Johnny and Marty along the other. The cookstove and a pine-log fire warmed the rooms. Candlelight cast a warm glow. Everybody had cleaned up and dressed especially nicely. Even the cowboys had clean silk bandanas. Beth had pinned her hair up in a bun. Curly wisps dropped here and there. She looked soft and loving, especially when she smiled. Amanda wore a newly made calico dress. She was proud to have helped Beth with the meal. She looked adorable.

We joined hands to make a ring around the table and said our thanks. Beth ended with "All right, everybody, dig in!" We passed the food around till we each had a full plate. As we ate, Will spoke on what we had done since coming to Idaho. There was a touch of pride in his voice.

"Ben, Early and I got to the Raft River a year ago this past August," he said. "We had quite a surprise when we found the bottomland had been claimed by ranchers for their cattle. That turned out to be a blessing in disguise. This year, those ranchers bought our whole harvest save for what we kept for our own stock. And next year, when we plant more of the acreage we don't keep in pasture, they'll buy our whole harvest again. Even with this Panic, people will want beef, the Raft River ranchers will raise beef, and we'll grow some of what those beeves eat.

"We were fortunate to find the cave and the low land, we've worked hard, we've had lots of help, and we're grateful. We're grateful to be here as a family and to have friends as guests," he said with a nod to Johnny and Marty. "We're especially grateful to you men for all the help you've been. I wish more of our friends were here, but they're with their own families today, and that's good."

"You folks have done a lot in a year and a bit," Johnny said. "You've set up a ferry, cleared, watered and farmed a big stretch of land, and built a house, mill and barn. You've started an orchard, and you have farm animals and stock. You've worked very hard, you've done well, and we've been glad to help."

"Yep, you bet we have," Marty said. "We like cowpunchin', but cowboys, bunkhouses and chuckwagons get kinda tiresome after a while. It's nice havin' a real family to set at a meal with."

After apple pie, Marty played fiddle, Ben played banjo, and we all tapped our toes and sang. Johnny and Marty stayed the night and rode for the Raft River in the morning. It had been a fine Thanksgiving.

42

With December came river ice and deep cold. We hunkered down for the winter. We were well-stocked with food, cordwood and animal feed. Cold and snow forced us to make fewer trips to Marsh Basin and Oakley Meadows. On milder days, we fished through the ice or hunted deer out in the sage. Beth kept Amanda and me current with our reading and lessons. Ben made three trips to Rock

Creek. He came back from the second with a guitar. Will wondered with a smile if one day Ben might come home with a piano.

By February, I was eagerly looking forward to spring. Will planned how we would plant our acreage. All the cultivated land save for bluegrass pasture, orchards and the kitchen garden would be planted to corn, wheat, oats, hay and lucerne. There would be more hay and lucerne than anything else.

When the plowing and planting started in early April, we worked from first light to past sundown every day. By June, Will had twice asked Johnny and Marty over to help for a few days. I liked working alongside the men.

About mid-afternoon on a spring day, I had taken the team and wagon and returned from the fields to the house to help Beth in the kitchen garden. Toward sundown, I stood on the porch looking northeast, where Will and Ben walked across the green pasture, coming home. Their hand tools rested on their shoulders. Clouds passed quickly in front of the sun, causing it to cast broad stripes of moving light and shadow. The earth beneath Will and Ben seemed to be receding as it projected them forward. They were two big, strong six-footers striding across the land. They looked like giants. They looked like the pioneers Will wanted us to be. Ben raised his free hand and waved with a large gesture. I returned the wave, then yanked the bell cord once. The ring seemed to expand like the circular waves that roll away from a stone tossed into a still pond. Beth came out from the kitchen.

"Is something wrong, Early?" she asked.

"No, I was just celebrating," I replied. She smiled and returned inside. Will and Ben stowed their tools in the barn shed, came up on the porch, and the three of us went in to supper.

With that spring, we fell into the routine of farming. We watched the weather, hoping it wouldn't be too wet, too dry, too hot or too cold. We watched the river, hoping it wouldn't rise too high or fall too low. We watched for jackrabbits, hoping we could keep them at bay. We watched ourselves, hoping we would stay strong and healthy. We kept up with the latest equipment, hoping it wouldn't break down, and our earnings would cover its cost. We worried over the animals—taking care of the turned calf, the lame mule and the bloated horse. We nursed a snake-bit dog, bringing him back from near death. We lived by the seasons and at the mercy of nature.

I turned 14 that April and began to mature. My voice changed, and in a short time I outgrew three pairs of britches. I shot up like a well-watered weed. I ate about twice as much as either Will or Ben. Soon, I could rest my chin on top of Beth's head. Amanda looked at me with amazed eyes. I seemed to be transforming as she watched. In a few months, the growth, the heavy farm work and the huge amount of food I ate turned me from a boy into a young man.

When we were busy sowing in the spring, I did my school-work after supper. But between plantings, I worked on my lessons with Beth during the day. One of the things Amanda and I liked about Beth as a teacher was that she didn't stick strictly to our schoolbooks. She often used our natural interests as starting points for our lessons.

I was interested in nature and wildlife, so one spring day Beth gave me an assignment to collect and identify at least 10 wildflowers. I was to sketch them, note their colors and characteristics, and identify them by both their common and scientific names. Up to that point, most of the identifications I had done with Hart's help were animals.

I collected, sketched and recorded details for 12 wildflowers. I already knew the common names of a few, and by showing my sketches and descriptions to several people in Marsh Basin, I learned the names of the others. The 12 common names were larkspur, long-leafed phlox, globe mallow, evening primrose, arrowleaf balsamroot, wild onion, lupine, beardtongue, monkey flower, cymbal-leafed buttercup, death camas and sego lily.

I sent the names, sketches and descriptions to Hart, and about a month later I had the scientific names back from him. He said he had asked a botanist colleague for help with the Latin names and apologized for taking longer than usual to send the results to me. I had fulfilled Beth's assignment and had generated an interest that has stayed with me to this day.

Some days, Beth, Amanda and I took binoculars and notebooks and went for long walks. I carried water canteens and our lunch in a haversack. I took my Winchester, more for protection than hunting. We learned to leave the dogs behind because they scared away the wildlife we were out to see. We dressed so much alike that, from a distance, anybody might have thought we were three boys walking through the sage.

Spring days were often unpredictable. A bright morning sky could turn dark and gloomy by afternoon. We set out one such morning, hopeful that the sky would keep its clear blue. We walked northwest, past the row of poplars out into the sage. We were looking for birds and wildflowers. Beth suggested we walk a big loop, returning by way of the mill and north bank.

Amanda's strawberry curls fell from beneath her slouch hat. She was a quiet girl, slight and delicate. She loved working with Beth in the kitchen, around the house and in the garden. In the afternoons, they sometimes took a moment to sit where the sunlight came through the west window and softly lit a comfortable chair. They looked like older and younger versions of the same person. Beth read aloud to Amanda and then turned the book to have her read. Amanda stumbled over a word here and there, and Beth gently helped her.

Amanda loved to be wherever Beth was, and on that spring day the three of us walked west through the sage. I named the plants and wildflowers I knew, and took notes and made sketches of some I didn't. I pointed out the wild onion blossoms that looked like little pink umbrellas, the yellow squawbush flowers that make a drink like lemonade and the red prickly-pear cactus blossoms, with yellow pistils and stamens inside.

Beth suggested we sit silently on a rock outcropping to watch and listen. The sun had warmed the black basalt, and there was no wind. The air was about 70 degrees, and the only clouds were low above the western horizon. Bees buzzed from flower to flower, and there was what seemed like a singing contest going on between horned larks and meadowlarks. Both easily out-sang the sage sparrows. Two red-tailed hawks danced an aerial ballet high above us to the east.

Through the binoculars, I spotted a bird I had seen before but hadn't identified. I asked Beth to make notes about its features as I said them aloud. The bird was busy building a nest in big sagebrush nearby. It was about eight or nine inches from tip to tip and brown overall, but had a grayish back and brown-streaked, dusky breast. It had yellow eyes and white spots on the tip of its tail. It didn't chirp; its song was a melody. Sometimes, the song was short; it paused and then repeated. Other times, it was long and continuous. Beth sketched the bird's shape. It was like a robin's but smaller. I sent the description and sketch to Hart in my next batch. He identified the bird as a sage thrasher.

We continued walking west and after a few minutes heard an odd sound the breeze brought our way. It drew us to a large grassy area surrounded by thick stands of big sagebrush. Several sage grouse cocks strutted about in the open. The hens stood nearby in a cluster, calmly watching. The cocks' tail feathers stood erect like fans made of spikes. As they strutted, the cocks beat their wings in strong, rapid arcs from their rumps to their swelled chests. The beats made a rustling sound as the wingtips crossed the white chest feathers. As the wings came forward, the cocks inflated two bare-skin pouches on their chests. Then, as the wings fanned back, the pouches deflated, and a gurgling, plopping sound burst from the birds' mouths.

The cocks strutted, repeating the movement and sounds over and over. At intervals, a hen broke from the cluster, approached a cock submissively and they mated. We stood in silent wonder for maybe 15 minutes, watching the oddly spectacular ritual.

"What are those funny birds doing, Mama?" Amanda asked.

"They're mating, sweetheart," Beth replied. "You've seen our hens and roosters mate. Sage grouse mate a little differently. They're following nature and making more of their kind." Amanda seemed satisfied with Beth's answer.

We moved to the edge of the sage away from the birds and ate the lunch I had carried in my haversack. When we finished, we turned south. Following that course, we would reach the river some distance below Hawkins Rapids, turn upstream, walk along the bank to the rapids, then past the mill and on to the homeplace.

We came upon what we first thought was a deer lying on its side in the grass and surrounded by tiny wildflowers. The length of its back was toward us, and its legs lay flat, stretching away. It didn't move as we approached. As we drew close, I saw a fresh, open wound in its shoulder. It was almost round and about the size of a dinner plate.

"Is it dead?" Amanda asked.

"Yes, dear," Beth replied, "I'm afraid it is."

The grass and flowers partly hid its shape, and as we stood over it, I realized it was too heavily built to be a deer, and its hoofs were wrong. I circled around its head to its belly side.

"It's a horse, a foal!" I said with great shock and surprise. I felt a chill run up my spine. The foal was freshly dead. The blood in its wound was still wet. There were no other marks on its body, and no sign of coyotes or buzzards. There were a few large flies but no maggots. I dropped to one knee, grabbed the hoof of the outside hind leg and lifted it.

"It's a filly," I said, "but I don't understand. I've never seen any horses but our own on this side of the river. And it's not a newborn. I'd guess it's about two weeks old."

"Maybe its mare escaped from one of last year's wagon trains and wintered here," Beth said.

"Maybe, but for the timing to be right, the train would have to be traveling with an already pregnant mare," I said. "And where is she now? I wonder if she's one of the ranchers' mares. Maybe she swam the river, wandered about and had her foal."

"If a rancher had lost a mare," Beth said, "we'd have heard about it. Maybe the foal is from an Indian pony."

"It's a real puzzle," I said. "We've never seen Indians on this side of the river."

"Can we bury it, Mama?" Amanda asked.

"I'd like to, dear," Beth replied, "but we don't have a shovel. I'm afraid we'll have to leave her for the scavengers."

"What a shame she died," I said, "she's such a pretty filly."

As we left her and walked on, the breeze carried a death stench to our noses. The mare lay dead in taller grass about 100 feet farther. Her hindquarters were eaten away, and the wound was thickly spotted with buzzing black flies. Her eye was covered with squirming maggots. The odor was overwhelming. I motioned to Beth and Amanda to circle upwind. I untied my bandana from my neck and held it over my mouth and nose. I approached the mare and looked at her hoofs. They were shod. I walked to where Beth and Amanda stood.

"She's wearing shoes," I said, "so she's not an Indian pony. I can't figure it out. What happened here?"

"I don't know, Early," Beth said, "but the mare must have died first."

"Right, but not in birthing," I said, "the filly is too old."

"Yes, later," Beth said.

"That must be it," I said. "The mare survived the birth but died days later. Then the filly couldn't live without her mare's milk. She couldn't live on graze alone, so death took her."

"The coyotes and buzzards have been here, and they'll be back," Beth said. "There's nothing we can do. Let's go on to the river."

"I wonder if we'll ever find out whose mare she was," I said. Beth didn't reply. She took Amanda's hand, and we walked on.

On the north side, due to the slope of the Plain, you could see the green belt that lined the river from wherever your head was above the sage, and you weren't down in a sink or swale. The green belt was more willows than anything else, but there were black cottonwoods, river hawthorns, water birches and chokecherries too. The catkins had fallen from the male cottonwoods a week or two back. Now the leaves were out, the sweet smell of resin filled the air, and the cotton pods were forming. The chokecherries were in full bloom, showing cylindrical clusters of tiny white flowers.

We spotted robins, warblers and sparrows among the trees, and hawks and turkey vultures high above. I wondered if from a soaring bird's point of view, the river looked like a long rope, green at the edges, stretched in an arc across the land, and kinked and twisted here and there.

The willow thickets kept us from getting down to the bank, but we saw swallows, gulls and a kingfisher over the river, and at one point were close enough to flush a pair of mallards. Amanda stopped us with a finger over her lips and a quiet "Shhh" so we could listen for a killdeer's plaintive cry.

Just below the rapids, a stiffening wind made us turn and look at the western sky. It was black across the width of the horizon and rising fast. To the east, the sky was clear blue, but black clouds were quickly taking over. Lightning bolts shot down in rapid succession from south to north. The thunder came moments later, rolling and rumbling over the Plain.

"I bet Will or Ben is ringing the bell," Beth said, "but we can't hear it because the wind is wrong."

"If we run, we might make it to the mill before the storm's on us," I said. Without a word, we started running. If it were a straight line, we might have made it, but having to dodge sage and rabbit brush slowed us down. I stayed behind Beth and Amanda, as if to protect them. The storm was on our heels and chasing fast. The first big raindrops hit the ground around us—plop, plop, plop—so loud I thought it must be raining eggs. Lightning cracked big, sharp and very close. I turned to see a cottonwood in flames behind us near the bank.

Amanda stumbled and fell ahead of me, and I tripped over her. Beth came and grabbed Amanda's hand. We were up and running again, now drenched and dirty from the fall. I saw the mill ahead. In a minute or two, we were there and inside, with the door shut behind us. Lightning struck the rod on the roof with a sharp, ear-splitting crack. The building trembled. I thought of Louis. I was glad he had built a sturdy mill and protected it with a lightning rod. We huddled together in a corner and waited.

Five minutes passed. Rain pounded on the roof, and wind swirled around us, howling. Ten minutes more. Lightning struck east of us. Thunder came a few moments behind. The storm was passing but still violent. There was the loud clamor of a wagon outside and men struggling with panicked horses. I got up and opened the door. It was Will and Ben, each down from the bench and holding a horse's harness at the head. They were drenched.

"Are you OK?" Will screamed above the din.

"Yes, we're all OK," I yelled back.

"Stay inside, close the door," he yelled as May Belle jerked her head back. I did as Will said.

"It's passing," I said to Beth and Amanda. "Will and Ben are here with the wagon and team. Everything's all right." I looked at Beth, Amanda and myself. We looked as if we had been swimming in mud.

Will and Ben came inside after they had calmed and tied the horses. They were dripping wet.

"I'm glad you're safe," Will said. "I started ringing the bell as soon as we saw black clouds rising in the west."

"We thought so," Beth replied, "but the wind didn't let the sound reach us."

"Lightning struck a cottonwood close behind us," I said. "We ran to the mill house."

"I'm glad you're not any taller," Will replied, smiling. "We have no dry clothes, so the best we can do is wait out the storm and then head home. I hope there's not much crop damage."

"Will our garden be all right, Papa?" Amanda asked.

"Your young plants might have been hurt," Will replied, "but it's early yet, so you can always reseed. It'll be OK, sweetheart."

"I'll help you fix things up if they need it, Amanda," Ben said.

"Thank you, Ben," Amanda and Beth said in unison.

We waited about 20 minutes until the rain had backed off to a sprinkle. Will and Ben untied the team, held their harness at the head and brought them around to face east. Beth, Amanda and I climbed into the bed, while Will and Ben took the bench. Will slapped the reins on the team's backs, and we started home.

43

The cottonwood near the cave mouth was an oddity. It was an eastern cottonwood, like those much closer to the Mississippi. It wasn't native to Idaho Territory like the narrowleaf and black cottonwoods along the Snake and other streams. That left the question, how did it get here? I could only guess.

Years before we came, maybe a traveler heading west and crossing the Mississippi in late May or early June when the cotton pods are ready to burst picked a handful and carried them across the Great Plains. Perhaps he planted the cotton in moist places as he went, places he thought it had a good chance of sprouting and surviving. Maybe he camped in what became our cave. And perhaps he had iron tools that he used to break through the roof to make a smoke hole. We'll never know.

Sometime before we came, the eastern cottonwood had divided into two trunks a short way above its base. Its bark had become gray and deeply furrowed. Its crown had grown and spread so the overall tree was shaped like a V, and now the top was just above the level of our porch floor. We could sit on the porch, look toward the river and peer down into the cottonwood's crown. A light breeze flipped the leaves and caused sections to move independent of each other. A stiffer breeze brushed the entire crown, causing it to sweep and rustle as a whole.

In spring '74, a pair of mourning doves built a nest of twigs in the crook of two branches a short way down from the top of the crown. The female laid two white eggs. Sometimes, as she sat to warm them, the male walked on her back. After the eggs hatched, both parents fed the squabs food they gathered and regurgitated. Soon after the young left the nest, the male performed the court-ship ritual again, complete with cooing, noisy wing flapping and gliding that ended with a flamboyant tail display. Days later, the female deposited two more white eggs in the nest.

I often came upon the adult pair on our porch. They rose almost vertically to escape, fluttering their wings and making a soft chattering sound. From early spring through the summer, they produced four pairs of squabs. By late September, all were gone somewhere south.

On a late October afternoon in '74, Will, Ben and I were repair-ing an irrigation ditch near the northeast corner of the sink when we heard the *George Hawkins* bell ringing with pauses between. We stopped work, loaded our tools in the wagon and headed home. We were about as far from the house as we could get and still be on our land, so it took awhile to reach the bench.

With the crops harvested, there was a clear view to the house from some distance. We saw Beth and Amanda on the porch looking in our direction. As we drew close, Beth called out that there was a stranger on horseback at the ferry landing on the south side. The ferry sat at the bank on the north side, and Beth had called to the man to wait. There seemed to be no cause for alarm, but seeing a stranger nearby was so unusual that Beth had become a little excited.

He was a large man sitting on a big bay horse. He had a loaded pack horse alongside. He wasn't wearing a gunbelt and holster, but he had a rifle in a sheath tied to his saddle. He wore a dark coat and a wide-brimmed brown hat. Will picked up a Winchester and handed it to Ben as we walked toward the landing. We boarded the ferry and angled it with the current. As we started across, the man dismounted and stood beside his horse, holding the reins. As the ferry approached the landing, the man walked down the bank. He was a coarse-looking man with big, meaty hands.

"Hello. Good afternoon," he said with a gruff voice and a German accent.

"Hello, welcome to the Hawkins place," Will said, a little warily. Ben and I stood back by the ferry as Will approached the man.

"I haff cattle by Goose Creek," the man said. "I'm looking the land over."

Will stopped. His posture changed. He seemed to be examining the man very closely.

"Henry, is that you?" Will asked in a disbelieving tone.

"Yes, Henry, Henry Schodde," he said. "How do you know my name?"

"Henry, I'm Will Hawkins. Do you remember me? Natchez, Mississippi. I was with my father on our steamer. You saved our first pilot's boy from kidnapping. Our cook served you a big meal as thanks."

"Mein Gott! Ya!" the man said. "I was Heinrich. You told me, 'This is America, you are Henry.' Ya! Vill Hawkins! Hello, hello. How are you? What are you doing here?"

"That bell you just heard is from our steamer, the *George Hawkins*," Will said. "But there are no more steamers for us. This is our place now. We've been farming here two years. These are my sons, Ben and Early," Will said, turning toward us. "Remember the story I told when we were in camp down toward Dover between the rivers?" he asked us. "This is Henry," he continued before we could reply. "This is the man who stopped the wagon and saved Amon from being kidnapped."

Ben and I were a moment clearing our heads. We stepped forward and shook hands with Mr. Schodde.

"Henry, can you stay for supper?" Will asked. "Come across on the ferry, meet my wife and daughter, we'll show you around our farm, and then we'll sit for supper. It's sure to be a beautiful sunset."

"Why sure," Mr. Schodde replied. "I'd love to."

He walked his horses onto the ferry, and we started across.

"So, you have cattle at Goose Creek?" Will asked.

"Ya, 'bout 50 head," Mr. Schodde said. "Jack Fuller and I brought them down from the mountains for the winter. I think there's enough grass."

"We looked at Goose Creek before we settled here," Will said. "I think you're right. There is enough grass. How is it that you chose Goose Creek?"

"I was living in Toana, Nevada, on the other side of the Goose Creek Mountains," Mr. Schodde replied. "Jack and I ran the cattle through a pass and down the creek to winter here on the Snake River. Goose Creek is good, but it won't water enough land. I will look for a way to water the land for crops with Snake River water. If I can do it, I will settle here."

Mr. Schodde stayed for supper and spent the night. Before he left in the morning, he asked if we would have lucerne and hay to sell if he settled on Goose Creek and expanded his herd. Will replied that we would. We promised we'd stop to visit on our way back and forth to Oakley Meadows. He said he'd do the same if he went to the Raft River. Goose Creek was a little closer and a quicker ride than Marsh Basin, so, unless the ranchers on the Raft River had a wagon near the Snake, that made Henry Schodde and Jack Fuller our nearest neighbors, or so we first thought.

We looked for them at Goose Creek the next time we went to Oakley Meadows but didn't find them there, only some of their cattle. We followed a fresh trail about five miles farther down the Snake and came upon Mr. Schodde, George Smith and Alex Morton working on the bank. They were just above the rapids that lay about 30 miles downstream from Hawkins Rapids. Since Mr. Schodde had settled near the lower rapids, we began calling them by his name.

They had two projects under way. One was a cabin set back from the river, and the other was a waterwheel. The waterwheel was huge and looked very much like a steamboat paddlewheel. When it was finished, it would sit in the river at the head of Schodde Rapids, lift water in buckets as the current kept it turning, and transfer the water to a flume that carried it to Mr. Schodde's land. In the coming years, Mr. Schodde would build 10 more waterwheels and irrigate land on both sides of the river. Even with many acres under cultivation, his herds became so large that he continued to buy lucerne, corn and hay from us.

The spring of '75 was very soggy. May brought one rainy day after another. Low spots in the fields and pastures became mud holes. On a particularly wet day, I brought the dairy cows in from the pasture and milked them in their stalls. I also brought the horses and mules to the barn, but I left the beef cattle out to graze. The following morning when I led the animals to the pasture to turn them out, I discovered the beeves had pushed two

sodden fence posts down on the north side, trampled the barbed
wire and walked off toward the lava fields. I couldn't see them,
and there was no way to tell how far they had gone. There was
fresh grass and water as far north as they wanted to wander.

I returned the beasts to the night pasture, went to the house
and told Will what had happened. He asked Ben and me to saddle up and ride out to find the cattle. He said he'd stay behind. It
wasn't raining when we left, but we took our rain gear along just
in case. With the soft, wet ground, following the cattle tracks
was easy. We came within sight of the lava with only tracks and
manure as signs of the beeves.

The lava was a huge field that had formed about 2,000 years
before. It spread for miles. Only birds could see the extent of it. If
you put your palm down flat on a table and spread your fingers,
the field would be the whole back of your hand, and your fingers
would be long, tapering stretches of lava. It was a combination of
aa—rough, sharp and jagged—and pahoehoe—smoother, rounded
and swirled lava. How it flowed when molten and how it cooled
and dried made the difference. Between the fingers of lava were
grassy areas called kipukas. In some kipukas, there were vernal
pools and ancient juniper trees. We suspected the beeves were
headed for the grass, water and shade in the kipukas, but we had
no idea how they knew those attractions were there.

We were probably seven or eight miles north and east of the
homeplace when the rain started. It was a steady downpour
and, in spite of our slickers, we were drenched in no time. We
had been up this way before and knew there were caves beneath
some of the lava domes. It was just a matter of finding one that
wasn't too long a hike over rough lava. We got lucky on our third
try—very lucky as it turned out. The cave we found was about
five feet high, 30 deep and 50 wide. People had been there before
but not any time recently. The cave floor was littered with very
old bones, small and large. The small bones were rabbit, and we
figured the large ones had to be bison since there weren't horses
or cattle up this way long ago. Parts of the roof were blacked
from the smoke of cooking fires. We had stumbled upon a shelter
used by some ancient people. They had left stone tools and other
artifacts behind. Ben and I decided the cave would be our secret.
I wondered if we'd ever be able to find it again. There were no

distinctive landmarks in sight, especially in a pouring rain.

We laid our slickers and clothes out to dry and waited on the rain. We explored every square foot of the cave, then lay down and dozed off. When we awoke, the rain had backed off to a drizzle. We dressed in damp clothes, left the cave and walked back to the horses.

We found the cattle at the mouth of a kipuka nearby. They were grazing and gradually moving north, occupied only with eating. We turned them south and drove them home, arriving after dark to find that Will had patched the fence together and left the mules in the pasture.

At the house, Will told us we had done a good job in finding the beeves and bringing them home. He told us we needed two things—fence posts and barbed wire—and he didn't want to wait to order the wire from Corinne via the mail coach at Oakley Meadows and have the freighter haul it up from Kelton. He wanted Ben and me to take the big wagon to Kelton, order the wire by telegraph, wait for the train to bring it in and get back as quickly as we could. We were to go south through Marsh Basin and check with George and Alex for fence posts. If they could have a load ready for us to pick up on our way back, good. Otherwise, we were to return by the Raft River Valley, go up Pole Canyon and cut trees for posts there.

44

Ben and I left for Kelton first thing in the morning. We were lucky the rain had stopped and the sky had cleared. The road south was muddy, and Cañon Creek was running high as we made our way through the Early Mountains. George and Alex had no posts on hand and were too busy with other work to have more cut and finished by the time we returned. We planned to stop at Pole Canyon on our way back.

Kelton was bustling, as usual. We checked for barbed wire with the hardware merchant first. He had none but said if we were going to order by telegraph, we should ask for Glidden wire, a new brand that was better than the old Kelly wire. We went straight to the telegraph office and ordered two coils from Corinne. The return message said the wire would be on the morning train. Before registering at the Rosevears' hotel, we took the horses and wagon to the livery. I had an unfortunate accident there. I tore my britches and gashed my thigh on a nail that jutted out from the end of a loose stall rail. I pretended the wound was nothing. Actually, it hurt like the dickens, and I wasn't too comfortable with the sight of my own blood. Ben looked worried for me. He dabbed the wound with water from a horse trough and tied his bandana around my thigh. If that didn't stop the bleeding, he said, we'd see the druggist or find the doctor, if there was one.

We had our supper in the hotel dining room and stepped outside afterwards. My thigh felt tender, and I limped a little, but the bleeding had stopped, and we felt the wound would heal itself. There was loud piano music coming from a saloon two doors down from the hotel. Ben couldn't keep his attention away from the music.

"Do you want to go to the saloon?" he asked.

"Will said we shouldn't, remember?" I replied.

"That was two years ago. We're older now," Ben said. "I don't think Will would mind. That piano sounds good. Let's just take a look."

We had nothing else to do, so I was easily persuaded. There was so much noise and such a mix of people in the saloon that we didn't even draw a glance when we went in. We took seats at a table near the stairs. Ben kept his gaze glued on the piano player. I sat wide-eyed, looking at the people. There were several women in fancy dresses that revealed more than the clothes women usually wore on the street. There were a lot of cowboys. Most were playing cards at the tables. Some stood at the bar, talking and slapping each other on the back. There was a well-dressed man who looked as if he had just gotten off the train from a big city. Three waiters with white aprons tied about their waists circulated around the room, carrying drinks from the bar to the tables and empty bottles and glasses back. The piano player played very fast and loud. He had green garters around both his arms above the elbows to keep his cuffs off the keyboard. The music he played was new to me. After a while, he stopped playing, spun around on the piano stool, stepped up to the bar and motioned to the bartender. The bartender drew a large glass of beer and gave it to the piano player. Ben leaned toward me and said, "Stay right here. I'm going over to talk to the piano player."

Ben stood at the bar talking with the man for a minute or two. The man nodded several times and then motioned to the piano with his free hand. Ben stepped to the piano, took his hat off and laid it on top. He sat on the stool, pushed his sleeves up and began to play. He started with a flurry that covered the keyboard from one end to the other. Only the piano player seemed to notice at first, but as Ben continued to play, heads turned and, one by one, people stopped talking. The well-dressed man took special notice, nodded and turned his chair to face Ben and the piano. I didn't know what Ben was playing or where he learned it, but he was drawing a lot of attention. When he finished the first tune, the room was quiet for a second, then everyone burst into applause. Ben turned a full circle on the stool, smiled, touched his forehead with his fingertips and gave a little wave, as if tipping his hat.

He turned back to the keyboard and started a much slower, quieter tune. It sounded like a lullaby. He began to sing:

> *Oh, give me a home*
> *Where the buffalo roam*
> *Where the deer and the antelope play*
> *Where seldom is heard*
> *A discouraging word*
> *And the sky is not cloudy all day*

Ben sang the verses, and more people joined in on each chorus. If you can imagine a saloon full of rowdy cowboys turning misty-eyed, that's what the room looked like. By the end of the song, you'd have thought the audience was young schoolgirls. But Ben didn't give them an inch. He finished *The Western Home* and launched into a rousing dance tune. The applause and cheering were like thunder. Ben had the room in his grip. The piano player looked stunned.

As Ben continued to play, one of the waiters stopped at my table.

"Hey, sonny, kinda young to be in a saloon, ain't ya?" he asked. Before I had a chance to answer, the youngest of the fancy-dressed women stepped in.

"It's OK, Billy," she said, "he's with me." She sat next to me, and the waiter backed away. She had long, curly blond hair, and her pretty face wasn't as painted as the other women's. "Hi, honey, my name's Rebel, what's yours?" she asked.

"Early, Early Hawkins," I replied, with some hesitation.

"Is that your friend at the piano?" she asked.

"Ben's my brother," I replied.

"Naw!" she exclaimed, "you two boys is the wrong color to be brothers."

"It's a long story," I said, "but he *is* my brother."

"How'd y'all get a name like 'Early'?" she asked.

"Folks squeezed Earl and Lee together," I replied. "How did you get a name like 'Rebel'?"

"Honey, I'm from Tennessee," she replied.

"Then we're neighbors," I said, "I'm from Kentucky." Just then, she caught site of the bloody bandana around my thigh.

"My lawd, honey, what have y'all done to your leg?" she asked, almost shrieking.

"It's OK," I replied, "I cut it a little on a nail."

"Oh, no, honey," she said, "I done some nursin', and a cut like that ain't OK. You best take care of that, or y'all could lose your leg."

"I washed it out, and the bleeding stopped," I said, "it really is OK."

"No," she insisted, "y'all are dead wrong. Now, listen to Rebel. Come with me upstairs, and I'm gonna fix that leg." She stood up and yanked me by the arm. "Now, come on," she said, "don't be no mule. I'm gonna fix that leg." She pulled me up from my seat and just about dragged me up the stairs. We went into a room off the hall, and she closed the door. She led me to a dresser where there was a basin of water. I could hear Ben playing and singing down below.

"Come right over here," she said, "and I'll undo that bandana." She bent down and struggled to untie the knot. It wouldn't give, so she knelt and worked on it until it gave way. She gasped when she saw the wound.

"Honey, you'll have to drop your britches so I can do this properly," she said.

"Drop my britches?" I asked.

"Yes," she said, "Now, don't argue with Rebel. Y'all have a

terrible gash there and with your pants in the way, I cain't get at it. Set here and pull your boots and britches off. When y'all get 'em off, I'll fix the wound and mend your trousers." I sighed and did as she said, accepting my fate and trying as hard as I could to hide my embarrassment. I stood at the dresser while she moved the basin to the floor, knelt at my thigh, wet a cloth and cleaned the wound.

"My lawd, Early, you're a grown man," she said. "Shore couldn't tell by that sweet, young face. Now stand still while I dry you and put a proper bandage 'round your leg." She gently patted me dry, then wound a bandage around my thigh and knotted it. "How's that feel, too tight?" she asked.

"Feels fine," I replied.

"Come set with me on the bed while I mend your britches," she said. She went to a night table beside the bed and pulled a tin box out of the drawer. We sat and she opened the box. She chose a needle and spool of thread, and spread my britches across her lap. "Maybe y'all can help me thread this," she said, handing me the spool and needle. When I took them from her, she let her hands linger on mine. She looked me square in the face. "Now, Early, I don't want y'all bein' nervous or scared or nuthin'," she said. "We can set this mendin' aside for a spell. There's some more important things I want to show you."

For the next hour or so, Rebel introduced me to pleasures I hadn't known before. I'm glad my first time was with an experienced woman. I told Ben later that he had played and sung the right tunes at just the right times.

Rebel mended my britches, and we went back down to the saloon. Ben saw us coming down the stairs, caught my eye and gave me a big, knowing grin. He played two more tunes and turned the piano back over to the house player. Everybody applauded loud and long. As Ben walked toward me, the well-dressed man stood and motioned to him to come to his table. He smiled broadly, looking very open and welcoming. Ben sat talking with him for a few minutes, and he gave Ben what looked like a calling card. They stood, shook hands, and Ben returned to my table.

"You look like the cat that ate the canary," he said as he sat down.

"You're looking mighty pleased yourself," I said.

"That man just offered me a job as a headliner in his opera house in San Francisco," he said.

"San Francisco, California?" I asked.

"Yup, and they plan to tour the country and maybe the world," he replied.

"Are you going to go?" I asked.

"I don't know, Early," he replied, looking me in the eye, "I want to talk to Will and Beth." He was smiling, and his deep brown eyes were glistening. At the same time, he looked a little puzzled, as if he was facing a dilemma. We rose from the table and walked to the hotel in silence. We didn't speak again until we were in our room undressing for bed.

"What did you do upstairs with that blond tart?" he asked.

"She's no tart!" I exclaimed. "She cleaned my wound, bandaged my thigh and mended my britches."

"What else did she do when she had your britches off?" he asked, grinning.

"Well, you know, Ben," I said, "she taught me some things."

"Good for you, brother," he said. "I learned those things with Maria in Smithland. And my music led me to learning a lot more at Rock Creek. Women are wonderful beings, you know."

"I think that's something I'm just starting to appreciate," I said.

We were at the depot waiting with the wagon when the morning train came in. We loaded the wire and headed north. Pole Canyon was a good two days' drive from Kelton. We cut enough junipers and young firs for about two dozen posts, trimmed them and loaded them in the wagon. After one more night in camp along the Raft River, we reached the ferry landing across from the homeplace, four days out of Kelton. Beth and Amanda ran the ferry across to meet us. Ben would have news to tell at supper, but I wouldn't tell mine.

When we sat for supper, Beth asked how our trip went. I replied that Ben had more to tell than I did. He looked at me and grinned, knowing I couldn't tell my story, and that he would have to tell his. He didn't go into a long build-up. He simply said that a man named Thomas Maguire from San Francisco had heard him play and sing, and offered him a job in his opera company. Beth smiled, looking pleased and proud. She praised Ben and said she was happy for him. Amanda asked if she could take the train to San Francisco and visit him. Will didn't look surprised. He said he knew that sooner or later Ben would be leaving us—there was no opportunity for him here in Idaho Territory unless he wanted to make a life of farming or ranching. Beth and Amanda seemed to have concluded that Ben would go. Will asked Ben if he had decided. Ben replied that he thought he should at least go take a look. He added that he would wait until all the crops were planted.

"This sounds like a good opportunity for you, Ben," Will said. "If you decide to accept the offer, I hope it goes well. We'll miss you terribly. Farming this land without you will be tough, but Early is getting bigger and stronger everyday, and if we can count on our neighbors to help with the harvest and threshing, we should get along all right."

"Thank you, Will," Ben said. "I owe my life to you, and I'll never forget you and Beth and what you've done for me."

"We did what any decent people would do," Will said.

"You did a lot more than that," Ben said. "You gave me a home and a family. You made me what I am. If I decide to stay in San Francisco, I'll miss you and the homeplace. I'll send a letter to San Francisco by the mail coach and let Mr. Maguire know when to expect me."

Ben left from Oakley Meadows in early June. He and I drove down together in the wagon. He took his instruments and a canvas bag Beth had made for him. Will went across with us on the ferry, while Beth and Amanda watched from the porch. They had already said their tearful goodbyes. Beth looked at Ben with great love and pride. She embraced him, kissed his cheek and wished him well.

"Remember, Ben, we're here if you need us," she said. "We hate to see you go, but we know it's an opportunity for you. Please write and tell us how you are."

I led the team off the ferry onto the southside landing. Will stood with Ben on the ferry deck. I was too far away to hear what they said. They shook hands firmly, then stood apart for a moment. They came together in a bear hug, then parted, and Ben walked off the ferry toward the wagon.

"Let's go before I change my mind," he said. He didn't try to hide his tears. As we started to drive away, the ringing bell followed us. We turned to see Will heading back across, and Beth and Amanda standing at the bell, tugging on the cord together. The strong, steady rings continued, fading gradually as the distance between us and the homeplace grew. We were far down the road into the sage before we lost the sound of the bell.

We camped one night and the next day saw the mail coach's dust trail to the west as we approached Oakley Meadows from the north. We were closer, but the coach was driving faster. I started to move to quicken our pace.

"We don't have to run," Ben said. "It'll take them some time to change horses and transfer the mail and freight."

We came to the station as the men were trading the teams. The coach passengers had gotten out to stretch their legs, and the driver was tossing the mail sack down from the roof. I went to tie our team while Ben moved to the tailgate to get his baggage. I walked back and met him there. We stood facing each other. I was almost as tall as he was, but he was much bigger. We had been brothers since '64, and I had become so used to him that I had kind of lost sight of him. Now, as we stood at the wagon, I was struck by what a magnificent man he was.

"See you, brother," he said. "If I stay, I hope you'll come visit."

"If we can get away, maybe we all will. I hope you'll come back to the homeplace now and then," I said.

"I better go," he said, "it looks as if the team's ready." We shook hands, then bear hugged, just as he and Will had. We caught each other's eye as we stood back. We had both welled up with tears.

"I'll help with your baggage," I said.

We walked to the coach and passed Ben's bag and cases up to the roof. He climbed into the coach from the outward side as the other passengers entered from the station side. He sat by the rear window, facing front. The driver and guard moved to their seats. The driver released the brake and slapped the reins on the horses' backs. "He-ah, gettup," he yelled. Ben leaned out the window and waved his hat as the coach lurched and began to move away. I waved my hat as dust chased the coach. In a few moments, the sound faded and the coach became a speck moving through the sage. I dropped my hat to my side and watched until the coach disappeared. For a moment, I felt terribly empty and alone. I looked across the road to where Bill Oakley, the stationmaster, stood leaning against the rails of the horse corral.

"Howdy, Early," he said. "I think there's a letter here for you. You want to set for a spell before you go back?"

"Sure, Bill," I replied as I walked toward him. I think that was the first time I called him "Bill." It had always been "Mr. Oakley." I don't know why I changed. The letter was from Rebel, down in Kelton. I couldn't have been more surprised, but I didn't want to open it with Bill there.

"Where's Ben off to?" he asked.

"San Francisco," I replied.

"Yup, the big city," he said.

"He got a job with an opera company," I said.

"Yup, he's a hell of a singer," he said. "Hate to see him go, though."

"I can't stay long," I said. "I want to see how far north I can get before dark."

"Sure, but take some bread and jerky with you," he offered.

"Thanks, Bill," I said, accepting his offer.

I drove almost half way home before stopping for the night. I picketed the horses in fresh grass along the creek. At sundown, I sat in the wagon bed and read Rebel's letter. She asked after my leg wound, said she missed me and wondered if I would visit again. I smiled and pondered the thought as I chewed on Bill's bread and jerky. I slept under the stars in the wagon bed that night, surprised that Rebel had written me a letter.

In the morning, I drove west of Goose Creek to Mr. Schodde's place before turning for home. He wasn't there or anywhere in sight. I figured he must have been out tending to his beeves. His cabin and corrals had been up for at least six months now, and his place had started to look like home. It was the only homestead for miles around. One waterwheel turned in the river at the head of the rapids, bringing water to his fields. He had started building another wheel on the bank. I went in and left a note saying I had stopped to visit, and added we had bales of freshly cut lucerne if he needed any.

I got home close to the end of the day. Will came in from the barn, and the four of us sat for supper. We exchanged long silent looks, and I know we were all thinking the same thing: It just wasn't the same without Ben there.

We had our first letter from him in July. He said he was doing well and thought he would stay in San Francisco, at least for a while, to see what opportunities developed. Although Maguire's Opera House was new, they were drawing good-sized audiences with "light musical amusements." The company had started rehearsing *Thespis*, a comic opera by Gilbert and Sullivan from London, England. Ben's part was Sparkeion, a newlywed groom. All this sounded very far away from farming in Idaho.

45

During the summer, when the water was warm, we bathed in the bigger, rock-lined irrigation ditches. Otherwise, we heated water on the wood stove and filled a tub in the kitchen. Also in summer, I enjoyed swimming in the river. The water was usually low and slow enough then that there was no danger, especially if I stayed close to the bank.

Whenever the ferry had been left at the south landing for whatever reason and I was on the north side, I either rowed or swam across, current allowing, to get it. I had two techniques for rowing across. For the first, I hugged the north bank and rowed straight upstream, judging the distance I had to row by the speed of the current. Then I turned across the flow and, with a combination of angling the bow and using the oars, I crossed to the ferry at the south landing. For the second technique, I started at the north landing at an upstream angle and rowed as hard as I could to beat the current and cross to the south landing.

My swimming technique was like the first rowing technique, except I walked upstream along the north bank, always farther than I had to row, then dove in and swam south, letting the current carry me down to the landing. Whether rowing or swimming, winding up at the south landing took a lot of trial and error before I was able to hit it just right. As hard as I tried, there were many times that I wound up below the landing. After I mastered both rowing and swimming across the river without being swept too far downstream, I did it just for fun, regardless of where the ferry was.

In the summer of '75, Amanda was nine years old. She insisted she was strong enough to row and swim across the river like me. I said she wasn't, but she wouldn't hear it. I finally gave in and offered to row over with her so she wouldn't try to cross on her own. We each took an oar, and I taught her both rowing techniques. Her rowing wasn't as strong as mine, so I took the downstream seat and adjusted the bow angle so we hit the south landing. I also promised to teach her how to swim over so she wouldn't try it without me. I delayed as long as I could, but she pestered me, and, before July ended, I had to make good on my promise.

Although I didn't tell Amanda the first time we swam, I walked her much farther upstream before we dove in than I would have if I had been alone. She was always energetic, and she was getting feisty as she got older, so I guess I shouldn't have been surprised that she was such a strong swimmer. I swam downstream of her and watched her so I could help if something went wrong. As it was, though, I had to slow us down as we swam cross-current so we wouldn't reach the south bank at the marshy area above the landing. When we scrambled up the logs and out of the water, Amanda stood up straight, faced me squarely, put her hands on her hips and said, "See, Early, I *told* you I can swim the river!" I laughed and replied, "Yup, you sure can."

Among the people we came to know during our visits to Marsh Basin were two families who lived southeast of town. Of the two, the Weatherman place was closer in. They had come from Kansas to homestead in the Basin. By the summer of '75, Sigmon and Julia Weatherman already had six kids. Maggie, one of their three daughters, was Amanda's age. Farther from town, and out along a creek that came to bear their name, was the Howell place. The Howells had come to the Basin from Utah. One of their seven sons was my age. His name was Charlie.

Especially with Ben gone, I was glad to have a boy to pal around with now and then, and Amanda liked having Maggie as a friend. But the distance between us made seeing our friends difficult. Marsh Basin was almost four hours from our place on horseback and about an hour more if we drove a wagon. Even during the long summer days, that meant if we started from the homeplace at first light, took care of whatever business we had in Marsh Basin and wanted to get home before dark, Amanda and I had barely any time to spend with Charlie and Maggie. The same was true if they came over to the river. They lived on farms as we did, and their warm-weather days were as full of chores and farm work as Amanda's and mine. We had to plan our get-togethers so our play didn't interfere with our work. That usually meant getting ahead in the fields, then riding to the Basin and spending a night or two, or Charlie and Maggie coming to the river and staying with us.

They rode from the Basin on horseback to spend a few days at our homeplace in late August. They had left at sunup and got to the south-side ferry landing just after 10 a.m. Charlie hailed me, and I ran the ferry across to bring them and their horses over. Charlie rode a gray gelding, while Maggie's mount was a paint pony. After turning their horses out in the pasture, the first thing Charlie and Maggie wanted to do was swim in the river. Amanda and I, especially Amanda, took them up on that idea immediately. She led us up the bench on the north side with great excitement and not a little pride. She was eager to show our visitors how to swim the river. The level was low and the current slow, so swimming to the south-side landing was easy, even for our creek-dwelling friends. We walked upstream on the south bank, sat in the sun for a few minutes and swam back across to the north landing. The swims were fun and the start of what we hoped would be a great visit.

Later, while the girls busied themselves with girl things, Charlie and I packed lunch in a haversack and walked down toward the rapids with our fishing poles. Our plan was to try our luck from the bank wherever the willows let us get close. We wove our way through the brush and willows to the water's edge at four or five spots, but the fish weren't biting. I pointed out several water-bird species to Charlie. They were new to him since he didn't live at the river.

We relieved the August heat by diving in here and there. I noticed that the level had risen and the current had quickened during the course of the day. We figured there must have been big thunderstorms somewhere upstream.

I showed Charlie our grain mill just above the rapids. The boil and rush of the water was unusually strong for late summer. We skirted the rapids and cast our lines into the pool below, but the fish still weren't cooperating. It was getting on toward late afternoon, so we turned for home. I hoped Beth wouldn't be disappointed that we weren't bringing fish for supper.

We had walked about two-thirds of the way back and were at a low spot in the road where thick willows blocked our view of the river, when Will came racing down the slope ahead riding bareback on a plow mule. He barely slowed as he passed, yelling, "Drop your poles and run down!" We had no idea why we should, but we did as he said. We ran to a break in the willows where Will had left the mule and his boots and clothes on the bank. He was out in the river struggling across the current. We looked upstream and saw why. Amanda and Maggie were adrift in the skiff, moving down. They both gripped the only oar, desperately trying to use it like a rudder to steer toward the bank. Charlie and I looked at each other, excited and scared.

"The rocky point that juts out into the river below," I said, "where we stopped before—let's go there—the current's going to take them all farther down." We ran to the mule, I jumped up, and Charlie leapt up behind me. We took off running downstream. Luckily, the mule had a halter and a long lead. Will must have stripped off the harness and grabbed what he could at the barn. We raced to the rocky point, jumped to the ground and looked upstream. Will had reached the boat. He was in the water hauling it with the bow line. The girls struggled with the oar in the upstream oarlock.

"This might work, Charlie," I said. "We'll use the mule as an anchor. Let's wade him into the river as far as he can stand. You hang onto his tail behind, and I'll stretch out his lead in front. Maybe we can reach them." We pulled our boots off, dropped our britches and shirts on the bank, and waded into the river in our underclothes. We stretched out a good 20 feet. We yelled to Will and the girls to make sure they saw us. They struggled mightily with the river. I grabbed the lead with my left hand and wrapped it one turn around my wrist. I stretched as far as I could toward Will with my right hand as he swam and the current brought them down. The water swirled around my chest as I tried to keep my footing. I leaned out as they came near. Will's hand reached for mine, and we locked on. His grip felt like an iron claw clamping down. The boat swung around at the end of the bow line, but we had it and the girls were safe. Will pulled his legs up beneath him and stood beside me. He looked exhausted, but he managed a smile and so did I.

"Pull him back, Charlie," I yelled as I slacked off on the mule's lead. He inched back, and we hauled the boat and the girls to the bank. They looked relieved as we helped them out.

"Maybe you can tell us what happened, Amanda," Will said.

"Papa, we were rowing across just fine until one oarlock broke, and we lost the oar in the river," Amanda said.

"Why are you wearing fancy dresses and high-button shoes?" I asked.

"We were going to a tea party," she replied. Both girls looked a little sheepish.

"A tea party?" Charlie asked.

"Yes, a tea party at the south landing," Maggie replied. Will, Charlie and I looked at each other and laughed.

"Well," Will said, "we're sorry you missed the party, and we're glad you're safe."

"Thank you for saving us, Papa," Amanda said.

"Yes, thank you, Captain Hawkins," Maggie added.

"Oh, it's all in a day's work," Will said with mock modesty in his voice. He paused. "Now, there are five of us here, a boat and one mule. Beth must be worried sick. She's probably coming this way looking for us. If you'll wait here, I'll ride ahead, fetch my boots and clothes, ride on to the house, and come back with a wagon and team. We'll load the boat and be home in time for supper." The rest of us nodded in agreement.

"Can you pick up our fishing poles on your way back?" I asked. Will said he would, mounted the mule and turned to the girls before he rode off. "No rowing while I'm gone, right girls?" he asked, smiling. They said nothing and only smiled in return, knowing Will was teasing.

With Will gone, Charlie and I gathered up our boots and clothes, and disappeared into the brush to strip off our wet under-clothes and dress in our britches, shirts and boots. Then it was just a matter of waiting for Will to return with the wagon and team. He came about an hour later and, as he had said, we were home in time for supper. At the table, we learned that Beth, sur-prised to find herself alone at the house, had rung the bell and, getting no response, saddled her mare and rode down toward the mill looking for us. Will had met her on his way up, assured her we were all right, and they had ridden back together. Everyone agreed we had had enough adventure for the first day of Charlie and Maggie's visit.

Nothing quite as exciting as the girls' getting turned loose on the river happened during the rest of our friends' stay. Charlie and I spent the better part of one day upstream from the home-place, fishing. As we sat on the bank with our lines in the water, we talked about the river and wondered aloud about where it came from and where it went. I told Charlie that when we first came to Idaho, we rode down along the river from the crossing at old Fort Hall. Neither Charlie nor I had been any farther down-stream than Schodde Rapids. We had heard stories about the deep canyon, a place called Cauldron Linn and Shoshone Falls farther down. We thought we ought to see them. We agreed that early spring, when the river was high and planting wasn't yet under way, would be the best time to go.

There was a tug on Charlie's line. When he stood up and pulled back on his rod, whatever had taken the hook nearly launched him into the river. There was no clutch on Charlie's reel, and the fish was stronger than he was, so he had no choice but to let it run with the line. Otherwise, the line or Charlie's hex bamboo rod would snap. Luckily, the fish ran upstream. He would tire, the line would slack a bit, and Charlie could start reeling him in little by little.

As it was, landing the fish took awhile. Charlie and I traded the rod back and forth because we each got tired before the fish did. When we finally got it to the bank, I used a driftwood branch as a gaff to haul it up onto dry land.

The fish was an unusually large cutthroat trout. It was eas-ily 30 inches long and must have weighed close to 50 pounds. We gutted it there on the bank but didn't take its head off. We ran a length of line from gill to gill through its mouth and wrapped another around its tail to make it easier to carry. We each took a line and walked the cutthroat home. We amazed Will, Beth and the girls with our catch, had fresh trout for supper that night and two meals the following day.

A short time later, Amanda and I rode to Marsh Basin to spend a few days with Maggie and Charlie. Charlie and I loaded a pack mule and rode south, as if on our way to Kelton. Near the pass, we turned onto the logging road and followed the ridge line up Will Peak. By local reckoning, the peak was about 10,000 feet. Our plan was to camp near the summit and return the next day.

We held the beasts at a slow walk through the dry grass and the few junipers that remained on the slope. The horses bobbed their heads rhythmically as they struggled with the grade. We stopped every so often to let them rest.

The thickly timbered water courses stretched down the mountain's flanks like long, curved fingers. Aspens in the upper reaches had already started to show their fall colors. A wide band of Douglas fir circled the peak, but the summit itself was treeless and grassy.

We made our camp on the shore of a small lake that lay in a bowl below the peak. The beasts were happy to be picketed in a meadow of fresh green grass. We shouldered our rifles and walked off to kill something for supper. The best we could do was a marmot. Charlie got it with one shot.

The longest view from the peak was to the north. A patchwork of farm fields lay below in Marsh Basin and off east toward the Raft River. Golden ripe grains, rows of green corn, and stretches of lucerne and timothy hay awaited the harvest. Beyond the fields, the Early Mountains rose above the Plain. Creeks meandered toward the Snake, which cut its own blue path from east to west. Barely visible on the far side of the river was one small cultivated patch surrounded by an endless sea of sage. It was our homeplace, where my heart lay.

46

My favorite place to sit and write in the record was on the shade porch overlooking the river. I spanned the arms of a rocker with a smooth board, set my inkwell on top and was ready to scratch down the words with my gold-nibbed pen.

The porch usually caught a breeze on even the warmest summer days. If I paused and looked up from my writing, I saw the crown of the cottonwood ahead, the water well, hitching rail and corral below, and the kitchen garden and barn to the left. Chickens scratched for grubs, and now and then a rooster crowed, not caring that it wasn't dawn. The ferry sat at the landing on the near bank, and the cable stretched across to the far side. Beyond the river lay miles of sage and then the mountains.

The cottonwood murmured when the breeze was light and rustled when it stiffened. The mourning dove cooed for his mate, and here and there a jumping fish splashed. If the breeze swirled just right, I smelled sage, turned earth, fresh water or all three. It was a peaceful scene.

Toward sundown on most days, the river turned a deep blue, and the distant mountains went purple, showing shadows and texture not seen at midday. Birds fled to their night roosts, and a hush came over the land. One by one, stars pierced the darkening sky. As twilight turned to night, it was time to gather my things and go in to supper.

Charlie had a hard time getting permission from his folks and Mr. Weatherman—Maggie's father and Charlie's teacher—to go exploring downriver. His folks asked who would do his chores at home. Plowing and planting season was coming up. Who would do the early spring work Charlie usually did? Mr. Weatherman asked how Charlie would keep up with his lessons at school. The school term was drawing to a close. How would Charlie make up for the schoolwork he would miss? His folks knew Charlie and I planned the trip together, but Mr. Weatherman didn't. When Charlie told him he wanted to explore downriver with me, Mr. Weatherman came up with an idea.

He said he knew me, that I was Captain Hawkins' boy. He had spoken with me, and he knew I was interested in nature. He knew I corresponded with Hart Merriam and that I had ridden across the Plains to Idaho from Kentucky. He knew I kept our family's record, and that it went back four generations to Daniel Boone's time.

Mr. Weatherman suggested this to Charlie: If he would make up the lessons he would miss, and he would return from the trip with a journal to read to his fellow scholars, he would have his teacher's permission to go. He reminded Charlie that the class had studied Lewis and Clark and Frémont, and had learned that great explorers keep journals. Mr. Weatherman told Charlie that, with my help, he wanted him to record a detailed account of where we went, what we saw and the people we met. He wanted Charlie to write and make sketches in the journal every day. He said to collect samples of unusual rocks, plants, shells—anything Charlie could carry that wouldn't spoil.

Charlie's folks and I liked Mr. Weatherman's idea more than Charlie did. Charlie liked farming, hunting and fishing, but he wasn't much for books and writing. Yet keeping the journal was the only way he would be able to go on the trip, so he agreed. He rode Knight from Marsh Basin to the south ferry landing on Sunday, March 19th, 1876. He had tied his baggage behind the saddle in a canvas duffel.

We packed a mule and saddled our horses the next morning at first light. As we mounted outside the barn, Will stood between us, holding the horses' bridles. "Now, I know you men won't do anything foolish," he said. "I expect you back in a week. The ground is almost ready to work, and there's plowing and planting to do. Have a safe trip, and come back with good stories to tell." I liked that Will respected me, trusted my judgment and let me be free. He had treated me that way as far back as I could remember. His guidance gave me confidence and maturity most boys my age didn't have.

Charlie and I started downriver on the north bank at sunrise. We decided we would keep the same pace that Will, Ben and I had followed across the Plains four years earlier. At about 20 miles a day, we would be on familiar ground all the first day and part of the next. We went into camp for the first night in a little cove across and down from the mouth of Goose Creek. The bank sloped gently to the river's edge. It looked as if somebody planned to make the cove the northside landing for a ferry they had started to build on the south bank. We didn't know whose ferry it was because nobody was around.

We picketed the beasts and laid out our camp. We baited hooks and threw a set line into the river, hoping we'd have fish for breakfast. We walked out into the sage, looking for rabbits or grouse. We quickly bagged a sage hen and went straight back to camp, eager to start a fire to take away the evening chill. The temperature was still dipping below freezing on most nights.

After supper, I asked Charlie when he planned to start his journal. He said he hadn't thought about it. I reminded him of his promise and suggested he had to write in the journal at least once a day if he wanted to keep up. He protested that we hadn't really done or seen anything worth writing about. He said all we had done was ride along the river for about 25 miles. I wanted to demonstrate to Charlie what writing a journal was about, so I recited a long list of plants and birds I had seen that day. The most unusual birds were hundreds of migrating Canada geese resting along Goose Creek. We could hear them honking from where we sat. Then I described the weather we had had that day and what the signs were for tomorrow. I pointed out that Will Peak and the other high mountains south of us were snow-capped, as were the Sawtooth Mountains far to the north. But Ben Butte, the Early Mountains and the Plain were low enough to be snow-free. I mentioned our set line and the sage grouse we had killed, cleaned and eaten.

Charlie got the point but wanted me to write the journal. I said I was keeping my own notebook and would help him, but Mr. Weatherman and his folks expected a journal written by him, not me. He grumbled as he rummaged through his baggage and came up with a notebook, a stick pen and nib, and a cork-stoppered ink bottle. We talked and Charlie wrote for about an hour. Then we dug a shallow trench, shoveled hot coals from the fire in, covered them with dirt and our tarp, spread our blankets, and went to sleep.

We rose to morning frost and were quick to start a fire. There was a trout and a Utah sucker on our set line. We cleaned them and baked them in the Dutch oven we had brought along. Somehow, food always tastes better in camp than at home.

We came opposite Henry Schodde and Jack Fuller's place early in the afternoon. We had plainly seen their waterwheels, cabin and corrals from some distance back. Mr. Schodde was busy with some cattle just past the homestead, but Jack wasn't around. About 25 or 30 head had formed a circle with Mr. Schodde and a calf in the center. He had tied the calf's fore and hind legs and had it on the ground. We couldn't tell what he was doing, but the herd looked very worried. They were moving about and bumping into each other but not breaking the circle. Their baying sounded like moans. After a few minutes, Mr. Schodde untied the calf. It got to its feet and ran to its mother. The ring broke up and scattered. When the noise quieted, I put two fingers in my mouth and whistled as loudly as I could to get Mr. Schodde's attention. He turned our way and waved, but I think we were too far away for him to recognize us. He walked to the river's edge and peered across. I cupped my hands around my mouth and called over.

"It's Early, Early Hawkins."

"Hello," he yelled, and waved in a big arc.

"We're headed downriver," I yelled.

"Stop on my side on your way back," he yelled. We tipped our hats, waved and continued on our way.

"If we find a place to cross, maybe we should come back on the south side," I said to Charlie.

"Sounds good to me," he replied.

Not far ahead we came to the mouth of the canyon and went into camp, where we had certain access to water. I had heard this spot spoken of as The Cedars. The trees had survived travelers' axes because they were on islands in the river. Farther down, the canyon deepened, showing hundreds of feet of black basalt cliffs between the river and the rim. Charlie remarked that the country here and below was very different from that around Marsh Basin or the Hawkins place. With the birds I had pointed out along the way and the plants we had collected during our noon rest, Charlie said he would have plenty to write about in his journal.

In the morning, we were under way barely more than an hour when we came to Caldron Linn. A voyageur with the 1811 Hunt Expedition had perished there when his canoe struck a rock, and he was hurled into the cataract. The man's death was proof to later explorers that the Snake was not navigable much farther than The Cedars.

Caldron Linn wasn't a waterfall. It was more like a rocky chute. The river narrowed to about 40 feet, turned south and then sharply north, and dropped steeply between two rock ledges. The combination of gravity, water and rock was deadly.

Charlie and I picketed the beasts back from the rim and followed a narrow switchback foot trail down the cliff toward the river. The deeper we went, the louder the rushing water echoed between the canyon walls. At the bottom, we had to yell to each other to be heard. It was early spring, and the river had been steadily rising as snowmelt above sent water down a hundred creeks into the Snake. Hawkins and Schodde rapids were little ripples next to the angry torrent that was Caldron Linn. We sat amazed and safe while a few feet away countless tons of raging water vaulted and tossed and pitched as they rushed to the much calmer river below. Charlie smiled impishly and yelled in my ear.

"I don't think we want to cross here to get to Schodde's on the way home."

"No," I yelled back with a big grin, "I don't either."

We lay on our bellies at an eddy up from the big drop and cupped water into our mouths with our hands. We filled two canvas bladders we had brought down, looped them over our shoulders and climbed the trail up to the rim.

The farther west of the canyon mouth we rode, the more raptors we saw. They rode updrafts from within the canyon, where we guessed their nests were, rose above the rim and soared out over the sage to search for prey. The sparrow hawks were easiest to identify. They fluttered their wings and hovered before diving to snatch a lizard or vole. A soaring red-tailed hawk swooped down to glide just above the rim and was fiercely attacked by a prairie falcon. The hawk quickly learned he wasn't welcome, rose on an updraft and veered north and away from the canyon.

At the mouth of a dry creek, we started to see miners' shacks and men working rocker boxes along the gravel bars in the canyon on the south side. Nearby, there was a small, stone-walled building that looked like a store. A broken line of shacks continued for miles, then there was another camp with a stone building. Even at midday, nearly the whole camp was in the shadow of the canyon wall. Sunlight fell only on a bit of the camp, then on the river and the north bank and wall. Long, rickety ladders leaned against the vertical wall. There was a rowboat pulled up on the gravel bar on the south side and no one but us on the north side.

A few miles farther, we heard the roar of falling water and came to falls we judged to be about 175 feet high. The river split around a massive rock tower and fell straight down to a large pool below. Sunlight shining through the fine spray made rainbows that added color to an otherwise black-rock and white-water scene. These falls weren't grand enough to be the famous Shoshone Falls. They had to be farther down.

Just below the double falls, there was a large camp in the canyon on the south side. Rowboats sat on both banks. There was a string of shacks up from the bars on the north side and, about in the center east to west, a low, stone-walled building set in a cove of boulders. Another stone-walled building sat on a rock ledge about 100 feet east of the first. Men worked rocker boxes and sluices here and there on both sides of the river. A man standing about half-way between the two stone buildings turned and looked up at us astride our horses, peering down at him from the rim. He looked to be holding a rifle at his side. He took his hat off and waved it over his head. We took our hats off and waved back. He pointed to a trail that started in a notch at the rim and wove its way down to the canyon floor. He traced the path of the trail with his pointing finger, then motioned with his hand as if pulling us toward him. It was mid-afternoon and close to time to go into camp. Charlie and I figured the riverbank was better than the dry rim, so we accepted the man's invitation and started down the trail.

As we approached, we realized he was holding a hoe rather than a rifle. He had been working in one of several garden ter-races between the bank and the wall. He was a Chinaman, but he wasn't dressed like the Chinamen in Kelton. He wore a mix of Western and Chinese clothes. He had boots and britches like ours, then a black silk Chinese blouse with a high neck but no collar. The front had toggles and loops instead of buttons. Over the blouse was a vest like those a lot of men wore. His cowboy hat had a creased crown and curled brim. It was a little too big, so it sank down to his ears. A braided pigtail hung down his back almost to his belt. He leaned on his hoe and smiled as we came near. He was missing several teeth.

"Hello strangers," he said, "I am Mista Ah. Welcome to my claim." We dismounted and I introduced us.

"Hello Mr. Ah," I said, "I'm Early Hawkins and this is Charlie Howell. We're headed for Shoshone Falls. How far down is it?"

"Ah, 'bout three mile I think," he said. "But you not go today, too late, you stay suppah and sleep, OK?" I looked at Charlie and he nodded.

"Yes, thank you, Mr. Ah," I said, "we would be happy to stay. Is there good grass to picket our animals?"

"Oh, yes, Mista Hawkins," he replied, "good grass little bit upstream. Leave saddles here and we go. I show you." We dropped the saddles to the ground, unpacked the mule, traded the beasts' bridles for halters and led them upstream with Mr.

Ah showing the way. "Watah here first," he said, pointing to a little cove in the bank, "then we go to grass." He patted Spirit's neck and added, "Pretty hoss." We watered and picketed the beasts, and turned back toward the stone buildings.

"What will you plant in your garden?" I asked as we walked.

"Oh, plenty vegetables," he said, "and I sprout beans. You see laytah." We reached his stone-walled cabin. There were wooden cabins strung nearby downstream and several Chinamen working rocker boxes near the riverbank. Mr. Ah welcomed us inside. He was short and easily walked through the doorway. Charlie and I removed our hats and ducked. Once inside, we stood upright. The walls were native stone built to enclose boulders in some sections. A wood frame topped the walls, and a thick canvas roof stretched across the frame. Woven grass mats covered the floor. There was a cast-iron stove in a far corner with a flue leading out through the roof. A wide shelf lined one wall in what looked like a kitchen area. There was a free-standing cabinet alongside the shelf. Narrower shelves were mounted on the other walls. Several oil lamps sat on the shelves, and two lanterns hung from the roof frame. Soft cushions lay on the grass mats and lined one wall. A gold miner's retort sat in the corner to the left of the doorway, and a .20 gauge shotgun and .32 caliber pistol hung on a rack to its right. Mr. Ah's cabin looked cozy and comfortable.

"Like coffee before we go for fish?" Mr. Ah asked. We said yes. Mr. Ah took a large pot from the stovetop and poured coffee into three blue and white porcelain cups. He handed the filled cups to Charlie and me. They had no handles. "I think I have fish on hooks in river," he said. "Fish are suppah. We go check aftah coffee. Here, sit, make self at home," he said as he motioned to the cushions along the wall. We sat, leaning against the rocks, sipping coffee and looking at Mr. Ah with great curiosity.

"Mista Hawkins, Mista Howell, you boys, that right?" he asked.

"Yes, you're right, Mr. Ah," I said, "Charlie and I are 16, well, almost 16."

"And your mama and papa?" he asked.

"My family is in Marsh Basin," Charlie replied, "and Early's is on the river about 65 or 70 miles up. Our families have farms. Have you been upriver?"

"No, I come through Boy-see, but first from San Francisco,"
he replied.

"Were your born there?" Charlie asked.

"Oh, no, China, Guangdong, China," he replied. "I crossed
sea on sailing ship many years. I work gold mines California,
then railroad, then keep shop, then here for flour gold."

We finished our coffee and walked to the riverbank to check
Mr. Ah's set lines. He had quite a haul—two trout, two mountain
whitefish and three suckers, enough for supper and breakfast,
he said. Mr. Ah quickly gutted and cleaned the fish on a rock at
the bank, leaving the entrails and heads for whatever scavengers happened by. We returned to the cabin, where Mr. Ah fried
some of the fish on the stove in a deep iron pan. About halfway
through the frying, he tossed several handfuls of sprouted beans
into the pan. After a few minutes, the three of us sat on cushions
and leaned against the rock wall with china plates of fish and
green sprouts in our laps.

Charlie and I ate as if it was our last meal, while Mr. Ah took
things very slowly, savoring every mouthful. The food wasn't
going anywhere but into his belly, so I guess he felt no reason
to rush. We cleaned our plates at the river and sat there for a
few minutes. A light breeze carried the smell of cooking fires our
way. Two Chinamen came across the river just below, pulled
the rowboat up on the bar and walked down toward their cabin.
Charlie and I exchanged smiles as we watched the setting sun
give the black canyon walls a touch of orange.

We gathered our dishes and returned to the cabin. Mr. Ah lit
a long, thin stick in the stove and used it to light the oil lamps
and lanterns. Just as he finished, three other Chinamen came to
visit. Mr. Ah introduced them as Mista Ding, Mista Wang and
Mista Li. Each man carried a glass jar with a flexible tube coming out near its base and a tiny bowl mounted on its top. The men
wore the same slippers and silk outfits the Kelton Chinamen
wore. Each had a long braided pigtail hanging down his back.
As they sat cross-legged on the floor cushions, each man reached
over his shoulder, grabbed his pigtail and pulled it around to the
front so he wouldn't sit on it.

Mr. Ah went to the cabinet and returned with a colorful little tin can. He removed the lid, took out what looked like small

tar balls and dropped them into the bowls on top of the men's glass jars. It was then I realized the jars were pipes. Mr. Ah held the stick he used to light the lamps over Mr. Ding's pipe bowl. By then, there was no flame on the stick's end, just a glowing ember. Mr. Ding drew on the pipe several times. Mr. Ah relit the stick in the flame of an oil lamp he kept beside him, then held it over Mr. Wang's pipe bowl. Mr. Wang drew on his pipe, and Mr. Ah moved on to Mr. Li and repeated the steps. The three men sat silently, seeming to pass into another world. There was hardly any smoke, and it didn't smell like tobacco. Charlie and I looked quizzically at each other and then turned to Mr. Ah.

"What are they smoking?" I asked.

"Opium," said Mr. Ah. "You want try?"

"No," I said.

"Yes," Charlie said.

"Charlie," I said, "Will said not to do anything foolish."

"I smoked a cigar," he said. "That wasn't foolish, so neither is this."

"OK, Charlie," I said in a disappointed tone, "suit yourself."

Mr. Ah went to the cabinet and came back with a glass-jar pipe like the others. He took a little ball of opium from the can, dropped it into the bowl and handed the pipe to Charlie.

"I heat only, not light," Mr. Ah said. "I hold hot coal over bowl close but not touch opium."

The three visitors seemed to have dropped into a half sleep and barely noticed us. Charlie took several draws on the pipe. First, he seemed to slump, as if his bones weren't holding him up anymore. Mr. Ah took the pipe as a slight, oozy smile came across Charlie's face. He looked at me through heavy eyelids, rolled down onto his side, curled up and fell asleep. I checked to make sure he was still breathing. Mr. Ah and I looked at each other as if to say, "Oh, well." I went out, fetched our bedrolls, covered Charlie, spread mine on the grass mat alongside the door, lay down and went to sleep.

We had a hard time rousing Charlie in the morning. Mr. Ah poured him a big cup of strong coffee to help. Breakfast was the last of the fish from the previous day's catch, again cooked with sprouted beans.

Charlie fetched the beasts upriver as I washed the breakfast things and packed our baggage. The morning was cold enough for coats and gloves, and to see our breath. When the beasts snorted, clouds of vapor rose above their heads. We packed the mule, saddled the horses, thanked Mr. Ah, said goodbye and started up the trail to the rim. As we climbed, I mentioned to Charlie that he probably shouldn't write in his journal about smoking opium. He agreed.

47

We looped around a big side canyon below Mr. Ah's claim, and in less than an hour began to hear the roar of the falls. The river itself didn't look much different above the falls than it had for the past three days. Before the drop itself, the canyon opened to a bowl with most of the curve on the north side. There was a ferry crossing the river just above the falls. We kept back from the rim and followed the arc to a spot a short way downriver. We left the beasts and walked to the edge on foot. The curve of the canyon put us some distance from the falls. Charlie and I fell silent and stared. It was one of the grandest sights I had ever seen. First, the water split and ran around huge towers of rock that spanned the river's width. Then it dropped over several ledges to form low falls and pools. Finally, it fell at least 200 feet in a jaw-dropping display of sound and fury. The rock face behind the water jutted out unevenly and at different angles, creating caverns between wide sections of falls. Mist rose from the pool below and filled the caverns. Later, Charlie wrote in his journal that the falls were spectacular.

We walked back to the beasts and retraced our route to the trail that led to the ferry. It was a slow, careful descent. The ferry lay on the south side when we reached the river. We waved to attract the keeper's attention, then waited as he crossed. It was a current ferry like ours, with a cable stretched between anchor towers on each bank. But rather than a pulley system to turn the bow with the current, this ferry had a steering oar like a broadhorn. The keeper was a big man who handled the oar with ease. He brought the ferry to the bank and greeted us in a booming voice.

"Hello, lads, I'm Robert Morrison, and I'm here to take you across the mighty Snake." He rolled the "r's" in his name and dwelled on them, making them stand out. "Two lads, two horses and a mule." he said, "That would be two dollars and a half, but since you're just lads, make it one dollar and two bits.

"It's barely 9 in the morning and he's drunk," Charlie whispered. "Are we sure we want to do this? The falls are mighty close."

"He's crossed twice since we saw him," I whispered. "The boat and rig look strong. I think it'll be OK." I dug into my pocket for the coins and handed them to Mr. Morrison. "A dollar and two bits it is," I said.

"Thank ye, lad," Mr. Morrison said. "If you'll walk your beasts and yourselves on board, we can be on our way." Spirit and Knight moved onto the ferry easily, but the mule resisted a little. We got him on board and tied the three beasts to the rail. Mr. Morrison pushed off the landing and leapt aboard the stern. He moved quickly to the oar and turned the bow with the current. "Where are you lads from, and where are you headed?" he asked.

"We've come from about 70 miles above, and now we're on our way back," I replied. The ferry's pace quickened as we moved away from the bank into the stronger current.

"Did you see the Caldron Linn then?" he asked.

"Yup, we did," Charlie replied. "It's a frightful stretch of water."

"Aye, that it is," Mr. Morrison said. "It was named by some of my countrymen back in '11."

"What country is that?" I asked.

"Why, Scotland, of course, laddie," he replied. "If you'll hold this oar, I'll play you a Scottish reel on my fiddle." Charlie and I took the oar from him and struggled to hold the angle. He went to a wooden chest that was fastened to the deck and withdrew a fiddle. He started a lively tune, whirling and gliding in a dance about the deck as he played.

"You're right," I whispered to Charlie, "he *is* drunk. If he goes over the side, he's a goner." As he danced, he bumped his back into the mule's nose. The animal was already unsettled, probably by the roar of the falls, and the jostling didn't help. The mule yanked on his reins and rose slightly on his haunches, pulling his front hoofs off the deck and baying loudly. His nerves affected the horses. When the three beasts moved, the ferry tipped dangerously. "Whoa, Mr. Morrison," I called out loudly, "you'll have us all going over the falls. Take the oar, and I'll calm the mule."

He stopped playing, looking a little sheepish.

"It's all right, lads," he said as he took the oar in one hand, holding the fiddle and bow in the other. Charlie took the fiddle and bow from him and put them back in the chest, while I rushed to settle the mule. In a minute, things were calm, and we reached the south landing. "Thank ye, lads, for a fine crossing," Mr. Morrison boomed, apparently unaware that Charlie's and my hearts were in our throats. We managed one weak thank-you between us. We walked the beasts off the ferry, mounted and started away, happy to be back on solid ground. "Good day, lads," he called to us from the ferry, "come back anytime. Next ride's free, and I'll play a different tune."

There were three mining camps in the canyon on the south side of the river between Shoshone Falls and Caldron Linn. The first, Shoshone, was opposite Mr. Ah's claim. The second, Springtown, was about five miles above the double falls. The third, Drytown, was at the mouth of the dry creek. White men ran trading posts at each of the camps, but all the miners we saw were Chinamen. Springtown was the camp we had seen earlier that, at least at this time of the year, was almost completely in shadow. When we stopped at the trading post, we learned the double falls were called Little Falls and that Rock Creek Station, where Ben had often gone to play and sing, was eight miles south.

We camped along the dry creek that night. Early the next morning, we looked down at Caldron Linn from the south rim. Charlie noticed what we both first thought was a red-tailed hawk coming, gliding west in the canyon between us and the river. As the bird drew closer, we realized it was much too big to be a hawk. It was a golden eagle. Its wingspan must have been six or even seven feet.

We reached Henry Schodde and Jack Fuller's place about midday and found only Mr. Schodde at home just finishing his noon meal. He was very glad to see us and insisted we sit and eat, which we did. Mr. Schodde didn't get many visitors, so he was eager to talk. He told us the Bradley and Russell Cattle Company was building the ferry we had seen on our way down. They would use it to cross cattle to graze them on the north side. Then Mr. Schodde must have asked us about 20 questions: Why did we go downriver? Why on the north side? What did we see down there? Where did we cross? When were we due back home? Did we want to spend the night? He was so curious that Charlie went out to get his journal and I to get my notebook so we could give him thorough answers. He said he had heard about Shoshone Falls and wanted to go see it, but it was hard to get away, seeing how Jack was gone to Nevada. We told him if he pushed and went on the south side, he could get there and back in two days. We said he should go in the spring when the water was high. He was so excited by our stories, we thought he might just take up and leave the next morning.

We didn't spend the night with Mr. Schodde but continued along and went into camp at the river about half way to Goose Creek. That night was particularly clear and dry, with millions of stars all around. We reached Cañon Creek before noon the next day. We decided we would spend the afternoon comparing notes and making sure Charlie's journal was complete. We camped there that night and divided our baggage in the morning. I continued up to our place, while Charlie followed the creek toward home.

I didn't see him till the next time I was in Marsh Basin about two weeks later. We met at Mr. Burstrom's store near the Howells' place. The first thing I asked Charlie was how his report went. He said very well. His fellow scholars applauded after he spoke and then asked lots of questions. Mr. Weatherman praised Charlie's work, and his folks said they were proud he had done such a good job. They said if Charlie ever wanted to go exploring with me again, it was OK with them.

I had gotten my own fine reception from Will, Beth and Amanda. Will and I started turning the ground the next morning. It looked as if it would be a fine spring and a good year.

48

We spent the better part of April making the ground ready and then sowing grains and hay. Our mules pulled the sulky plows, harrows and seed drill. We used mules for almost all the field work, saving the horses for riding and driving. With grain and hay sown and irrigated, we turned to corn. After we plowed the ground and smoothed it with harrows, the two-row corn planter dropped kernels into furrows it had made. Will talked about the farm as we walked the field.

"Between Henry Schodde and the Raft River ranchers," he said, "we can sell as much feed as we can grow. But with Ben gone, you and I can work only so much land. Whatever we do, we'll always need extra help at harvest time, but to use more land and get the most out of it, we should add at least one man year 'round. I want to find a good hired hand. A married man would be best. He'd be more settled. But to have a man and his family on our place, we'll have to build another house.

"As far as I can tell by pacing the ground, we've fenced 160 acres. We might have more. At some time, I expect the Homestead Act will apply to our land, even without a survey. We've already met the prove-up requirements on a quarter-section by clearing the land, building a house and barn, farming some of the ground and making pasture of the rest. We can build a house for the hired help up the bench past the night pasture and orchard. Within a few days, I want to pace the land and pick a site. When we get it under way, we can ask George and Alex to help."

Will went on to say he would ask around about a hired hand in Marsh Basin, but he'd also mail notices to the *Idaho Statesman* in Boise and the *Daily Reporter* in Corinne, and we'd wait to see if anything happened.

At the close of the day, after we had bedded the mule down and stored the seed corn we hadn't yet planted, we walked to the house and up the stairs to the shade porch. Between us, we must have had half a cornfield's worth of mud on our boots. As we sat by the door to pull the boots off, warm light and the aroma of fresh-baked bread seeped out from inside. The twilight sky was purple going to black, the wind was calm, and the young cottonwood leaves were still. The door creaked a little as I opened it. We went in in our stocking feet to Beth and Amanda and supper.

Late one afternoon about two weeks later, Will and I were cultivating in the fields when we heard the bell ringing. Because there were long pauses between the rings, we knew not to be alarmed. It was close to quitting time, so we headed home. As we neared the house, we saw a wagon and team at the south landing. A man and woman had stepped down and were standing beside their fully loaded wagon. We tied our mules and walked to the bank where we could call across the river. The man cupped his hands around his mouth.

"Is this the Hawkins place?" he called.

"Yes," Will called back. "What's your business?"

"I'm your hired hand," came the reply.

"We'll come over," Will called back.

From the ferry, the man at the landing looked like a barrel with arms, legs and a head. The woman looked much the same, only a little smaller. We stepped off and Will introduced us.

"I'm Billy Latham and this is my wife, Annie," the man replied.

"Pleased to meet y'all," Annie said.

"We seen your notice in the paper and came as quick as we could," Billy said. His wide chest wouldn't let his short arms hang at his sides. They sort of jutted out from his shoulders. His face was like the full moon. He had a respectful, agreeable manner. Annie looked as if she was Billy's sister rather than his wife. She had the same polite, courteous manner. They were young, not kids, but young.

"Were you working on a farm west of here?" Will asked.

"Yup, we were," Billy replied, "out Overland Road near Boise City. The farmer got hisself kilt in a accident, the family went East, and the farm went under."

"Did you grow up on a farm?" Will asked.

"Yup, both did," Annie replied, "in Tennessee."

"We could have been neighbors then," I said. "We're from Kentucky."

"That's right nice," Billy said, with an innocent smile.

"Do you have children?" Will asked.

"Nope," Annie replied, "we tried, but the doc says we cain't have none."

"We want to build a house for the hired help up yonder," Will said, pointing upriver. "Until that's done, we don't have a place for married folks to live."

"The weather's good, and we have a tent," Billy said. "And whether you're buildin' with stone or wood, I'm your help. My daddy taught me both. Show me where you want the house, and I'll start tomorrow."

"You're a very persuasive man," Will said.

"A hard worker too," Annie said.

"I'll tell you what, then," Will said. "Let's cross the river, you can meet my wife and daughter, we'll have some supper and talk it over. You're welcome to stay the night."

"Yes, sir, Mr. Hawkins," Billy said, "sounds right good."

"Billy," I said, "just so you know, folks 'round here call Will 'Captain Hawkins.'"

"All right, 'Captain' it is," Billy said. Annie nodded and smiled.

We bedded down our guests' horses in the barn and walked to the house, where Will introduced Billy and Annie to Beth and Amanda. They had already set two extra places at the table and were ready to serve supper. As we ate, Will explained our farming operation and outlined our goals. He told Billy what we expected from a hired hand and what we could pay. Billy nodded and smiled as Will talked. He looked comfortable, as if he was on ground he knew. Annie asked what she could do to help. Beth replied that she could work in the kitchen garden and help put food by. And once the new house was built, it would be hers to keep up. Beth added that Annie knew as well as anyone that there was always work to do on a farm.

When we finished eating, Annie rose to help Beth and Amanda clear the table. Will asked Beth if he could speak to her in the next room. When Beth returned, she told me Will wanted to speak to me. I went in, and he asked me how I felt about Billy and Annie coming to work with us. I replied that they seemed all right, but added that you don't know a horse till you ride it. Will smiled, paused and asked whether I thought we should give them a try. I said I did, and he replied that he, Beth and I agreed.

Will offered Billy and Annie the job, they accepted, and we shook on it. Beth said she wouldn't have Billy and Annie living in a tent until their house was built. She said she knew how difficult it could be for two women to live under the same roof, so she would help Billy and Annie set up housekeeping in the cave.

"Now, I say 'cave,'" Beth said, "but I don't want you thinking of some dripping, dreary place with bats. It's the cellar under this house. Will and Early and our other son, Ben, lived there when they first came to Idaho. I'll show it to you tomorrow."

In the morning, Beth and I helped Annie get settled in the cave while Will and Billy planted corn. Will said we would start on the house as soon as the corn was in and irrigated. Will showed Billy the house site we had chosen. It was on the bench a short way back from the bank about half a mile upriver from our house. After supper, we worked on the plans and calculated what lumber, shingles and windows we would need. I rode to Marsh Basin to take the order to George and Alex, and to ask if they could help us build the house. They said they would come to our place with the materials in two or three days and would stay until the house was finished.

I spent the night at Charlie's place. When I returned home the next day, Will and Billy had gotten a good start on collecting the rock we would need. By the time George and Alex came, we had started on the walls. With five of us working, we finished the house in two weeks. It was a large cabin with fireplaces at each end and a shade porch all around. Inside, it was divided into three rooms. Its front door faced the river.

Will commented that Billy was indeed a hard worker, and he had learned stonework and carpentry from his daddy very well. Will said Annie's kitchen wouldn't be complete until we could bring a cast-iron cookstove up from Kelton. Judging by how well Annie did helping Beth with the garden and making meals for five hungry house builders, waiting for a stove wouldn't be a problem.

When George and Alex were gone and all but the finishing touches on the cabin were done, we loaded a wagon with Billy and Annie's things and helped them move in. They looked pleased and happy, as if they had found a comfortable home.

At supper that night, Will asked me how I felt about taking a wagon and team to Kelton to fetch a stove for Annie. I immediately jumped at the idea and, almost as quickly, Beth spoke up to say, no, Kelton was too far, and the trip was too dangerous for a 16-year-old boy to make alone. I silently wondered if she knew I was thinking about more than a stove in Kelton. Will said he couldn't afford several days away. I suggested that Billy and I go. If we went by way of Marsh Basin, I said, and drove our two strongest mules from dawn to dusk, we could be back in five days at most. Will and Beth looked at each other, neither saying a word, then Will turned to me, smiled a very small smile and nodded. I thought I saw a twinkle in his eye.

When the table was cleared, I rode Spirit up to Billy's and told him if he could be at our barn at first light, he and I were going to Kelton to fetch a stove. Annie was delighted. She said she had never had her own cookstove before.

The sky was still dark and strewn with stars when Billy came to the barn in the morning. The black in the east slowly gave way to deep purple and the purple to lavender as we got two mules in harness and hitched to the wagon. We loaded our baggage and drove to the north landing. The lavender sky gradually yielded to burnt orange. The river was like molten copper as Will, Billy and I crossed. Will said goodbye at the south landing. As Billy and I started south, the orange in the east became a blazing yellow, and the sun crept over the horizon, bathing the land in soft light, making the dew glisten and giving the roosters something to crow about.

The drive down went well. We reached Kelton just past sundown on the second day. Billy didn't want to stay in the Rosevears' hotel, so we camped at the edge of town. I waited till he was sound asleep and snoring, then slipped away to the saloon where Rebel worked. Her face lit up like the Fourth of July when she saw me standing near the door. She took my hand and led me upstairs. I felt many pairs of eyes following us as we went. In her room, I explained the other reason I was in Kelton and said I had to be back to Billy before he woke in the morning. She guaranteed I would, and we got down to pleasures.

Billy hadn't moved an inch since I left him the night before. I held our coffee pot up and banged it with a spoon to wake him. He was up and around in seconds.

Billy was a work machine. Since he came to our place, I had seen him do only three things: work, eat and sleep. He couldn't even sit and take in the scenery when it was my turn to drive on the way to Kelton. He sat on the bench next to me whittling spoons out of wood he had brought along. If there was any such thing as an ideal hired hand, Billy was it.

We had our breakfast and were at the hardware store waiting when the owner came to open shop. It took four of us to load the stove into the wagon, then Billy and I were on our way home. With the extra weight, we figured the drive back would be slower and longer than going down. We reached the south landing toward the end of the third day. Annie had her stove, and she and Beth had enough wooden spoons to last awhile. I was pleased to have seen

Rebel again, and if anyone at home knew I had, they didn't let on.

One of the sows farrowed a litter the day after we got back from Kelton. Billy and I were in the pen when she delivered one after another after another. She lay on her side to let them suckle. There were more little pigs than the sow had teats. They fought with each other for the milk. The runt squealed and squirmed and greatly annoyed the other pigs and the sow. I crouched down and put the squealer on a nipple, but that made things worse. The other pigs pushed the squealer off the teat, and it went right back to squealing and wiggling and making trouble. Billy reached down, grabbed the squealer by its hind legs, swung it high and smashed its neck over the pen rail.

"Squealers ain't good," he said, "they just mess things up for the sow and the others." Billy held the dead pig limp at his side for a moment, then tossed the carcass over the pen fence. "The dogs'll find it 'fore long, and it'll be gone," he said. Seeing that the sow and her little pigs looked content, we left the pen.

That spring, Billy and I set up an apiary out in the sage beyond the sink. We bought working hives from a beekeeper in Marsh Basin. We placed them far enough away that the bees didn't annoy our animals at pasture but close enough that we could walk out for the honey. With a steady supply of honey, we didn't have to buy sugar, and Beth liked that.

One day, I was on my way out to harvest honey when I stopped to climb atop a rock outcropping. As I sat peering across the sage through my binoculars, what I first thought was a honeybee landed on my thigh. It was about the size of a honeybee, and it was striped yellow and black, but it was carrying a small, black insect, which I knew honeybees didn't do. I guessed it was a yellow jacket. It turned over on its back and quickly devoured the insect, rotating the body as it ate. Then it returned to its feet and buzzed off, leaving two tiny, uneaten wings on my pants leg.

Every once in a while, usually on a Sunday afternoon, I tried to lure Billy away from working by tempting him with one attraction or another. That spring, I offered fishing, hunting, swimming and just walking through the sage to look at whatever was out there. But Billy was hard to convince; he always had work to do. One Sunday, I managed to interest him in walking by showing him some of the notes and sketches I had made on other hikes. "You mean you seen all them things right out here?" he asked. I guaranteed him I had. We started from his place, walking east to our fence line, then northeast through the sage. We each carried a haversack and a Winchester, and Billy took a forked stick. Why, I didn't ask.

We had walked about 10 minutes past our fence when a jackrabbit darted out and ahead of us. It ran, then hopped, then ran again. I didn't raise my rifle, but Billy quickly got the rabbit in his sights and dropped it with one shot. He gutted and bled it on the spot, emptied the contents of his haversack into mine and stored the rabbit inside his.

We hadn't walked much farther when a big rattler surprised us. It had been lying stretched out, warming itself in the sun. It heard us before we saw it. It rattled, flipped over and coiled like a bullwhip. My reflex was to jump away and raise my rifle in the direction of the noise. Billy quickly moved behind the snake.

"Don't fire. Keep in front of him, but stay back," he said. "Move sidewise a little to hold its attention." As I moved, the snake followed me with his head, darting his tongue in and out. The tongue and the rattle were menace enough to keep my heart racing. Billy looped his haversack strap over his head and laid the sack and his rifle on the ground. He looked at me, then back at the rattler. He pounced on the snake, trapping it with the forked stick just behind the head. He reached down and picked it up, replacing the stick with his thumb and finger. The snake hung down about five feet. It was as big around as my wrist. Billy held it at arm's length, keeping its tail down with the stick. Its mouth was open, showing its long fangs. It was angry but helpless.

"No use killin' it," Billy said with a big smile. "It gets mice and rabbits, and that's good for us."

With that, Billy whirled around and flung the rattler as far as he could. It landed with a rustle and thump about 50 feet away. I breathed a sigh of relief, we gathered our things and walked on.

Annie was about as good a worker as Billy. One day early that first summer, she had spent the better part of a morning in the garden, pulling weeds from the long rows and picking enough green beans to fill two sacks. After the noon meal with us, she sat in a straight-backed chair beside the table with a big mound of beans at her elbow. She had one large bowl on her lap and another nestled between her thighs in a hollow she had made in her apron. She held a sharp knife in her right hand. She plucked beans from the pile with her left hand and, with very rapid movements, cut their ends off and quartered them, dropping the waste ends in one bowl and the quarters in the other. She moved so fast I was amazed a bloody finger didn't drop in with the beans. She left two bowls of cut beans for Beth, packed the remainder in a sack, cradled it in her arms and walked home.

49

Our trip to Marsh Basin for the July 4th centennial picnic marked the first time the whole Hawkins family had gone anywhere together since we came to Idaho. Billy and Annie volunteered to stay behind so the family could go.

We left early on the morning of the third and spent the better part of the day getting to Marsh Basin. Will drove a two-mule team with Beth beside him and our baggage behind. I rode Spirit, and Amanda rode Patches, her pinto pony. Beth had baked fruit pies and bread for the picnic and had carefully packed them with our things.

We stabled the animals at Pearson's White Front Livery and registered at the Yeaman House first thing. After supper in the hotel dining room, we walked through town to the picnic site. George Smith and Alex Morton were erecting a frame above a puncheon dance floor they had built. The frame would hold hanging lanterns to light the floor after dark. Tables and chairs sat in a ring on the ground around the dance floor. Beyond the ring on one side, several men were setting up a baseball diamond, while on the other side, men were putting water troughs and hitching rails in place where teams and saddle horses would be shaded by the poplars.

July 4th dawned bright and warm in Marsh Basin. One hundred years earlier in Philadelphia, the Continental Congress had adopted the Declaration of Independence. Today, we would celebrate the centennial with food, games, dancing and fireworks. Families came on foot, on horseback or by wagon throughout the day. There was scarcely a settler in the valley who wasn't at the celebration at one time or another. Cowboys came from the Raft River, Henry Schodde and Jack Fuller came from their spread west of Goose Creek, and Bill Oakley came from Oakley Meadows. It was the first time I had seen so many of our neighbors together in one place.

I spent most of the day with Charlie. He beat me in the sack race—he came in first, and I was second—but I outthrew him in the ball-toss. We played outfield alongside each other, and our baseball team beat our rivals 14 to 12. I had brought my Winchester, thinking there would be a shooting contest, but the men ditched the idea, saying there were too many children running wild on the grounds, and shooting would be too dangerous.

Late in the afternoon, travelers passing through Marsh Basin brought word that on June 25th instant, Lieutenant Colonel George Armstrong Custer and about 200 soldiers of the 7th Regiment, U. S. Cavalry, had been wiped out by Sioux, Cheyenne and other Indians on the bank of the Little Big Horn River in Montana Territory. Custer had disobeyed his general's orders and blindly ridden into a massacre.

After a big supper, we lit the lanterns over the dance floor, and three musicians started to play. Frank Riblett played fiddle, and two men I didn't know played banjo and guitar. I thought of Ben and knew he would enjoy playing at this celebration. I first danced with Beth and then a Goose Creek girl named Sadie Carpenter. Charlie danced with Mary Baker and looked as if he was sweet on her. Amanda was delighted that a shy boy named Bobby Dunlap asked her to dance. Will and Beth hadn't been to a social like this in years, and it was good to see them dancing and enjoying themselves.

When the musicians took a rest, several men set off fireworks out past the baseball diamond. Everybody cheered the big explosions and shooting stars. Ralph Howell, Charlie's father, said the fireworks had come to Marsh Basin from China by way San Francisco and Kelton just for this occasion.

The music and dancing began again, but it was getting late, and people started saying their goodbyes and heading home. We returned to our hotel only when Amanda couldn't stay awake any longer. It had been a fine day.

With the help of men from Marsh Basin and the Raft River, we had a plentiful harvest in fall '76—the most grain and hay we had ever brought in. The work days ended with the cutting and threshing crews diving into the river, drying off, then going up to the house for supper. Annie was a big help to Beth in feeding the extra mouths. Some of the men slept on the shade porch, while others lay in the haymow.

The kitchen garden and the orchard were big producers that season too. The apple, pear and cherry trees had begun bearing two years earlier. Close care, mild weather and steady growth pushed the yield up each season. Putting the fruit by kept Beth, Annie and Amanda very busy, yet they found time to bake fruit pies. I loved eating the wedges while they were still warm.

When you're living in the days, they go by with aching slowness. But when you look back on them years later, they seem to have fled like a deer from a cougar. Time at our place on the river often passed with nothing much out of the ordinary happening. Our days were brightened with an occasional letter from Ben, a poem from Amanda, a rainbow, a powdery snowfall or an especially glorious sunset.

I turned 18 and Amanda 12 in the spring of '78. Early that June, we rode to Marsh Basin to visit Charlie and Maggie. Charlie had finished school, didn't want to homestead a farm right away and planned to become a freighter. The freight line running within a few miles of his family's place made things all the more convenient.

We learned the Overland Stage Company was about to start a loop through the basin along its route between Kelton and Boise City. That was good news for the Hawkins family because Marsh Basin was about half as far from home as Oakley Meadows.

Eastbound travelers in Marsh Basin brought word of Indian trouble on Camas Prairie out toward Boise City. A band of Fort Hall Bannacks under Chief Buffalo Horn had killed two cattle ranchers on the prairie, burned the King Hill station buildings, stolen a corral of stage horses, ransacked houses and barns at Glenn's Ferry, and cut the boat loose to drift down the river. On the south side, they chased off freighters who had come to cross. The Bannacks got murdering drunk on whiskey they found among the goods. They killed and mutilated other overlanders who had driven up to the crossing, not knowing what they were getting into. Last the travelers knew, the Bannacks were headed south through Owyhee County toward Nevada, raiding as they went.

Trouble had been brewing on Camas Prairie for years. Ranchers ran cattle on the land, and farmers turned, planted and fenced it, shutting several tribes out of country where their people had dug camas root for thousands of springs. Things boiled over in late May when hogs some Snake River ranchers turned out on the prairie rooted out camas the Bannacks felt was rightly theirs. Hearing this story, I wondered if it was Buffalo Horn's braves on their way to Camas Prairie who chased Spirit and me years before. I felt lucky to have outrun them.

In February '79, the Idaho territorial legislature approved the formation of Cassia County by splitting off about 5,100 square miles of eastern Owyhee County. In June, citizens chose officers, renamed Marsh Basin "Albion" and made it Cassia County's seat. Since our homeplace was in Alturas County, we couldn't do county business in Albion, but it was good to have a growing town nearby.

That summer, silver was discovered in the Wood River country northwest of us. A year later, the mines had drawn enough attention that the Overland Stage Company began twice-daily service on a spur line up to the mines. Stages and freighters crossed the river at Starrh's Ferry, down from Goose Creek near Fuller and Schodde's place. George Starrh and his brother, Tom, both Albion farmers, built the cable-and-leeboard ferry to answer a need George had seen while placer mining for gold at the river.

In late March 1880, Henry Schodde stopped at the homeplace on his way to the Raft River. He and two cowhands were driving his herd to Charlie Barnes' ranch. Henry told us he was leaving Idaho, at least for a while.

"I'm not getting younger, I just turned 44, and I'm lonely here by myself," he said. "Jack's long gone and I need more company than cows. I'm going back to Germany to see if I can find a wife. If there's a woman there who will live on a cattle ranch in Idaho, I'll bring her back. Charlie Barnes is taking my herd for a while. The Overland Company and the Starrh brothers will use my place near the landing for a stage and ferry stop."

"Henry, we hate to see you go," Will said. "We wish you well and hope you find a good woman and come back to the Snake River soon."

In fact, more than three years passed before Henry returned. He and his wife, Minnie, had been through a lot before we saw them early in the summer of '83. They married in Salt Lake City in 1881 and, rather than heading for Cassia County, pursued an opportunity in Nebraska. Their first child, William, had died in infancy there in '82. Their second child, George, had been born in Utah in April '83. Now, the couple would settle on the Snake River, reclaim and expand Henry's land and herd, and rear children. In time, the Schoddes' land, on both sides of the river, would total more than 400 acres. They would run about 5,000 head, mostly on public land, and have seven children—five boys and two girls, a good balance for a ranching family. Henry built the family's first house of native stone on the north side. Later, he built a frame house, and the stone house became the children's school.

Over time, Henry built wing dams in the river and 11 water-wheels that he used to raise water to placer-mine gold from the gravel bars on the south side and to irrigate bottomland for crops on both sides. Even with 200 or 300 acres in cattle feed, Henry continued to buy hay and grain from us. Local folks came to call him the Cattle King.

50

In his letters, Ben kept us up to date with what he was doing in San Francisco. He often remarked on how different life was in the city than in Smithland or on our Idaho farm. He had been very busy with rehearsals, performances and travel in the five years since arriving there, leaving too little time to come home to visit. His troupe had toured West Coast cities, and now they were preparing for a national tour. He knew the touring company would be playing Denver, Chicago, Saint Louis, New York and Boston, and he hoped they would add other cities closer to us so we could either see him there, or he could come to us.

In a letter posted from Saint Louis, Ben wrote that the troupe had added a three-week run in Nashville, and on their return to San Francisco they would play Salt Lake City. That meant on their way west they would pass through Kelton. Ben wrote he would take leave of the touring company, ride the stage to Albion, visit with us and catch up with the troupe later. He added that while in Nashville, he hoped to see Maria if she was not away with the Fisk Jubilee Singers.

Ben's next letter was posted from Smithland and contained news that surprised and pleased us all. He had met Maria in Nashville, and they had seen each other's performances. After two weeks together, they had taken the steamer *C. W. Anderson* to Smithland, where they were married, with Louis, Sally, the cousins and Maria's family on hand. One of the women in Ben's troupe had taken ill and returned to San Francisco. Maria had left the Jubilee Singers with Mr. White's blessing and joined Ben's touring company. That meant when the troupe completed its Eastern tour and was on its way back to San Francisco, Ben and Maria would visit our homestead together. We had a happy occasion to look forward to and started watching the days, waiting for Ben and Maria to come.

The fall 1880 harvest went smoothly. Farmers came from Albion and Goose Creek and cowboys from the Raft River to help bring in the crops. They brought machinery and teams of horses and mules to use alongside ours. We had brought in the corn, barley and hay, and were about halfway through the wheat on a bright, sunny afternoon when we had a visitor. I was working up high on the threshing machine when I saw a rider coming our way from the west. I called down to Will and the other men.

"Rider coming," I said as I pointed his way.

"Who's that?" Isaac Hunter asked. "Just about everybody we know is already here."

"I can't tell," Will said. "From this distance with the sun behind him, I can't make out who it is. I doubt there's trouble though. If there were, Beth would have rung the bell."

I held my hands over the front edge of my hat brim and squinted toward the rider. He must have seen me looking his way because he took his hat off and waved it over his head. I knew that motion, and the rider's identity suddenly hit me.

"It's Ben!" I screamed and waved back with great excitement. Several of the men gave each other puzzled looks because they had no idea who Ben was. I jumped to the ground, mounted one of the idle horses and galloped off toward Ben. He kicked his horse and galloped toward me. After a half-minute run, we met and circled each other, whooping and hollering like wildmen. We jumped down and backslapped and bear-hugged each other, still screaming like mad fools.

"Early, look at you, you're as big as I am, you look like a grown man!" Ben exclaimed.

"Well, Ben, I'm 20 years old, I *am* a grown man!" I exclaimed. "And look at you. How come you don't look like a city slicker?"

"I didn't want to wear my fancy clothes," Ben replied. "I'm here to help with the harvest."

"And I hope a lot more than that. Is Maria with you?" I asked.

"Yes, she is," he replied. "She's with Beth and Amanda and Annie at the house."

"Well, I want to see her," I said. "Will's with the men out yonder in the wheat. Let's ride to him."

Will had walked out through the wheat stubble toward us. As we rode up, he removed his hat and wiped his brow with his sleeve. He stood solid with his legs apart and wearing a smile as wide as the divide. Ben dismounted and he and Will shook hands and bear-hugged. Their greeting was just a tad bit calmer than Ben's and mine. Tears glistened in both men's eyes.

"Ben, you look great," Will said. "Is Maria with you? How is she?"

"Fine, she's fine," Ben replied. "She'll be very happy to see you."

"Well, what do you say we knock off early, go to the house and celebrate?" Will asked.

"I told the women I was coming out to work," Ben replied. "They're not expecting us till sundown. They won't have things ready if we go early. Come on, let's cut, let's thresh wheat. I want calluses. I want workin' man's hands."

We introduced Ben to the men he didn't know, and he got reacquainted with those he did. We got right down to work and kept at it till the sun was on the horizon. Some of us rode to the barn bareback, while the rest took the wagons. After taking care of the beasts, the men strode straight to the river, stripped to their underclothes and dove in. I stopped on the way to see Maria, then joined the men at the river. We were like kids at a swimming hole.

The women had fixed a big supper, which we devoured like people who hadn't eaten in days. The conversation at the table revolved around Ben and Maria, who told us about their wedding and the places their troupe had played. In Saint Louis, Ben had seen Johnnie Mack, the hack driver who had toured us around the city eight years earlier.

After supper, Ben and Maria sang some of the songs from *H.M.S. Pinafore*, the Gilbert and Sullivan opera they had been performing on tour. It was a first for everybody in the room.

We finished our harvest the following day, and the men went ahead to the next farm. Will and I would join them in two days, when Ben and Maria were on their way to Kelton.

Ben looked over the whole place and was surprised at how much had developed in the five years since he left. He loved us dearly and admired our lives but would return to San Francisco with Maria to make their home.

Ben and Maria worked with us during the days, and we visited with them in the evenings. They were very much in love, it was wonderful having them with us, and we hated to see them go.

Will had predicted that one day the Homestead Act of 1862 would apply to unsurveyed land. That prediction came true in 1880 when Congress extended the act's provisions. Will began the process that would eventually end in his gaining title to the approximately 160 acres we had been squatting on since August 1872.

Rather than traveling to the land office in Boise, Will worked with Charles Cabb, an attorney-at-law in Albion, and used the U. S. Mail to provide the proof the government needed before the land office could grant title. The process took time, what with documents repeatedly passing back and forth and all. Will had to confirm by witness affidavits the date we first lived on and began to improve the land, and to testify to just what we had done.

To be honest, we didn't fulfill all the requirements to the letter of the law—to the spirit, yes, but not the letter. Our land was so remote, and the government was so eager for settlers, that the land office wasn't inclined to investigate or hold us to fine points. By spring 1881, we had been farming and building on the land for nearly nine years. Will provided the necessary witness affidavits and other documents, ran legal notices of our claim in the Idaho *Statesman* as the law required and, after several months of process, he had our provisional grant deed. The provision was that as soon as there was a land office nearby, if government surveyors were not to conduct cadastral surveys as they had already done on the south side of the river, then contract surveyors had to conduct a metes and bounds survey. That way, the government would know exactly where the land was and what its dimensions were. When that information was recorded, the deed would be final.

51

Amanda had become a voracious reader soon after she learned how. She always did very well with her lessons, leap-frogging ahead whenever Beth introduced a new subject. In fact, twice when we visited Marsh Basin, later Albion, we discovered Amanda was far ahead of other schoolchildren her age.

But the older she got, the less Amanda liked living on our isolated farm. Although she loved her family and didn't dislike our way of life, she dreamed of bigger things. In spring 1881, when she was 15, she read an item about Vassar College in *Harper's Weekly*. She decided then and there that as soon as she turned 18, she would attend Vassar.

Amanda composed a long letter to Samuel L. Caldwell, the president of the college. She told him about her background, interests, studies and ambition, and included her impressions of many of the books she had read. She asked Mr. Caldwell what Vassar's admission requirements were and what preparation he would advise so she could meet them.

Amanda's eagerness didn't speed the reply any. She had a letter from Mr. Caldwell, posted from Poughkeepsie, New York, nearly a month later. His response was almost as long as Amanda's original query. He said he was very impressed with Amanda, encouraged her in her ambition to attend Vassar and laid out a study plan that would lead to her admission. He said the college administered admission exams in several Western cities every year and suggested Amanda should look into taking the test in Saint Louis or Chicago when she was 17 or 18.

Will and Beth were taken aback by all this, especially coming from their 15-year-old daughter. Poughkeepsie, New York, was very far away from the Hawkins place on the Snake River, Idaho, they said. And they didn't mean only in overland distance. A young woman apart from her family and roots, traveling cross-country and living on her own? How would she manage? Although Will and Beth had questions, they didn't discourage Amanda. They didn't want to crush a young girl's dream.

Amanda diligently followed Mr. Caldwell's plan and regularly corresponded with him to be sure she was on the right track. She came up with solutions for every problem that arose about her attending Vassar. She would travel to Saint Louis or Chicago for the admission test with a chaperone, she said. That could be me, or Will or Billy. Or, for that matter, Judge Rogers or Dr. Miller from Albion. Some of her ideas were impractical, but she was as determined as a bull when a cow is ready. If she couldn't travel all the way back to Idaho for the vacation periods, well, then she would take the rail cars to Paducah and stay with Louis and Sally in Smithland. They would be happy to have her, she said. There was no stopping Amanda when her mind was made up. She decided she would attend Vassar College, so it was a sure thing.

Early in 1881, the Oregon Short Line Railway started to grade and lay track from the Union Pacific line at Granger, Wyoming. They headed out of that country, moving across southern Idaho Territory and then into Oregon to Huntington. The construction crews built a water tank and a sidetrack every 25 miles or so to provide water for the steam locomotives. By summer 1883, the track layers had reached a point about six miles north of our homeplace. The railway company built a sturdy depot there and named the stop Minidoka. It was a Dakota word meaning fountain, spring or well, although there was nothing of the kind at that point in the sage.

Minidoka was the rail stop closest to Albion, the seat of Cassia County in Marsh Basin about 30 miles south. Passengers and freight to or from Albion came and went at Minidoka. A town began to grow up around the depot, and passenger coaches and freight wagons ran regularly between Minidoka and Albion. They crossed the river at the ferry Uncle Jimmy Story had built in spring '82 just below what we called Hawkins Rapids. After the railroad, the rapids became known as Minidoka, like the town.

Minidoka was the kind of town where a young boy could ride his pony to the depot in the morning, check the posted schedule, then return during the day to watch the trains come and go. That might sound like a small thing, but for a boy growing up on a farm or in an isolated town surrounded by endless sagebrush desert, trains coming and going were grand events.

Soon after the Oregon Short Line Railway began running scheduled trains through Minidoka, I started seeing a weathered old cowboy at the depot. He wore a battered, wide-brimmed hat and boots that looked as if they had been in a thousand pairs of stirrups. On all but the worst days, he sat against the wall on the sunny side of the building in a rocking chair. He had long strips of rawhide tied in coils and stored in a wooden crate to his right. On his left, he had samples of his braidwork spread out on a Navajo blanket. He might show a bridle and headstall, a coiled riata or a set of reins. Or he would show a bosal and hackamore with a breastplate and hobbles. His braiding was tight and beautifully finished. As he sat rocking slightly, he braided, creating tack to display and sell. His fingers moved quickly, with a certainty earned from years of experience. He talked with passersby without interrupting his work. One day, after I had seen him several other days but hadn't spoken to him, he spoke to me.

"Hey, young feller, need some tack for your pick of the remuda?" he asked. He didn't look up at me as he spoke. Standing close beside him as he braided, I noticed he wasn't looking directly at his hands either. It was then I realized he was blind. The first question that occurred to me was, how does he do such beautiful braidwork without sight? The second question was, how did he know I was a man, let alone a young man. I asked neither.

"Well," I replied, "not for this dappled gray, but we have others in our barn that might need new tack. I'm here at the depot every so often. I'll check to see what we might need and let you know next time I see you."

"Sure thing," he said in the clipped way that was so common in the West. Most folks spoke with great economy. I introduced myself and told him I had a farm on the river about six miles south. His name was Jack Lounsbury. He was from the Arizona cattle country. He had come to Minidoka to be with his brother and family. His brother would start a business here. Over time,

Spirit, our other horses and our mules wore something of Jack's braided tack.

Hardy Sears was a friend of ours who drove stage and freight between Minidoka and Albion. Later, he bought Mr. Bartholomew's hotel in Minidoka, and his sons Willis and Charlie drove the teams. Early one spring morning in '84, Hardy showed up at our ferry landing on the south side of the river. He was driving a light freight wagon drawn by a two-horse team and trailing a saddle horse behind. I was tending the irrigation gates along the bench. Hardy hailed me, and I ran the ferry across to meet him. He said he had urgent business down the Raft River Valley and asked if I would drive the wagon up to Minidoka, pick up some freight and a passenger named Lyle Blue, and deliver them to Albion. He said he had left a saddle horse in Albion that I could ride back to our place. I was happy to oblige.

I ferried the wagon and team to the north side, packed food, water and my Winchester, and started up our road to Minidoka. The train wasn't due for more than an hour and it was a pretty day, so I took my time, enjoying the wildflowers and the birds that darted about. The young horned larks liked flying along the ruts just ahead of the horses, about a foot or two off the ground. A group of them appeared out of the brush, sped along ahead of us and then disappeared, only to be replaced by another group that did the same, and so on.

As I approached the depot, I saw the locomotive's plume of smoke and the caboose receding into the distance to the west. Either I was late or the train had come and gone a little early, leaving one passenger, a valise and a pile of freight on the platform. From the wagon, the passenger looked to be a cowboy. He stood at the far corner of the depot with his hands on his hips and his back to me, looking north, as if he was surveying the country. He was tall and lanky. He wore a pistol holstered low on his right hip, boots, dark britches, a striped white shirt, a black vest and a wide-brimmed hat.

I jumped down from the bench, tied the team to the hitching post and mounted the stairs to the platform. I walked across toward the cowboy and as I got within earshot, asked, "Mr. Lyle Blue?"

He turned around sharply, smiled and said, "No, it's Lily, Lily Blue." It was a woman with the biggest, prettiest green eyes I had ever seen. I knew she saw my jaw drop to my knees and my eyes bug out of my head, but she didn't let on. I recovered as quickly as I could and stammered, "Miss Blue, I'm Early Hawkins, and I'm here to drive you down across the river and on to Albion."

"That's fine, Mr. Hawkins," she said. "I'll help you load the freight and my valise. Let's be on our way." A chill shot up my spine. I froze for a moment, staring into her eyes and overcome by her very pretty face. My heart beat double time.

"Mr. Hawkins?" she asked.

"Yes, Miss Blue," I stuttered. "Let's be on to Albion." I must have blushed as red as a tomato. She seemed completely unfazed. I felt like a schoolboy at his first social.

"I'll back the wagon so we can load the freight," I managed. I turned, crossed the platform, went down the stairs and climbed to the bench. Just then, I realized the team was tied and had to jump down, untie them and climb back up. Miss Blue stood by her valise, calmly waiting. I couldn't look at her; I was too embarrassed. I brought the wagon around and backed up to the platform. We loaded the freight and climbed up to the bench. She sat beside me, looking entirely comfortable.

"Do you want to drive or shall I?" she asked, with a hint of a tease in her voice.

"I think I can handle the team," I said. I slapped the reins on the horses' backs, and we were on our way south.

We drove along in silence for an awkward minute or two. Searching for something to open a conversation, I asked, "Where are you from?"

"Wyoming," she replied.

"What brings you to Idaho?" I asked.

"Cattle business," she replied.

After another awkward silence, I said, "I hope you don't mind my asking, but isn't it unusual for a young woman to be in the cattle business?"

"Yup, I'd say it is unusual," she replied.

Another awkward silence, then, "Well, then, how is it that you're in the cattle business?"

"My father had four daughters and no sons," she replied.

"Two of my sisters like pink, frilly things, and the other's still a kid, so I'm in the cattle business."

"We met a Wyoming rancher named Tom Sun when we came across 12 years ago," I said.

"Heard of him," she replied, "but he's down near Rawlins, and our ranch is close to Cheyenne."

"What's it called?" I asked.

"Blue Sky Ranch," she replied, "3,000 head on 10,000 acres of open range."

"You *are* in the cattle business," I said.

"You haul freight and people?" she asked. I had begun to wonder whether she would volunteer a question.

"Nope, I'm just here for today, helping a friend of mine," I replied. I deliberately didn't go any farther, hoping she would be curious enough to pursue the point. She was.

"What *do* you do then?" she asked.

"We have a farm on the river a few miles over yonder," I said as I pointed southeast.

"How big?" she asked.

"A quarter section," I replied.

"What do you grow?" she asked.

"Lucerne, corn, wheat and hay, mostly," I replied. "We sell to the ranchers here."

"Any cattle?" she asked.

"A few head for our own beef and a couple of dairy cows," I replied.

"Pretty country," she said, "wide open. I like that."

That's the way our conversation went. Her questions and answers were short and to the point. She seemed to be a typical Westerner—not given to much talk. We crossed the river at Story Ferry and continued down to Cañon Creek. I suggested that when we entered the draw through the Early Mountains, we could stop at a shady spot, water the horses and have something to eat. She said she'd like that.

Hardy had left a blanket in the wagon. I spread it beneath some water birches and laid out the food I brought from home. We had chicken, hard-boiled eggs, and young greens and carrots I had taken from the kitchen garden. As we sat and ate, Miss Blue relaxed and got more talkative.

"Did you go to school?" she asked.

"No," I replied, "the school was too far away—in Albion. It was called Marsh Basin then. My mother taught me and my younger sister at home, and I read a lot. Did you finish school?"

"Yes, in Cheyenne," she replied. "My mother insisted her daughters go to school. She wanted me to go on to university, but my father stepped in and said he needed me on the ranch. If he had had a son, I probably would have gone to university."

"That would be unusual," I said. "There aren't many university men in the West, let alone women."

"If the West is to grow and prosper," she said, "people will have to be educated, and I don't see why women should be left out."

"Don't get me wrong," I said, "I don't think women should be left out either."

She removed her hat, and her curls dropped nearly to her shoulders. Her hair was light—almost blond—and very thick. From a distance, given the way she was dressed and with her hair tucked up under her hat, it was easy to mistake her for a slim man. But here, up close, face to face, with her cascade of curly hair, her huge green eyes and her smooth skin, any fool could see she was a beautiful young woman.

She stood, walked to the creek, knelt, lowered her head to the water, dipped her hands in and gently splashed her face. She looked very shapely as she knelt. She removed the bandana from her neck, soaked it, wrung it out and retied it. She stood, came back to the blanket, put her hat on, tucked her hair up beneath it and faced me.

"Are we ready to go?" she asked.

"You bet," I replied. I gathered what was left of the food and put it and the blanket in the wagon. We climbed aboard and were on our way. I turned to her as she turned to me. Our smiles were hints of affection.

As I reined the team to a halt at the Albion Hotel, I asked Miss Blue how long she planned to stay.

"Two days," she replied. "I'll be leaving on the afternoon train the day after tomorrow."

"Can I take you to the depot then?" I asked.

"I'd like that," she replied, looking me straight in the eye and smiling.

"I'll be here first thing that morning," I said. I carried her valise into the lobby, and we said our goodbyes. I drove the wagon to Hardy Sears' place, mounted the horse he had left for me and rode home.

52

I couldn't get Lily Blue out of my head, not that I wanted to, actually. I thought of her eyes, her hair, her smile, her direct manner, her voice. I thought how unusual it was that she dressed like a cowboy and was in the cattle business. She was an individual; she wasn't afraid to be different. I liked that.

I thought that since Lily Blue had asked about our farm, she should see it and meet my family. I worked out the details in my head. There wouldn't be enough time if I went for her in our wagon, so I thought I'd go on horseback and take another horse for her. The only problem I could foresee was her valise—we wouldn't be able to carry it on horseback. I decided I'd take two canvas sacks for her things. I'd leave the valise at Hardy's and ship it to her in Cheyenne by rail later. I hoped she'd like the idea and go along. If not, there was always Hardy's coach.

I was so excited by Lily Blue and her coming to our home-place that I left the farm early the next afternoon, planning to stay the night at Hardy's and to be at the hotel first thing in the morning.

She was sitting on the porch bench when I rode up at about 8 a.m. She was dressed as she had been when we met. She didn't seem at all surprised that I hadn't come with a wagon.

"Good morning, Miss Blue," I said rather loudly as I dismounted.

"Good morning, Mr. Hawkins," she replied as she stood. "I suppose you have a plan for my valise."

"Why, yes, I do," I said. "I brought two canvas bags that I think will hold your things and lie nicely behind our saddles." I untied the bags and stepped up on the porch. "I can ship your valise to Cheyenne by rail if that's all right."

"Yes, that will do," she said. She stepped to the edge of the porch and put her hands on her hips. "Those are fine-looking horses," she said, surveying our mounts.

"The gelding is mine, and the mare is my mother's," I said.

"Does your mother ride well?" she asked.

"Yes, very well," I replied.

"Good," she said.

Miss Blue picked up her valise, placed it on the bench and opened the lid. She quickly moved the contents into the canvas bags, putting things in order as she went. She fastened the straps and lifted one bag as I took the other. I followed her down the stairs, and we tied the bags behind the saddles.

"I'll take your valise inside and leave it with the desk clerk for Hardy to pick up later. I'll have it on the eastbound train to Cheyenne in a day or two," I said.

Miss Blue was mounted and testing the mare when I returned from the lobby. She sat the horse very well, and the mare instantly knew who was in charge. I mounted Spirit and we started out of town.

"Your train at Minidoka's not till afternoon," I said. "I'd like to show you our farm on the way."

"I'd like that," she said.

We rode at a trot toward the draw through the Early Mountains. Miss Blue rode as if she was born to the saddle. Willows lined the creek along the way, and when we reached the canyon itself, cottonwoods and water birches joined the willows. The young cottonwood leaves quivered in the gentle breeze. An occasional gust sent them spinning as the wind swept each tree, making the leaves move in concert. First there was a whoosh as the gust brushed the crowns. Then an almost musical rustle rose and gently settled as the wind backed away.

We passed through patches of light and shadow that followed the pattern of the ridge line. Morning sun came through the low spots and lit the opposite hillside, while the high points blocked the light and cast shadows.

We moved out of the canyon and onto the sagebrush plain, riding side by side in the ruts of the wagon road. Miss Blue turned to me with an impish smile and a gleam in her eye.

"So, Mr. Hawkins, would you like to race?" she asked.

Before I had a chance to answer, she kicked the mare, and took off like a shot. I was so surprised, I was 10 lengths behind before I got Spirit up to a run. He was getting a little old for this kind of thing, but he gave it everything he had. At a long curve just ahead, Miss Blue stayed on the road, but I took to the brush inside the curve to the right. She turned over her left shoulder to look behind and saw nothing but empty road. She didn't realize I was on her right closing the gap until I was nearly beside her.

Spirit liked a challenge and knew exactly what was going on. If he could help it, he wouldn't let me lose a race. With an extra burst of speed, we crossed onto the road just ahead of Miss Blue and the mare. She was a superb rider. If the mare had been as fast as Spirit, I wouldn't have had a chance. Miss Blue and I pulled up, had a good laugh and congratulated each other on the race.

When we reached the ferry landing, Beth waved to us from the porch. She returned to the house and, with Amanda, came out through the cave. They started the ferry across to meet us.

"You have a wonderful farm here, Mr. Hawkins," Miss Blue said as we waited.

"We've been here close to 12 years," I said. "We've had our ups and downs, but overall we've done well. We have about 160 acres in crops and pasture. We sell almost everything to the local ranchers."

"So you said," she said. "You're right to be proud."

When the ferry reached the landing, I tied it and opened the gate for Beth and Amanda to step down. I introduced Miss Blue. The three women seemed comfortable with each other right away. It was very much like Beth to suggest that we call each other by our first names. Lily said she'd like that. I was struck for a moment by the fact that I was standing on our ferry landing with three women. Two were already very dear to me, and the third was becoming so.

"You're just in time for dinner," Beth said. "Will will be in from the fields in a few minutes. Let's cross to the house." Amanda walked beside Lily as she led the mare aboard the ferry. Amanda had just turned 18, and I guessed that Lily was only two or three years older. A fast friendship seemed to be developing between them. I walked beside Beth as I led Spirit. She turned to me and smiled. No words passed between us, but I understood two things: Beth knew I was sweet on Lily, and she approved.

"Early," Beth said when we reached the porch, "if you'll ring the bell for Will, Amanda and I will take Lily in and get cleaned up for dinner. Will's not far; he should be here shortly."

Lily removed her gunbelt and asked me to loop it around the horn of the mare's saddle. The women went in, while I waited outside for Will. When he came, we went in together, and I introduced him and Lily.

"Miss Lily Blue, this is my father, Captain Will Hawkins," I said, trying not to sound too grand and formal.

"I'm very happy to meet you, Miss Blue," Will said, obviously surprised and pleased.

"And I'm happy to meet you, Captain Hawkins," Lily said.

"We decided to use first names," Beth said as she came toward us from the kitchen, smiling.

"Yes, we did," Lily said. "Is that all right with you, Will?" she asked.

"Certainly is," Will replied. "Welcome to our home, Lily."

We sat for dinner, and everyone got caught up on Lily, her family, where she was from and what she was doing here on the Snake River. She wanted to know more about us and how we started the farm. Each of us told pieces of the story.

After the meal, Amanda showed Lily the house and cave as Will, Beth and I cleared the dishes. When Lily returned, she commented on the patchwork quilts Beth and Amanda had made during the past winter.

"Your quilts are so bright and colorful," Lily said, "they're just lovely. I'd want to hang one in a frame on a wall rather than spread it across a bed."

"Well, how nice, thank you," Beth replied, "but we mean them to be practical. They're very warm on our long winter nights."

We walked with Lily along the bench. Beth and Amanda pointed out the young growth in the kitchen garden and explained what they would plant and harvest through the summer.

"We eat a lot fresh, but we put a lot by too," Amanda said.

"We're usually busy putting by straight through summer into early autumn," Beth added.

Will asked Lily to please visit again, said goodbye and returned to Billy and the cultivating work in the fields. Beth and Amanda excused themselves, asked Lily to please stop at the house before we drove to Minidoka, and left me to show her the rest of the farm.

We walked past the barn, night pasture and orchard. I pointed to Billy and Annie's place and told Lily about the house and our hired help. We paused where the beef cattle and dairy cows grazed in the sink pasture's green grass.

"They look well fed and healthy," Lily said. "They don't look half wild like the cattle we have out on the range."

As we walked back toward the house, I pointed out the mountains we had named for ourselves.

"I doubt those names will stick," I said, "people are already calling the rapids 'Minidoka.'"

"Did you name Ben Butte after the brother you mentioned at dinner?" Lily asked.

"Yes, my older brother, Ben," I replied. "He and his wife, Maria, live in San Francisco. They're players in a musical theater company. They're both excellent singers and musicians. We see them every so often. We miss them a lot."

Lily and I returned to the house so she could say goodbye. Beth and Amanda thanked her for visiting and asked her to please come again. Lily was very gracious and assured Beth and Amanda she would return.

We mounted and rode north toward Minidoka. Before the homeplace got too far behind, Lily reined the mare to a halt and turned to survey the scene. The poplars formed an L at the edge of the sink. The house stood on a knoll beyond them. The top of the cottonwood rose above the house roof. The barn stood nearby to the left. Acres of pasture and fields lay across like a many-colored ribbon, while the river formed a baseline along the far edge of the homestead. Beyond the river lay sagebrush desert and, in degrees of distance, the mountains. It was midday, and the spring sun lit the scene in bright, crisp light.

"I like it here," Lily said as she turned and looked at me warmly.

"I'm glad you do," I replied. I had begun getting used to being with her, but my heart still fluttered as we spoke.

We rode on to Minidoka and waited on the depot platform for the eastbound train. When it came, I helped Lily with the canvas bags and paused with her at the stairs until the engine was ready to go. We stood facing each other saying goodbye. She removed her hat and let her curls drop. I removed my hat. She stepped closer, took my hands, stood on her toes and kissed me lightly on the cheek.

"Please write to me," she whispered.

"I promise I will," I replied, softly.

The engineer blew the whistle, saying it was time to go. Lily mounted the stairs and took a seat on the near side at the window. She smiled and waved as the train pulled away. I waved my hat over my head until I was sure she was out of view.

I stood still for a moment, feeling mixed emotions. I was happy I had met Lily, and I was sad to see her go. Right then, I started planning a trip to Cheyenne.

At home, when I mentioned Lily's valise to Beth, she suggested I tuck a quilt inside before shipping it to Cheyenne. I liked that idea, and Beth included a note in her beautiful hand:

> *"Dearest Lily,*
> *Please accept this gift and remember us with* *warmth on those cold winter nights. We enjoyed* *meeting you and hope you will visit again soon.*
> *Love from the Hawkins Family"*

After her visit, Lily and I exchanged several letters and even a telegram or two. She loved the quilt we sent and was touched by the gesture. She invited me to visit Blue Sky Ranch.

I had an idea to write to Hart, asking him to identify a biological specimen I had seen. Here's what I wrote:

Today I observed a vertebrate specimen, apparently primate, having bipedal, erect ambulation. Estimated height was 173 cm. Two superior limbs terminated in hands, each having five digits—four fingers and an opposable thumb. Vision was frontal and binocular. The eyes were large, with green irises. Ears were close to the head on opposite sides at eye level. The specimen was warm-blooded and held a constant temperature. The face was hairless save for eyebrows and lashes, but the head was covered with luxuriant golden hair. The nose was small, central to the face and straight, with two symmetrical nostrils. The mouth was full, with regular, white dentition. The corporal epidermis was smooth, cream colored and sparsely populated with downy hair. Two ventral mammary glands stood across the upper torso. Diet was omnivorous. The specimen vocalized in dulcet tones and responded to visual, auditory, olfactory and tactile stimuli. Please identify.

In about two weeks, I had Hart's reply:

Homo sapiens, female; pursuit and retention advised.

53

As soon as our crops were planted, I took my first trip to Cheyenne. I thanked my lucky stars we had hired Billy and Annie because without them, I wouldn't have been able to leave our place in the spring for more than a day or two.

I rode the Oregon Short Line from Minidoka to Granger, Wyoming, then the Union Pacific on to Cheyenne. The route took me through the magnificent Rocky Mountains and across the continental divide.

I expected Lily to meet me at the Cheyenne depot and was surprised to find her father there instead. We had never met, of course, but he somehow picked me out of the crowd. He wasn't dressed as you might expect a rancher to be. He wore a dark, three-piece business suit and a cravat. He was cordial but left no question that he was serious and in charge. He introduced himself as Hobart Blue and insisted I call him Bart. He explained that Lily couldn't meet me because she was out on the range with the hands, branding new beeves and castrating young bulls. He looked at me sidelong as he said that.

Bart drove directly to the Cheyenne Club, which was housed in a large, impressive new building in town. The club's members were the most prominent cattlemen in the territorial capital. Bart introduced me to several men who expressed what I thought was an unusual amount of interest in me, my family and our life in Idaho. It wasn't until later at the ranch house with Lily and her family that I realized what was going on.

The family regarded me as a serious suitor of their eldest daughter. And that could only be because Lily portrayed me that way. As a man with no sons, Bart saw his eldest daughter's potential husband as the heir to everything he had accomplished. His daughter might be smitten with me, but I had to pass his tests. If I was to take over his ranch one day, he wanted to be damn sure he was leaving it in good hands.

But Lily was the only part of the Blue Sky Ranch I was interested in. I had no intention of removing to Wyoming and eventually taking over the ranch. My family and farm were on the Snake River in Idaho. I assumed the woman I married would live with me at our homeplace. I said nothing of this out loud during my visit. I did something else though: I fell head over heels in love with Lily.

Amanda met me at the Minidoka depot when I returned from Cheyenne. She was jumping with excitement. She had heard by wire the previous day that the Vassar admission exams would be given at Washington University in Saint Louis on June 10th and 11th. It had been decided that I would chaperone my sister to Saint Louis, so I had barely unpacked my baggage when I was packing it again for the trip.

We stayed at the Planters' Hotel, as Will, Ben and I had in '72. Amanda was busy with interviews and written exams for the better part of both days. I learned that Johnnie Mack was no longer driving a hack, and that Tom Dodge was up the Missouri on his way to Fort Benton. I visited book shops, walked along the levee and crossed to Illinois on the Eads Bridge. I wrote to Louis and Sally, saying they should look forward to seeing Amanda in September on her way to Vassar. I was that sure she would be going.

Amanda told me about her first day's interviews and exams as we ate supper. She had met Mr. Clement, other administrators and some faculty members. She had written three separate exams. She said she had made a few small mistakes, but overall, she felt she had done well. She spent the rest of the evening preparing for the second day. Then, that second evening over supper, Amanda said that Mr. Clement had as much as told her she would be accepted. She was so excited, she could barely eat. Her diligence and hard work had paid off. She would soon realize her dream of attending Vassar College.

With the Oregon Short Line well on its way across Idaho in 1883 and the Wood River mining country booming, Eastern financier Jay Gould bankrolled a spur line from the main OSL tracks north to Hailey. In late June '84, Will rode the OSL cars west from Minidoka and up the spur line to the land office in Hailey. He wanted to have our land surveyed and secure our ownership.

The government men at the land office told Will the south side of the river had been surveyed in 1874 using the standard township and range system. But, they said, the government had no reason or plan to survey the north side. If Will wanted our ground surveyed, the government could contract with a two-man team to conduct a metes and bounds survey, but Will would have to pay for it. Will had already decided on a survey when he got the provisional deed, so he agreed.

The government men said they would make the arrangements and wire Will two weeks ahead of the survey date. They asked how the surveyors would find the homeplace. Will told them to have the men come to Minidoka on the afternoon train, then ride the only southeast wagon road to the river.

The wire came in early July, and two weeks later a pair of young Irishmen—brothers Jim and Dan Finnegan—rode in with their equipment packed on a mule. They would spend the night, do the survey the next day, then return to Hailey on the morning train the day after that. Beth took having overnight guests in stride, as she did with almost everything.

Before sundown that evening, Will and I rode the land with the surveyors, showing them its dimensions and extent. Will said he had carefully paced the ground and figured we had fenced something very close to 160 acres.

"You'll know by sundown tomorrow," Dan said. I figured he and Jim were close because there was an easy and constant banter between them. Nothing one did escaped the other's notice. There was affectionate ribbing back and forth about everything—the boots one wore, how the other tied his bandana, the condition of one's hat, how the other sat his horse and so on.

"Well, ya know, Dan's hoss ain't got no bones under her flesh," Jim said. "He picked 'em out one at a time and fed 'em to his hungry hound dawg. And that's why his hoss slumps so bad."

"Yeah, she's a mite swayed," Dan allowed, "but y'all should see my dawg. He's a real healthy mutt."

We turned the horses and mule out into the night pasture and walked to the house to sit on the porch. Jim pulled a whiskey flask from his gear bag and asked if we wanted a nip. When Will and I declined, Jim asked if we minded if he and Dan had one or two. Will had no objection, so our guests started passing the flask back and forth. Before long, they were tipsy, their banter was coming fast and furious, and they were slapping their knees with laughter.

"C'mon, Jim," Dan urged, "bring out your flute."

Jim pulled a tin whistle from his bag and started to play. Dan immediately jumped to his feet and began to dance a jig.

The tune came around and he sang:

> *I'm on my way*
> *I'm goin' today*
> *I'm goin' to Erin Ryan's*
>
> *She's a pretty girl*
> *I'm all in a whirl*
> *I'm goin' to Erin Ryan's*

We clapped our hands and tapped our feet as Jim played faster and faster. Dan sang and danced faster and faster to keep up. Finally, he collapsed to the floor, flat on his back with his arms outspread, laughing and laughing.

"You got me that time, Jimmy," Dan managed through his laughter. "I owe you one."

Jim and Dan bedded down in the cave. They were up at dawn, swimming in the river. After a big breakfast Beth served, they got straight to work on the survey. Their equipment was a large compass and two tall poles connected by a 16-foot chain. They started at the north landing by taking a bearing where the bluff met the river and proceeded from there. We got to our work and let them get to theirs.

Our ground was very close to rectangular in shape except for the river boundary, which meandered a bit. I can't imagine Jim and Dan measured the entire west-east stretch of the land by repeating 16-foot chain lengths. They must have had a way to project a few lengths down a long, straight line. They had finished their compass and chain work by dinner time. When the table was cleared, they did their calculations and offered the results.

"By our figurin'," Jim said, "you have 159.6 acres fenced on three sides and bounded by the river on the fourth."

"Will," I said, "it looks as if your pacing was right on the mark."

"Must be these boots," Will replied with a smile.

"We'll report our findings and turn our papers over to the land office tomorrow," Dan said. "You should be able to square your deed anytime after that."

That night, in contrast to the night before, Jim and Dan sat quietly on the porch listening to coyotes howling in the distance, counting the shooting stars and watching the river flow. When Beth came out to ask if she could get them anything, Dan said, "Naw, but thanks, Mrs. Hawkins. Nice place you got here, ma'am."

"Yes, thank you," Beth replied, "we like it."

Jim and Dan said their goodbyes and left early the next morning. Will rode the OSL cars to Hailey the following week and recorded the deed on our surveyed 159.6 acres along the river. The papers confirmed the homeplace was ours.

Lily came to visit for two weeks in August, arriving on the 6th. From the moment she stepped down from the wagon, I knew she didn't expect to be treated like a guest. Everything about her said, "This is a farm, there's work to be done, let's get to it."

She worked in the house and garden alongside Beth, Amanda and Annie. Will, Billy and I spent our days with the irrigation gates and ditches, in the barn or pasture tending to the beasts, and in the fields.

August 6th happened to be the night of the full moon. As the sun neared the western horizon, the moon cleared the distant ridgeline in the east. For a minute or two, the two disks hung at opposite poles, staring at each other across the Plain. Lily and I watched from the porch, two specks on the Earth, itself seemingly suspended midway between the sun and moon.

The twilight roused yipping coyotes in the thickets along the river. As the rising moon cast its eerie light across the sage, coyotes slipped upland to pursue the night's prey. Later, as the moon neared the top of its arc, it was so bright we read a newspaper page by its light.

Each night, the waning moon rose about an hour later than the night before. As it dimmed, it yielded more of the sky to the stars. As the heavens turned, the Big Dipper came to rest lying across the northern sky, its handle stretching west and its cup open to the stars above. Late one night, as Lily and I strolled back from the rapids below, a shooting star streaked into the Big Dipper's cup and vanished, as if doused by unseen water. Lily gasped and raised her fingers to her lips. She turned to me, her eyes wide and glowing with wonder. I held her and kissed her softly. We walked on to the house. I felt like ringing the bell to announce to the world that I loved Lily.

We stole time away to ride the fence line, hike through the sage or stroll the riverbank to the mill and rapids. Lily was not a timid or retiring woman—she was game to do almost anything. After supper one evening as the orange sky began its gradual turn to violet, then black, I offered to demonstrate how I swam the river. There was a combination of challenge and mischief in Lily's eyes and voice as she said, "Not without me, you won't." She shed her outer clothes as quickly as I did mine, we swam across, walked upstream on the south side and swam back to our starting point. As we stood dripping wet on the bank, we touched hands, turned and embraced. During her visit that August, we established a bond that would go unbroken for the rest of our lives.

At the start of Lily's second week with us, Beth left for San Francisco to be with Maria and Ben for the birth of their first child. As Lily and I returned from driving Beth to the Minidoka depot, I thought out loud about how the coming of the Oregon Short Line had changed our lives.

"Before the railroad, we were much more isolated," I said. "Albion was a day south, and Kelton was two days beyond that. Now, with Minidoka only six miles from home, the outside world is almost on our doorstep. You're about 30 hours east in Cheyenne, and Ben and Maria are about 50 hours west in San Francisco. And everyone is only minutes away by telegraph."

Lily remarked that even with the railroad, telegraph and newspapers bringing the world so close, her family's life on Blue Sky Ranch near Cheyenne was little affected by most distant or even nearby events. She said the weather still touched them more than anything. Drought or an extremely cold winter could have a devastating effect on their herds and their fortunes. Of course, if beef prices crashed or the railroad stopped running, they would be hurt, but most events they read of in the newspapers had no effect.

Looking back on this now, Lily's point is clear. Events that in time would profoundly change the way people everywhere lived meant nothing to us then in the rural West. The papers said the Bell Telephone Company was formed in August '77, and before that year was out we read that Thomas Edison had introduced the phonograph. Then, in the fall of '79, the papers announced that Edison had invented the electric light. It would be many years before those advances reached the ranches and farms of Wyoming and Idaho.

However, there *were* events that affected me personally, while still others affected our farm and family. In late 1876, Mark Twain published *The Adventures of Tom Sawyer*. Since I had come from a river town and had read and loved Mark Twain's earlier books, *Tom Sawyer* had special meaning for me. Then, in 1880, *Ben Hur*, a novel by Lew Wallace, appeared. General Lew Wallace lived in Smithland while stationed at Fort Smith during the War, and the story locally was that he started the novel there. Those facts made reading the book almost an obligation. Actually, it was an exciting novel that I enjoyed.

Something like the coming of the sulky plow or the Buckeye mowing machine affected our farm and us more than any of the bigger things Lily and I discussed as we drove. On the farm, a late freeze or the like had a huge effect. We lived or died, succeeded or failed by our wits, our hard work and at Nature's mercy.

Lily took a new direction. "My youngest sister is fascinated by tales of gunfights," she said with a little giggle of disbelief. "She clips gunfight stories from the newspapers and keeps them in a scrapbook. She sees our Blue Sky cowboys as gunfighters who are quick on the draw and out to fill rivals with lead. She tries to pit one group against another and to egg them on to fight it out. The cowboys find it all very amusing."

"I'm amazed that some gunfights become so famous," I said. "In '81, Pat Garrett killing Billy the Kid and the Earps shooting the Clantons in Tombstone got more publicity than President Garfield being assassinated. You'd think it would be the other way around."

"Maybe that's just here in the West," Lily replied, "and maybe it's because we're still territories and not states. I wonder if it was different in the East."

Just then, we capped a rise and the tops of the poplars came into view. We were home. Beth returned from San Francisco a few days after Lily left for Cheyenne. Maria had given birth to a healthy boy, and mother and son were doing well. Ben and Maria named their first child Brad. I wouldn't see my nephew until he was nearly two years old.

54

Amanda left for Vassar in early September 1884. I went with her as far as Saint Louis. I bought her a nicely bound journal in a bookstore there as a going-away present. I hoped she would start her own personal record.

Louis and Sally met us in Saint Louis, and Amanda went on to Smithland with them. Then Louis and Amanda traveled to Poughkeepsie together. The night I got back to the homeplace in Idaho, I found a poem that Amanda had left under my bed pillows. Here it is:

Lonely Bird

I am a lonely bird
I have a roost but no mate
I have a nest but no young
I sing a plaintive song
I hear no reply
I wait in vain
Spring and summer come and go
With fall I will fly
Perhaps ne'er to return

During her years at Vassar, Amanda did return but only in the summers. Otherwise, she went either to Smithland or to the homes of friends she made at school and who lived closer than Idaho.

Canvassers had agents out selling subscriptions to Mark Twain's new novel, *The Adventures of Huckleberry Finn*, in fall '84. It was due to be published in December. I subscribed, but didn't get my copy until February '85. The day I picked it up at the Minidoka post office, I read in the Omaha paper that a monument to George Washington had been dedicated in the District of Columbia two days earlier.

There were enough long, cold nights left that winter for me to sit near the fire and read *Huck Finn* once, then again and again. Although I had never had adventures quite like Huck's, I saw myself as him and my old friend Nothet as Jim.

In July that year, the news in all the papers was that General and former President Ulysses S. Grant had died. He finished writing his memoirs just a few days prior. Mark Twain called him "a truly great man." He was only 63 years of age.

Hunting through a New York *Times* newspaper a westbound passenger had left at the Minidoka depot, I saw that a new Gilbert and Sullivan opera called *The Mikado* had opened at the Fifth Avenue Theater on August 19, 1885. The critic gave it a good review, but he thought the libretto was better than the music. I wondered if Ben and Maria would ever play in *The Mikado*.

Lily's and my letters and visits continued through '84, '85 and into early '86. Our letters passed in a steady flow back and forth, and one of us traveled east or west every chance we got. While at the Blue Sky Ranch, I learned more than it turned out I would ever have to know about cattle and the cattle business. We drove herds, roped and branded, birthed calves, made young bulls into steers, and shipped hundreds of head off to slaughter and the market. Bart patiently explained the details of the dollars and cents end of the business. He was determined to convince me that my future lay in ranching.

The Blues were well-connected in Cheyenne society, so we spent many evenings at stage plays, dinners and other social events. In Albion or Minidoka, we scarcely had the like, so these affairs were a pleasant diversion for Lily and me.

In late winter 1886, as we sat together before a fire roaring in the stone fireplace at the Blue Sky Ranch, I proposed to Lily and she accepted. We decided on a summer wedding but not on where we would live.

Neither of our families was religious, so rather than standing with a minister in a church in Cheyenne, Lily and I were married by a justice of the peace in the flower garden of the Blue Sky ranchhouse outside of town. Will, Beth and Amanda came with Charlie Howell from Minidoka, and Ben, Maria and Brad came from San Francisco. Lily's parents, her sisters, the ranch foreman, several hands, and many friends and neighbors filled out the bride's side of the aisle. Lily's sister, Marianne, was her maid of honor, and Ben was my best man.

Lily looked radiant in the soft white dress she and her

mother had made. As she walked down the aisle on Bart's arm, I thought I felt my knees knocking. I turned my head slightly toward Ben and said, "Hold me up" under my breath. He whispered, "Steady, brother."

Lily and I stood side by side and exchanged our vows. When the justice pronounced us husband and wife and gave me permission to kiss the bride, we turned to each other and I took Lily's hands. She looked up at me with her huge, beautiful green eyes. They were misty, and her lips were parted in a slight smile. I was sure I was shaking, but when I brought my hand to her chin, it was steady. We kissed softly and when we withdrew, we were each beaming through tears welling up in our eyes. I was transfixed by her glow, and for a moment we were the only two people in the garden, for that matter, in the world. The music swelled and we were brought back to Earth by a thunderous cheer from the guests. That moment with Lily is deeply engraved in my memory, and no other experience, save perhaps the births of our children, is its equal.

A wonderful party with music and dancing followed. When Ben and Maria sang the wedding-night duet from Gounod's opera *Romeo and Juliette,* everyone stood silently. Even the children seemed stunned. Lily's eyes filled with tears of joy, and she rushed to Ben and Maria to thank them when they finished. As performers, Ben and Maria had gone far beyond what any of us ever imagined was possible. I was immensely proud of my brother and his beautiful wife.

After the party, the guests bade us goodbye at the new Cheyenne depot. We had reserved a Pullman sleeper on the 4:25 Union Pacific hotel express. Lily and Maria wore city dresses with the full bustles that were fashionable for ladies at the time. Maria was accustomed to the style, having lived in San Francisco for years, but Lily looked a little uneasy. She and her mother had made Lily's dress from a Butterick pattern. It was not the kind of dress that ranch women were used to.

We spent our wedding night in our private Pullman compartment. I thought of Rebel and silently thanked her. Without having been with Rebel, I would barely have known what to do.

The country between Cheyenne and Kelton was familiar, but west of Kelton was new territory. We traveled through magnificent open country before crossing the Sierra Nevada and descending into California's Central Valley. We were in San Francisco less than three days after leaving Cheyenne. The trip was a new experience for Lily and me, but not for Ben and Maria. They had crisscrossed the continent many times with their musical theater troupe.

Lily and I spent a week in San Francisco as Ben and Maria's houseguests. They had a beautiful home, many friends and knew the city well, so we had a wonderful time. I enjoyed romping with Brad, who was then almost two years old.

Lily and I had two experiences during our stay that overshadowed the rest. One was an art gallery showing of work by Winslow Homer. A painting called *Snap the Whip* struck a chord in me. My companions moved on as I stood staring at the line of boys in a field near their schoolhouse. Years before, I could have been one of those boys. Lily came back, touched my elbow and asked if I was all right. It was almost as if she had awakened me from a trance.

The second experience was unlike any other in my life. Ben, Maria and other theater people in San Francisco had arranged a benefit for Thomas Maguire, the impresario who had recruited Ben to star in his company 11 years before. Mr. Maguire had since moved to New York, where he had fallen on hard times. The San Francisco players felt they owed Maguire a great debt and brought him back from New York for the benefit.

A Studebaker Brothers carriage brought Mr. and Mrs. Maguire from their hotel to a dinner party at Ben and Maria's home. As much as everyone coaxed Ben, he would not reveal just what we would see later at the theater. When we arrived there, not even the marquee revealed the performance. It said nothing but "Surprise Guest Tonight." Word of the mystery show had spread only by mouth. The hosts gave their personal guarantee that paying customers would get their money's worth.

The theater was nearly full when our party entered. With Mr. and Mrs. Maguire in the lead, we were escorted to front row center. Only a patch of carpet, a high-backed chair, a small table and a lectern were on the stage. We settled into our seats and joined the audience's buzz of anticipation. A few moments later, the lights dimmed, and a slim man in a dark three-piece suit walked onto the stage from the wings. He had a full moustache and thick, dark hair. He carried an unlit cigar. When the lights came up, a chill ran up my spine, and a gasp of recognition hit me and others in the audience. I turned to Lily with my mouth agape, "Lily, it's Mark Twain!" I said, probably much too loudly. We and the entire audience burst into applause. Ben and Maria and the Maguires beamed. Everyone stood. Many cheered. Mark Twain first looked stunned, then bemused. He waited until the audience calmed down and sat. He paused, scanning the lower theater and the balcony. His timing was perfect.

"Well, I didn't know if you'd remember me," he said. The audience roared. He had us in the palm of his hand from the first moment.

"A little better than 20 years ago, I spent a six-month sojourn in the Sandwich Islands. Being without an income when I returned to San Francisco, I had the foolish idea of giving a lecture. I rented a new opera house at half price from a man I had known in Virginia City. He had left Nevada to escape his reputation, much like me, and had come to San Francisco.

"A short time ago, while I was in Keokuk visiting Grandma Clemens with my wife and daughters, I had a telegram from friends of that man, asking if I could come for a special occasion. I prefer traveling by steamboat, but since I was already nearly half way here, and with a little help from the Union Pacific, here I am to honor my friend Thomas Maguire."

With that, Mr. Twain gestured to Mr. Maguire, who stood, faced the audience and bowed. The full house gave him a hearty round of applause. When the clapping died down, Mr. Twain continued.

"We came through the lakes, then down the Mississippi to Keokuk from Saint Paul. Shortly after nightfall on our first evening on the river, the pilot entered a shoal crossing. He rang the bell, calling for leads. Alone on the hurricane deck, I heard the leadsman chant the depths, drawing out each syllable as he watched the line. Presently, he came to the origin of my *nom de plume*, repeatedly calling out 'Mark Twain, Mark Twain' in a cadence familiar to me from my youth. My young daughter, Clara, appeared and approached me urgently. She gave me a mild scolding. 'Papa,' she said, 'I have hunted all over the boat. Don't you know they are calling for you?'"

The audience laughed warmly. Mr. Twain paused, then went on.

"I'm happy to be with you tonight, but it will be one night only because I must return to my family. My daughter, Susy, is writing a biography. Until she chose me as the subject, I thought she was a bright little girl. Yet, I am obliged to return to her so she can finish."

Mr. Twain spoke for about an hour, occasionally pulling his watch from his vest pocket and checking the time, and repeatedly re-lighting his cigar, which refused to stay lit. He called San Francisco "heaven on a half-shell" and referred to Washington, D. C., as "a stud farm for every jackass in the country." He walked the stage as he told stories about the Sandwich Islands, about Virginia City and about being passed by a Pony Express rider when coming across to Nevada by stagecoach.

He excused himself for an intermission and, when he was ready to return for a second hour, blew a cloud of smoke onto the stage from the wings to announce his entry. He began by reciting from memory a long passage from *The Adventures of Huckleberry Finn*, the novel he had published the previous year. It was a touching story about the friendship between Huck and Jim. He acted out each part, changing his voice and diction so the audience could follow.

Mr. Twain spoke as a good-natured man who was disappointed in himself and his fellow humans, who saw the high purpose and folly of life. He said that man "would be better underground inspiring the cabbages," that man "is God's favorite after the housefly," that man "loves his neighbor as himself but cuts his neighbor's throat if his theology isn't straight." He reserved his kindest words for children. Then, at the end, he said it was time to go because his teeth were loose. He left the audience happy, satisfied and thinking. We gave him a standing ovation. He left the stage and, when the applause continued, returned for a bow. Then he was gone.

Our group leaned forward, looking at each other one face after another. Our eyes were glowing, and we were all smiling broadly. Mr. Maguire spoke first.

"Shall we go backstage and meet Sam Clemens?" he asked. We didn't hesitate for a second. "Yes!" was our unanimous and enthusiastic reply.

Mr. and Mrs. Maguire led us through a side door into the dressing room area. It was strangely quiet, especially after the noise of the theater. The only other person in Mr. Twain's dressing room left as we entered. Mr. Maguire and Mr. Twain greeted each other heartily, Mr. Maguire congratulated Mr. Twain on his lecture, and they shared a private joke about Virginia City. Then Mr. Maguire turned to us.

"Sam," he said, "I'd like you to meet some friends of mine." He introduced Ben and Maria first. "This handsome young couple are Mr. and Mrs. Ben York. Ben and Maria were my star performers, and they, with others, are responsible for our being here tonight. They are now in rehearsal and will soon open in *The Mikado*."

"Ah, that's a favorite of mine," said Mr. Twain. "I'm certainly glad I didn't appear opposite *The Mikado*. I would have spoken to an empty house."

"If our production had conflicted with your appearance, Mr. Twain," Ben said, "we would have gone dark for the evening in your honor."

"That's very kind of you, Mr. York," Mr. Twain said, "and it's the only way I would have filled any seats." Mr. Maguire turned to Lily and me.

"And Sam," he said, "This fine young couple are Mr. and Mrs. Early Hawkins. Early and Lily have just been married and are in San Francisco on their honeymoon."

"Congratulations," Mr. Twain said, "marriage is a fine institution that I highly recommend. Mrs. Clemens and our daughters are more dear to me than anything. I, of course, am a burden they bear very well."

"Thank you, sir," I said.

"Yes, thank you," Lily said.

"Hawkins," Mr. Twain said, "I heard a story years ago about a Captain Hawkins who left a thief standing in his underclothes on an island in the Cumberland."

"That's Captain Will Hawkins," I said, "he's our father. Ben and I were on the packet *George Hawkins* when Will walked that man down the stage and left him on Dover Island."

"You're rivermen!" Mr. Twain said, "I knew it the minute you walked in the door. You know, it's true. It's a small world, and it's shrinking a little more every day."

"I've read all your books since *Roughing It*," I said.

"Well, you don't look any the worse for it," Mr. Twain said. "Any internal afflictions I can't see?"

"No, not at all," I replied. "I'm much the better for it, and that's not even counting the laughter."

We spoke a few minutes longer with Mr. Twain, thanked him and bade him goodbye. Hearing his lecture and meeting him were the highlights of our stay in San Francisco.

55

In November '86, we had an excited letter from Amanda. Two weeks before, she had attended the unveiling of the Statue of Liberty in New York Harbor. If that wasn't grand enough, she had met and been very impressed by Antoine Bouchard, a member of the French diplomatic delegation. He asked permission to call on her at Vassar and she consented.

When Lily and I were first married, we had to live apart. Bart needed her on their ranch in Wyoming, and Will needed me on our farm in Idaho. It took a natural disaster to bring us together.

With declining prices and tightening credit already hurting Cheyenne cattlemen in the winter of '86-'87, severe weather dealt a death blow to many. Cattle couldn't get at the grass on much of the range due to heavy snow and long, bitter cold. In January, a freak chinook wind melted the snow so rapidly that the meadows and valleys where most of the grass lay became swamps and shallow lakes in a day or two. Deep cold, heavy snow and biting winds returned immediately, locking the grass under a shield of ice that the starving herds couldn't penetrate. Cattle died by the thousands, breaking many ranchers. Bart sold their spread and moved into town, where he became a wholesale merchant. Lily came to live at the homeplace in early spring.

Billy and Annie had the second house, so until we could build another for Lily and me, she and I would live with Will and Beth in the main house. We could start plans for the third house right away, but building it would have to wait till the crops were in and we had a little time on our hands.

In mid-May, Henry Schodde stopped at the homeplace on his

way to the Raft River on cattle business. He said he had brought a fine stallion up from Nevada and asked if we had mares we wanted to get in foal. Lily asked Beth about our maiden mare. Beth replied that the timing was perfect. The mare was of age and due to come into season in about a week. If the breeding took, the mare would foal next April, Beth said. Henry added that he had kept the stallion on oats, bran and hay, plus fresh-cut young grass, clover and lucerne since April to better his chances in the breeding months.

Beth suggested that she and Lily take the mare to the Schoddes' place, and asked if Will and I could get along without our women for a few days. We replied that we thought we could. Will asked if they were sure they could handle a maiden mare with a stallion. Beth and Lily said they could, especially with Henry there to help.

I took Beth and Lily across on the ferry just after sunup two days later. They rode downriver on the south side, trailing the maiden mare behind, then crossed to the Schoddes' north-side ranch on Starrh's Ferry. This is what Lily told me about what happened at the Schoddes':

The stallion was a fine-looking chestnut. He hadn't covered a maiden mare before. He had sired many good offspring but only with brood mares. Henry kept the stallion alone in a corral apart from the intended mare. He tested each mare until she showed she was ready, then led the stallion to her.

When Beth and Lily felt our mare was fully in season, Henry led the stallion nearby and within her sight. She seemed a little fidgety, but that was to be expected from a maiden. She showed no sign of refusing the stallion, so Henry led him away, and Beth and Lily prepared the mare and her corral for servicing. Lily stood at the mare's head, holding it a little high to prevent her from kicking, if she had that notion. Beth stood beside her hindquarters, out of her kicking line. Henry led the stallion into the corral through a gate opposite the mare's head, plainly within her sight. She showed no outward objection, so Henry circled to her quarters near Beth. The stallion curled his lip and smelled the air. He seemed eager to mount the mare.

In an instant, the mare dropped her head, turned her quarters toward the stallion and kicked, catching everyone by surprise and knocking Beth to the ground. As Beth rose to her feet and

Lily struggled to calm the now frantic mare, the stallion reeled around, nearly lifting Henry into the air, and kicked violently at the mare. A hoof caught Beth in her right temple, splitting her head open and knocking her to the ground. Her blood poured into the dust as Lily and Henry fought to settle the horses. Lily got to the gate, led the mare out, and Henry followed with the stallion. They ran to Beth, who lay unconscious in the dirt. She didn't respond. Henry wrapped his and Lily's bandanas around Beth's head, and they carried her to the house.

Minnie put her youngest in his crib and quickly shooed her other two children outside. Henry and Lily lay Beth on the big bed. Minnie came with a pan of water, and they tried to stop Beth's bleeding. They struggled, but it was no use. Beth's irises didn't respond to the light. She was dead. Minnie was overcome with grief. Henry held her as they both sobbed. Henry reached out to Lily, who stood trembling at the bedside.

"Come with me, please, if you can," he said. He took two pistols from a cupboard near the door and walked to the corrals with Lily. He handed her a pistol as they approached the mare and stallion. The horses stood calmly apart from each other in separate corrals.

"We cannot have these reminders," he said as he entered the stallion's corral. Lily had seen instant justice before and knew what Henry meant to do. Her face was wet with tears, and she was still trembling. She entered the mare's corral. She watched Henry for the timing. Two head shots rang out, and the horses fell to the ground, dead.

"I will butcher them later for the coyotes and buzzards," Henry said. "For now, we will take care of Beth and Minnie." As they turned to go back to the house, Lily saw Henry's elder son and daughter standing outside the corrals, staring wide-eyed through the rails.

Lily and Minnie sobbed as they cleaned Beth's wound, smoothed her hair and brushed the dust from her clothes. They straightened her body on the bed and covered it with a muslin sheet.

"What will I tell Will and Early?" Lily asked.

"You can only say what happened," Minnie replied. "It's a tragedy."

"I will build a coffin," Henry said, "and in the morning we

will drive her home in my wagon."

They reached the south-side landing in late afternoon. That morning, Billy and Annie had driven to Albion, and I had brought the ferry back to the north side. Will and I had spent the day sowing seed in the fields and were still there when Henry's wagon reached the landing. Henry swam Lily's horse over and brought the ferry back. They crossed with the wagon and team, and tied the horses to the corral rails up from the north-side landing. The coffin lay lengthwise in the wagon bed. They walked to the porch, and Lily rang the bell, fast and hard.

Will and I heard the alarm and knew from its urgency that something was very wrong. We vaulted into the wagon and drove hard for the homeplace. We saw Henry and Lily from a distance, walking toward us. I brought the team to a halt, we jumped to the ground, and rushed to Lily and Henry. Lily was crying uncontrollably and Henry looked grave. I held Lily, and she buried her face in my shoulder.

"What is it, Lily?" I asked.

"There's terrible news," she sobbed. Will and Henry stood by helplessly. There was an air of gloom.

"My stallion kicked Beth in the head," Henry said. "She is dead. I am very, very sorry. It's my fault. I am very sorry."

Will and I stood shocked in disbelief. The grief hit me with the weight of an anvil. Will looked as if he collapsed into himself. I held Lily in one arm and reached for Will with the other. We stood like three slumping pillars, holding onto each other and weeping. Will let go his grip and turned to Henry.

"Don't blame yourself, Henry," he said. "Horses are unpredictable, stallions more so. Just when we think they're ours, we learn they're not. Where is Beth now?"

"She's in a pine box on my wagon at your corral," Henry replied.

"Let's go to her and choose a place for a grave," Will said.

Henry's team stood in the cottonwood's afternoon shade, flicking their ears and swishing their tails to unsettle the flies. The breeze flipped a few cottonwood leaves here and there. Sunlight dappled the pine box when a gust opened the crown. Eddies gurgled as the river flowed across the landing, unaware of our grief.

"She loved her garden," Will said. "Let's place her at its edge, within sight of the house."

I went to the shed beside the barn and returned with two long-handled shovels. Henry, Will and I dug for nearly an hour, taking turns. Lily sat at the landing, silently watching the river. The four of us carried the pine box to the grave. Will loosened the lid. I couldn't bear to look. I turned Lily away. Will leaned in and whispered, "Goodbye, my love, rest in peace." Will nailed the lid, and we lowered the box into the ground. Will gently spread the first shovelful of dirt on top. We filled the grave and tamped the covering earth firmly. We spread the remaining dirt around the site.

"I'll cut a headstone," Will said.

"I'll ride to Minidoka and send wires to Ben and Maria, to Amanda, and to Louis and Sally," I said.

"I'm so very sorry," Henry said.

"Thank you, Henry," Will said.

"Let's go to the house. We should have supper," Lily whispered.

That supper was the saddest meal I've ever had. My mind was on Beth, and I wondered what Will would do. I wondered what we all would do.

After the meal, I saddled Spirit and rode to Minidoka to send the wires. When I returned, Billy and Annie were there, kneeling at the grave, holding each other and weeping. I knelt with them and was overcome with grief.

Amanda went to Smithland and came west with Louis and Sally. Brad was sick in San Francisco, so Maria stayed with him, but Ben came to the homeplace. The tragedy brought us all together for the first time since Will, Ben and I left Smithland 15 years before. The family had a lot of catching up to do.

Henry, Minnie and their children came from Goose Creek, and many friends came from Albion, Minidoka and the Raft River. We gathered at the grave. Will, Amanda and I took turns reading lines from Percy Bysshe Shelley, Beth's favorite poet. As we read, one of the barn cats, white and just past being a kitten, wove in and out of the legs of the people assembled, rubbing each ankle as she went. A meadowlark had perched in the garden nearby. Its eager, flutelike song seemed to say, be hopeful, continue. Ben sang a requiem in Latin. Even the cowboys wept.

Ben left for San Francisco and Louis and Sally for Smithland after a day or two. Amanda would be with us for the summer. Will, Billy and I got back to tending to the farm and beasts, and the women to the houses and garden. We took things day by day.

Will immersed himself in work. He was busy from sunup till sundown and often beyond that. As always, he was strong. But every so often, he stopped because something had reminded him. He looked wistful for a few moments, and a tear glistened in his eye, or a slight smile crossed his lips. He didn't seem to be aware of leaving us momentarily, of losing focus. In a few seconds, he resumed whatever he was doing, as if he hadn't been away.

Jumping ahead in the timeline about three years: If things weren't especially busy, Will started riding to Minidoka every so often and being away for a few days. I suspected he had a woman friend there, but then one day I saw his horse in the livery. So wherever he was, he must have gone by train. Maybe he was in Shoshone or Hailey or Pocatello. I never asked, he didn't say, and if it was a woman, he never brought her to the homeplace.

Returning to the timeline: When the crops were in, we started on the third house. The site was up along the bench within shouting distance of Billy and Annie's place. The new house was very nearly a duplicate of theirs. We brought the materials from Minidoka and had it up in three weeks. When we finished, Will announced the third house would be his, that Lily and I would have the main house. We protested, but Will's mind was made up. Amanda asked if she could live in the new house with him until she had to return to Vassar. Will looked at her with a mixture of deep love and great sadness. After a long silence, he consented.

That July, it was 1887, on a Sunday evening after we had all gathered for supper at the main house, Lily told us she was quite sure she was pregnant. There are but a few moments in a man's life that touch him at his core. From May to July, I had two of those moments. A life had ended, and a new one was stirring in Lily's womb.

56

Our first child came with the onset of spring on the evening of Monday, March 19, 1888. About two weeks earlier, when Lily felt the time was near, she had me build what she called a "birthing chair." It looked like a high-backed chair missing a seat. Its sturdy arms were fastened to a slanted back and supported by uprights.

Delivering a baby was no mystery to Lily. As a girl, she had been present with her mother at several cousins' and neighboring children's births. She had seen the birthing chair at some of the births she witnessed, knew it worked well for at least those women and wanted it for her first delivery.

Lily's contractions began before dawn that Monday morning. They were mild and followed no regular schedule. She didn't wake me. She rotated from lying on her back in bed, to walking barefooted through the house, to using the chamber pot. When I awoke, she was already in the kitchen preparing breakfast. She said nothing about the contractions, knowing many hours would pass before they got serious and regular, and the baby was ready to leave her womb.

Annie was coming early that morning to work with Lily at our house. Annie's mother was a midwife, and Annie was close to being one herself. With Annie's and her own experience, Lily had decided without telling me that I wouldn't be needed till much later. She packed a lunch for Will and me and shooed me out of the house, knowing I had spring plowing and sowing to do.

A light rain had moistened the ground, and the weather was mild. Conditions were ideal for turning the soil and sowing seed. Working with separate teams for the sulky plow and the harrow and corrugator, the three of us set nearly 10 acres to wheat and had the new seed irrigated before sundown.

When we returned to the barn, Will and Billy began stowing the equipment, hanging the harness and seeing to the mules, while I went to the house to check on Lily and Annie. The sun had set and I felt the evening chill coming on as I mounted the stairs to the porch. Inside, lanterns lit the rooms, a fire glowed across the hearth, and a large pot of stew simmered on the woodstove. I didn't see the women in the kitchen or front room, so I called for Lily from just inside the door. Annie's voice came from the direction of the bedrooms, "In here, Early."

I walked to Lily's and my bedroom where I found Annie sitting in the corner chair and Lily pacing back and forth across the floor at the foot of our bed. Her belly was enormous.

"She's in late labor, between contractions," Annie said. "Everything's fine. She's almost full open. It won't be long now." Lily turned and walked to me.

"You'll be a proud papa soon," she said as she took my hands and kissed my cheek. Just then, the next contraction came. Lily winced in pain and buckled slightly at the knees. I grasped her hands to support her.

"Should you lie down?" I asked urgently. She couldn't answer as the pain coursed through her. I moved around behind her, where I could stand closer and support her under her arms.

"I'm ready to crouch," she said as her breath returned. "I'm ready to push."

I helped Lily to the birthing chair. She backed into it, crouched and supported herself by placing her arms over its arms. Her water burst immediately into the pan between her feet.

Annie slid a large pan of warm water nearby. The next contraction came and Lily clenched her jaw and pushed. Beads of sweat came to her brow. There was a brief period of relief. She reached down and felt the crown of the baby's head beginning to emerge.

"He's coming with the next push," Lily said. "Catch him, Early."

I crouched in front of Lily and looked into her eyes. I saw love and determination and a kind of pleasure. The next contraction came. She closed her eyes, clenched her jaw, moaned and pushed. I got to my knees and extended my hands below Lily. There was a quaking and a swoosh, and suddenly I held our firstborn son in my hands. For a moment, I was overcome. It seemed so vividly real, yet I thought I must be dreaming. Tears streamed down my face, and a huge smile of wonder spread my lips. This is so impossibly miraculous I thought as I beheld him.

"It's a boy, Lily," I said, "you were right, it's a boy." He snorted and gasped and let out a piercing cry. I thought I had never heard such a beautiful sound.

Annie came with a length of string and tied the cord. She handed me scissors and pointed out where to cut. I snipped the cord and little lines of blood came to the severed ends.

I bathed our son in the warm water, gently stroking him clean. The water calmed his cries. Annie handed me several layers of clean muslin to wrap him. I looked at Lily. Minutes had passed, but she had barely moved. She looked at once relieved and overjoyed. A few moments later, she delivered the placenta. We let it lie where it fell. Annie helped Lily up and to the bed. I brought our son to her and laid him on her breast. She looked upon him with great adoration as he returned her gaze. She offered her nipple, and he suckled. Lily smiled a smile of pride and contentment.

I had helped birth I don't know how many foals, calves, little pigs and puppies, but nothing compared to this. I was overwhelmed and, as Lily had said, a very proud papa. We named him Thomas.

Shortly after Thomas' birth, George Montgomery and his stepson, Andy Smith, came up from Albion to build a ferry across the Snake River. They looked at our ferry and J. J. Story's and asked us what problems we had. Ours wasn't a public ferry but Uncle Jimmy's was, so he wasn't eager to reveal information that would help the new ferry compete with his. We talked freely about the main problem we had had since building the ferry at our homeplace. Story, and for that matter, the Starrh brothers, had the same problem.

The three ferries were propelled by the current and crossed the river in a north-south direction. That meant there were many days when the prevailing west wind was strong enough to stop the ferry or slow it to less than a crawl. The wind hit the ferry broadside and canceled the effect of the current. There was nothing we, Story or the Starrhs could do but wait till the wind died down.

George and Andy chose a spot where the river bent sharply south. That meant their ferry crossed in an east-west direction. A strong west wind hit the head of the ferry when it moved west and its tail when it moved east. As a headwind, a blow from the west hit a much narrower breadth of the ferry. It slowed the boat, but didn't stop it. As a tailwind, it sped the ferry up.

Story's Ferry was about a mile below Minidoka Rapids, while George and Andy built theirs about five miles farther down. The distance to both Albion and Minidoka from either was nearly the same. But because stage drivers and freighters could cross at almost any time regardless of the wind, they favored Montgomery's Ferry. And then George, his wife, Alice, and their boy, Andy, were unusually hospitable people, so that added to their advantage.

Andy was easily six feet tall and had a big, open face and manner. Although he was 18 and 10 years my junior when he first came to the river, he and I became fast friends.

For the first several years of the Montgomery Ferry, George and Andy traded jobs back and forth. One operated the ferry while the other drove stage and ran freight between Minidoka and Albion, then they switched.

In winter, when thick ice covered the river and the ferry couldn't run, the family retreated to Albion. They drove stage and carried freight when there was business, but they didn't live at the ferry landing till spring returned and the ice broke up.

Amanda graduated from Vassar in June 1888. We were too busy farming to attend the ceremony, but Louis, Sally and Antoine were there. Antoine had been courting Amanda since they met nearly two years earlier. On her graduation day, he proposed marriage and Amanda accepted. Since they would be living in France after their wedding day, Amanda suggested that their marriage ceremony ought to be held at the homeplace in Idaho. Of course, Antoine agreed.

Now, we were simple people in Idaho, but we weren't ignorant. We read and kept up with events, but, after all, we were farmers. Antoine and his kin were a family of diplomats. They were used to riding in fine carriages on the streets of Paris, New York and Washington. The fanciest thing Lily and I had ever done was honeymooned in San Francisco. So the sight of Antoine, his parents and his sisters dressed in their finery bouncing along in farm wagons from the Minidoka depot to the homeplace was something to behold.

But they never looked down their noses at us. They put up a very good effort to fit into our way of life at the homeplace. We fixed up the main house and the cabins as best we could to make our guests comfortable.

The wedding was a beautiful affair. Of course, the Bouchard family's clothes were a cut above whatever Amanda's wedding party, Judge Rogers and our guests could muster. But that didn't matter. It was an outdoor ceremony conducted just up from the landing. The river, the bluff that led to the cave, the rushing cottonwood, the corral and the green kitchen garden formed a frame that enclosed the wedding scene. Billy and I had built a bower and a small platform where the ceremony was performed. Antoine's father was his best man, and Maggie Weatherman was Amanda's maid of honor.

Will looked very dignified. But his pride and joy were colored with more than a trace of sadness. It had been just a year since Beth's death, and here was Will giving away his daughter, a beautiful young woman who was the spitting image of her late mother. There wasn't a dry eye in the audience as Judge Rogers read his words, and the bride and groom recited their vows. I stood beside Lily, touching shoulders and arms. I was recalling our wedding, and I know she was too.

We had cleared out the large front room in the main house for the reception. The music and dancing were wonderful, if diminished a little by Ben and Maria's not being on hand to perform. They were touring with a show and couldn't attend.

When we waved goodbye to Amanda and Antoine at the depot, we knew it would be a long time before we would see them again. They were going off to live in France. They would be coming to America on diplomatic visits, but our getting to Washington or New York when they were there or their getting to Idaho would be difficult. We hoped for the best.

In the 1888 presidential race, seven men rose to challenge the incumbent, Grover Cleveland. The campaign centered mainly on import tariffs. Cleveland, a Democrat, wanted to reduce them, saying high tariffs discouraged trade and caused prices to rise. His Republican challenger, Benjamin Harrison, influenced by American industrialists, advocated protectionism and still higher tariffs. Although Cleveland won the popular vote by nearly 100,000 ballots, Harrison won the electoral vote with 233 to Cleveland's 168 and, thus, the presidency.

In early fall, a few weeks before the November election, a group from Albion rode up the mountain we called Will Peak to camp at the lake near the summit. They had a lively discussion about naming the mountain and lake. When they returned to town, they suggested the mountain be named for the winner of the election and the lake near its peak for the second-place finisher. The idea caught on, so when the election results were known, Will Peak became known as Mount Harrison, and the lake became known as Lake Cleveland.

The area that eventually was named for Bannack Chief Pocatello became a crossroads when Fort Hall was founded in 1834. Early explorers' and trappers' routes, then emigrant trails, then stage and freight lines came from the east or south to cross the Snake River and go north, or parallel it and go west.

When Fort Hall Indian Reservation was set aside in 1868, whites were expelled and white immigration to that area stopped. But Chief Pocatello granted a railroad right-of-way and a town-site in the early 1880s. That led to further reduction of Indian lands and growth of a town that was incorporated as the city of Pocatello on April 29, 1889. If we boarded the eastbound after-noon train at Minidoka, we could be in Pocatello before nightfall.

On July 3, 1890, Idaho became the 43rd state. There were celebrations in Minidoka and Albion. We chose Albion because, as the bigger town and the county seat, its celebration was bound to be more exciting. And it was. There was a grand parade fea-turing the Albion Civic Band and 13 girls on horseback, each representing one of the original states. Andy Smith played flugelhorn in the band. As he marched by, he turned his head toward us and winked, not missing a note. Fanny Cubine, the girl Andy later married, paraded on a white horse. She and her mount represented Virginia, the state where she was born. A dance followed the parade. We had a wonderful time.

Everyone we knew felt that as a territory our interests weren't being served by the federal government as well as they should be, and we lacked the privileges and power of the states. We welcomed statehood and the bigger voice that went with it.

57

I had a letter from Hart Merriam in early June 1890. He said he had organized a biological survey expedition to Idaho that would begin in July. He planned to send three men ahead to outfit the expedition and begin the field work. He would join them in August. It looked as if the group's itinerary would have them passing through Shoshone on their way to the falls in early October, but he couldn't give an exact date.

Hart wanted us to meet and asked me to telegraph and let him know if a short visit would be all right. I immediately wired him from Minidoka, suggesting that he could ride the Oregon Short Line cars from Shoshone to the Minidoka depot, where I would meet him. After his visit, I would deposit him at the

depot for his return to Shoshone. He responded that he would
let me know a date by wire as soon as he could. He added that
he was looking forward to visiting our farm and meeting the
Hawkins family.

Hart came from Shoshone on the afternoon train on October
8th. Meeting a man for the first time after corresponding with
him for years is an odd thing. I had built an image of him and
had certain expectations. I'm sure he had done the same with
me. And although we had exchanged family photographs the
year before, and I had some idea of what to expect, a man in the
flesh is very different from a man on paper.

Hart was several inches shorter and larger in girth than I
was. He wasn't fat but what people called "stocky." Unlike his
photograph, where he had only a moustache, he now sported
a full beard. He explained he shaved only when his wife was
along. His canvas trousers were tucked inside high snake boots.
He wore a loose wool jacket over a muslin shirt. A fedora contained his tightly curly hair. He wore spectacles and carried a
canvas duffel and a rifle case.

He recognized me right away, giving me a hearty greeting.
He was warm and eager from the start. He stood on the depot
platform and drew a deep breath as he surveyed the Plain.

"Beautiful country, Early," he said. "I can't tell you how good
it feels to be in Idaho after being cooped up in Washington so long.
Is this your wagon here? Let's jump in and get down to the river."

As we drove, I pointed out the mountains to the south. Hart
spotted several birds, including a magpie.

"You know," he said, "people say magpies prey on mourning
dove eggs and nestlings, but it's not true. My colleague, A. K.
Fisher, studied both species in the field and found no predation
at all." Hart leaned over the side to inspect the ground as we
rolled along.

"Stop! Early, please stop!" he suddenly urged. I pulled back
on the reins and yelled "Whoa!" to the team. Hart was on the
ground before the wagon came to a halt. He kneeled to inspect
something in the dirt, then stood, unfastened his trousers and
began to urinate on whatever he had seen.

"Damn velvet ant," he said with contempt. "One of those
damn cowkillers bit me once, and I've been punishing them ever

since. The bite hurt more than anything I've ever felt."

We saw a narrow plume of woodsmoke rising and bending east before the homeplace came into view. From the next rise, the poplar windbreak, the houses and barn, the orchard, the pastures, the newly cut fields, the cottonwood, and the river spread out before us in the late afternoon light. The trees were dressed in their fall coats.

"Now, there's a pretty sight," Hart said, "you and your family should be very proud, Early."

"Thank you, Hart," I replied, "we like it here."

Will and Billy were hoisting hay into the mow as we drove up. They stopped their work and walked to our wagon as Hart and I stepped down.

"Dr. Merriam," Will said as he extended his hand, "I'm Will Hawkins, Early's father. Welcome to the Hawkins place. And please say hello to Billy Latham, the best hired hand in Idaho." I thought I saw Billy blush a little under his weathered skin.

Hart was not a shy and retiring man. As I unhitched the team and walked them to the barn, Hart jumped right into an animated conversation with Will and Billy. They were still at it when I returned.

"Let's go in to meet the womenfolk and see what's for supper," I said. I picked up Hart's duffel, he grabbed his rifle case, and the four of us walked toward the house.

The wonderful aroma of freshly baked bread greeted us as I opened the door. Lily and Annie had six adult places set at the table. The seventh was a child's place for Tommy. It had a riser seat and was between Lily's place and mine. Tommy played with toys on the hearth, while Lily and Annie were busy with last minute fixings in the kitchen. They turned away from the cookstove and came to the door as we stepped in.

"Lily Hawkins and Annie Latham," I said, "I would like you to meet Dr. C. Hart Merriam."

"I am very pleased to meet you," Hart said, "but please, ladies, please call me 'Hart.'"

"Why certainly, Hart," Lily said, "and please call me Lily."

"And me, Annie," Annie said, "I ain't one for puttin' on no airs."

Hart tossed his head back and laughed heartily at Annie's request.

"Well, Lily," Hart said, "excuse me for making a professional observation upon just meeting you, but it looks as if you're very well along."

"Why, yes, I am," Lily said, "I expect it will be another week, two at the most. Perhaps you would like to stay and assist with the delivery, doctor?"

"I'm afraid I'm due back in Shoshone day after tomorrow," Hart said, "and then I'm to catch up with my men. They're on their way to the falls. Do you have help nearby, Lily?"

"I delivered Tommy, my first, here at home 2-1/2 years ago with Early's and Annie's help," Lily said. "That went well, and I expect this one will too. We're hoping for a girl."

"You women are so strong," Hart said. "I'm always impressed. If we men had the babies, the population would plummet." We all nodded and chuckled in agreement.

"Supper is nearly ready to serve," Lily said. "Do you men want to wash up before we sit?"

"Sure," I replied, "we can use the pump outside, then we'll fill our bellies. Maybe Hart can tell us about his survey so far."

"I'd be happy to," Hart said, "but I don't want to bore you with biology."

Supper was beef from a steer Billy had butchered about a week before, plus green beans, carrots and potatoes from the kitchen garden. Just-churned butter on warm, freshly baked bread rounded out the meal. Our orchard apples and flour milled from wheat grown in our fields went into the dessert pie. We had produced everything that was on the table and in our bellies. That was satisfying to know.

Whenever Will ate with Lily, Tommy and me, we sat him at the head of the table. It was his rightful place, and where he sat that night. Conversation flowed freely as we ate. Hart spoke of the collecting he and his men had done so far in Idaho and what they planned for the 10 days or so before the expedition disbanded in Humboldt Wells, Nevada.

Will recalled meeting William Henry Jackson, who was on his way to join the '72 Hayden Expedition to Yellowstone, and how coincidental it was that Hart was on that very same trip. Now, here we were 18 years later enjoying supper with Hart on the Idaho homestead we had come so far to build.

Yes, Hart added, who could ever have predicted that 16-year-old boy would become a physician and go on to head the Bureau of Biological Survey at the United States Department of Agriculture? Life's turns sometimes amaze the mind, he said.

I continued the thought by noting that it's a long way from steamboats on the Cumberland to buckboards on the Snake River Plain. Or, Lily added, from Boston parlors to Wyoming cattle range to an irrigated farm on the sagebrush desert.

"I believe I'm ready for 'nother slice of that apple pie," Billy said. There was agreement all around.

The conversation turned to what we would do the following day, the only full day Hart would be with us. He said he would like to take a break from collecting, but if I wanted to show him the farm and walk the riverbank with him, he would be very happy to observe and make notes.

"I notice you have Winchesters on your gun rack there," Hart said. "I have a Remington, do you like to shoot, Early?"

"Why, yes, I do," I replied. "I hunt mule deer and an occasional pronghorn here on the Plain."

I saw a sly little smile cross Will's lips. I knew he thought Hart was challenging me to a shooting contest, and I knew he thought Hart didn't have a chance.

"Well, you know," Hart said, "I'm a fair marksman. Good enough that my neighbors banned me from the Locust Grove turkey shoots near my father's house in upstate New York. Maybe we can fire a few rounds together tomorrow."

"Are you a betting man, Hart?" Will asked.

"Well, yes," Hart replied, "I've been known to place a wager now and then. Are you that confident in Early's eye, Will?"

"Early's getting a bit old to split a cornstalk at 50 yards," Will said, "but I think he's still got a good shot or two in him."

Old? I thought to myself. What's Will talking about? I just passed 30. Will is setting Hart up, I knew. Will and I exchanged knowing smiles. We'd have some fun the next day, and we knew that when Hart lost the wager, we wouldn't take his money. We'd just give him a drubbing and a ribbing.

If I described Hart in one word, it would be "enthusiastic." From the moment his feet hit the floor in the morning, he radiated energy. He applied his enthusiasm to everything and swept people up in the excitement. Until I met Hart, it was hard to imagine anybody getting excited about common, everyday things. When I saw him enthuse about the bacon, eggs and warm bread Lily served for breakfast, I knew the day ahead would be different.

I took the day off to be with Hart, while Will and Billy gathered hay from the windrows. Hart challenged me to a shooting contest first thing, but I begged off, suggesting we wait till the sun was higher, the light brighter, and Will and Billy were in for their noon meal.

I wanted to show Hart the whole place and the stretch of river down to the rapids. We mounted and rode the bluff road upriver toward our eastern fence line. As we rode, I pointed out the kitchen garden, barn, night pasture, orchard and houses on the river side, and the pastures and fields on the inland side. I told Hart about living in the cave when we first came, about how we grubbed sage and, over time, dug the ditches, built the houses and barn, planted the windbreak and orchard, and cleared the whole homestead for crops, pasture and living space.

Hart and I noted that in the 18 years since we began corresponding, he had gone to Yale and medical college, and had become a physician and then a renowned naturalist, while my family had started on wild land and created a working farm that supported three Hawkins generations and two hired hands. Our achievements were very different, but both were praiseworthy.

The brisk east wind carried the sweet smell of newly cut hay. As we neared the fence line, we saw Will and Billy, with the wagon and mules, off in the northeast hayfield. They were out just about as far as they could work and still be on our property.

As we turned at the fence to ride west, Hart asked what wild mammals we saw regularly. I told him about the mule deer that came from the Sawtooth Mountains to winter on the Plain, the pronghorns and badgers we occasionally saw, and the rabbits and coyotes that were common. I said the hawks liked the mice and voles, especially when the harvest drove them out of our fields.

We rode on past the barn and main house, and down the mill road toward the rapids. Hart asked how I felt about Idaho recently becoming a state. I replied that it had been a long wait and that we were glad to have a bigger voice in regional and national affairs. Our first chance to vote would be two years ahead in the 1892 presidential election.

I showed Hart the mill and credited Louis with its design and construction. It had been serving us faithfully since we built it in '73. We rode past the rapids to Story Ferry, where we visited for a bit with Uncle Jimmy. He had a long wait between crossings and was happy to have the company. He showed us his new Winchester rifle, which got Hart thinking we ought to get back for our shooting contest and noon meal.

Will and Billy were already at the house when Hart and I rode up, and Lily and Annie had the meal spread out across the table. I knew Will had some mischief up his sleeve when he turned the conversation to shooting and asked Hart what he was willing to wager. Hart was confident, almost cocky. He said he had $100 in his purse, and if that wasn't enough, he would put up his rifle itself. Will replied that $100 was plenty, that he wasn't inclined to strip a man of his rifle. Hart was eager to finish the meal and start shooting.

We cut a dozen cornstalks from the garden and walked a safe distance down from the house along the riverbank. We chose an open spot and planted the stalks about three feet apart in the mud along the bank. We paced upland about 50 yards and scored a line in the earth. We agreed to shoot without braces and either standing or from one knee, whichever was the shooter's preference. We flipped a coin to decide who would shoot first and at which stalks. Hart won the toss and chose the six upriver targets.

He loaded his Remington deliberately, dropped to one knee and took his aim. His first shot missed the easternmost stalk altogether. I also shot from one knee. My first ball nicked the westernmost stalk, but it stayed upright. Will stood silently behind us, grinning. Hart acknowledged I had the edge. His second shot split the next stalk and sent it into the river. Mine did likewise. Our third shots both missed their marks. His fourth shattered its target, while mine uprooted the stalk and sent it into the river nearly whole. He nicked his next, and I missed mine.

We were neck and neck; the sixth shot would decide the contest. Will was still grinning. He knew I had purposely missed my fifth shot to build the suspense. Hart's last shot clipped the stalk about midway up its height. The top half fell but stayed attached, as if on a hinge. I cleared my throat and carefully took my aim. I fired and watched the sixth stalk explode and sail into the river in pieces.

Hart looked momentarily stunned. Will and Billy cheered, Billy danced a little jig, and Will slapped me on the back with hearty congratulations. Hart extended his hand and said, "Nice shooting." He reached for his purse, but Will stopped him.

"Naw, Dr. Merriam," he said, "we were just joshing you. We don't want your money. It was all in good fun. Early's been the best shot in two states since he was 10. He's never been beat. But you're welcome to try anytime."

Hart had a good laugh. He was a good sport about it all, even if a little embarrassed. Will and Billy excused themselves and headed back to the far eastern field to gather another wagonload of hay. Hart and I walked farther upland, looking for rabbits for supper. We had promised Lily and Annie a few cottontails.

We had bagged three and were probably about a mile out when we heard the bell urgently ringing. The rings were rapid and very strong.

"That's for us, Hart," I said. "There's trouble at home, and I doubt Will and Billy can hear. The east wind's bringing the bell to us and keeping it from them."

We took off running as fast as we could. I wished Spirit was with me. I needed his speed. My longer legs got me out ahead of Hart. I reached the porch probably a full minute ahead of him. Annie was frantically ringing the bell. I bounded up the stairs.

"What is it, Annie? What's the matter?" I shouted above the ringing. She stopped but the tone lingered.

"It's Lily!" she screamed. "She's in awful pain! It's the baby!"

I stepped to the edge of the porch and looked west for Hart. There was no sign of him.

"OK, Annie," I said, "Hart's on his way. You and Lily and I have done this before, and we can do it again. Let's see what we can do to help Lily."

"No, Early," Annie said, "This is different. There's no head. Lily is opening, but the baby's head isn't there."

I had helped enough cows and horses and dogs to know what was going on. The baby was in the breech position. This was dangerous. I looked again for Hart. No sign. I gave the bell a few more loud, rapid claps and rushed inside to Lily with Annie.

The birthing chair stood nearby, but Lily was on our bed with her skirts up above her waist and obviously in great pain. I went to her while Annie went for a pan of water. Just then I heard Hart's steps on the stairs.

"In here, Hart," I shouted, "in the front bedroom! It's Lily, it's the baby!" He burst into the room, sweating, trying to catch his breath, and already stripping his jacket off and rolling his sleeves.

"Water! Hot water, Annie!" he shouted, "and muslin, clean muslin cloth. Remove her clothing, Early, this is no time for modesty."

"I think it's breech," I said.

"You're probably right," he said as he moved his hand across Lily's lower belly, pressing gently as he went. Lily said nothing. She winced and groaned in pain. Sweat poured out of her, and I could see the pain in her eyes,

"You'll be all right," I said. "Dr. Merriam, Annie and I are here. You and the baby will be all right." Lily arched her back, raised her hips and drove her shoulders into the bedstraw mattress. She clenched her teeth and groaned in pain.

"Early," Hart said, "get my bag. I have ether there. Bring it and a clean towel. And if you have whiskey, bring it."

I passed Annie on my way out. I heard Hart tell her to leave the water and bring another pan, as hot as she could make it. When I returned with the bag and whiskey, Lily looked calmer. She was talking.

"That wave passed," she said, "but there will be another soon."

"Lily," Hart said, "I want you to sit up a little and drink as much of this as you can as quickly as you can." He handed her a full glass of whiskey. As she sipped, Hart continued. "Lily, you and the baby will be all right. I want to tell you exactly what we're going to do. I want you to finish that glass and then lie back. I want you to put this towel over your nose and mouth and breathe slowly and deeply. The baby is in the breech position, but I can turn it. You are already fully dilated. I'll reach inside, turn the baby, and you'll deliver it head first. This will be painful, but the ether and whiskey will help. You can do this, and you and the baby will be fine. Are you ready?"

Lily locked her eyes on mine. Beads of sweat dotted her face and involuntary tears spilled from her eyes. I felt immense love and respect for her at that moment. I took the whiskey glass from her, held her close and eased her onto her back. Hart handed me the ether towel, and I held it gently over Lily's nose and mouth. She took slow, deep breaths.

"That should be enough," Hart said. "Keep it ready in case she needs more as I work." Lily drifted into a semi-conscious state. Hart had scrubbed his hands and forearms, and held them in the nearly scalding water Annie had brought. He bent Lily's legs farther at her knees and had me slide a pillow beneath her hips as he raised them. "I know this is tough to watch, Early," he said, "but your wife and I need you here."

Hart gently reached up inside Lily. I saw movement in her lower belly. She groaned in pain. Hart removed his hand, and in a moment I saw the crown of the baby's head.

"It's all right," he said, "the cord is not around the baby's neck. Lily has to push now. Talk to her, Early. Tell her gently that she has to wake up now and push."

Lily was nearly fully conscious when the next wave of labor pains came. She bore down and pushed. I could see the contractions as the baby's head emerged. Lily took short, quick breaths, then a deep, long breath that she held as she pushed. I stroked her head, patted the sweat from her face and spoke to her softly, telling her she was doing fine, and the baby was coming.

"The baby's head is out now," Hart said, "I'm turning the shoulders to ease them out."

Until that moment, it hadn't occurred to me to ask after Tommy. When Annie returned, I did.

"He's asleep in his bed," she said, "I just looked in on him."

"Did you hear that, Lily?" I asked, "You've always said, 'That boy can sleep through anything,' and he has." She smiled a wistful little smile, and I knew everything was going to be all right.

"It's a boy," Hart said, with relief in his voice. The gender didn't matter. We were all relieved that the baby and Lily were all right. Hart cleared the baby's throat and nose, held him up by his ankles and smacked his bottom. We smiled then cheered when he let out a loud cry. Hart tied and cut the cord, and laid the baby on Lily's breast.

I was overcome with emotion at that moment. Tears flowed from my eyes and streamed down my face. My insides felt as if they had become my outsides. I felt profoundly humble. I hugged Lily and the baby and nuzzled against Lily's neck. She smiled and breathed a long, gentle sigh.

"I am so proud of you, love," I whispered, "nothing I've ever done or will ever do can equal what you've just done. I feel so small and so big at the same time. I love you deeply, my Lily." She turned and kissed me gently on the forehead. I felt her hand squeeze my shoulder. We held each other and gazed at our new baby boy.

The afterbirth came. Hart put it in a pan, and Annie carried it outside. It seems crude to say she gave it to the hogs, but that's what she did. Like everything on a farm, it was put to good use.

As Lily rested in bed and nursed the baby, Hart and I cleaned the rabbits and helped Annie prepare the evening meal. Toward sundown, we heard Will's and Billy's voices calling to the team that pulled the hay wagon. Hart and I went out and helped pitch the last load to fill the mow. We said nothing of the baby. We spoke only of the rabbits we had killed and how they would make a fine supper. We washed up at the outside pump and went in.

"Where's Lily?" Will asked when he saw only Annie in the kitchen.

"In here," called Lily from the front bedroom.

We walked to the bedroom. I entered first and went to Lily's side. Tommy was beside her as she lay holding the sleeping baby. Annie followed, then Will, Hart and Billy. I saw the surprise and pride on Will's face. Billy's mouth fell agape and then broke into a broad grin.

"Captain Will Hawkins," Lily said, "I would like you to meet your new grandson, Clinton Hart Hawkins." That Lily had chosen a name was a complete surprise to everyone, including me. And, of course, it was entirely all right. We all smiled, and there were bursts of cheers and applause. Hart blushed through the ruddiness that weeks outdoors had produced.

"Thank you, Hart," I said.

"Yes, thank you, Hart," Lily added, "thank you for our second son."

"You did it, Lily," Hart said, "I just helped a little."

"Without you, Hart," Lily countered, "the baby and I would likely both be in our graves."

At the supper table, Annie, Hart and I recounted the story for Will and Billy how the birth came about. It by no means escaped us how fortunate we were that Dr. Merriam had come when he did.

Hart checked on Lily and the baby before I drove him to the depot to catch the morning train west. Mother and son were doing well, and Hart predicted they would continue to do so. As I stood on the Minidoka depot platform with one hand in my pocket and the other returning Hart's wave as the cars pulled away, I reflected on how utterly astounding the intersection of our lives had been. We would stay in touch but wouldn't see each other again. My last thought as the train and its plume of coal smoke receded into the distance was that even this, one of the most profound, most humbling experiences of my life, was fleeting. But Lily and I would have Clint to remember it by.

58

The United States Geological Survey completed its initial irrigation surveys from Minidoka Rapids west past Schodde Rapids in 1890. George Montgomery was first along the river to know of the surveys and told Henry Schodde, Jimmy Story, the Starrh brothers and us. He suggested we meet at his place at the ferry to talk about the effects, which we did.

We sat in the Montgomerys' front room, where Alice served coffee with slices of chocolate cake she had baked. George had spoken with the surveyors. They said the government was considering sites for irrigation projects. George had had some experience with irrigation projects. He said they mean canals, dams and lakes behind the dams, and that means no more free-flowing river. That means no constant current.

"You know like I do that we all depend on the current," George said. "Without it, ferries don't cross the river, waterwheels and mill wheels don't turn, and gates don't collect water for crops."

"Not only that," I added, "with the news of last year's flood in Johnstown, Pennsylvania, people aren't going to like the idea of a dam."

"George, if the government has decided to build an irrigation project here, what in the world can we do about it?" Tom Starrh asked.

"That's a good question, Tom," George replied. "I suppose we can start by letting the right people know we're against it."

And that's what we did. The men chose me to write a letter telling our objections to any irrigation project along our stretch of the Snake. I wrote three copies, and we all signed them. I sent them to Governor George L. Shoup, Congressman Fred T. Dubois and the Secretary of the Interior John W. Noble. Eventually, we received polite replies from all three men, none took sides on the issue, and that was the last we heard. Nothing came of the irrigation surveys, at least not then.

Summer droughts and severe winters in the late '80s changed the local ranching industry. The open range could no longer support big ranches and large herds. There were more sheep and fewer cattle in eastern Cassia County. The cattle ranches were broken up into smaller spreads running fewer head. Ranchers began grubbing sage, fencing fields, setting up irrigation systems and growing winter feed. Still, they couldn't make the switch quickly enough to support their herds, so they became more dependent on farmers like us. To answer the demand, we cut back our grain acreage and sowed more timothy hay and lucerne.

On a crisp, early spring day in '91, a few days after we had sown our lucerne and hay, I was working with a team and the sulky plow turning the ground in the kitchen garden. Billy followed with another team and the harrow. A west wind kept the dust away from Lily and the boys, who watched from the shade porch. Will had gone to Minidoka.

A stranger approached the south landing from upriver. He rode a big black with a heavy mane and long, full tail. That tail was unusual for a horse in this country. The custom was to thin the tail so it wouldn't gather burs and sage. The rider reined the black to a halt at the landing. He removed his hat and waved it over his head, signaling he wanted to cross. I raised the plow, moved the team to a patch of grass and stepped down. I called to Billy to let his team graze. I went up the cave stairs into the house and returned with a Colt pistol tucked in my waistband. Billy met me at the corral. I asked him to cross with me to meet the stranger. We strode to the landing, untied the ferry and started over. The rider dismounted and stood beside the black, holding a close rein.

As the ferry neared the south landing, I called "Hallo!" The stranger raised his hand in greeting but didn't speak. The black turned skittish, raising his forefeet and tugging at the reins. The stranger calmed him. As Billy and I walked up the landing, I realized our visitor was but a boy, maybe 15 or 16 years of age. He wasn't armed, and he looked a little green. His clothes and boots were near new. I spoke first.

"I'm Early Hawkins and this is Billy Latham. What can we do for you?"

"I'm Eddie Burroughs from the Bar Y on the Raft River. My brothers sent me to see about getting alfalfa from your first cutting," the boy said.

"I guess I'll just have to get used to calling it 'alfalfa'," I said. "It's our habit to call it 'lucerne.' We'll have plenty cut and baled about mid-May."

"Just in time for round-up," Eddie said. "My brothers will like that."

"You're with George and Harry Burroughs and Lew Sweetser at the Bar Y?" I asked. "I didn't know there was a third Burroughs brother. Are you new to the country?"

"Just came from Chicago about two weeks back," he replied. The black snorted and pushed Eddie's shoulder with his nose. The horse had no bit, only a hackamore, with a shoestring for a headstall.

"Your horse looks mighty scarred up," Billy said. The black had spur marks from his mane to his tail.

"No one else can ride Whiskey Jack," Eddie said. "It took me a week of gentling to gain his trust. He's said to have killed a man. Word is he was beaten by a Mexican who owned him. If you treat a horse mean, he'll be mean. Not me, I treat him like a friend."

"Can you lead him onto the ferry?" I asked. "It's near dinner time, and my wife will be happy to set another place."

"Sure I can," he replied. "And thanks for the invitation. I'm so hungry I could eat a . . . " Eddie grinned and stopped himself. "Well, let's just say I'm real hungry." We crossed and Billy and I unhitched the teams and turned them out to graze. Whiskey Jack would spend our dinner hour alone in the corral.

As we entered the house, Tommy came running across the room squealing "Papa! Papa!" He ran straight for my legs, wrapped his arms around them and hung on for dear life. I bent down and hoisted him up to eye level.

"Say hello to Billy, Tommy," I said, "then we have a guest I want you to meet."

"Hi, Billy!" Tommy said, almost screaming. Billy playfully stuck his fingers in his ears and mouthed, "Hi, Tommy!" making no sound.

"OK, Tommy, now calm down a little," I said. "This is Eddie. He's from the Bar Y Ranch, and he's here to have dinner with us."

"Oh, goodie!" Tommy exclaimed with slightly less volume than his greeting to Billy. Tommy stretched his arms toward Eddie. I watched for a reaction from Eddie and didn't see him reel back, so I passed Tommy over to him. Just then, Lily and Annie came in from the kitchen.

"Well, I see you've met our bundle of energy," she said, smiling at Eddie. "Our second, Clint, is napping peacefully, but Tommy never seems to tire."

"Lily Hawkins and Annie Latham," I said, "I'd like you to meet Eddie Burroughs from the Bar Y Ranch."

"Hello, Mrs. Hawkins, hello Mrs. Latham," Eddie said, "I'm pleased to make your acquaintance."

"Oh, Eddie," Lily said, "you don't have to be so formal. Call me 'Lily' and call Annie 'Annie.' You're just in time for dinner. If you want to wash up, we'll have the meal on the table in a few minutes."

We sat for dinner and asked Eddie about his trip from Chicago and how things were going on the Bar Y. He said his parents had taken him out of school and sent him west, thinking it would calm his wild streak. As a greenhorn at the ranch, he was taking a lot of ribbing from the veteran cowhands. His brothers had started him out grubbing sage, but he proved to be close to worthless at it, so they made him the mail carrier. He rode the 60-mile round trip to American Falls every day, carrying the mail there and back. If supplies were needed, he drove a team and rig, but most days he rode horseback with leather mailbags strapped behind his saddle. That's how he came to tame Whiskey Jack. The Bar Y cowboys gave him the most ornery horse they had, thinking Eddie would spend more time in the dust than the saddle. They stood bug-eyed when Eddie mounted the black, rode him like a house on fire till he calmed down, then turned him into something like an agreeable pet.

Eddie was a talkative boy with a vivid imagination. He was good dinner company, and we were happy to have him. At the close of the meal, he asked if I had a nib pen, inkwell and paper. I gave him a large, blank sheet and the writing set I used for the record. He sat at the table beside Tommy and proceeded to draw the Hawkins place as seen from the south bank of the river. The cabins were at the far right, then, moving west, were the orchard, night pasture, barnyard, barn, garden, and, atop the cave, the main house. The cottonwood, poplars, corral, ferry and landings completed the scene. Alongside the drawing to the right, Eddie drew our faces, each about the size of a dollar coin. There were Lily and Early, Billy and Annie, Tommy, and even our Clint, all smiling. I said Eddie would have to add Will's when they met. At the bottom of the drawing, along the south bank of the river, Eddie wrote "The Hawkins Place."

I watched the drawing evolve with something akin to awe. Even Tommy fell silent. Eddie worked with sure strokes, showing no hesitation and making not one false line. When he finished and held the drawing up for us to see, a chill shot up my spine. For a moment, I was speechless. I'm sure I heard Lily gasp before she moved beside me and grasped my elbow.

"Eddie, I'm beside myself," I finally managed. "I've never seen anything like it. I'll have to make a frame and hang the drawing on our wall."

"Oh, Eddie," Lily added, "it's wonderful. Thank you."

"It's nothing, really," Eddie said, "I love to draw."

"No, please, Eddie," I said, "it's not 'nothing.' It's a very special something that we will cherish. Thank you."

That was the first of many visits from Eddie Burroughs. Will missed him the first time but wouldn't again. Eddie formed a close bond with Tommy. They spent hours together, with Eddie spinning fantastic tales full of grandly named characters off on wonderful adventures and performing heroic deeds. It was as if Eddie held Tommy in a spell. Their visits together were among the few occasions I remember seeing Tommy calm and quiet for any length of time.

Eddie stayed at the Bar Y till soon after he turned 16 years of age in September. His parents called him back to Chicago and school. Years later, he returned to Idaho as a young man. I'll write more about him when I reach that point in the record.

59

Election Day 1892 was the first time we were eligible to vote for president. Lily and I rode to the polls in Minidoka to cast our ballots. As it turned out, we helped Grover Cleveland regain the presidency by voting for James Weaver, the People's Party candidate, thus drawing support from President Harrison. No candidate gained a majority, but Cleveland outpolled Harrison in the electoral college and won.

On the way home, Spirit came up lame. I dismounted and doubled up with Lily for the rest of the ride, trailing Spirit slowly behind. Earlier, I had noticed what looked like swelling around the pastern in his right hind leg. I had stood him in the cold river, and that seemed to help, but it proved brief.

He developed ringbone and in spite of removing his shoes, keeping him from work and turning him out to pasture, the problem persisted. Firing, which was probably as painful for me to administer as it was for Spirit to undergo, did no good. The joint became heavily calcified and completely immobile. Apparently, it became painful to even stand on because Spirit took to lying on his side in the pasture and in his stall. I moved him to the birthing stall so he would have more room. I couldn't bear to put him down. After all, we had been together for more than 25 years. I decided to make him as comfortable as possible and let him live out his days.

Late one afternoon the following spring, after the pastures had greened and we had begun putting the crops in, Spirit didn't come to the gate with the other horses to be led to the night pasture and barn. I stood up on the gate rail and saw him lying on his side in the green grass in the far corner. I walked out to him. He didn't raise his head and snort as he usually did when I approached. I knelt and felt his nostrils for breath. There was none. I put my ear to his chest and heard no heartbeat. Spirit was gone. The light that had been with me since I was a young boy had flickered and died. I wrapped my arms around his neck and spoke my goodbye into his ear. My tears wet his forelock.

I walked to the house, told Lily and went on to the barn, where I got two lanterns and a long-handled shovel. I returned to Spirit and started digging. It was too late in the day for buzzards, but the coyotes would have at him if I left him till morning. I made mounds of earth on each side of the grave, put the lanterns on top and lit them.

It takes a big, deep hole to bury a horse. After a while, Lily came out with the boys and my plate of supper. Tommy, who had just turned 5 years of age, innocently asked, "What are you doing, Papa, what's wrong with Spirit?" I told him in a straightforward but gentle way that Spirit had passed on, and I was going to bury him where he lay. Tommy's eyes grew wider, his jaw dropped a little, and his chin began to quiver. He drew close to Lily's skirt and said, "Oh, poor Spirit, bye-bye Spirit," and then grew silent.

It was past midnight by the time I felt the hole was big enough. The waning, gibbous moon had risen, adding its light to the lanterns' glow. Coyotes sang in the distance to the north and east. With the digging, I had unearthed a pile of rocks, including a big one with a flat face.

I went to the barn, harnessed a mule team, coiled a thick rope and returned to the grave. I wound the rope around Spirit's legs, hitched it to the team and dragged him into the hole. I untied the rope, climbed out and stood on the edge of the grave, peering down at my lifeless horse. I removed my hat and held it over my heart. I said my final goodbye, paused and began filling the hole.

I shoveled the earth in layer by layer, tamping it firmly between each one by walking back and forth on it. When I reached the top, I walked the mules across the earth, filled the depression they made and tamped it again. I dug a central place for the big rock, sank it, filled around it and spread the smaller rocks across the grave. I finished at about 3 a.m.

When I met Will at the barn just past sunrise, I had had barely three hours sleep. He noticed and asked if I was all right. I told him Spirit had died, and I had been up most of the night burying him. He looked at me with great sympathy in his eyes.

"I would have helped if you had asked," he said, "but I understand why you didn't. He was a good horse, and I'm very sorry he's gone." Will asked if I knew what killed Spirit, and I replied I didn't.

After supper the following night, I took a hammer and chisel and engraved the big stone on Spirit's grave. I cut his name in large letters across the top, then his birth and death places and dates beneath. Below that, I chiseled, "A Good Horse." As the grass grew up around the smaller rocks, I removed them, leaving the engraved flat rock as Spirit's monument. It was just a symbol. His true monument was in my memory.

When Spirit died, I had been bringing a new colt along for nearly three years. He was just about ready to ride. At birth, he had had a large head and a shaggy mane. He was a dark bay. About that time, I had read that there were only 1,000 bison left on the Great Plains. Where countless millions once roamed, there were now but a few. I named my new colt Buffalo in their honor. There could never be another Spirit, but Buffalo grew to be a good horse.

60

When the ice broke up in the spring of '93, Uncle Jimmy Story found he had gotten too old to do the hauling, lifting and other heavy work at the ferry. He sold the operation to another Jimmy—Charlie Howell's younger brother, James R. Howell. Jimmy Howell and his wife, Anna, both 21 years of age at the time, had an infant son, Charles, named for Jimmy's older brother.

Besides running the ferry, Jimmy saw another opportunity where the current was swift just below Minidoka Rapids. He built a waterwheel at the steep north bank like those Henry had built at Schodde Rapids, and for mostly the same purposes. The waterwheel lifted water from the river for placer mining flour gold above the bank and for irrigating the kitchen garden Jimmy and Anna put in alongside their cabin.

The Howells had an unexpected boost in ferry crossings when Albion Normal School opened in January '94. Students came from throughout the state to train to be public school teachers. Most came by the OSL to Minidoka, then continued to Albion by stage, crossing at either Montgomery Ferry farther down or Howell's Ferry near the rapids. By that time, Hardy Sears had bought Mr. Bartholomew's hotel in Minidoka, renamed it

Sears Hotel, and his sons, Charlie and Willis, were driving stage between the depot and Albion.

Ice usually closed the river to ferry crossings in December. We had to wait for it to firm up and thicken before we could cross on foot, then, later, leading a horse, and finally, driving a team and wagon.

In December '93, as they did each year, George and Alice Montgomery left their ferry site and moved the family to Albion for the winter. When the ice broke up in early spring, the family returned to resume crossings and driving passengers and freight between Minidoka and Albion.

In mid-May '94 to everyone's surprise, most likely including theirs, Andy Smith and Fanny Cubine were married in Albion. The newlyweds spent their honeymoon running the ferry and lived with the Montgomerys at the site for a short time. Soon, they built a cabin on Rice Island about five miles below the ferry. They moved to the island with three cows, intending to raise cattle. The worst flood in memory came in early June, swamped the island, floated their cabin and drove them back to Albion.

By the time they returned to live at the river in mid-'97, they had two children, Austin and Mabel, and had both worked at the Comorah Mine south of Albion, Andy as a miner and Fanny as a cook.

Andy liked to fish and in searching for good places to cast his line, he had found a spring gushing from a low basalt bluff on the north side of the river nearly 10 miles above our homeplace. The water ran steadily and unbroken a short way down to the Snake.

Andy walked the land there and decided it was good ranching country. He would build a cabin and barn, direct water from the spring to the homesite, grow a kitchen garden, and raise cattle. He hauled framing beams and uprights, floor planks, clapboard lumber, windows, doors, shingles and hardware from Albion and Minidoka, and got his project under way.

He led a team on his saddle horse and pulled a damaged rail longways through the sage to the ranch from the Oregon Short Line. Turned crossways and dragged by the team, it was a brush rail used to clear ground for the buildings, corrals and Fanny's kitchen garden.

When Andy came and went south, he crossed at our ferry, and drove his team and wagon up the bluff road. We had opened the fence and put in a gate at our eastern boundary. Will, Billy and I stole time away from our own summer work to help Andy with his buildings and his water system.

Before summer was out, Andy, Fanny, their two children and a few cattle and horses were living at the ranch. The odd thing was Andy hadn't yet filed a homestead claim, although he had been to the land office in Hailey and had looked over the surveyors' maps. He found the spring was in the township's Section 16. In any township, Sections 16 and 36 were always the school sections and couldn't be claimed.

Andy had seen that Sections 8 and 17 were good land downhill from the spring, and he built there, though it wasn't until December '98 that he filed a claim on the southernmost part of 8 and the northernmost part of 17. He claimed 158.7 acres, part bottomland and part upland. He could irrigate almost all by gravity from the spring. As his herd grew, he would graze them on the vast, unclaimed public range.

Andy was excited about the prospect of working his own land, but Fanny didn't much like the idea. She wasn't against ranching, but she objected to the location. At nearly 10 miles distant, following the course of the river, we were the Smiths' nearest neighbors. The Oregon Short Line tracks were about six miles straight north, and Minidoka was about 12 northwest as the crow flies.

With Andy out on horseback with the cattle, Fanny felt isolated on their ranch at the spring, especially with small children. Their third, Clara, came in January '99. I told Fanny that until Minidoka sprang up after the railroad came in '83, our nearest neighbor was 25 miles away and on the other side of the river. That didn't settle her any.

Andy had plenty of work to keep him busy on the ranch, but he always found time to fish. He made a one-man bull boat by forming a frame of cut willows and stretching cowhides over it. He lashed the hides to the frame with rawhide and sealed the seams with pine pitch. His habit was to launch the boat at his place, taking along a paddle and his fishing gear, and float downstream. By the time he reached our place, he had usually caught enough cutthroat trout and suckers to supply supper for all of us and his own family. We would thank Andy for the fish, put his boat in the wagon and drive him up to his claim.

On a day in spring '99 when the river was very high, I had returned from business in Albion and was halfway across on our ferry, when I looked upstream and saw Andy coming down in the bull boat. He was sitting in his usual posture, wearing his wide-brimmed hat and guiding his line in the water. I assumed he would come to our landing and looked forward to fish for supper. I didn't look back for Andy until I had reached the north side, tied the ferry and was leading Buffalo off. There was Andy floating by midstream. He waved his hat, smiled and called out, "Hallo, Early!" I was so dumbstruck it took me a few heartbeats to recover, wave and call back. I stood watching as he drifted by, wondering out loud to myself, "What the heck is Andy doing?"

I learned the next day that Andy had shot the rapids in his bull boat and landed safely at Montgomery Ferry with a big load of fish. George took Andy's feat pretty much in stride, but Alice was upset, and when feisty Fanny found out, she laid down the law: "Andy, you're a grown man with a wife and three small children, and I forbid you to ever do such a reckless thing again." Andy grinned and gently brushed off the warning, but he never did such a reckless thing again.

Having lived at the confluence of the Cumberland and Ohio rivers, Will and I were no strangers to floods. The berm along our Snake riverfront protected us from all but the highest water. The gap in the berm—the north landing—was our only vulnerable spot. We built a removable barricade across the landing to close the gap. As long as we kept our irrigation gates shut, hauled the ferry up the landing and got the barricade in place behind it, we had always stayed dry.

Before the OSL and telegraph came across southern Idaho, we had no early warning of coming high water. We had to rely on observation and intuition. After the telegraph, word came from Idaho Falls, where there was a gauging station about two miles below town. If the upper river flooded, we heard about it downriver.

In early June 1894, news came by wire that the highest flow rate ever seen—75,000 cubic feet per second—was recorded at Idaho Falls, about 100 miles above the homeplace. The flow rate was more than seven times the mean and, at 12.5 feet, the river had risen almost 11 feet above its lowest point.

There was diversion for irrigation above Idaho Falls but none below. We might get some relief from flooding at low points along the 100-mile distance, but there was still a lot of water coming our way. It was the first time since we came in '72 that there was a real danger of the river spilling over the berm and flooding the bench.

I got the word in Minidoka and raced straight home. Will and Billy were in the fields mowing lucerne. I rang the bell strong and fast. I saw them driving the mule team hard down the bluff road and met them at the barn.

First, we hitched six mules to the ferry, rolled it up the landing on rounded logs and tied it front and rear to the cottonwood and cable tower. Next, we got the barricade in place behind the ferry, then quickly moved to the cave door. We sealed it as best we could with hides and sacks of sand. The river's pace had quickened, and it was rising fast.

Watching from the shade porch, we made a decision about the kitchen garden. Lily and Annie went to work picking and pulling everything that was even close to ready. Will, Billy and I led the beasts out of the barn to the day pasture in the sink. We drove the hogs there too. We carried everything movable in the shed and barn from the ground floor up into the haymow. There was nothing we could do about the orchard but hope that a flood wouldn't kill the trees.

Next, we ran to Billy and Annie's and Will's houses. By the time we got the movable things either up into the rafters or across the bluff road into the sink, the river was racing and steadily climbing the berm at the bank. We ran to help Lily and Annie finish stripping the kitchen garden.

We had done as much preparation as we could. We would take turns standing watch through the night. We hung lanterns around the perimeter of the shade porch. We had our supper and waited.

Water began spilling over the berm just past sundown. Within minutes, it floated the ferry and spread to the cottonwood. It swamped the corral and garden and reached the cave door. We could see only a silhouette of the barn, but we knew the river had invaded its ground floor. And if it was there, it was into the orchard and the two cabins farther up the bench. For a moment, we wondered if it could possibly rise above the bluff and flood the sink, but no, that would take another Bonneville Flood, and this wasn't it.

The river crested three feet up the bluff wall and took fully a week to gradually return to its banks. We were another two weeks cleaning up and getting the homeplace back to normal. Although the kitchen garden was a total loss, we were in early June, so Lily and Annie replanted everything that would be ready before the first frost.

Since we started farming our claim, we had often wished the soil was a little better at retaining moisture. It was alluvial and aeolian above a volcanic base. The only humus it contained was what we had created by spreading manure and plowing stubble under. Now we were glad it drained quickly because that fast drainage saved the cottonwood and the orchard. A layer of silt covered every place the water had reached. Clearing the ditches was the first and hardest work we had to do to recover.

In 1895, D. W. Ross, Idaho's state engineer, did further inspection and surveys, covering the same ground west of Minidoka Rapids as the United States Geological Survey had five years before. In late July, the USGS set up a gauging station at Montgomery Ferry and began recording the height and flow rate of the river. As it had been after the 1890 survey, we heard nothing definite about an irrigation project after the '95 work. But this time there were rumors and lots of speculation.

"Why would they be measurin' the river if they didn't have somethin' up their sleeve?" was a repeated question.

"Betcha they're gonna build a dam and ruin us all," was one neighbor's worry.

I wrote to Charles Walcott, the USGS director, and asked if there were plans for an irrigation project near Minidoka Rapids. He replied there were "no such plans at this time." Even with that assurance, many people's minds weren't eased.

61

My fondest memories of our boys are from when they were very young, wide-eyed, eager and not yet wise to the ways of the world. I delighted in seeing them riding their ponies, running with the dogs or walking barefoot along the riverbank, their fishing poles over their shoulders, stopping here and there to skip stones.

One of their favorite things was jumping from the rafters in the barn down into the loose hay. I stood a long ladder on the floor of the haymow and leaned it against the upper crossbeam. The boys scampered up the ladder and walked out across the beam with complete abandon. Fear never seemed to occur to them. They flew off the beam and turned somersaults in the air. They were the haymow acrobats, screaming and whooping with glee.

When the boys were small, I could keep them amused for long periods with simple things. One was voice disguisers I made from cornstalks and fish bladders. I cut three-inch lengths of cornstalks, hollowed out the pith and cut a notch just in from each end, one on top and one on bottom. I wrapped pieces of fish bladder around the ends, fastened them and poked small holes through. I didn't want to demonstrate the disguiser myself, so I gave one to each boy and instructed them to enclose one end with their lips, covering the notch, and laugh. They looked a little doubtful at first, but the strange sounds widened their eyes and had them laughing uproariously. They took to talking through the disguisers and delighting in their unrecognizable voices. They fooled Lily by standing out of sight behind the kitchen wall and talking to her through the disguisers. She was startled. "Who's that? Who's in the house?" she asked as she came around the corner drying her hands on her apron. She broke into a big smile and lots of laughter when she saw her two sons, themselves laughing impishly.

Tommy and Clint were quite alike, which made rearing them a lot easier than if they had been opposites. One difference was that Clint was more competitive. That came about because he was younger than Tommy, yet felt he had to do whatever his older brother did. If Tommy got a pony and learned to ride, Clint had to have a pony and learn too. When I taught Tommy how to milk, Clint had to learn alongside. When the river was low and slow, and

I took Tommy to teach him to swim, Clint couldn't wait till he was older; he had to learn with his brother. In Clint's eyes, as long as he did whatever Tommy did—even if in anybody else's view not as well—he was pleased and proud. Tommy was patient with and protective of Clint, and the younger boy looked up to his older brother.

On summer Sundays, we floated a line from the aft end of the ferry and took the boys in tow as the current pushed the rig across. Once we reached the opposite bank, we switched the line to what became the aft end and towed them back. One hot afternoon in August '95, when Lily had made us all new swimsuits in the latest fashion, our summer day turned into a nightmare. Will had neared the south bank with the boys in tow, while Billy, Lily and I sat at the north landing facing the river. Annie was at home. Billy had set fishing lines just west of us. The three dogs had waded into the river and were paddling about. A loud, gruff voice caught us by surprise from behind.

"Afternoon, neighbors," the voice almost snarled. We turned to see a coarse man astride a scarred black horse. He trailed an equally ragged pack horse. "Mighty nice day for a swim," he growled. Before responding, I turned over my shoulder and whispered to Billy.

"While I keep this man busy, see if you can calmly walk past him to the house and get my pistol and rifle. Stay behind him when you come back." I turned to the stranger.

"Good afternoon, friend," I said. "You startled us. We're not used to strangers approaching on this side of the river." He wore a pistol and carried a rifle in a leather sheath, both on the left side. Billy walked by him.

"Came through the gate to the east," he replied, "headin' for the mines."

He looked past me, leering at Lily. His clothes were greasy dirty, stained with who knows what. His boots were beat up, the crown of his hat was crushed, and the brim looked as if he had chewed notches in it. His face was dark, deeply creased and covered with grizzled stubble. He had the look of a man who had been living outdoors a long time. He was missing several teeth, and those remaining were jagged and brown. As I stood and moved a few steps closer, I smelled a stench about him. I was barefoot and unarmed. If his intent was evil, he had me cold.

"What can we do for you today?" I ventured.

"Nothin' much," he said, "maybe some water for my horses."

"Sure, be my guest," I said as I motioned to the trough behind him at the corral.

As he dismounted and led his horses to the water, Billy came out the cave door carrying my Winchester in one hand and Colt pistol in the other. The stranger glanced at him menacingly. Billy stood near the door. I didn't turn to look, but I knew it would be a few minutes before Will and the boys reached the north landing. The stranger turned about, looking our homestead over as his horses drank.

"Nice place you got here," he said. His tone was dark, not friendly.

"Thanks, it suits us just fine," I said. "What are you after in the mining country?"

"Money from suckers," he sneered. He was looking past me again, higher this time, probably at Will nearing the landing. I felt him sizing up the situation, calculating his odds. He faced three men, one armed, two not, a woman and two small boys. His eyes slowly returned to mine. I stared at him. He looked down as his horse pulled its head from the trough. The tension eased. He mounted, then reached down and grabbed the pack horse's lead.

"I'll be goin'," he snarled, "much obliged for the water." He rounded the corral and headed up the ramp to the bluff road. Without looking back, he turned west. Will came up alongside me, and Billy joined us.

"I don't like the looks of it," Will said.

"Neither do I," I said. "We should check the gates, east and west. I doubt he closed them. I wonder if he'll be back."

"Keep the two barking dogs with you tonight," Will said, "and I'll take Woo to my place with me." Tommy had given Woo his name. "Woo" was the only noise he could make. He sounded more like an owl than a dog. He had gotten into some chicken bones as a pup. By the time I cut and pried them from his throat, he had lost his bark.

The night passed peacefully. It was hot and still, with no moon. Night sounds drifted through the wire window screens. The dogs slept on the porch. They were used to coyotes singing in the distance, and didn't howl or bark in reply. We went about our work the following day. There was no sign of the stranger, and his memory began to slip from my mind.

Well past the next midnight, we awoke to howling and screaming and a terrible ruckus coming from the barn. I leapt from bed, pulled my britches and boots on, grabbed my pistol and bolted from the house. I stopped dead in my tracks, ran back, handed Lily my Winchester and told her to stay together in one room with the boys.

I looked toward the barn from the porch. There was only starlight, and I saw nothing but silhouettes. The howling and screaming continued, joined by panicked noise from chickens, hogs, horses and cattle. It was as if the whole barnyard had exploded. I wondered where the dogs were and why they hadn't barked. I raced to the bell and rang it as hard and fast as I could. I needed Will and Billy. I could barely see outlines of beasts on the bluff road and around the barn. The horses and mules were out of their stalls, the hogs out of their pen and the cattle out of the night pasture. I skipped down the porch stairs and ran up the bluff road toward the barn and the terrible howling.

The barn doors were wide open. The howling sounded like a siren. I lit a lantern, held it high and walked toward the noise. A coyote hung on a rope by its tail from the beam above. Its hindquarters were bloody and crippled. It howled and snarled and bared its teeth. It tried to lunge at me. There was a muzzle on the floor beneath it. I went to the shed, returned with a hand scythe and lopped the coyote's head off. In the silence, I heard my heavy breathing, then people running. Will and Billy appeared at the door. Woo was with them.

"What the blazes is goin' on?" Will asked excitedly. "The animals are scattered all over the place. Where are the dogs? Why aren't they barking?"

"I don't know, I don't know," I replied. "Somebody's been here." Then it hit me: "It's a decoy! He's after Lily and the boys!"

I dashed past Will and Billy, running toward the house, my pistol in one hand and the scythe in the other. I raced along the bluff road, stumbling in the dark. I was a crazy man. Tears streamed across my temples into my hair. I reached the house and leapt up the porch stairs. I ran through the open door and to the bedroom. The boys were there bound and gagged, but Lily was gone. The stranger had been there. I smelled him. I was enraged. I tried to keep my wits about me. I ripped the boys' gags off and cut their ropes. I held Tommy by the shoulders.

"It's OK, Tommy, you boys are all right. Where's Mama? Tell me what happened," I insisted.

"He took her! The bad man took her!" Tommy cried. I knelt and enclosed both boys in my arms.

"It's OK, boys," I assured them. "Grampa will be here in a second, and I'll go after Mama." I heard Will and Billy on the stairs, then in the room behind me.

"The stranger took Lily, the boys are OK," I said as I rose and turned. "I'm going after him."

"I'll go with you," Will said.

"No," I said, "this is my fight. You and Billy stay with the boys and gather the beasts. I'm sure he went west. I'll find a horse and go after him."

"Take two pistols, a rifle, plenty of ammunition and a rope," Will said.

"Collect them for me—and some food," I said. "I'll be back as soon as I can find a horse and saddle him. Billy, come along and help me." I took a lantern from the porch and trotted up the bluff road with Billy, whistling and calling for a horse. I thought of Spirit. If he were still alive, he would have been at the porch steps waiting for me. I made out the silhouettes of two mules just past the barn. Then there was the outline of a horse, his head bowed, calmly grazing the grass along the road. It was Buffalo. I passed the lantern to Billy and coaxed Buffalo to me as I slowly walked toward him. I asked Billy for his belt, removed mine, linked it with Billy's and looped it around Buffalo's neck like a collar.

"OK, Billy," I said, "I'll lead Buffalo to the barn and saddle him. You start gathering the beasts." Billy nodded in the lantern light.

"Bring Lily home safe," he said, "and kill that bastard."

I looked into Billy's eyes for a moment. I probably will kill the bastard, I thought. He had violated everything most dear to me. I probably will kill him.

I trotted Buffalo to the barn, lit a lantern and quickly saddled and bridled him. I mounted and we galloped to the house. Will had everything ready, with food and extra bullets packed in saddlebags. I tied the rifle sheath and bags on Buffalo, and double-checked his cinch. I had already sweat through my nightshirt. I tucked it in my britches and strapped the gunbelt around my hips.

"Take Woo," Will said. "He's a good tracker, and he won't give you away barking. Bring Lily back safe, but leave the stranger dead for the coyotes and buzzards. Good luck, son."

I kicked Buffalo and took off west on the bluff road. Woo ran ahead but stopped at the open gate, sniffing and wooing at something on the ground. I dismounted and pulled Woo away. The barking dogs lay by the post in pools of blood that glistened in the starlight. Their throats were slit. There were slabs of fresh meat nearby. The stranger had lured them away with the meat and killed them. I walked Buffalo past the gate, closed it and mounted. Woo jumped about excitedly at Buffalo's feet.

"OK, Woo, let's find them," I said as I kicked Buffalo ahead. I reckoned the stranger would leave the road shortly past the gate. He knew at least I would follow, and staying on the road would make it easier for me. It was up to Woo to find the trail. The starlight was bright but not enough for me to see a track. Woo stopped, sniffed the ground and air and started northwest into the sage.

If it had been a cloudy night, I would have faced an impossible task. Starlight silhouetted the sage, lit the ground enough to show passageways and let me see Woo's outline ahead. I reckoned the stranger had maybe 30 minutes on me, but I had no way to know how fast he was moving.

If I had an advantage, it was that I knew the country. I had ridden and walked this ground countless times. I saw a faint glow of light in the near distance to my right. It was Minidoka. I knew he wouldn't go there. The Big Dipper lay across the northern sky above the town. It reminded me of a summer night with Lily. A shooting star had fallen into its cup and caused her to reel with wonder. My Lily. I couldn't lose her. I followed Woo. I wanted to find the riders before daylight. If I didn't, he would see me coming across open country, and there was no telling what he would do.

I kept my eyes on the distance as much as I could. I hoped to catch a silhouette as the riders topped a rise. As I rode, I wondered why the stranger hadn't just burned the barn. That would have brought me running. Then I realized it would have brought Lily running too, and he couldn't have taken her without killing me and maybe Will and Billy. He must have tied his horses out of sight near the house, done his dirty work at the barn, then run back along the river as I ran east on the bluff road. He was shrewd. I reminded myself to be careful.

I had been riding for maybe an hour when I saw their silhouettes less than a mile ahead. Two riders, one close behind the other, topped the railroad grade and disappeared down the other side. The stranger was headed for the Wood River country. Whatever he intended to do with Lily, he first wanted to put distance between them and the homeplace. I quickened my pace. My plan was to get ahead of them. I would reach the railroad grade and ride hard west on the south side. I would cross beneath a trestle I knew about a mile ahead, ride hard north and get in front of them on their trail. If the stranger saw me toward the northwest, he wouldn't be as suspicious. If he didn't see me, I would get the drop on him.

The ground beside the railroad grade was clear, letting Buffalo race at a full gallop. Now Woo was behind us. He couldn't keep up with Buffalo. We reached the underpass, crossed the grade and ran north, dodging the sage. I was taking a chance the stranger would continue on the same line he had set. If he didn't come toward me, Woo would have to find his new track. There was a big rock outcropping ahead, almost perfectly placed. I ducked behind it, dismounted and tied both Buffalo and Woo to the big sage. I slipped my Winchester out of its sheath, untied the saddlebags and climbed up the backside of the rocks. I found a perch near the peak with a clear sight southeast. First light was just coming to the horizon. I scanned the distance, but it was still too dark to make anything out. I reached into the saddlebags for rifle bullets and found the binoculars. Will had good foresight. I slowly scanned the near distance. There they were! Two silhouettes about a half mile out heading straight for me. The starlight slightly illuminated Lily's white nightshirt. They rode at a walk. The stranger's head was bowed, as if he was sleeping, but Lily's was upright. Their track would bring them just below me to the southwest. I had a perfect line of sight for a rifle shot.

I loaded the Winchester and both pistols. I sighted the rifle along my line of fire. I wouldn't be able to leave it exposed. I

would have to wait until he was at close range, I had a sure
shot and could drop him with one bullet. If I missed or wounded
him slightly, things would get complicated. I watched through
the binoculars as the stranger and Lily slowly approached. Lily's
wrists were bound together and to the horn. She was barelegged
and barefoot. She wore only the nightshirt she had been sleeping in. The stranger's head was still bowed. I decided on a chest
shot. His head was too small a target under his hat and in the
faint light. He came within range. I let him come closer, almost
below me. I raised the rifle and sighted on his chest. All in a
moment, Buffalo whinnied behind the rocks, the stranger's head
jerked up and I fired. The shot cracked the early morning, Lily
shrieked, the stranger flew out of his saddle, fell heavily to the
ground and lay still.

Lily instinctively kicked her horse and ran ahead, pulling the
stranger's horse with her. If there was to be more gunfire, she
would be out of the way. I watched the man on the ground for
a moment. He didn't move. I scrambled down the rock pile and
walked toward him, holding him in my rifle sights. He lay crum-
pled on his side. There was enough light now that I could see blood
oozing from his chest. I rolled him onto his back with my boot. He
was dead. I had shot him through the heart. I stood staring for a
moment, then turned to where the horses had stopped. I ran to
Lily. She sat slumped forward in the saddle. She was sobbing. I
untied her hands and lowered her gently to the ground. I held her.
She was the most valuable thing in the world to me. We stood in
a silent embrace. The top edge of the sun broke above the eastern
horizon. The vast Snake River Plain lay before us. I turned slightly
so both our faces met the sunrise. The warm light bathed us.

"Are you all right, my love?" I asked. I felt her head nod against
my chest.

"Are the boys all right?" she asked softly.

"Yes, they are," I replied, "they miss their mama."

"Let's go home," she said.

"Will said to leave the stranger for the coyotes and buzzards,"
I said. "I'm inclined to agree." She nodded. I went to his horses,
dropped their saddles and packs to the ground and removed their
bridles. I smacked their croups and sent them running into the
sage. I carried my barefooted wife to Buffalo and helped her into

the saddle. I went to the rocks and returned with the saddle-bags. I passed the canteen to Lily. After she drank, I drank, then I poured water into my hat for Buffalo and Woo. I untied them and leapt up behind Lily. I enclosed her in my arms, held the reins, and we headed home. When we rode in, I told the others Lily was not hurt, and there would be no more trouble from the stranger. We never mentioned that ugly incident again.

62

In early February 1896, two sheepmen were shot dead in their camp on Deep Creek in western Cassia County. After Sheriff Harvey Perkins and Coroner Dr. R. T. Story investigated, Jack Davis, better known as Diamondfield Jack, and Fred Gleason were charged with the murders.

The evidence against Davis and Gleason was purely circumstantial, and any clear-thinking observer at the time would have excused them. But in place of clear thinking, a galaxy of ignorance, prejudice, politics, ambition, religious differences, incompetence, cowardice, economics and grudges threatened an innocent man's life and kept the case going for nearly seven years.

Davis was convicted in spite of Gleason's being acquitted by the same evidence in a separate trial. Then, after two other men confessed to the killings, Davis' conviction was upheld. He came within a hair's breadth of being hanged in Albion in early '99 and again in mid-1901. On both occasions, he was saved by riders racing on horseback from the Minidoka depot to Albion with reprieves.

Public sentiment that had been strongly anti-Davis at the start turned equally strongly pro-Davis as the case progressed and the facts became known. Still, some people, including one of the original prosecutors, steadfastly proclaimed Davis' guilt. Talk locally began in February '96, continued through Davis' pardon in December '02 and goes on today more than 50 years later. I bet it will still be heard 50 years from now.

Some distant events carry more personal meaning than others. In early July 1896, I read in the Pocatello *Tribune* that Harriet Beecher Stowe, the author of *Uncle Tom's Cabin*, had died. I remembered reading years earlier that when Abraham

Lincoln met her during the Civil War, he said, "So you're the little lady who started this big war." The newspaper story didn't note her response.

If you don't keep pace with progress, it will march right by and leave you in its wake. Generally that's true, but sometimes progress doesn't fit, so you just let it go by. You stick with what you have until something that does fit comes along.

After the '96 harvest, Heb Potter, one of the Albion farmers we shared equipment and threshed with, visited kin in California's San Joaquin Valley. He came back with stories about bonanza wheat farms covering a section or more. At harvest, the farmers used a Houser combine, a machine called that because it combined a header with a thresher. The only operation it didn't do was grind the grain to flour. Combines cut and threshed over a million acres of wheat a season, about a third of California's total. And some combines, Heb said, were pulled through the fields by steam tractors rather than horsepower.

The farmers in our co-op talked about buying a Houser combine and even considered a steam tractor. But in the end we decided our separate header and thresher, both powered by horses or mules, worked just fine. None of our farms was bigger than a quarter section and even counting our other grains, we didn't have enough acres to make a combine pay, with or without a steam tractor. We would wait for progress that fit to come along.

We divided our grain harvest crew into three teams and rotated the men among them so no man did the same job through the harvest. The first team worked the header, the second followed with the thresher, and the third drove the wagons full of grain to the mill.

And since we still threshed from the field rather than from the stack, Lily and Annie could count on having as many as 20 hungry men to feed for two or three days at harvest time. The women didn't complain—they liked the socializing. Otherwise, they might go weeks with no one to talk to but each other, Billy, Will, me and our boys.

In early June '97, I grieved with everyone else when I read Mark Twain had died. But then I laughed with everyone else when I read he wired from England, saying the reports of his death were exaggerated. Mark Twain was never without his wit.

The Albion *Times* didn't have a telegraph, so we got most of our outside-world news from the Idaho *Statesman*, the Pocatello *Tribune* or Eastern papers the OSL brought to Minidoka. We read in the Omaha paper that by 1898 both Cuba and the Philippines had revolted against Spain. First President Grover Cleveland and then President William McKinley pressed Spain to end the dispute by granting the colonies independence, but Spain would hear nothing of it. McKinley sent the battleship *Maine* to Havana harbor to show United States Navy strength. On February 16, the *Maine* exploded and sank, killing 266 American sailors. Spain claimed the explosion was internal, and the United States claimed it was external—a mine. In April, Congress declared war on Spain.

With our country at war, some young men at Bill Langley's saloon in Albion talked about volunteering to fight. When they sobered up, they decided they would probably be better off farming or ranching in Idaho.

Other Americans did fight in Cuba and the Philippines though. Theodore Roosevelt was one of them. We didn't know it at the time, but he would become president and have a big effect on our lives a few years later.

The Spanish-American War ended in December with a treaty signed in Paris. At least for the time being, Cuba was independent, and the United States got the Philippines, Puerto Rico and Guam.

By April '98 when Eddie Burroughs returned to Idaho, he had become a young man of 22 and had shortened his name to Ed. The Bar Y had changed since he left nearly seven years earlier. Although Ed's brothers, George and Harry, were still in the cattle business, they and their partner, Lew Sweetser, had expanded into mining.

The three men had seen placer miners with hand-operated sluice boxes up and down the Snake River for years. They thought they could use their engineering knowledge to find a more efficient and profitable way to separate gold from river sand and gravel. In '93, they formed the Yale Dredging Company and in '94 began operating the *Yale*, a small, steam-powered dredge, from a base at the mouth of the Raft River. The *Yale* pulled sand and gravel from the river bottom using a chain-and-buckets system. Coarse and fine material were separated in mechanical sluice boxes, the rough stuff was dumped back into the river, and the fine was hauled to burlap screens on the riverbank. From there, flour gold was extracted with mercury, melted and formed into bars.

The *Yale* didn't make the partners rich men, but the results were good enough to cause them to expand the operation. They formed the Sweetser-Burroughs Mining Company and gave it a Minidoka mailing address. By '96 or '97, they had built the *Argus*, a steam-powered dredge about the size of an Ohio River packet. They towed it to dredging spots between Minidoka Rapids and Schodde Rapids with a small, steam-driven tugboat.

The *Argus* worked around the clock and on a much larger scale than the *Yale*. Rather than a chain and buckets, it had a suction nozzle that vacuumed sand and gravel up from the bottom. The whole operation, starting with coarse rock and finishing with gold bars, took place on the dredge. The partners spent 4-1/2 cents per cubic yard to extract the rough, and each of those yards yielded 10 to 20 cents of gold. That was the formula under ideal circumstances and, of course, circumstances had a way of not always being ideal. Nevertheless, word was the partners made $50,000 a year in their best years.

By late '98 or early '99, mining was going well enough that Sweetser and the Burroughs brothers built the *El Nido*, a two-story, 30-by-60-foot, 18-room houseboat where the partners and, later, their wives lived. The company's employees, four or six men, lived on a separate, smaller houseboat.

George, Harry and Lew were occupied with flour gold mining and had W. S. Sparks running the cattle operation when Ed came for spring roundup in '98. Ed visited us soon after his arrival and several times when he and other cowhands came with wagons to haul bales of lucerne back to the Raft River.

Tommy had just turned 10 that spring, and Clint would be eight in the fall. Although Ed didn't generate the squeals of delight he enjoyed when Tommy was a toddler, he still fascinated the boys with his fantastic tales and drawings. The boys were especially taken by Ed's stories of his time with Troop B, 7th U. S. Cavalry at Fort Grant, Arizona Territory.

Ed loved horses and ranch work, but had no affection at all

for mining. In June, with spring roundup over and the Bar Y herd in summer pasture, Harry helped Ed buy Victor Roeder's stationery store in Pocatello. Ed renamed it Burroughs' and dove right into being a retail merchant.

One Saturday that summer, Tommy, Clint and I rode the OSL cars into Pocatello to visit Ed at his store on West Center Street. Roeder's—now Burroughs'—was a well-established store with a steady stream of customers. Ed kept the newsstand full of magazines and newspapers. There was a cigar counter and books, lines of writing paper, pens and sheet music. Soon, he added Kodak cameras and photographic film developing and printing services. He established a newspaper delivery route and often delivered the papers himself, riding his black horse, Crow. The Pocatello *Tribune* noted the sale of Roeder's to Ed and encouraged its readers to visit Burroughs'.

The boys and I had a fine time visiting Ed that day. He made photographs of us and sent prints by mail after he developed the film. I made a photograph of him standing behind his camera and tripod. We had known Ed as a cowboy, and here, dressed in a businessman's coat, high collar and tie, he looked out of place.

Seeing his popular retail store in Pocatello, anyone who didn't know Ed might think he was a young man who had found his place and whose ambitions as a merchant would carry him far. But I knew him. I knew his love of adventure, his imagination and his way with horses and children. I knew he spent every spare moment writing stories and poems, and drawing cartoons, people and scenes. To me, he didn't seem cut out to be a retail merchant in Pocatello.

In early '99, Victor Roeder returned from California and bought the store back from Ed. Ed helped his brothers with the roundup that spring and by summer he was gone—first to New York and then to Chicago to work at the American Battery Company, his father's business. He would return to Idaho in 1903 and stay until spring '04 but not at the Raft River. He rejoined George and Harry at Stanley Basin and then Parma, Idaho, where they had moved the dredging business. We wouldn't see Ed again, but occasionally there was a letter or whimsical poem or story in the mail, usually with a photograph or sketches he had made. We missed Ed and remembered him with affection.

63

As we did every year, in the summer of '99, we mowed the hayfields and left the hay to dry in long windrows. Whether cut or standing, hayfields attract mice. They come from the sage to the irrigated ground for cover, food, and to nest and multiply. Mice, in turn, attract both harmless and poisonous snakes.

When the wind and sun had dried the hay, we went into the fields with a wagon, a mule team and pitchforks. Will drove between the rows as Billy and I pitched from opposite sides of the wagon.

We had just returned from hauling a full load to the haymow and had begun refilling the wagon, when tragedy struck. Billy picked up a big forkful of hay and had it about head high when a very angry rattler jumped from the hay and hit him twice, first on the face and again on the arm. Billy yelled and reeled back, dropping the pitchfork and hay. The snake fell to the ground and slithered away.

Will jumped from the springseat and ran to Billy, who had fallen on his back, stunned. I ran around the wagon to Billy and Will, carrying my pitchfork.

"He's bit bad," Will said, "let's get him to Doc Noth in Minidoka."

"That ol' rattler was faster'n me this time," Billy managed, holding his fingers to his cheek.

I leapt into the wagon and spread the loaded hay to make a flat bed. We helped Billy up and into the wagon. I stayed with him in the bed as Will drove hard for the east gate, bouncing over windrows as we went. Will passed me the knife he kept in a sheath on his belt.

"Wrap your belt above the arm wound and yank it tight. Cut crisscross on the fang marks and suck out as much venom as you can," Will yelled over the beating hoofs and clatter of the wagon.

The areas around the punctures on Billy's cheek and arm had begun to swell and turn a sickly blue-black. I made the arm cuts with the point of the blade. Billy barely flinched as black blood oozed from the wounds. I had tasted my own blood before, but Billy's tasted different. As I sucked and spit, I figured it must be the venom.

It was probably about six miles from the east gate to Minidoka. Will had the mules running like racehorses. I remember thinking, what would we do if Doc Noth wasn't there?

We came into town like an explosion—lots of noise and a big plume of dust. As Will reined the team to a halt outside Doc Noth's, people ran from all directions to see what the commotion was.

"Snake bit, snake bit bad," we said as two onlookers helped us carry Billy inside.

"How long ago?" Doc Noth asked as he examined the wounds.

"About 30 minutes," I replied, "is he going to make it?"

"Hard to say," Doc Noth replied. "I'll do my best. I can make new incisions, cup the wounds and then dress them. His weight will help. We can't keep the tourniquet on his arm throughout."

The whole left side of Billy's face was swollen, lumpy and dotted with the black and blue of poisoned blood. His left arm had swelled to nearly double size. The skin was stretched taut, looking as if it would burst. Black liquid oozed from the wounds. A spasm wrenched Billy, he turned his head to the side and threw up.

Doc Noth went to work. His movements were quick and efficient. When he finished, he checked Billy's pulse, looked at the pupils of his eyes and felt his forehead with his palm. Although Doc Noth tried not to show it, he looked more than concerned. He looked grave. He focused on Billy's face wound as if to say: A big man might survive one quickly treated arm bite, but a second wound on the face is deadly.

"Is Billy a married man?" Doc Noth asked. Will replied that he was, and Doc Noth suggested sending a boy on a fast horse for his wife, which we did.

When Annie came about an hour and a half later, Billy was barely conscious. The blue at his temples and beneath his eyes was a sign of death. We sat with him, doing what we could, alternating between sobs and silence. He died at sundown.

Grief is part of life. We just have to accept that. The undertaker came up from Albion to prepare the body. Will and I built a coffin.

With Billy gone, Annie didn't want to stay in Idaho. She would return to family in Tennessee. She packed their personal things, and in two days was set to go. Will and Annie said their goodbyes at the homeplace. He gave her $700 to add to what she and Billy had saved.

Lily and I drove Annie to the Minidoka depot. As we came to the top of the rise beyond the sink, Annie asked me to stop. She

wanted to take one last look at the homeplace. We stepped down
from the spring seat and stood three abreast beside the wagon.

The line of tall poplars turned the corner from the west to the
north border of our land. They rushed, then swayed gracefully
when the wind caught them. Beyond the poplars, the pasture
and fields were a living checkerboard. Cattle and horses grazed
in dark green Kentucky bluegrass. Tiny purple flowers dotted
deep green lucerne. Pale yellow tones separated the timothy
from the oats from the wheat. Lines of black basalt crossed the
fields enclosing blue stripes of water. The main house sat on the
far western end of the rise that stretched east to a distant fence
line and gate. To the left of the house, the barn, orchard and the
other two houses formed a textured line along the bench. The
cottonwood rose between the house and the ferry, which sat idle
at the north landing as the blue Snake flowed behind it. It was
a pretty scene.

Lily stood beside Annie with her arm around Annie's waist.
Annie tilted her head against Lily's shoulder. She reached into a
pocket of her skirt, withdrew a fringed handkerchief and patted
her eyes.

"They were good years," she whispered.

"Yes, they were good years," I replied.

We picked up the coffin at Doc Noth's, took it to the depot
and waited for the eastbound afternoon train. It was a funeral
train that day. The agent and two strangers helped me load the
coffin into a freight car, while Lily and Annie waited at the passenger car steps. We hugged Annie and said our goodbyes. She
mounted the stairs and took a seat at the window on our side.
The conductor signaled the engineer and pulled the stepstool up
into the car. The whistle blew, the big crank turned the wheels,
and the train rolled slowly out of the station. We waved, and
Annie waved, and Lily blew her a kiss.

Billy and Annie had been with us for 23 years. They were
good people. We were heartbroken about Billy, and we hated to
see Annie go. Will's words, "Billy Latham is the best hired hand
in Idaho" couldn't have been more true.

With Billy and Annie gone, we had to find a new hired hand.
I placed a notice in the Albion *Times* and let our need be known
about town and in Minidoka. The only response was from an old,

bent man. We had to turn him down because he wasn't fit to work.

The following day, a tall, lanky young man approached me in Minidoka, where I had taken a wagon and team to pick up some lumber.

"Mr. Hawkins?" he asked.

"Yes, Mr. Hawkins," I replied.

"I heard tell you're lookin' for a man to work," he said.

"Yes, I am," I said. "It's farm work. Are you a farmer?"

"Born and raised," he replied.

"Where?" I asked.

"Iowa," he replied.

"How is it that you're here in Minidoka?" I asked.

"It's as far west as my money took me," he replied.

"Why did you leave Iowa?" I asked.

"My mother died, and she was my only protection against my father," he replied. "I told him if he didn't treat me better, I would leave. He didn't, so I left."

"When did you eat last?" I asked.

"Yesterday," he replied.

"Are you a hard worker?" I asked.

"Sunup to sundown, six or seven days a week," he replied. "Been at it since I was a kid."

"May I look at your hands?" I asked. He extended his arms toward me, opened his hands palms down and slowly turned them up. He didn't have to say anything. He knew the evidence was there. "Ride south with me to our place and meet my wife and father. If things look right all around, we'll try you out for a month. If you do well, you have the job. If not, I'll bring you right back here where I met you. I have slices of ham and some fresh-baked bread in the wagon. You can eat your fill on the way down." His eyes lit up, and his broad smile revealed a missing upper left front tooth.

"I guarantee I'll do well, Mr. Hawkins," he said. "I'll be the best hired hand you've ever had."

"Be careful about that," I said, "you've got some mighty big shoes to fill."

He was an eager young man. He talked openly as we drove toward the homeplace. His name was Bud Raines, and he was all of 19 years old. He was easily six feet tall, but he couldn't

have weighed more than 150 pounds. He explained that he had
his father's given name, but where he came from, juniors were
always called "Bud." He hesitated when I asked what his given
name was. He finally revealed it was Cornelius. I told him I
thought his decision to call himself "Bud" was a good one.

I introduced Bud to Will and Lily. They took an immediate
liking to him and he to them. Bud was very impressed with the
homeplace and didn't hesitate to say so. I showed him around,
pointing out the cave, ferry, kitchen garden and irrigation system.
We walked east along the bluff road past the barn and orchard
on the right and the pasture on the left. When we reached what
had been Billy and Annie's house, we stepped inside.

"This will be your place," I said. "It'll be your responsibility
to keep it clean and orderly. There's a fireplace for warmth and a
stove for cooking. You'll take most of your meals here. Now and
then, Lily and I will have you over for dinner or supper. Your closest neighbor is Captain Hawkins. His house is the next one east.
Maybe you and he will share some meals." Bud was silent. He
seemed stunned and relieved at the same time. Finally, he spoke.

"This is like a dream," he said. "Much obliged, Mr. Hawkins.
I'll do right by you."

"Yes, I think you will," I replied. "Tomorrow we'll have some
ditches to clear."

"I'll be ready at sunup," he said.

"That's good," I said, "meet us at the barn."

64

For at least 15 years after we started farming our place, we
had very little trouble with pests, either animal or plant. For the
most part, we were protected by our isolation. Predators kept the
small-mammal population down, and insects like grasshoppers
and Mormon crickets didn't find us or decided our place wasn't
worth the 25-mile trip from the nearest neighbor's farm. We grew
our own seed, so there was no chance of importing weed seed from
other growers. Once we cleared, tilled and irrigated our land, we
controlled invasions from the surrounding wild land fairly easily.

It's hard to know just where the invaders came from later
on, but as the people population grew, so did our pest problems.

Downstream, farmers broke the soil and built wheels to lift water from the river. Upstream, Andy Smith planted lucerne for his cattle, and ranchers on the Raft River grew lucerne for their herds. In Minidoka, many families had kitchen gardens. Pests had more opportunities nearby, and they found our place.

Around Idaho Falls far above, farmers diverted water into canals and ditches and irrigated thousands of acres. We suspected that was the main source of the weed seed that sprouted and flourished in our ditches. We unintentionally imported it with our irrigation water.

We had lined some of the ditches with lava rock, and weeds weren't much of a problem there, but they were thick in the bottoms and up the banks of the earthen ditches. Water weeds slowed and sometimes stopped the flow. Bank weeds gave cover to rodents, mostly pocket gophers. Their burrowing undermined the banks and caused them to collapse. Clearing the ditches of weeds and gophers became a necessary and never-ending job.

For the water weeds, we modified a disk harrow and hitched mules to drag it, one walking on each side of the ditch. It was a two-mule, three-man job and the work Bud did on his first morning with us. Will was getting too old for the hard work of pitching the weeds once they were disked loose, so Bud and I took turns following with the pitchfork. Will led one mule and Bud or I led the second, while the other of us pitched wet weeds up over the bank. Bud did well. He worked long and hard without complaint.

We cut the bank weeds with scythes and spread them on the flat ground to dry and rot. The barn cats quickly learned that cutting time was a chance to snag pocket gophers. When they saw me, and then Bud and me, walking to a ditch with a scythe, they lined up and eagerly followed us as if we were Pied Pipers.

It started with one cat that happened to be at a ditch when I was cutting. He noticed that gophers came to the surface from their burrows and pulled the cut weeds down below. The cat watched to see which way the gopher was facing when it came up, positioned himself behind the gopher and waited. When the gopher reappeared, the cat pounced, sometimes catching the gopher before he ducked underground, sometimes reaching into the hole with one paw and pulling the gopher out, and other times missing his chance.

That cat somehow let the others know about the gopher feast, so weed-cutting time became a cat parade. At any one time, we had 15 to 20 adult cats. We never fed them. They ate what they hunted—gophers, mice, voles, ground squirrels, baby rabbits and, if they were very quick, small birds.

Cutting the banks exposed pocket gophers and other small mammals not only to our barn cats, but to wild predators too. Coyotes, hawks, snakes, foxes, and even the occasional badger or bobcat grabbed the chance for an easy meal. I came to look upon the predators as partners. As long as they didn't come too close to the barn and houses, they were all right with me.

The electric lights and telephones we had read about being in distant cities eventually came to the bigger towns in Idaho but not yet to us in the small towns and rural areas. Boise and Caldwell got the telephone in '84. Boise had electric lights in '86 and then electric streetcars in '91. Hailey got the telephone in '83 and electric lights in '87. These innovations changed the way folks lived, but a more profound agent of change lay close ahead.

Charles and Frank Duryea began building horseless carriages together in the early 1890s in Springfield, Massachusetts. Then, in 1898, Charles formed the Duryea Manufacturing Company in Peoria, Illinois, to continue building motorcars without his brother. By 1899, the word "automobile" had been coined to describe the machines.

In mid-1900, a Los Angeles man bought an automobile from Charles Duryea, who shipped it west on the transcontinental rail line. When the train reached Granger, Wyoming, a switching error sent the box car containing the automobile up the Oregon Short Line instead of straight west on the Union Pacific. When the mistake was discovered by the mechanic Mr. Duryea had sent with the automobile, he decided to roll it off the westbound morning train at Minidoka. He would wait for the eastbound afternoon train to Granger rather than ride all the way to Oregon and return the next day.

Having just sent a wire, Lily and I were at the depot when the local freight agent and the mechanic slid the boxcar doors open, set up a plank ramp and rolled the Duryea out onto the platform. I immediately saw why an automobile was first called a horseless carriage—that's exactly what it looked like, a carriage with no horse. Clever, mechanically minded men had taken a common horse-drawn carriage, removed its tongues, installed an engine and a system of gears to transfer the power to the rear wheels, mounted a steering tiller ahead of the front seat, and were ready to drive.

But this engine wasn't powered by steam. It was an internal combustion engine that burned gasoline, a distillate of crude oil that men pumped out of the ground. To start the engine, Mr. Duryea's mechanic inserted a crank into a hole at the side of the automobile below the seat. He gave the crank several hard turns, and the engine roared to life. The mechanic withdrew the crank, proudly turned to Lily and me and asked, "Would you good folks like to go for a ride?" We turned to each other, then back to the mechanic and said, "Sure!"

As Lily and I climbed into the seat behind the mechanic, he introduced himself as Mr. Mueller. I introduced us as Mr. and Mrs. Hawkins.

"I understand we have plenty of time before the afternoon train is due," Mr. Mueller said, "so where would you like to go?"

"Well, there's the stage road to the ferries at the river," I replied, "and there's the wagon road to our place, also on the river."

"If we drive to your place, can I get a decent lunch?" he asked. "The food on the trains has been awful."

"Why, certainly, Mr. Mueller," Lily replied. "We Westerners are well-known for our hospitality."

"If we're going that far," I added, "we should take our team and wagon to the livery. I'll step down and take care of that if you want to follow me there, Mr. Mueller."

"Lead the way, Mr. Hawkins," he replied.

That done, we were on our way to the homeplace in the Duryea automobile.

Now, I have seen surprised looks on people's faces on any number of occasions, but none of them comes close to matching our family's looks of wonder when we drove up to the main house in the Duryea. They were just beside themselves. Of course, Tommy and Clint were first to speak.

"Can we go for a ride, can we, can we?" they excitedly asked.

"Did you trade for the team and wagon?" Will asked, only half jokingly.

Bud was least impressed. He said he had seen a motorcar in Des Moines. Mr. Mueller countered with a question, "Would you like to drive this one?" That drew Bud into the excitement.

"Early and I have ridden all the way from Minidoka," Lily said, "so why don't we step down, and maybe Mr. Mueller can drive you all down the mill road. You can show him the rapids, and by the time you return, we'll have dinner ready."

There was rousing agreement, so that's what we did. We had a very pleasant dinner that Mr. Mueller pronounced better than anything he had ever had in a dining car. I told the boys if they promised to behave, they could drive back to Minidoka with Mr. Mueller and me to retrieve our team and wagon. They made the promise and kept it. They were as calm as two smoldering volcanoes during the ride. We thanked Mr. Mueller and bade him goodbye at the depot. He returned our thanks and said the pleasure was his. On the way home, it occurred to me that the 20th century had just begun.

65

We had never met Bert Perrine, but we knew of him as the owner of a hotel and ranch in the canyon in the Blue Lakes area about three miles below Shoshone Falls. He and his wife, Hortense, were hosts to ordinary and famous people at their Blue Lakes Hotel, and they grew fruit on the ranch.

Whether we asked about the fruit Lounsbury's or Whittier's store carried in Minidoka, the answer was always, "Oh, that's from Bert Perrine's place, the Blue Lakes Ranch." Depending on the season, there were fine-tasting peaches, plums, apples, cherries, strawberries and even watermelons.

But Bert Perrine didn't limit his business interests to his hotel and fruit ranch. In late June 1900, he filed water-rights notices in Cassia County at Albion and Lincoln County at Shoshone for 3,000 cubic feet per second to be diverted both south and north of the Snake River for irrigation, domestic and manufacturing purposes. Then, with $30,000 from Stanley Milner of Salt Lake City and support from the State Land Board for a preliminary study, Perrine and others drew survey lines from The Cedars, the campsite below Schodde Rapids, down about 65 miles on the south side and 35 on the north.

They proposed to build a dam at The Cedars that would raise the low river 38 feet to irrigate about 241,000 acres on the south side and about 30,000 on the north. By early October, Perrine, Milner and three other men had incorporated as the Twin Falls Land and Water Company and filed with D. W. Ross, Idaho's state engineer, a proposed segregation map showing a dam and canal headgates. The company wanted to sell nearly 300,000 acres of irrigated land to farmers and other settlers. It looked as if the growth Will had foreseen almost 30 years earlier was about to occur, but it would happen some 35 to 100 miles west of us.

Some pages back, I wrote of a conversation I had with Lily about how events of great consequence elsewhere seldom affected us at the homeplace. President William F. McKinley's assassination in September 1901 was the first in a chain of events that *did* have a profound effect on our lives.

McKinley was first elected president in 1896. The country had been in an economic depression under Grover Cleveland and the Democrats since '93. McKinley pledged to cut unemployment and produce industrial growth by protecting American goods with high import tariffs. Rather than traveling the country, he campaigned mostly from his front porch in Canton, Ohio. William Jennings Bryan, McKinley's opponent, campaigned widely after gaining great support with his fiery cross-of-gold convention speech. But he lost the popular and electoral votes by a wide margin. McKinley's vice president in his first term was Garret Hobart.

McKinley won the presidency again in 1900, repeating his defeat of William Jennings Bryan. For his second term, his vice president was Theodore Roosevelt. Roosevelt had been elected governor of New York State in '98 after acclaim as a hero of the war in Cuba. Upon McKinley's death in September 1901, Roosevelt was sworn in as president, the youngest man ever to hold the office.

In mid-June 1902, with the Idaho delegation voting in favor, Congress passed the Reclamation Act. Some called it the Newlands Act after its main backer, Senator Francis Newlands of Nevada. President Roosevelt signed it into law.

The act created the Reclamation Service and authorized it to explore 16 Western states and territories, including Idaho, to determine where irrigation projects might be located. The act did not use the word "dam," but, as George Montgomery had warned years before, irrigation projects meant damming rivers, creating reservoirs behind the dams and digging canals and laterals out from the reservoirs to irrigate the land. The purpose was to attract homesteaders who would make arid and semiarid land productive. The irrigation projects were to be financed by selling 40- to 160-acre plots and water to the homesteaders.

The day I read in the Idaho *Statesman* that Congress had passed and President Roosevelt had signed the Reclamation Act, I received my copy of *The Virginian*, a novel by Owen Wister. I had read some of Wister's short stories and was looking forward to his first novel. Standing outside the Minidoka post office, I opened the book and found this dedication:

To
THEODORE ROOSEVELT

Some of these pages you have seen, some you have praised, one stands new-written because you blamed it; and all, my dear critic, beg leave to remind you of their author's changeless admiration.

The two men had been classmates at Harvard University. Years after the great success of *The Virginian*, Wister wrote a biography of Roosevelt.

When the Reclamation Act became law, D. W. Ross, the Idaho state engineer who had been instrumental in getting the Twin Falls Land and Water Company's irrigation project under way, became the Reclamation Service's district engineer in Idaho. He surveyed the Snake River from its headwaters in Wyoming to Minidoka Rapids, looking for irrigable land and dam sites.

Land in areas under consideration for irrigation projects would be withdrawn from public entry, meaning no further homestead claims could be filed on it. In mid-November 1902, Secretary of the Interior Ethan A. Hitchcock withdrew from entry a huge tract of land above and below Minidoka Rapids on both sides of the river. The Minidoka Project, as it came to be known, was under consideration. If a dam at the rapids and a reservoir behind it were approved, the Hawkins place would be in their path.

In a December report, Ross recommended commencing the Minidoka Project immediately. In early spring 1904, a consulting board reviewed the report and its cost estimates, and reported favorably to the Secretary of the Interior. On April 23, Hitchcock approved the project and allotted $2.6 million for its construction. Privately owned land within the project area would be either bought or taken by judicial condemnation proceedings. Word was that a government man would come around within six months to make offers to landowners.

After nearly 32 years, we were about to lose the homeplace and our land. Lily and I felt betrayed and empty. Although Will was deeply disappointed, he assured us that the family would be all right. He said he had anticipated the loss and had made preparations he would reveal soon.

The Reclamation Service's plans to irrigate Western lands didn't affect the Twin Falls Land and Water Company's private project below Schodde Rapids. In February '03, engineers began preparations for construction of Milner Dam at The Cedars. The dam and the rapids were named for Stanley Milner, the Salt Lake City businessman who provided the seed money. With the dam built and canal digging under way, engineers closed the gates at a ceremony in March '05, and Lake Milner began to fill. It didn't grow wide, but long and narrow. Tom Starrh moved his landings as the water rose. His ferry would have a broader reach to cross.

With the dam and lake, the current that once turned Henry Schodde's 11 waterwheels all but stopped. He sued the company for violating his water right, rendering his wheels worthless and threatening his livelihood. Without the wheels to lift river water, he couldn't irrigate his land or run his placer-mining operation. The lawsuit started its slow progress through state and federal courts. The final decision was handed down by the United States Supreme Court in 1912, after Henry's death. As Henry's heir, Minnie had pursued the case and lost.

While our little world was being turned upside down, the greater world outside kept moving on. In mid-1903, Henry Ford sold the first Model A, then went on to create an industry. Neither

Charles Duryea, the man who built the automobile we rode in, nor his brothers kept with the business. Ford had the greatest success at that. The Ford Motor Company sold 15 million Model T automobiles before introducing its second Model A.

Then, near the end of '03, Orville and Wilbur Wright flew the first heavier-than-air, powered aircraft at Kitty Hawk, North Carolina. I wondered, do earthshaking things always happen when centuries turn? After all, the Lewis and Clark Expedition began in 1804. Now, 100 years later, the world was changing in big, important ways, and the pace of change was accelerating. In his lectures, Mark Twain spoke of his century—the 19th—and longed for it.

We were past the '04 harvest and three weeks into October by the time J. H. Lowell, the government man, came to the homeplace. He had already been upstream to the Samson-Gifford spread near Bonanza Bar and to Andy Smith's ranch at the springs.

Mr. Lowell rode down the bluff road from our east gate. Andy had told him he was sure we wouldn't mind. The dogs startled his bay mare as they barked around her legs. The dogs weren't accustomed to strangers riding in from the east. Will and I came from the barn and calmed them. Mr. Lowell bade us good morning, dismounted and introduced himself. He was polite enough, a government man just doing his job. We understood he didn't make the laws. He followed in their wake, smoothing the water and settling the chum.

Mr. Lowell came, he said, to make us an offer on our land. He had already come to agreements with Samson, Gifford and Smith, and he was sure we would come to one too. He took a sheaf of papers from his saddlebag.

"I see you got your patent on just under 160 acres in '83," he said.

"We started farming this ground in '72," Will said, "long before the government or anybody else thought about irrigating it. It's private land, our land, we hold the deed. Does that count for anything?"

"Mr. Hawkins," Mr. Lowell said, "the United States Congress and President Roosevelt made a law that will let thousands of citizens turn hundreds of thousands of acres of Western wasteland into a breadbasket. That counts for more than 160 acres of private land."

"Mr. Lowell," Will said, "I appreciate that, yet I can't help but think if the name on my deed was Newlands or Roosevelt or Dubois rather than Hawkins, this patch of private land would count for more."

"Maybe so, Mr. Hawkins, maybe so," Mr. Lowell said. "D. W. Ross has looked your land over and has authorized me to offer you $5,000. The payments per acre for project land vary according to how long the owner has been on the land and how much he has improved it. Your per-acre payment is at the top of the scale."

"That's about $30 per acre," Will said. "I have to tell you, Mr. Lowell, that after 32 years working this ground, being forced off for $30 an acre doesn't dispose me kindly toward the government."

"I understand, Mr. Hawkins. I wish things were different," Mr. Lowell said, "but that's the best I can do. You retain the right to make entry on up to 160 acres of project land."

Will had voiced his protest, but he knew Mr. Lowell was just a man doing his job. If there was injustice involved, it didn't come from him.

"The hired hand and my grandsons are up to Minidoka," Will said, "but my daughter-in-law is in the house. Let's go inside where there's a table to spread your papers. Maybe Lily has a pot of coffee on the woodstove."

She did. We sat down with Mr. Lowell, and Lily poured us each a cup of hot coffee.

"It's a fine home you have here, Mrs. Hawkins," Mr. Lowell said. "It saddens me to know you'll have to give it up and leave."

"Yes," said Lily, "we've been wrestling with that since the news of the project came through."

Mr. Lowell laid out the papers, we read them, and Will signed. He had no choice but to sell. We were in the path of a United States government irrigation project and had to yield. We elected to stay one more year. We would sow in spring '05, harvest that fall and then be gone.

We were far enough upstream from the dam site that construction wouldn't affect us or we it, but we would lose the mill at the rapids as soon as work began. Later, when the dam was built and the engineers closed the gates, the Snake would exceed its banks and gradually creep over the land north, south and east. The river would become a lake, and the Hawkins place would be at its bottom, inhabited only by fish.

When Beth died, the light in Will's eyes dimmed. With the sale of the homeplace, that light dimmed lower. He had worked for more than 30 years to create a home for his family, a legacy that would be passed from generation to generation. Now, the Hawkins place would soon and forever be underwater. Forces beyond our control had cast our fate.

We learned later that Samson-Gifford's nearly 430 acres had gone for $13,160, and Andy's almost 160 acres had sold for $1,900. Andy wanted $2,500 but $1,900 was as high as Mr. Lowell could go. The sale was a godsend as far as Fanny was concerned. She hated the isolation of the ranch at Smith Springs. The family moved into Minidoka where Andy and Fanny opened Smith's Meat Market. Andy went from ranching cattle to butchering them and selling cuts.

Things turned out differently for Jimmy Howell and his waterwheels below Minidoka Rapids than they did for the Schoddes. After the dam, the current slowed enough so it no longer turned the big, wooden wheels. But recognizing its responsibility, the government granted a permanent water right that would stay with the land. Jimmy and any future owner would pay $50 per year for 480 acre-feet measured at the site. If available water didn't meet that amount, the landowner would share in the shortage with other gravity canal water users.

66

The day following Mr. Lowell's visit, as Will and I were working an irrigation trench together, he turned to me and said,

"Early, it's time you and I went on a short trip together."

"Where to?" I asked.

"Let that be something you find out once we get there," he replied. "We'll leave on the afternoon train day after tomorrow and be away for a few days. One light duffel should do us fine. Lily and the boys will be safe here with Bud."

Tommy drove the team and wagon to the Minidoka depot two afternoons later. Three generations of Hawkins men, each an eldest son, sat across the spring bench. We didn't talk much on the way up. Tommy pointed to a V-formation of Canada geese honking overhead. "Heading south for the winter," he said.

We rode the OSL cars east to Pocatello, changed trains there and continued south for more than an hour. The mystery was deepening for me. We got off the train at the Oneida depot. We didn't know it then, but years later the town's name would be changed to Arimo. There was a young man waiting for us there with three saddle horses.

"Early Hawkins, this is your cousin, Carl Hawkins," Will said. "Carl, his father and three brothers came to Idaho from Missouri and made entry on a homestead west of here in '89."

Carl was less surprised to see me than I him. "If we ride steady, we can be there before dark," he said.

We crossed a creek a short way from the depot, then farther ahead, another. We stayed to the right of the second creek and followed it up a gradual grade of sage toward a line of mountains. There seemed to be no pass through them, so I figured wherever we were headed must be on this side. As we drew closer to the mountains, however, a narrow gap appeared between them.

"That's Big Tom Mountain to the right, and this is Garden Creek Gap," Carl said. "There's been talk of blasting a wagon road through, but it hasn't happened yet. There are a couple of places where we'll have to dismount and lead the horses, so let me go first."

We entered the gap single file and rode carefully at a walk. There were layers upon layers of rough exposed rock close on both sides. It seemed as if some unseen hand had helped the creek carve its path. Around a sharp bend, we surprised a bobcat standing in a small pool trying to snag a trout with its paw.

As we descended the opposite side, the exposed rock gradually gave way and the trail widened. We were in a basin, surrounded by hills and mountains. The sun had already slipped behind the peaks to the west. In the dimming light, I saw our path leading to buildings and cultivated land. Beyond them, at some distance, a lake glimmered faintly.

At the base of a low hill and in the center of a cluster of buildings stood a large ranch-style house. It was well-constructed of stone, logs and sawn lumber. A shade porch stretched across its front. Coal-oil lamps glowed in the windows, and woodsmoke rose from three stone chimneys. A barn sat to the right and rear. A corral and outbuildings formed a long arc behind the house. Several dogs ran out to greet us. We rode to the barn and bedded the horses down.

As we stepped inside the house, four men came up and welcomed Will. Carl introduced me to his father, Aleada, and three brothers, Louis, Frank and Bell, all grown men. There were no women.

"You're just in time for supper," Aleada said, "Let's sit and eat." The table was set for seven, with pots, serving bowls and candles running down its center. As we ate our fill, our hosts asked how things were at our place on the river and how our trip down was. Both Will and I responded with bits and pieces of information. In the back of my mind, I wondered how Will found these cousins and what we were doing at their farm.

When the last of us finished eating, the four sons cleared the table and Aleada went to a cabinet and returned with a ceramic jug and a tray holding seven glasses.

"Even though I got religion some years back," Aleada said, "I ain't given up the hooch. Got me a fine still up the draw out back. There's nothin' like a little taste after a good meal. Join me, gentlemen?"

Will and I nodded that we would. Aleada half-filled three glasses and passed two to us. Before we drank, the sons came back and took their places at the table. Aleada passed the jug, and his sons half-filled their glasses. He raised his glass and offered a toast:

"Here's to success for the Hawkins clan, whoever and wherever they might be." Each of us either repeated "Success" or uttered a little cheer and drank from his glass. Aleada drained his glass and poured another. After a few minutes of gulping from the refill, he loudly asked, "Well, Will, how long are you gonna keep Early in the dark? Why don't you tell him what's goin' on here? Matter of fact, tell all of us. Let that hooch loosen your tongue so's you can tell the whole story." By then, Will had drunk nearly all his half glass and was ready to talk.

"I've been quiet about this because, although I prepared for it, I really didn't want it to happen," Will began. "But now it has happened. We have to leave our farm on the Snake River because the government has taken it for an irrigation project. We could start over on another homestead nearby, but I can't bear to stay near where we worked so long and hard to build something for ourselves that's now gone forever. I decided when the government began to survey in '89 and '90 that if it came to losing our farm, I'd rather go somewhere else, and I'd rather leave Beth at the home-place she knew and loved. I hoped Early and Lily would agree."

"After that first survey," Will continued, "I had my suspicions, but nobody really knew. The irrigation ball had gotten rolling in the West and in Washington, and something was bound to happen. About that time, I heard from Louis in Smithland that some Hawkins cousins had moved from Missouri to Idaho and had homesteaded south of Pocatello. I did some digging and found Aleada and his boys."

"When my wife died," Aleada said, "we had nothin' to hold us in Missouri. My kin were down in Alabama. I kept hearin' what Greeley said about goin' west, so that's what we did. We came up from Ogden and found this basin. There wasn't nobody here. It was good land, sheltered and well-watered. I filed on 160 acres and Carl, who was the only son old enough, filed on another 160. Since we were first, we put our name on the biggest creek and the basin itself."

"That's how I found you," Will said. "The railroad men in Pocatello told me there's a tiny town named Hawkins west of Oneida in a place folks call Hawkins Basin. I rode the cars to Oneida, borrowed a mare, came through the gap and found you in your first cabin."

"And I didn't know you from Adam," Aleada said. "You had to convince me we was kin."

"Yep," Will said, "I did it by tracing the tree back and showing you which Hawkins went to Alabama and begat you."

"That you did," Aleada said, slapping his knee and laughing, "that you did. You told me who my pappy was. How'd you know?"

"I remembered he came upriver to one of our New Year's Day Hawkins family reunions in Smithland," Will replied. "I was a young boy, and you weren't born yet. He bounced me on his knee and gave me rock candy. How could I forget that?"

"That's good enough for me," Aleada said. "He gave me candy too. Belle used to say that's why I ain't got my own teeth."

"What happened then, Will?" I asked.

"I told Aleada and Carl they had 320 acres between them," Will said. "With the other sons not yet of age, some of the best land might slip away before they could file on it. I said I would file on 160 choice acres in your name. As the other sons came along, they could file. The finest land would all be in the Hawkins name. They would build a cabin on your land and work it to meet the prove-up requirements. If one day you needed the land, it was yours. If not, it was theirs. I came as often as I could to help.

"Then, when the government surveyed again in '96 and put the gauging station in, and when Bert Perrine started something west of Schodde's, I thought we would be in the way pretty soon. When the Reclamation Act passed in '02, I knew we were goners. It was just a matter of time, a short time.

"As much as it pains me to leave the homeplace on the river, this is where we'll come if Early and Lily agree. The land has been good for almost 15 years. Aleada and his sons have done right by it. We'll put up a barn and a house or two so everything will be ready when we leave the homeplace next fall."

"I do agree," I said, "and I think Lily will too. Is this where you came all those times you left the homeplace for a few days?" I asked.

"Yes, it is," Will replied.

"I thought you had found a woman friend somewhere," I said.

"Surely not here in Hawkins Basin," Will laughed. "There's not an unmarried woman for miles. Ask your young cousins here. They have to ride the cars up to Pocatello or down to Ogden just to see a girl in a skirt."

We walked our ground with Carl in the morning. It was rolling land on the valley floor, bordered on one side by Hawkins Creek. The cousins had kept it planted to wheat and oats. The yield had been lean in dry years, but only severe drought would prevent bumper crops now that the reservoir and irrigation systems were in.

Carl pointed out the timber on the surrounding mountains. There was plenty of pine and maple for the logs and lumber we'd need for houses and a barn. And there was juniper for corrals and fenceposts.

I judged the basin to be about two miles wide and five long. Nestled in the surrounding hills and mountains, it was a pretty spot. It wasn't the Hawkins homeplace on the Snake River, but it was a pretty spot.

When we returned home, Will and I walked from the depot to the homeplace. As many times as I had come down the Minidoka road, I was still taken with the vastness of the Snake River Plain and the majesty of the mountains that rose in the distance. When we came to the rise above the farm, the poplars and cottonwood greeted us with their fall colors. The homeplace looked like a peaceful bit of paradise. I would miss it so.

In spring '05 as we sowed our last crop, the newspaper stories were about U. S. engineers getting the Panama Canal under way. The French had tried there and failed, and Americans had abandoned a canal attempt through Nicaragua. Then the U. S. took up the project in Panama. It would be nine years in the building and hailed as one of the greatest engineering and construction feats of all time.

67

Opening night at the Rupert Opera House was Friday, October 13, 1905. By calling their new dancing and amusement hall an opera house, C. W. Scott and Claude Hickok made it out to be much grander than it was. The building was little more than a one-story clapboard structure with a raised stage at one end of a large room. But for Rupert, a town sprouting where just before there was nothing but sagebrush, a dance hall or theater or opera house was a big step forward.

Ben, Maria, Brad and Brad's wife, Melody, were coming for our final harvest, and they wanted to perform at the new opera house. Their show was Saturday, a week after the opening. We advertised in the Rupert *Record* that the York Theater Troupe would be appearing, fresh from engagements in San Francisco, California, and Virginia City, Nevada. The troupe consisted of the four Yorks. Andy Smith recruited an orchestra made up of musicians from Minidoka, Rupert and Albion. If Scott and Hickok could call their hall an opera house, Andy could call his pieced-together band an orchestra. They rehearsed with the troupe evenings in the week leading up to the performance.

On the night of the show, every seat in the house was full. The overflow stood in the rear and along the side walls. With the harvest in or nearly so, people had come from miles around.

The Smiths, Sears, Howells, Montgomerys, Schoddes and many
other families we knew were there. For some like us, it had been
the last harvest. Soon a lake would build behind the dam and
end farming along that stretch of the Snake forever.

There was a buzz of anticipation in the audience. The house
lights dimmed, the footlights came up, and Ben walked from the
wings onto the stage. He was carrying a banjo. There were scattered whistles and claps and cheers from the crowd. He stopped
at center stage, just back from the footlights and overlooking the
orchestra. He very deliberately wrapped the banjo strap around
his neck, adjusted the instrument's position and plucked a few
notes. He looked toward Will, who was sitting with Lily, Bud,
the boys and me in the first row. He nodded, smiled and tore into
a fired-up version of *Blue Tail Fly*. Toes started tapping throughout the hall. In a minute or two, *Blue Tail Fly* merged into a
rousing *Turkey in the Straw*. Ben didn't sing, he just played. He
was paying tribute to Will. He was expressing his gratitude.

His pace gradually slowed, and *Turkey in the Straw* merged
into the first few notes of *Oh! Susanna*. Ben began to sing. His
voice was rich, mature and resonant. He sang from his heart:

> *I come from Alabama with my banjo on my knee*
> *I'm goin' to Lou'siana my true love for to see*
> *It rained all night the day I left*
> *The weather it was dry*
> *The sun so hot I froze to death*
> *Susanna don't you cry*

He called to the audience to join him for the chorus:

> *Oh! Susanna, don't you cry for me*
> *I come from Alabama*
> *With my banjo on my knee*

Ben had captured the crowd. He varied the pace of the song,
singing strongly and filling the hall with his lone voice on the
verses, then blending in with the audience as they sang and
clapped and stomped through each chorus. Ben was three songs
into his performance, and everyone was having a fine time.

Only Will and I knew why Ben had chosen those songs and what their significance was. I looked down the row at Will. The years had toughened and lined his face, thinned his hair and weakened his once strong, straight body some. But that Saturday night he seemed to glow. His smile was wide as he clapped and sang, his eyes were big and bright, and his cheeks were wet with tears of joy.

Ben brought *Oh! Susanna* to a close, then Maria and Melody joined him at center stage. Melody was carrying a flute. Ben and Maria faced each other, clasped hands and turned slightly toward the audience. Melody stood a step away, raised the flute to her lips and started a tune that sounded familiar but that I didn't recognize immediately. Ben began to sing:

> *I wandered today to the hill, Maria*
> *To watch the scene below*
> *The creek and the old rusty mill, Maria*
> *Where we sat in the long, long ago*
> *The green grove is gone from the hill, Maria*
> *Where first the daisies had sprung*
> *The old rusty mill is now still, Maria*
> *Since you and I were young*

Maria joined him on the chorus:

> *And now we are aged and gray, my love*
> *The trials of life nearly done*
> *Let's sing of the days that are gone, my love*
> *When you and I were young.*

And they continued, verse, chorus, verse, chorus. It was the song Ben had sung on the *George Hawkins* when we went to Cairo for the Great Race. Ben and Maria had changed it slightly to fit the new occasion. Again, the audience was taken with the performance, but Ben and Maria had sung the song for Will.

As they finished *Maggie*, Brad came from the wings and met Ben, Maria and Melody at center stage. Melody blew one note on her flute to give the singers the pitch. Ben began in a baritone that filled the room:

Swing low, sweet chariot . . .

and the three joined in *a cappella* for four-part harmony:

> *Coming for to carry me home*
> *Swing low, sweet chariot*
> *Coming for to carry me home*

Will surprised me and, I suppose, everyone else in the hall when he stood and began singing with the four on stage:

> *I looked over Jordan and what did I see*
> *Coming for to carry me home*
> *A band of angels coming after me*
> *Coming for to carry me home*

I stood for the chorus, as did maybe a dozen people scattered through the hall:

> *Swing low, sweet chariot*
> *Coming for to carry me home*
> *Swing low, sweet chariot*
> *Coming for to carry me home*

By the next verse, half the people in the opera house were on their feet:

> *If you get there before I do*
> *Coming for to carry me home*
> *Please tell my friends I'm coming too*
> *Coming for to carry me home*

Everyone in the hall was standing and singing by the last chorus:

> *Swing low, sweet chariot*
> *Coming for to carry me home*
> *Swing low, sweet chariot*
> *Coming for to carry me home*

At the last line, Ben stepped forward and motioned like a conductor to bring the song to a close. The crowd stood silently for a few moments, then sat. There was no applause.

Melody played an introductory phrase on the flute, then the four singers began *a cappella*:

> *Let us pause in life's pleasures and count its many tears*
> *While we all sup sorrow with the poor*
> *There's a song that will linger forever in our ears*
> *Oh! hard times come again no more*
>
> *'Tis the song, the sigh of the weary*
> *Hard times, hard times, come again no more*
> *Many days you have lingered around my cabin door*
> *Oh! hard times, come again no more*

They sang verse, chorus, verse, chorus through to the end. It was the first time I had heard anyone sing that song with such deep feeling. Other singers made it sound like a march. I thought the Yorks captured what Stephen Foster meant. I'm sure Ben chose *Hard Times* to show sympathy for those of us whose farms had been taken by the government for the Minidoka Project. Yes, we had been paid, but no amount of money can make up for the loss that's in the heart.

Before coming to the homeplace for the last harvest, the Yorks had been touring with a musical comedy called *Little Johnny Jones*. George M. Cohan wrote it, and it had been a big hit on Broadway in New York City. With no sets and only four players at the Rupert Opera House, the Yorks couldn't stage the whole show, but they could sing the songs. Andy Smith and the orchestra accompanied them.

If the audience had turned somber at hearing Stephen Foster's *Hard Times*, George M. Cohan's *Yankee Doodle Boy*, *Give My Regards to Broadway* and *Life's a Funny Proposition After All* turned them right around. Ben introduced their final song of the evening, *Why Did Nellie Leave Her Home?*, saying it was the first Mr. Cohan had sold for publication—as a boy of 16. The audience left the hall in high spirits, feeling they had gotten their money's worth.

The following day, Sunday, October 22, 1905, we finished what little of the harvest was left. In late afternoon, we unhitched the teams, unbuckled their harness, walked them to their stalls and groomed them for the last time at the homeplace. Shutting the barn doors late that day was like finishing a history book and closing its covers. In the morning, we would begin loading everything into wagons and hauling it to the Minidoka depot for shipment to the Oneida depot, south of Pocatello. We would ring the bell for the last time at the Snake River homeplace, remove it from its mountings on the shade porch and carry it to the farm in Hawkins Basin.

Lily and Maria had prepared a special supper. We gathered at the main house. As Will washed up, he discovered the knife he kept in a sheath at his belt was missing. He asked us to wait supper a few minutes while he took a lantern and one of the dogs out to the near field where he suspected he had dropped the knife. Of course, we obliged.

Those few minutes turned into 15, then 30 with no sign of Will. I stepped out onto the porch and looked in the direction Will had walked. I saw his light and heard the dog howling. Something was wrong. I pulled the bell cord strongly and quickly several times, thinking Will would signal with his light. Nothing. Ben and Lily came out from inside.

"Something's wrong," I said. "The dog's howling and I can see Will's light, but it's not moving."

"Let's go, Early," Ben said as he pulled a lantern from its hook and bounded down the stairs.

Ben and I ran straight for the light as the others stood peering into the darkness from the porch. The dog heard our steps as we approached and ran to us. We saw Will from about 20 yards out. He was lying flat on his back in the stubble. His lantern stood nearby. As we ran, we called out, "Will! Will!" but he didn't move or respond. We reached him and fell to our knees at his side. His eyes were open, and he was staring straight up into the black sky.

"Will! Will!" we cried again as we shook him. No response. I put my ear to his heart. There was a very faint beat. The right side of his body was rigid, as if frozen. He seemed to be struggling to speak. I pushed his hat back and put my ear to his mouth.

His breath was warm but no words came. I raised my head and looked in his eyes. They were fixed and showed no expression, as if he was staring at nothing. Ben and I looked at one another but spoke no words. We each knew what the other was thinking.

"Look!" Ben said, "his lips are moving. He's trying to speak."

I again put my ear to his mouth. He struggled mightily and faintly whispered, "Bury . . . me . . . Beth." Those were Will's last words. He died there, lying in oat stubble. Ben and I stood and faced each other. His eyes welled with tears, as did mine. We embraced and sobbed, holding each other up.

I lifted Will's feet one at a time and passed the lantern hoops over them. I took his ankles while Ben crossed Will's hands over his chest, buttoned one cuff to the other and lifted him beneath the arms. We walked toward the house at a slow pace. The lanterns swung slightly on Will's ankles as we walked. When we came within sight of the porch, everyone ran down the stairs and toward us. "No, oh, no," was all we heard, over and over, like a chorus.

We carried Will to Beth's grave and laid him alongside. I asked Lily, Maria and the boys to stay with him while Ben, Bud and I went to the barn. We tore boards off empty stalls and hastily built a coffin. We grabbed two shovels and returned to the grave site. Ben and I gently lifted Will's body, placed it in the box and nailed the lid shut. We started digging a grave beside Beth's.

Lily and Maria went inside and brought the supper out. Ben, Bud, Tom, Clint and I took turns with the shovels. When we weren't digging, we ate. When the hole was ready, we slipped thick ropes beneath the coffin, lifted it and gently lowered it in. We gathered around the grave, and each of us spoke words in turn.

Ben said, "Will, I owe you my life, I owe everything I am to you. I pledge to honor your memory for the rest of my days."

I spoke last. "Goodbye, my father," I said through tears. "I wish I could honestly say I'm half the man you were. Rest in peace, Captain Will Hawkins, with Beth."

As we shoveled loose soil into the grave, Ben sang the same requiem he had sung when we buried Beth. With the grave filled, we went to the rock pile for heavy stones to cover the loose dirt. We would cut a headstone in the morning. Will lay beside Beth, together in death as they had been in life.

When I returned to Lily's and my bedroom after Will's burial ceremony, I found a large envelope on the top shelf in our armoire. My name was written on it in Will's hand. Inside was his last will and testament, written out in longhand. He must have known the end was coming soon; he just didn't know when. His will was short and to the point:

I appoint my son, Earl Lee Hawkins, as the executor of my will. Please carry out my wishes as quickly and as simply as possible with as little participation by the legal profession and government authorities as practical. I have no debts, own my property with no mortgages or notes, and there are no legitimate claims against any of my possessions, so the resolution of my estate should not be a complex matter.

To my daughter, Amanda, I give my best wishes. Through your strong will, grace and intelligence, you have made a good, giving life for yourself. I approve of the course you have chosen, and I am extremely proud of you. Please do not take my not giving you money or possessions as a slight. You, Antoine and your girls are comfortable beyond anything my meager resources could add. You have been a bright light in my life, and I love you dearly.

To my son, Ben York, I give $2,500. You came into our lives as a gift, and you bore great gifts of your own. Having you as a son has been a joy and a privilege. I am proud to have contributed to your life and success in some small way, but truly, your many achievements are your own. You have used your talents well. I wish you, Maria, Brad and Melody the very best.

To my son, Earl Lee Hawkins, I give the balance of my cash money and all my real property and material possessions. Words cannot express my pride in you and my gratitude for your having continued the family traditions. My missions in life have been to do well, to be good, and to make sure that this family and the Hawkins name keep on. You have made that possible. I wish you, Lily, Tom and Clint the very best.

I could not have had a better family.
  This is my last will and testament, dated October 1,
1905 and affirmed by my signature below.

Will Hawkins
The Hawkins Homestead
Snake River, near Minidoka, Idaho

Witness: Andrew Harrison Smith

Epilogue
Thanksgiving 1954

Once we moved to our new farm in Hawkins Basin and began to till and sow, I turned the recorder's duties over to Tom. He and Clint would grow to be fine men, marry and have families of their own. Then those children grew, married and had families and so on.

Tragedy struck us and many others near dawn on April 18, 1906. Ben, Maria, Brad and Melody had just returned to their home in San Francisco from an engagement in Sacramento. Theirs was one of few brick houses in the neighborhood. The earthquake shook it mercilessly, causing it to collapse and crush the four sleeping troupers within. It was a great loss for us and audiences everywhere.

Bud stayed with us until his father died in 1908. He returned to Iowa and took over the family farm. He married a local woman, and together they had seven children.

After many tries and many rejections, Ed Burroughs finally got on the road to success in 1912 when *All-Story* magazine serialized one of his stories. In 1914, A. C. McClurg & Company published the same story as a book. Ed used his full name, Edgar Rice Burroughs, for that story, *Tarzan of the Apes*, and all those that followed.

Amanda spent her life in France as wife, mother and teacher. She and Antoine had three children, all girls. She died suddenly in 1939.

My Lily and I lived through World War I, the Roaring Twenties, the Great Depression, then World War II. She passed on in 1946. I think of her every day. Sometimes, when I lie in my warm bed alone at night waiting for sleep to come, I stare through the darkness at the ceiling I can barely see. My thoughts drift to Lily. Tears escape the corners of my eyes, run in little rivulets across my cheekbones and settle in the hollows of my ears.

I so enjoy walking in the valley. The sage grouse still strut in spring, the meadowlarks trill their pretty songs, and the hawks come for mice at harvest in fall. My greatest pride is my family, which has grown so big and spread so far that I have trouble keeping track. I love and cherish them all.

By Thanksgiving Day 1954, Lily had been gone eight years. I still missed her, especially on holidays when the family got together. After our turkey dinner, I talked with my great-grandson, Rob. Of all my sons, grandsons and great-grandsons, he reminded me most of Will. He had the same generosity, determination and air of competence.

"When will you be driving back to the university?" I asked.

"Monday morning," he replied.

"I'll tell you what, then," I said. "Come by in that jalopy of yours and pick me up. I'll ride as far as Minidoka with you and come back on the train."

"But Early," he said, "That's a long way, and you've been under the weather lately."

"Don't worry about me," I said. "I'll get back to Arimo OK, and your mother can meet me at the depot."

Rob was in my drive early Monday morning. His car was one of the first postwar Fords. Despite his hard work, the thing looked like a wreck. I was surprised it got him back and forth to the university. He held the door for me as I slipped into the passenger seat.

"Why do you want to go to Minidoka?" he asked as we started.

"Well, let's just say I want to recall some fond memories," I said. "And, Rob, if you would, please stop at the Chevrolet dealer's in Pocatello as we go. I want to talk to Dee Bogert there."

"Sure thing," he said, "it's along the way."

Rob pulled into Intermountain Chevrolet on West Center Street. The morning light bounced off the rows of shiny cars, making them gleam as they probably never would again.

"Now, Rob," I said, "this might seem like an odd request, but I want you to take your baggage and personals out of the Ford and pile them on that platform yonder. I have to go inside, and I'll be back in a minute or two."

"OK, if you say so," he said. If Rob had figured out what was up, he didn't let on. I saw Dee in the showroom through the glass. I waved and went on in.

"She's all set to go, just as you asked," Dee said.

"Fine, thank you, so am I," I replied.

We walked to the rear of the building, where a new '55 Chevy Nomad sat, sky blue and white, gleaming in the morning sun.

"She's beautiful," I said. "I love the whitewalls." Dee handed me the keys, held the door, and I slid behind the wheel. I turned the key in the ignition, and the V8 roared to life. The sound was sweet, and I was thrilled. You'd think it would take a lot to make a 94-year-old man feel young again. That Chevy did it in an instant. I thanked Dee and eased the Nomad around the building and up to Rob. The look on his face was worth a million bucks. Any old man can remember gratifying moments from his life. Being able to give that Chevy to Rob and seeing his reaction was one of mine.

After Rob calmed down and loaded his things into the Nomad, he took the wheel and we headed for Route 30 west. Will, Ben and I had come this way 82 years before. Looking back, it seemed the time had gone by in the blink of an eye.

"If we're going to make it to Minidoka for the afternoon train, we better step on it," I said. I liked the thrill of driving fast on a smooth highway.

"Well," Rob replied, "it's a new engine, and we do have to break her in easy. Minidoka's not even 100 miles, so we can take it slow and still make it in plenty of time."

Leave it to a youngster to spoil an old man's fun, I thought. Years ago, it had taken us days to ride this distance on horseback, and here Rob and I were taking it slow and getting there in a couple of hours. As we drove, we caught glimpses of the Snake River here and there. The country had changed but not all that much. We saw farm and ranch houses on both sides some distance from the road. Every so often, there was a store and filling station alongside the highway.

At the Raft River, we got our first look at the upper end of Lake Walcott. It was about here that Will, Ben and I had first talked to Nibbs Gamble. I've often wondered how things would have turned out had ranchers not claimed the Raft River Valley before we rode in.

The land along Route 30 west of the Raft River was still mostly in sage. Here and there, a man had plowed up some ground for potatoes or sugar beets. Looking north across the flats, we saw trees and tall brush lining both sides of the lake. Black Pine Mountain, Horse Butte, the Cotterel Mountains and Mount Harrison, as folks called them now, lay to the south. The farther west we drove, the wider the lake grew. The highway was quite some way from the lake shore, but the trees marked its line, and I knew when we had passed the dam. We crossed the Snake River at Montgomery Bridge, near where the ferry used to be. Rupert lay straight ahead.

"Would you like to double back along the north side and stop at the park for a few minutes?" Rob asked. "We have plenty of time."

"Sure," I replied, "I like that idea."

Rob drove us along the river road, around the pool below the dam and up into the lakeside park. The cottonwoods there were now about 50 years old. Even stripped of leaves in November, they were grand trees. We got out of the Nomad and walked a ways east along the lake shore up from the dam. We stood at the water's edge. It was a sunny, still day. The air was brisk. In the distance, across the lake, the lines of Horse Butte, the Cotterel Mountains and Mount Harrison stood against the clear blue sky. Out there, under the water, lay Will, Beth and Spirit. Out there, under the water, lay the homeplace, lay the lone cottonwood and many memories.

"Shall we go?" Rob gently asked, rousing me from my reverie.

"Yup, let's," I replied.

We drove west on Minidoka Dam Road, crossing the North Side Canal twice. At Acequia, we turned onto Route 24. The depot was less than six miles northeast. Magpies scavenged in the potato and sugar beet fields that lay idle along the road. Here and there, a farmhouse broke the monotony of the Plain.

The depot looked as sturdy and imposing as it had when it greeted steam locomotives decades ago. Rob walked with me to the ticket window and made sure I was set. He offered to wait until the train came. I told him there was no need, that he should go ahead. He turned and looked me square in the eye.

"Thank you for the Nomad, Early," he said, "thank you for everything."

"Call your mother and let her know you made it back," I said.

"Sure, I will," he assured me.

Rob headed west toward Kimama, Shoshone and the future. When the diesel locomotive pulled the long train into Minidoka, I boarded and headed east across the lava for Arimo, home and the big divide.

The End